WANT ME

He had claimed her and stood by the claim. She was safe, for the moment. She did not delude herself into thinking that her position of relative safety could not change at any moment, on a pirate captain's whim. No, she must not let down her weapon of seduction, especially not now, in sight of them all. She had only allowed one thought to be in her mind, one thought to blazon from her eyes. "Want me." And when her courage had faltered, she had added, "As I want you." Obviously, it had worked and worked well.

The captain stood next to her, his sword drawn, and sliced through the bonds that both held her and held her up. She closed her eyes and swayed momentarily before catching herself and then she forced herself to look into his eyes. They were the color of amber.

Eyes the shade of the sun on a late summer evening, eyes that flickered with compassion and strength, eyes that held her startled gaze with tidal force; he touched the heart of her with those heated eyes. And she knew with sudden and disturbing clarity that they were the eyes of a man, not a pirate.

TELL ME LIES

CLAUDIA DAIN

LEISURE BOOKS NEW YORK CITY

To my husband, who knew.

A LEISURE BOOK®

March 2000

Published by

Dorchester Publishing Co., Inc.
276 Fifth Avenue
New York, NY 10001

ISBN 0-8439-4692-X

TELL ME LIES

Chapter One

Caribbean Ocean, 1715

The sun was warm on her bared skin, as warm as the wind that swept gently across the surface of the sea. It was a gentle wind, for the sun was low upon the horizon, its raging heat spent for another day and it took the strength of the wind with it as it hovered near the undulating swells of the darkening sea. Though gentle, the wind was strong enough to lift the ends of her sun-streaked hair, sending them cascading around her shoulders to entwine in a tangled embrace just above her bosom; the wind was also strong enough to muffle sound with its own steady passage by her as it followed the retreating sun. It caressed her, this dying wind. This gentle, tired wind sent slender ropes of hair into her eyes and mouth where they caught and held, refusing to leave. And the sun, for all its running retreat to the far horizon, was still strong enough to light her hair with golden fire and heat her skin to a warm flush, still strong enough to catch the glint of unsheathed steel and dripping blood and eyes lit with the lust of a recent kill. Eyes filled with the certainty of having her. The ropes that cut into her wrists, holding her to her place in the bow, told her the same.

There was no way out for her.

The wind was cooling noticeably without the heat of the hot tropical sun to warm it and with each passing moment it was weaker, always weaker in its force. The golden throbbing mass of the sun was half buried in the blue-black waters that seemed to rise to engulf it. She watched it sink, faster and faster now, as if giving up. As if, instead of being pulled into the sea, it was diving in and willfully choosing to allow the dark waters to swallow it whole. When there was just a sliver of gold left trembling before the vastness of the sea, she turned away, unwilling to witness so eager a defeat. There was still enough light to see the blood-soaked deck and the blood-splattered bare feet of the pirates who had captured her. And without the sun, the wind lost the best of its force so that now she could hear very clearly what they said.

The sun was gone, leaving her in advancing darkness.

"Got more 'n I reckoned we would."

A score of eyes shifted in her direction, the vanished sun sending up its light to color the horizon pink and gold and purple . . . and to show her those glinting, greedy eyes. She was nothing but cargo to them; no, not cargo . . . plunder.

"Aye, an' if I 'adn't a plucked 'er . . ."

"Don't grab fer glory, Ned, 'twas Pierre who spotted 'er."

Ned grumbled loudly, wiping his blackened hand across his nose a few times before he fell silent. She had Pierre to thank that she did not lie dead with the others on what remained of her ship. She had no thanks to offer. Better dead than this coil.

No! she shouted within herself. *Do not run to death as that cowardly sun runs to plunge itself into the sea. No! Think of a way to survive! Life is too precious to throw away without a fight.* But what manner of fight would it be without a single weapon at her disposal and an ocean away from any aid other than divine?

"Pierre'll not hoard this booty. Nay, we'll divide th' spoils as always and share the wealth, as always."

"The captain divides 'a spoils, don' forget, and there's more to the cargo 'an what's trussed up in the bow."

"Aye, Red Jack would 'ave done us fair, but he's dead."

"And redder yet," someone chuckled mirthlessly.

"New captain now; he's killed for the right, but how will he divide?"

"He's always been right enough, I'm thinkin'."

"As long as he's not laughin'."

"He'll not smile when he sees 'er. Don't like killin' much and don't take to captives."

"But we've got 'er now and I'll slice the man who tries to throw 'er over."

Her mind whirled as she sorted through this information. She was booty. She was to be shared among them all. The captain divided the spoils of his plunder.

The sun was gone, but the wash of rosy light it left behind lit the men below her enough to shake her soul. They were ruthless animals, thieves, murderers, rapists. They were pirates. If she was passed among them she would be dead by morning. The will to live bubbled up again within her, stronger now. She did not want to die, not now, not yet. Not like this. *Think!*

The captain divided the plunder.

It was the captain's decision.

Perhaps she could appeal to him, beseech him to . . . she laughed helplessly inside herself. He was a pirate, a captain of pirates. He led pirates in acts of murder; he did not lead them in acts of mercy.

Piracy: oceanic murder and robbery. The law that ruled them was the law of profit, and the spirit that guided them was the spirit of self-interest. Profit and self-interest. What could she offer a captain of pirates that would appeal to those twin gods he served? She had nothing.

No, that determined will rumbled in the depths of her mind; *you have yourself. Use what you have to survive.*

She wanted to live.

She had to think rationally, as her father had taught her; she must not allow them to use her as a dumb animal. She had herself and her faith in a heavenly Father more powerful than any man, any pirate. But God seemed very far away. The sun had set and the darkness was growing. Melancholy warred with panic until she banished them both. She had to think of a way to survive, and she would . . . she would.

All she had to fight with was herself.

They seemed to want her.

If she could use that wanting against them . . .

If . . . if she could make the captain want her, want her to such a degree that he would not share her . . . Could she survive even that? She would have to; she could see no other way. The crew would not like it, judging from their comments and the way their eyes roamed over her bared skin and bound hands and moving hair. But he was their captain and he controlled them; of them all, he was the only one who could enforce such an unpopular decision. She dared not place her fate in the hands of one of the crew, especially Pierre, whom the crew thanked even now for his foresight and generosity. No, her best chance was with the captain. With the captain, she might survive. She had to survive.

Hating the departing sun that took its light and left her in growing darkness, she scanned the deck, illuminated now in the gentlest shades of rose and purple. She was losing the light. She had to find him before she was left in total darkness.

The band of pirates shifted and parted. They drew back in something like respect or fear and stopped their speculation as to the dividing of the spoils to allow a man to enter their midst. The captain.

He was tall and dark, his hair black and wavy and his skin dusky in hue. His eyes, even in this fading light, showed light, lighter than his skin, much lighter than his hair. He was well-muscled. His thigh ran red with a long straight slice to mark the source; a long cut, but not deep enough to pose a threat as it was already closing against itself. His features were cleanly drawn and regular, though she thought she saw a wide line of white scar tissue just beneath his jaw. He was relatively clean. He could have been worse. In her heart, she thanked God that he was not repulsive to her and prayed that she could win him to her. She had never thought to pray such a prayer and so fervently. She knew enough about the sex act to know that she must beguile him with the unspoken promise of splendor in her arms. He must want her enough not to contemplate sharing her. Beyond that, she knew little. She was a virgin.

God, she whispered in her soul, *count this not against me as sin. I must survive.* Surely God would not deal harshly with her. He had given her the will to live; He would not judge her too harshly if she but used the weapons at her disposal. She had but one weapon: herself.

But there was no more time for debate within herself. He stood before her, as did they all. They were building themselves up to set upon her. The light was nearly gone. The captain must see her. And want her.

With all her will she forced herself to relax against the pull of the ropes that bound her. More than that, following some inner instinct, she loosened the tension in her joints until her head arched back and her hips swayed and her breasts tipped toward him. And with every ounce of that stubborn will to survive, she called to him with her eyes, willing him to look at her. For a moment, she did not know what to call to him, what silent message she wanted him to hear; then she knew. She gave to him the urgent message of her heart and her mind and, God forgive her, her soul. Her eyes called out to him, "Want me."

The captain strode into the midst of his crew with his anger barely suppressed. They had a captive. They never took captives. He and Red Jack had agreed on that, anyway, though little else. But Red Jack was dead now and he was captain, finally, having killed the one man who stood in his way. It had not been a fight he had provoked, but he had won and that was all that mattered on a pirate ship at sea. He had won. And now he ruled them all, by fist or guile. He had waited long for this moment, and the woman was ruining it all. There could be no captives because there could be no witnesses. The captain's orders were: take the goods, kill as few as possible, and sail off. It was that damned Pierre's idea and look at the result: instead of stowing the marketable goods from that limping hulk, they were arguing about the woman.

Most ships lay to at the first sight of a pirate ship; why fight? Pirates didn't want lives, they wanted profits. There were no profits in dead men. Captives, hostages, whatever one wished to call them, were always trouble. Damn Pierre for his audacity in ignoring standing rules. And damn the woman for causing trouble just by being on his ship.

He had no thoughts as to how to handle this problem. Given to the men, passed from one to the next, she would likely be dead by morning if she was an innocent. An experienced woman would have more of a chance, though even at that, it would be a slim one. Damn the woman and damn Pierre for his mistake, if mistake it was. Somehow, he doubted it. Pierre was too wily for his own good, and too ambitious. A fight among the men with him thrust into the role of referee might be just what Pierre had planned since there was no chance of the issue of the woman being resolved to everyone's satisfaction. The problem was for the captain to solve, and if the captain did not? Then he might lose their loyalty; pirates served by common consent, usually wrung out of them by either fear or greed. There was no room for failure. Fail in their eyes even once and a sword was at your throat. If he failed to deal well in regard to the woman, Pierre would be only too happy to step up and take his place. And Pierre had brought the woman aboard.

A sideways glance at Pierre confirmed his suspicions. All eyes were where the woman was being held, all except Pierre's. Pierre's eyes were on him, waiting, watching, speculating. Damn Pierre.

The captain spared not a glance at his captive, but took his time gauging the mood of his men. They were eager, overeager, to begin reveling in the fruits of their plunder. Rum would overrun the blood-soaked decks, washing them without cleaning them, followed by the vomit of the intemperate. The woman, if she was lucky at all, would be untied to lie upon her back. If they were of a mood, they might take her where she stood with her hands tied behind her. The rising of the sun on this night of debauchery would mean the cleansing of the decks and readying themselves again to hunt fresh game on this vast ocean of opportunity. The woman would most likely not see the rising of the sun. Damn Pierre.

Lifting his eyes, he finally looked at her, this cause of all his trouble, and was shocked enough by what he saw

13

in the deepening twilight to forget Pierre and the men and even the plunder. She was blatant sexuality, wanton and soft with wanting, yearning desire. Her hair, darkest blond streaked with sun-warm strands, flowed and moved languorously over her rounded shoulders. She was round and full and soft everywhere, from her breasts to the mound of her belly to her hips and thighs. Her dress was torn at the hem to halfway up her leg and again where sleeve attached to shoulder. Forcing his eyes to leave the fullness of her breasts, he studied her face. Her brows were much darker than her hair and strongly arched over eyes of a very light color, ringed with black lashes. Her mouth was wide and slightly open, her nose was straight. He felt compelled to look again at her eyes. Never in his life had he been hit with such a jolt of desire. Never had he wanted a woman so much at first sight.

He suddenly had the solution to his dilemma, and damn Pierre.

"It's time to divvy up, Captain," Pierre nudged.

"Aye, it's time, Pierre," he answered softly.

The woman leaned away from the ropes at her back and sighed, licking her lips.

"It's a fair prize we've taken today," the captain began, "and the portions shall be meted out according to rank. You all know"—he glanced at Pierre—"that we do not take captives. As we now have one, I will take her, to keep the trouble she brings to a minimum."

"Nay, Captain, 'at's not a fair apportioning of th' goods," one of them argued, his hand on his cutlass.

"No?" he countered. "If I give her to you and you divvy her up between the lot of you, someone would cry 'foul' when she died before his turn. I would not have such a riot as would follow over a woman." Watching them think over that bit of irrefutable logic, he added, "Let's not quibble over a woman. They're as plentiful as barnacles on a hull in the next port."

"Which port?" one of them called eagerly.

"Any port," the captain laughed.

"But, Captain," Pierre cut in, "we are not in port now, and yet you have a woman and would claim her for yourself."

"Aye, that's true enough, Captain. You've got your portion and the woman."

Murmurs of "unfair" came at him from the throng that seemed measurably closer to him than a moment ago. He laughed again and spread wide his arms, forcing the men to take a step back. "Did I not say that I would take her for my portion? Did you think I would lay claim to both? Nay, she is my portion and all the trouble she brings with her. The captain's portion will be divided among you."

They quieted at that. The captain's portion was the largest; they would all be the richer for the further dividing of it. Also, he was right; there were plenty of women in the next port. Money was not so easily come by.

"Surely, you do not have to give up your portion for her?" Pierre pressed. "She is only a woman."

The captain looked at his first mate, reading the deceit in his black eyes. " 'Tis my portion to do with as I will."

Pierre shrugged dramatically and said for the benefit of the rest of the men, "It is not my share lost on so foolish a bargain."

"No," the captain agreed softly, his anger well sheathed, "it is not."

The decision made, she sagged in relief against the ropes. A strange relief, for her stomach was tied in knots and she struggled against the urge to gag. He had claimed her and stood by the claim. She was safe, for the moment. She did not delude herself into thinking that her position of relative safety could not change at any moment, on a pirate captain's whim. No, she must not let down her weapon of seduction, especially not now, in sight of them all. Perhaps later, when she was alone, after . . . Her

15

stomach heaved again. She was hardly safe. Now she must act on the promise of her eyes, though she barely understood what it was that she had done. She had not allowed herself to think during that angry debate of criminals, each with a hand upon his blade. She had only allowed one thought to be in her mind, one thought to blazon from her eyes. "Want me." And when her courage had faltered, she had added, "As I want you." Obviously, it had worked and worked well.

The captain stood next to her, his sword drawn, and sliced through the bonds that both held her and held her up. She closed her eyes and swayed momentarily before catching herself, and then she forced herself to look into his eyes. They were the color of amber.

Eyes the shade of the sun on a late summer evening, eyes that flickered with compassion and strength, eyes that held her startled gaze with tidal force; he touched the heart of her with those heated eyes. And she knew with sudden and disturbing clarity that they were the eyes of a man, not a pirate.

Her resolve, her will, was broken for an instant by the startling humanity reflected in his eyes, and she forgot to send forth her silent lure. The captain stepped back from her and frowned, black brows pulled low over those amber eyes. The sun and all its residue was gone now and the sky was the dark violet before full night. There were some lanterns on the deck, but no moon. God had taken away all His light and left her in the dark. And in that darkness she could see golden eyes studying her.

I want you, she thought with all her strength. *Want me.*

He stepped near her again, wrapping his hand around her arm, and pulled her after him. His frown was gone.

She could not slip again in her resolve. Surviving was possible now; she would not let it drift away for lack of strength. Blocking out everything else—the blood, the men, the spoils, even the ship itself—she allowed only one thought: *Want me as I want you.*

On that rested her survival. She meant to survive.

She was as soft and pliable as goose down, her eyes soft and dreamy, her step eager. Everything, except for that one moment when he had cut her bonds, proclaimed her eagerness for the coupling that would soon come. This woman was no innocent. Her every movement announced it. She was as experienced in receiving pleasure as she was in giving it, of that he was certain. Perhaps his bargain with the men was not so poorly made after all. It should prove to be an enjoyable week with her as his portion of the spoils of battle.

He thrust her into his cabin ahead of him, and she had time to make a cursory inspection before he stepped in after her and closed the door with an ominous thud. It was a sparsely furnished space, though she could hardly imagine that any space on a pirate ship would be luxurious, yet this room exuded a certain chill, a lack of personality, that startled her. It was as if no one at all lived in this room. That was all she had time to notice before the captain leaned against the door, pushing it closed. He watched her, his arms folded against his chest. Alone with him, she felt safer than she had on deck with his men all about her. His strength was undeniable and she was thankful for it; he would keep her safe, safe from them all. She turned to face him, hesitant gratitude shining from her eyes. Oddly, she had no fear of him, though he was bruised and bloody, the cut on his leg raw and irritated even in the weak light of the cabin. He was no animal; she had seen kindred humanity in his eyes. She only feared that he would not find pleasure in her arms. She felt safer unbound as well. At least now she could move.

She had nowhere to go.

Watching her, he again saw the same change in her

that he had noted on deck. It wasn't a change so much as a subtle shifting within her. Seeing her in better light, he knew that, though she was a woman used to sporting in a man's bed, she was no harbor doxy. Nay, her looks were too fine for that. Her skin was dark cream, her face delicate yet lush and heart-shaped. Her hands were not reddened with work. Her clothes, though not the apex of fashion, were of a fine weave and good color. She wore blue. Her dress matched her eyes. No harbor doxy would have that skin and those eyes. No harbor doxy would have been traveling on that ship, either; she would not have been allowed to board her. But it was more than that; intelligence sparkled keenly behind the sheen of her eyes. Before him, her arms crossed in imitation of his, stood a woman who could think, perhaps more than she could feel, for the spark of desire was deserting her even as he watched.

He studied her more intently. Perhaps the lighting on the deck had misled him. She did not seem the siren now; she seemed . . . nervous.

"I assured my crew that I was content with my portion. Are you not content with yours?"

She jumped slightly and then drew a deep breath. She had forgotten again, and after strictly lecturing herself not to; she had been lulled into a feeling of safety that was surely false. There was no safety here with this man, there was only survival, and survival beckoned sweetly enough right now. He had noted her fear, and that he must not do. He thought her content with him; he must think her pleased, and she must please him in return or he would cast her to the men without compunction. Had that not been what they all intended? He was a pirate. Human, of course, but just barely. She must never forget that. There was no safety with this man.

Again she inwardly repeated the words so familiar to her, *I want you. Want me. I want you.* Had she lived before saying those words, those simple declarative sentences? She couldn't remember. Her life depended on his believing the lie she silently told him, and told herself. *I want you. Want me.*

The captain watched her eyes soften with desire, saw the lethargy creep into her bones, saw the pulse quicken in her throat. Nay, no harbor doxy this, but perhaps a courtesan? A woman of quality who pleasured a man in all ways for a very handsome sum? Yes, she was likely a courtesan, smart enough to know her own worth and market it accordingly. He could allow that she was a very successful one, at that.

Controlling his throbbing lust, he approached her slowly. She was not coarse in her manner, for which he was grateful. He would match her in that. He was not to be outdone in etiquette by a well-paid whore.

"Have I taken your companion from you today?" he questioned politely. At her blank look, he asked, "Did you fear I would not know your quality and toss you to my men?"

Hope soared within her. Perhaps there were pirates who practiced mercy and one stood before her. He *had* rescued her from his men despite their clear displeasure and rapacious violence. She had not been deceiving herself in what she had read in his eyes. He had not abandoned all principle, all civility, all mercy even though he had succumbed to the lure of pirate profit. He was strong, and that strength would be turned to her protection. He would hide her in his cabin until they made port, and then she would leave his ship and no one would know that she had fallen into the hands of pirates and he would sail away to far-off ports. It would all be as if nothing had happened. He *was* a pirate with mercy.

"Yes," she murmured, unclasping her arms. But before she could say more, he went on.

"I am not such an ill-tutored rogue that I would fail to

19

recognize a practiced woman of pleasure when I am fortunate enough to find one." Eyeing her full bosom with anticipation, he added, "You are clearly at the top of your . . . ah, profession. You can't be worried over a lack of gentlemen. When I have consumed my portion"—his eyes flared like the fire in the lantern hanging from the beam—"you will be free to go. Reasonable?"

She scolded herself for her foolishness, doubly angry that she had so much trouble accepting the obvious. Pirates offered no mercy. There was no mercy for her here. His eyes lied. He was a pirate; he would be adept at lying, even the unspoken lie of compassion in his eyes. He was all smiles, all charm, and he had no plans to spare her. Hardly. He thought her a fallen woman and planned to use her as such, without having to pay, of course. And then he would release her; her mind clung to that. And if she wasn't what he thought her to be, what he clearly wanted her to be?

She managed a small smile in return. A smile so cool that it barely moved her mouth. "Reasonable," she answered with all civility.

He had the gall to bow crisply in her direction. How very well he played at mercy and compassion and civility.

The captain held his lust on a tight leash. Let her play at being the courtesan in a fine drawing room, he would have her soon. She knew it and he knew it. He could wait for a few civilized moments before plunging into her. What he would not do was drop his breeches and flip up her skirts like an untried boy. He would prove to her and to himself that she was not *that* irresistible.

He walked to a table bolted to the floor in a far corner of the small room. "Brandy?"

She had never touched it in her life. She had never had any intoxicants beyond a small glass of wine with meals. She knew she would need it now.

"Yes, please," she answered.

Nodding, he uncorked the bottle and poured two glasses. The room may have been unadorned, but his glassware was superb. Taking the glass from him, she waited for him to drink first, watching him, not forgetting her silent litany, not forgetting to want him, not forgetting to want him to want her. Strange that the brandy was of the same warm color as his eyes, though far, darker. His eyes were like poured honey, sweet and warm and thick with thoughts she could not read, but warm, as warm and golden as the sun which had so recently deserted her.

I want you, she thought. It was not such an unfamiliar thought now; no, it came easily and readily enough. He was not hard to look upon. No, he was just a step away from beautiful with his black hair and warmly luminous eyes.

Standing this close to her, he saw that her eyes were not blue, but green or a shade in between the two. They were the color of the water in a shallow tropical bay with white sand underneath. Strange that her eyes were the color of his beloved sea.

She did not sip her brandy but took a gulp that more than matched his. She did not stop until her glass was empty. She coughed only once. Then she stood, the glass dangling uselessly from her hand, waiting for him to attack her, praying that the brandy would work quickly.

"You have an unusual way of drinking brandy," he said with a soft smile. "You have a particular fondness for the drink?"

"Yes," she answered impulsively, holding out her glass for more.

Still smiling, feeling her smothered tension, he obliged her, taking another full swallow as he watched her tip her glass back until it was once again empty. She did not cough this time. He could read her need of it. Though a courtesan, she was no common whore; she was not one to

21

lift her skirts casually. Her clients were likely carefully chosen and a rapport established; at least he believed so of her. She was not at ease. He would have her so.

She did not move from her spot. She did not sway on her feet. She must be very accustomed to brandy and immune to its effects.

Her terror and her resolve were both so great that the brandy could scarce affect them. But she was able to breathe more easily; in fact, she felt a trifle warm across her breasts and belly. She did not move. She did not know what he wanted her to do. Submission was the only card in her deck, and she played it. And waited.

He could see her waiting, feel her nervous tension. Damn, did she expect him to attack her? Was she so certain of her appeal? He laughed softly at that; any woman would have appeal to a ship full of men in the middle of an ocean.

Any port in a storm.

But the storm within him did not rage so fiercely as all that. Not at all. Though he could admit to himself that he had never been so buffeted by the force of passion as he was now, with her. She stirred something up within him long buried and almost forgotten, an emotion that he did not care to examine and find a name for, an emotion that had nothing to do with what had consumed him for so many years: survival. No, with her in the room, on his ship, he did not think of survival. He wanted her. He would have her. He called it passion. Consuming, burning passion. But he would not let her see it.

The power of his lust for her battered her with an almost physical force. She would not have believed such a thing was possible. This path to destruction was very wide indeed. She had been told of it, of course, been warned against the lure of the sensual. She had listened and accepted, but she had not believed, not in her heart. How could she have believed that the urge to mate would supplant all other desires? She had never experienced such a thing, had never even seen it in others. Until now. The captain was awash with it, the current of his lust carrying him as surely as the sea carried the ship. But why was he doing nothing? Was this the normal way? Was there something she was supposed to do? He had brought her down here for one purpose and one only; she would not again be deluded into looking for mercy from him. He had no mercy. He had only lust, a lust that beat against her senses like a hammer. She could not dissuade him, he was a pirate, after all, but she could lose his favor and if she did, she would die. She would most surely die. God forgive her, but she did not want to die. The captain, studying her now with smoldering eyes and a relaxed stance that suggested more of contained tension than ease, was her bulwark against death. So she told herself, and every word of it was true, but the fire of his desire, so apparent in his light eyes, was causing an answering kindling within her. It was only desire that he gave her, she insisted, not strength and honor and compassion, not from him. He was a pirate and merciless. And he wanted her. But did he want her enough?

Her eyes searched his and she increased the fervor of her silent plea.

I want you, I want you, I want you, I want you . . .

The captain groaned softly and threw himself into his bunk, where he lounged with feigned ease against the bulkhead. He would not touch her, didn't dare to, or he'd disgrace himself by spilling his seed all over her torn blue gown. But he had shown her that he wouldn't attack her, and that demonstration of his willpower had taken up enough of his evening. It was time, past time, for her to keep the promise of her eyes. But he didn't dare touch her.

"Undress, girl, so that we may begin," he commanded quietly, "while I bind my wound with my sash. I would not have the metallic scent of blood spoil our interlude."

23

His words inspired her, though she kept her face a mask of submission. His blood would serve to hide her own; she would not betray her virginity to him, not when he so clearly wanted a practiced whore in his bed.

He had been waiting for her to begin it. She was at fault for not disrobing the moment they entered the cabin; she prayed that he was not terribly angry with her for the delay. But she had never taken her clothes off in front of a man before, not even her father. It was more embarrassing than she would have thought. And worse was to come, God help her. Closing her eyes to block out the sight of him, she tugged at the laces that held her gown together at the back.

He watched her hands go to her back, her tightly corseted bosom thrusting forward with the motion, her eyes closed and her head back. She was a skilled temptress, this one. This was how she would look at the moment of her pleasure; she was giving him an advance peek. Damn her.

"Open your eyes, girl, and look at me," he commanded, not so quietly now.

She obeyed him. To do otherwise would have put the knife to her own throat. How could she do this? He was devouring her with his eyes. There was a tick pulsing irregularly near his mouth. Oh God . . .

He was furious with her.

She stared at him, her face a mask of careful control, as she continued to remove her clothing. It was not done awkwardly, not by any means, but it was done slowly, almost lethargically, reluctantly, teasingly. This was worse than with her eyes closed. Shining eyes of jeweled aquamarine were leveled at him, taunting him with her self-control when his was so nearly spent.

"Do you dawdle, girl? Why, when all you do is delay the storm's fury?" he whispered, urging her to complete the task he had set for her. "We shall ride the crest of passion's storm together, girl, and when we are both foaming white, we will trough until the next swell of passion lifts us up. Again and again we will ride the storm. As the sea is unending and unstoppable, so is this," he promised.

She hardly understood him; his metaphors had no meaning for her, but her breasts tingled with sudden heat and there was a dull throbbing in the pit of her stomach. The exact meaning of his words escaped her. The meaning in his eyes did not. Burning desire and extravagant appreciation she read there, and she felt a small flush of pleasure that he was so pleased. She did not look for a reprieve that she knew she would not see.

When she was down to her corset and hose, she stopped. Her eyes never left his. To the best of her will, she had obeyed his command, striving to please him on this unfamiliar ground. But now . . . did he ask for more? Could she give him more?

"Why do you stop?" he chided. "Surely I must see all of my portion. 'Tis my right."

Yes, she was his plunder and he must see that his captain's portion was well met in her. Cargo, plunder, captive, girl: it was how he saw her, how he defined her. But, God, it was not true. She *would* survive this!

She was thankful that he did not set himself upon her like a starving dog. There was some dignity left to her in that he allowed her to quietly disrobe before he defiled her. Faint laughter at such a juxtaposition of words rose to turn her lips up in a wry smile. She had sunk far to be thankful that a pirate was gentle in his rape. It was the truth. She was not the woman she had been this morning. Now, survival shone brightly on any terms. And, truthfully, he had been nothing but gentle with her.

But the day was far from over.

The corset also laced in the back, in the English fashion. The ties did not trouble her, not this time, nay, they sprang easily apart, and with unintentional hesitancy she let the corset slip from her shoulders and down her arms, catching it at the last moment on her fingers before forcing herself to let it fall to the floor.

The captain did not see it that way. She was deliberately provoking him with her harlot's tricks, deliberately fanning his already scorching fire with her languid movements and inch by slow inch revelation of her nudity. Oh, what a fire burned in him. He had never in his life experienced anything like it. But he would not show her the effect she had on him, not when her eyes said, "Take me," and her face said, "Go rot."

And, as he had at every other moment in his life when faced with high stakes and an empty hand, he bluffed.

Never taking his eyes from hers, he smiled and invited, "You do that very well, as I'm certain you know. Would you be so kind as to do me the same service?"

She could make no sense of his remark and she heard no invitation. She heard a command, as all his wishes were to her. He must think her an idiot. Or reluctant. Pray God he thought her an idiot; to be considered reluctant was to be soon dead. This must be the way of the bedroom, the way between a man and a woman. Of course, she would not know that, but he did. Yes, it made sense, she reasoned, grappling with her panic at having to touch him in such an intimate and domestic fashion; a wife preparing herself for her husband and then doing the same service for him. Yes, she could see the logic of it. And the seductiveness. Intimacy and trust would be part of such a moment, the tender disrobing of a loved one in preparation for rest. But she was no wife. And he was not her husband. They were not going to rest on that narrow bed in the corner. For a brief flash, she had an image of her mother performing in just such a fashion for her father. She rejected that picture violently; to think of her mother and father now would spell her doom. There was nothing of them in this. She must think of nothing, of no one, but this man. This man, and his pleasure, was the key to her survival.

On shaky legs she walked to him. His eyes captured hers, compelling her to look at him. His eyes glowed like melting amber, and she felt the heat of the brandy sear her again, sending a throbbing pulse to beat at the tips of her breasts and at the juncture of her legs. It was disconcerting and distracting and oddly compelling. She didn't wonder at brandy's popularity. When she reached him, she knelt at his feet, preparing to start at his shoes, just as she did for her sisters. . . . Banish that image to rest with the others.

He was not in any way like her sisters. He was coiled energy and pulsing strength beneath skin bronzed brown by sun reflected off an endless ocean. He was leashed passion and boiling sexuality. He was a storm ready to break, yet he held off, waiting for her, allowing her to control the moment as best she could. He did not attack her. He gave her time. For that, she thanked him because he was the captain and he did not have to show her such . . . no, it was not mercy or compassion. It was because he followed pirate whim, and whims changed at the breath of the wind. In the storm of desire that now gripped him, the winds would blow violently and erratically.

His shoes she removed first and then his stockings; his breeches she would save for last. The captain leaned forward so that she could more easily remove his waistcoat of fine silk faille, a rich gray in color, though stained and sweat-soaked. He wore no matching coat. Odd that she was just now noticing what he wore. His eyes had captured her with their blatant passion; she had seen nothing else. His cravat was simply looped and gave her less trouble than her laces had done; the linen of his shirt clung to him damply and held a strong odor, an odor of salt and sea and dried blood. Impossible that she should be bending over a man, undressing him, her breasts bobbing and swaying less than an arm's length from his face. Impossible that she should feel his breath on her bared and sensitive skin. Impossible that his chest should be as dark as his face and rippling with long, sleek muscles. He was lithe and hard, one muscle lying in twisted cords next to another, overlapping in shared strength, twitching with suppressed energy.

He was not repulsive.

He should have been. He was a butchering pirate, fodder for the gallows, and a scourge to all decent folk. But he was magnificent in form and strength and gentle with her . . . and there was something calling out to her from the shadows in his sun-bright eyes, something of tenderness and pain and lost redemption. Impossible. He was a pirate.

He watched desire flame softly in her cool eyes as she touched him, brushing her fingers over his skin as she slipped his shirt from his shoulders. It was a caress, almost. She was good, damn good, at her game, feeding his passion while she kept hers in rigid check. It was a contest as to who would break first. He understood that as he read the careful distance in her eyes if not in her soft hands. She was a cool one, stoking the fire to a blaze without getting singed. And he was ablaze; he had never burned so hot or so bright, certainly never for so long as he had with her. She was a temptress, a naked and submissive handmaiden, her head bent to her task, baring his skin bit by bit as her ripe bosom brushed against his thigh. . . .

With the barest hesitation, she reached for the buttons on his breeches, his last remaining garment.

With no hesitation at all, the captain cursed and grabbed her by the arms, hauling her up the length of his torso until she lay sprawled across him.

"Damn you, girl," he choked out with a laugh, "you win."

28

Stunned by his curse and numbed by his action, she could only think, *Win what?*

The numbness did not last. His mouth invaded hers, anticipating a response that she felt compelled to give. Without knowing it, he tutored her. She mimicked his every move, his every groan, hoping to please him. Knowing she had to please him or die. His tongue plunged into her mouth and she responded in kind. His hands swept over her skin as hers did over his, feeling the thick muscles of his biceps as his felt the silky contours of her buttocks and waist. Lifting her up, he fastened his mouth to her breast, suckling like a babe. She watched, fascinated and horrified at once. Lifting her higher, he threw her onto her back, positioning his knees between her legs. Copying him, she lifted her head to lick his flat nipple, urging the tiny bud to erection. The space between her legs widened with the gentle pressure of his. Groaning, he fell atop her. She could only think that it was very odd that he did not crush her with his superior weight. His mouth, teeth and tongue in full play, slid from her mouth to her throat and shoulders and breasts before moving back up again to her mouth. And the space between her legs grew ever wider.

The captain, his mouth on her nipple, touched the juncture of her legs with the tips of his fingers. She was wet with her passion.

Without any thought at all as to the appropriateness of her response, she gasped and jerked under his touch.

"So, you are ready for me," he murmured against her skin, shifting until his mouth brushed her ear.

"Yes," she answered in complete ignorance as to his meaning, "I am ready." She knew what was to come, understood the anatomy and biology of copulation, understood that he would tear her and that she would bleed and that she must persuade him that her blood was his; her parents had been thorough and precise in their explanations, but she understood nothing of passion. Passion now left her dazed and weak, her limbs loose and her breathing harsh. She understood nothing of what she was feeling, but she was ready.

He hardly heard her. Plunging in to the hilt, having waited far longer for her than any man should have to wait, the captain shouted his satisfaction. He completely drowned out her loud gasp as he entered. She was a snug harbor for a man. Her "gentleman" must have been a doddering old man to leave her so tight. Two thrusts, three, four, and it was over. She was a delectable portion, after all.

"Yes, girl," he murmured against her throat, "you won most handily."

Not moving, a tear falling from the corner of her eye, she wondered, *Have I?*

Chapter Two

The pain of what she had just done tore at her. Her innocence was gone, shattered, and the battering ram who had done the deed lay on top of her, his weight now a very heavy one. She moved her leg gently against his, dislodging his binding sash, and was rewarded with the slick feel of his blood on her legs, knowing that his blood would mingle with her own, masking the proof of her virginity.

She was a virgin no longer.

But she was alive.

Forcing herself to look away from the pain, to save it for another, safer, day, she reminded herself that her survival was not assured. This man, this pirate, must continue to be pleased with her. If he tired of her . . . the crew waited in the same fashion that a pack of slathering wolves waited for a weak lamb to stumble and fall. No lamb she. She understood wolves. She would survive. The worst was behind her. That, in itself, was a relief. Of sorts. She had anticipated worse; beyond the shock of what she had done and a sharp burning when he had thrust into her, it had been nothing to send her screaming into the sea. Her path to survival could have been worse, and she thanked God for His mercy in that. She also had a clear understanding of exactly what it meant to be the captain's portion.

He would take her at will and at whim and she would be ready each time. If he ever found her lacking in her response, he would no doubt cast her aside. There would be no wanting her for his own, no happiness in her company for the simple reason that he enjoyed the richness of her mind and character. No, there would be none of that. He was a pirate and amoral. Everything he had done in the short time she had known him prophesied her fate if he grew tired of her: he had attacked, robbed, and destroyed her ship of passage; he had bought her from his crew for the express purpose of feeding his own animal lusts; he had just performed the most intimate of physical acts with a complete stranger. And after all that, he lay on top of her with a very satisfied smile and not a trace of repentance. He was like no man she had ever known. He was no man at all; animals behaved as he did, beasts of the wood and field who existed without conscious thought or moral conscience. More than ever she knew that he was a man she could not trust, no matter what his eyes told her. Ignore the pain and the longing there, she silently commanded herself, look to his actions to see the real man. She was not safe with him. She was just one step closer to living. She must continue to be what he wanted her to be, and what he wanted was without doubt.

He wanted a whore.

She would be a whore.

He felt her shift beneath him. He lifted the bulk of his weight from her and looked into her strangely colored eyes. They were luminous in their clarity and they showed no sign of either desire or fulfillment. Damn.

Irritated instantly, he frowned unconsciously. At that, sea green eyes beckoned him with the same look of brimming passion that already had whipped him into such a frenzy of desire. Damn again. She had not achieved release in their coupling and it galled him. That she should drive him to such loss of control and maintain such a firm hand on her own was beyond tolerable. She had not felt what he did, but she would. He would not allow a woman who sold herself to the highest bidder to best him at this game of desire and fulfillment; nay, he would not. Now that he understood the rules of this game she played, he would win it.

"And now it is I who shall win, girl," he whispered, his eyes going to her naked breasts where they pressed against his furred chest, "and you must see that I do or I shall not be fit company for one so lovely."

She could make no sense of his challenge, his command. She had won nothing but her temporary survival and lost everything else she valued. But somehow, somehow he was not pleased with her.

The captain, the edge taken off his lust, planned to take his time with her and he began by lightly rubbing his face against the mound of her belly, breathing in the scent of her. She smelled of vanilla and salt air, like the air from off a tropical isle reaching out to him on his ship. He wanted to bury his nose in the smell, wondering if it was her natural scent or one she applied. If the latter, it must have cost a fortune to cover herself in it. It was worth every cent.

Wrapping his arms around her waist, he lifted her toward his face as his mouth moved up to taste her. Her nipple, pale pink and tasting faintly of vanilla, rose in his mouth to meet his tongue. He arched her back by tightening his arms, and feasted on her right nipple. When it was darkly rose and hard, he smiled in satisfaction and attacked the other one with determination. Though he had just had her, his hunger for her had hardly been appeased. He wanted her again and with an even greater fervor. He told himself that it was to prove himself the master in this game of seduction and fulfillment. He would play upon her body with his hands and mouth until her breaking fire devoured them both. He would do it. He wanted her cool eyes of sea water green to boil and bubble with passion. For him. He wanted to close the distance she kept between them even as he suckled her. She was not unmoved. Her body bore the proof of that.

Unlocking his arms, he slid his hands up her back until they capped her shoulders, then edged her down the mattress so that her mouth met his. Invading her, in plunged his tongue and out again in a rhythmic dance that she followed easily. Her pebbled nipples pressed and rubbed against his chest. He slipped his hands between them and cupped her breasts possessively before lightly pinching her nipples to keep them hard and hot beneath his fingers.

But her hips did not lift to entice him. She did not moan. She did not thrash beneath his hands.

She struggled not to. He was unleashing sensations she could barely restrain. Rolling heat pulsed from her breasts to the damp juncture of her lost virtue. His tongue swept against hers in a hot dance of sensuality that she understood far better than she had before, but she kept her response to herself. The captain did not moan or thrash wildly, and as she followed his lead, she did not either.

Though he knew that she enjoyed his attention, there was a remote quality about her response that puzzled him. To be aloof while naked in a man's bed was not the way among women of her sort, and with a flash of insight he concluded that this was the essence of her success as a courtesan. She aroused a man's desire to conquer and consummate simultaneously.

She must charge a fortune.

Well, he had paid one.

His ardor was stronger now that it had been at first, but she concealed her rising uneasiness at the depth and breadth of his attention to her body. He would not be able to charge her with a lack of response. No, she turned into his embrace, raised her mouth for his kiss, returned caress for caress, initiating nothing, mirroring everything. She was alert and aware of each move he made and returned it in kind.

Of course, it was the careful plotting of each of her responses that irritated him so.

He had her measure now. Detached passion and the odd aura of vulnerability he had glimpsed as it flickered deceptively beneath her reserve was her trade. It was her lure, and he had jumped for it. Damn, but he would make her taste passion's lure herself before he let her go. He had paid for her. He would keep her until he had broken through her reserve and made her pant for him and him alone. *That* would be his portion, his portion of her, and he would fight until he got his due: passion from her to match his own.

She watched him in his frenzied attack on her body because he had told her to look at him earlier and had not said otherwise. She was afraid to look away or close her eyes, though it would have helped her composure. She did not like to see him bury his dark head between her breasts or watch his muscles ripple as he tightened his grip on her. She did not like the ruthless light that flickered in his amber eyes when he looked at her; it tore into her struggling composure with the fury of the storm he had promised her. But how long could this storm rage before she was rent as surely as a sail in the wind? Should he not be content now, his passions spent?

No slow seduction now. He would attack her on all fronts simultaneously and breach her defenses. She would melt. He was not at all ignorant of women and their pulse points. Aye, she would melt if he but put his back into it. And once breached, he would give her no time to rebuild her cool defenses. Nay, he would see her pant first. And he wanted that of her. He wanted her pleasure in their coupling to match his own, if not exceed it. He wanted to see her eyes glow like melting jade as she gave herself to him.

He kissed her deeply while his hands played unrelentingly upon her nipples. His mouth moved in a swift line between her breasts, stopping to suckle hard on each upthrust peak before licking a path to her navel where he plunged in with his tongue. He had the satisfaction of feeling her legs jerk in response.

His hands retreated from their duty at her breasts to slide down the sides of her hips and over the top to gather at the seam that hid her core. Lifting his mouth, nibbling a path to her right breast over the smooth slope of her belly, he laved and sucked as his fingers plunged and plucked. She bucked beneath him. Her skin was flushed pink and mottled around her throat and breasts.

The captain smiled against her skin.

His smile of impending victory was premature.

The girl beneath him ran trailing fingers, tentative and gentle, over his back to score his buttocks lightly before caressing his hips and creeping between them to clasp his member like a dirk.

In her ardent mimicry, she disarmed him.

The captain quivered as he moaned and thrust himself inside her, rocking against her warm cradle, feeling her hands on his buttocks, her breath against his neck, her hair in his face.

When the last of his contractions faded, he turned to look into her eyes. They were as clear and untroubled as a sheltered bay, and as unmoved.

Damn.

She lay still, taking his weight without complaint. He

was displeased, she could feel it. Why? She had given him measure for measure, stroke for stroke; what more was there to this mating? Not knowing what else to do in such a position, she gently stroked his back in long and even strokes, to calm him. As she did whenever her sisters were upset over some mishap. What else could she do? She had given him all she had, holding back only the private core of herself; her character, her personality. Her soul. He could not have that; that was not a part of their agreement. If she gave him all of her, she would lose herself, and she would not lose herself to him, a pirate. She did not trust him. She did not know him. And she did not trust the gentleness she sometimes sensed in him; she had seen his ruthlessness more clearly and more often.

He felt her caress and couldn't stop the wry laughter that erupted from him. She wanted more. Of course she would, for she had not achieved her own satisfaction in their bed sport. She sought her own release, and he could hardly blame her. Damn, but she must be as rich as a queen with such insatiability for sale.

"Nay, girl, I cannot stay, no matter how sweet the invitation. 'Tis my ship and I must be on deck to guide her."

Pushing himself away from her, he sat on the edge of the bunk and slipped into his breeches. "I have missed my own intent and managed to bleed on you after all, my dear. My sincere apologies." He nodded. "The scent of blood in bed sport is not to my taste, nor to yours, I would guess."

She did not answer him for fear her voice would crack with fear. She did not cover herself against his gaze, which slid to her again and again. She stayed as he left her. When he stood to don his shirt and tie his cravat, she watched him avidly, intently. He was beautiful in his wild masculinity; his dark hair had been tousled by her hands, his fingers were long and shapely, and his shoulders were broad and straight.

"Sleep if you can. No one will disturb you behind my door. You are safe here," he said, looking at her with a half smile. "I will be back at the end of this watch, to begin again," he promised, his golden eyes alight.

She watched the door after he had closed it. When she was sure he was gone, when his steps had faded away and no one else came to take his place, she sat up slowly, as an old woman would who has seen many lonely years and has little hope of seeing many more. Taking a deep breath, her feet dangling, she slid to the floor and made for the basin in the corner. Washing herself thoroughly, the water making a damp spot on the floorboards, she rubbed herself dry and put on her corset and gown, tightening the laces as smartly as she could. Without a comb or brush, the best she could do for her hair was a slapdash fingercombing. Her toilette complete, her civilized armor in place, she scrubbed away at the spot of blood staining the captain's sheets. When all trace of her innocence had been washed away by the cold water, she rubbed the place dry with the length of her skirt. She was a virgin no longer. He would never know she was not the wanton he believed her to be. There was nothing in this room to damn her. Finished, she stood and stared out the stern window of the captain's cabin, in all ways looking like a woman set to calmly wait.

She was far from calm. She was praying furiously. Though God had left her in the darkness, she was not completely despairing. He was Lord of All, darkness, too, she reasoned, her practical mind spinning. She was not alone, she was not alone, she was not alone, she was not alone . . .

Was she?

Chapter Three

He could hear the crew before he could see them. The issue of the girl had not been resolved to their satisfaction, not completely. The image of Pierre's black eyes studying him as he had claimed her rose again in his mind. New to the crew since Cartagena, an able seaman, Pierre was apt as mate; it was his loyalty that was in question. But then, pirate loyalty was always the question. Concerning Pierre, it was more a matter of ambition. The *Serpent* was a sweet vessel; Pierre would not be the first to want her for his own. Men before him had fought for the privilege. And died for the effort. But he had not died and the *Serpent* was his.

Giving them the woman would have satisfied them, for a time, but eventually blood would have been spilled in fighting for her. Not that Pierre would have a care for that when all the men who had a taste of her would have hailed him as hero; those that grumbled would have blamed the girl for dying before their turn, or turned on each other. The captain had seen many die and been responsible for the deaths of many more, but the thought of the girl lying dead on his deck disturbed him as nothing had in years. He was glad she had survived, but Pierre had disobeyed a standing order. There was no doubt in his own mind; Pierre was casting for captain. He was on deck now, feeding the men's discontent over losing her.

Standing in the shadow of the sunken doorway cut into the bulkhead on the main deck, the captain listened to them, preparing his strategy. To come at them like a bull would be to ask for a goring, and he did not relish a fight of fifteen to one. No, he had made a fair bargain and he would behave accordingly. If he led strongly enough, they would follow. Follow or be killed, it was that simple.

Smiling in resolve, the captain stepped into the open air of the main deck. The men quieted upon seeing him. It was a good sign.

"Stay on your course, John; we'll follow the Gulf Stream as she goes north," the captain cheerfully commanded.

Pierre, if for no other reason than to challenge him, argued, "It was my thought that we would about to the south. New Providence Island is a likely stop."

"Not for us," the captain answered with a wide smile.

A few of the older hands, those who had sailed with Dan for a voyage or two, slid backward until their backs hit the rail. Dan smiling was trouble, always. He was a man who used humor as a shield to hide his darker leanings, much the same way a mirror can be used to blind an opponent.

"But there will surely be more like the ship we just plucked coming out of the Bahamas. If we lay in and wait . . . wait in a friendly port with *our* arms full of women . . ." Pierre trailed off, the barb planted.

Dan smiled broadly, his eyes lit with golden fire.

Those who knew him best stayed with their backs to the rail.

"Pierre, when you have a ship of your own, you can circle New Providence until the wood rots beneath your feet. On my ship, we sail north."

It was the very lightness of his tone that convinced Pierre to lay off, at least on the subject of their route.

What Dan did not confess was that there would be no more taking of innocent ships, no more plunder, no more killing. No more pirates. He was done with it. And now that he was captain, he could do as he wished with his ship; the *Serpent* had always been his by law, now she was his by right. Bath, North Carolina, favorite harbor of Edward Teach and his blackbeard, would be his next destination. Bath held a dual identity: that of honest town and quiet host to pirates if they swept in. Dan would dump his pirate crew in Bath and hire on honest seamen; he would leave pirating behind him. He would leave *them* behind him.

Dan continued, "We'll skirt the coast till Boston, then strike east for the Azores. It'll be merry sailing with plenty of ships crossing our bow."

"Merry sailing for you, with a wench in your bunk," Pierre inserted, his black eyes dancing with mischief. "Was she worth the price you paid for her, Dan?"

Dan's smile was as warm as sunshine as his golden eyes met Pierre's black ones. What a pretty trap this man had set for him, but such an obvious one. If he answered that the girl had been worth the price, they'd all want her more than ever. It was the last thing he wanted; in fact, he planned to keep her exclusively in his cabin. Out of sight, they might forget about her. Though what man could forget her sunlit hair and ocean eyes? Certainly she had branded herself in his memory. But then, he had more vivid memories of her than his crew would ever have. He would not share her, of that he was certain and determined, if for no other reason than he had paid well for the privilege of her exclusive attention. No, he would not share her, but he would make her being out of their reach easier to bear with the lie now on his lips.

Laughing easily, Dan answered, "I had hoped, for the sake of my purse, to find her worth the price in goods I exchanged for her. Apparently, I am a poor sort for the intricacies of the marketplace."

A few of the men laughed raucously at that, the mood on deck lightening noticeably.

"But," Dan continued, "I am a fair man. I will not renege on my bargain. But, mates"—he laughed loudly—"you all have made the better deal!"

Hoots of laughter bounced from sail to board and out over the water. All but one joined in the laughter. Pierre burned, his black eyes as hot as coals. Dan had again taken his momentum and laughed it away, but Pierre had not shot his last round.

"Then pass her on, Dan, so we may test the truth of your words."

"The truth?" Dan questioned quietly, his mouth forming a slow and careful smile.

"What is true for you may not be true for me," Pierre hedged boldly. "I am easier pleased in my women. We all are."

Ignoring the men who stood around them in a tight circle, Dan faced Pierre and spoke so softly and so pleasantly that all, including Pierre, understood just how close he was to killing.

"Having made a bad bargain, I do not ask for a share of your portion." He smiled, his voice reasonable. "Do not ask for a share of mine." Dan reached out suddenly and clasped Pierre on his neck, his thumb pressing dangerously close to his windpipe. "Good or bad"—he paused, then said with quiet force, "she is mine."

Pierre backed away, literally, relieved that Dan eased his hold on his neck so that he could put some distance between them. But it was only for now. This was not the end of it. He meant to have the *Serpent* and he meant to captain her. Only Dan stood in his way. With the crew behind him, he would win. With the girl in the cabin, her legs spread for Dan in his bunk, he would have the time and the opportunity he needed to turn the tide in his favor. No matter how bad a bargain he had struck, no man left a woman alone in his bed for long, and while Dan enjoyed his portion, Pierre would work out his plan to have the *Serpent*. Taking the girl had been brilliant. It would all work out as he had hoped, he was sure of it.

He had watched as Dan had argued with Red Jack about the killing; always he argued about the killing. This time, Red Jack had attacked Dan, his sufferance played out, and Pierre had leapt at his chance. Killing Red Jack would have earned him the *Serpent*, and a ship of his own was all he wanted. But Dan had beaten him to it, killing Red Jack after a fight of just three blows. It was then that Pierre had taken the girl. She was a weapon in his fight for the *Serpent*, and Dan had risen to the bait. He had known that Dan could not stomach passing the wench, watching her life bleed out. He had known that Dan would set himself against the crew to protect her, whore or not. He knew exactly what he was about. The *Serpent* would be his within the week.

Now that he judged Pierre sufficiently cowed, Dan took the readings and plotted their course. It was one of the many fists he held over his crew; he knew how to navigate and he was the only one who truly did. Oh, he had passed on to John the basics and left it at that, but true navigation was both science and inspiration. He was prodigiously good at it.

His stomach rumbled in hunger. His thoughts strayed to the girl and anchored there. Damn. She was not for the

deck, she was for below, in his cabin, in his bed, naked. . . .
Damn. Why did his thoughts run to her? He'd had his fill of
her and then some, and she was within easy reach should he
want her again. Just a wench, bought and paid for in full.
Comely, sure, and eager to please, but also a mystery. There
was something about her, something in the careful passivity
of her expression that pricked him like an unwelcome dirk
in the side. Fire and snow, that was what she offered any
man who lay between her legs, and, despite his resolve, he
had not been able to melt her, though he had brought her to
a sizzle. Soon enough he would melt her reserve, he was
confident of it. She was a challenge, he'd give her that. Aye,
a challenge, and so he pondered her. Another rumble and he
had his answer. Of course, she must be hungry; he was.
That's why he had thought of her—hunger. Aye, hunger,
and he laughed silently and shook his dark head at his
own lie.

"Walter!" Dan called. Walter was old enough to be a
grandfather, the one man abroad he trusted to have contact with the girl he was going to keep to himself. Walter
was past the wenching stage of his life, preferring to
spend his money on drink when he was in port. Dan
hoped he died before life came to that.

"Aye, Cap'n," the grizzled old man answered, scoot-
ing forward.

"Fetch grub for my portion, if you would, and bring
her a hearty meal."

"Planning to work her hard, are you, Dan? Well, now,
you wouldn't want her to faint off on you for hunger."

"Stow it, old man," Dan laughed, "and make for Bert
while the food is hot."

"Oh, aye, I'm that eager to get another look at her."

"Right, it's the food that tempts you now, and don't
think I don't know it."

"It's food that fills me belly, but me eyes ain't all that
old."

Dan chuckled and watched Walter cross the main deck to the bow where the galley was located. His eyes were old enough, as was the rest of his body, poor old mate. He was balding and gray and stooped and missing an ear, but he was amiable enough and not as cruel as some. He was a good one for the job of fetching the girl food and drink.

Walter was not unhappy with the job himself.

"Dish up what you got, Bert," he commanded the cook, who was also the doctor, "as I've got to bring the wench her meal."

Bert did not bother to turn around at Walter's abrupt entry. He stirred the huge pot hanging over the fire once more before reaching for a pewter plate and scooping the contents onto it in one fluid motion. What he dished up was a stew of fresh fish and potato, a small loaf of barley bread with butter, and a large tankard of rum.

"He wants her well fed," Walter grumbled. "Lay on."

Bert obligingly added another full ladle to the plate and another loaf of the still warm bread, cocking an eyebrow at Walter in silent dismissal and disrespect as he handed over the plate.

Walter did not notice. His eyes were all for the food. Grabbing the plate, he turned and left as abruptly as he had entered, heading for the stern and the captain's cabin. Between the galley and his destination, he ate more than half of the stew and one of the loaves. The rum was easier to carry when he was more empty than full.

She started and turned with a swift jerk when the door flew open at the pirate's kick. Without a word, he set down the plate and tankard on the table, rubbing his butter-smeared hands on his breeches.

"No privacy on a ship, wench, so there's no point in acting like you've been caught on the pot. It's no secret what he's been doin' to ye down here in the dark."

She lowered her eyes at that, but raised them again when he continued.

"No, you'll be getting no privacy here, nor no privilege for sleeping in the captain's cabin. The captain's privilege belongs to Dan alone, and my privilege belongs to me, as I've fought for it. No privilege to you, girl, especially since Dan's not very pleased with his bargain, no, not to hear him tell it," he chuckled.

She listened to his tirade in silence. In silence, she watched him slam out much the same as he had slammed in.

The captain was not pleased with his bargain.

He was not pleased with her.

He had told the whole crew about his displeasure, his dissatisfaction, at what he had felt in her arms. At what he had experienced between her legs.

She would have to try harder, do better. But how? She had responded to his touch. She had not turned away. She had not closed her legs, though she had wanted to more than she wanted to breathe. No, that was not true; it was a fact that she wanted to breathe more. And had she not admitted that it had not been so very horrible? Yes, but she was feeling more guilty now, now that he was gone. He could not be as handsome as she remembered; her fear had played a part in that fiction, surely. He did not have eyes like costly amber. He did not smile with easy charm. He was not her savior on his ship of death, he was her captor.

He was not happy.

Dan was not happy with her.

His name was Dan.

She moved woodenly to the table and ate her food. It was not unappetizing fare, but she had no stomach for eating. No matter; she had no stomach for . . . other things . . . and she had managed. But not well, she reminded herself. She forced herself to eat, knowing that she would need all of her strength for whatever was to come.

His name was Dan.

Her stomach heaved and rolled at the memory of him. He was not happy with her, but she did not know why or how to change that fact. She pushed him from her mind and forced herself to eat, taking mouthful after mouthful with mindless precision until her plate was empty, as was the tankard. She would need her strength.

She stood listlessly, staring at the empty plate, pleased in a childish way at her accomplishment. She had eaten all her food and though her stomach tumbled, she would keep it down. She would, because she had to. That settled, she forced herself to look at the bed, the rumpled and damp bed: the place of her failure. How had she failed?

She had disrobed for him until she had stood as naked as a babe. She had knelt at his feet and removed the clothes from his body, smelling the salt of him, feeling the warm ripple of his muscles and the silkiness of his body hair. She had wrapped her arms around him, met his thrusts with careful submission, plunged her tongue into his mouth where she felt the sharp edge of his teeth. She had opened her legs for him.

She had watched him fondle her, kiss her, lick her, bite her. She had seen his dark head moving over her body, feeling the tender scrape of his skin against hers. She had felt the pillared strength of his manhood with her bare hands.

She had given him her virginity.

Her stomach rolled in earnest and she took deep breaths to subdue her rising nausea. The fish must have been bad.

For want of activity, to keep her hands busy, she made up the bed. The smell that rose from the sheets as she shook them made her feel lightheaded for a moment, but she persevered in her self-assigned task. That finished, she took her plate and tankard, so proudly empty, and set them outside the door. Easily done, as the door was unlocked. Puzzled about that, she surmised that the captain had no need for locks as no one would take what was his. She was his, for now, and a locked door was not where her safety lay; it lay with him and only him.

She had to please him.

She obviously did not know how.

She moved to the window and stared out. The stars were brilliant and cold and sharp in the night sky, but there was no moon to cast the sun's reflected light on the surface of the waters. The sun was a dim memory in this dark night.

Chapter Four

By the time Walter had shuffled his way back to the captain's cabin, the empty plate and tankard were waiting by the closed door. He found that odd, odd that she would stir herself to do even such a small thing to be helpful. He looked at the door, wondering for a moment about the girl, and then shrugged in renewed disinterest and walked away with his hands full of dirty dishware. She was of no matter, most likely would be dead soon enough.

Entering the galley, Bert turned to watch as Walter entered.

"How does she fare?" he asked.

"She ate right well and why not? It was good, hearty food and she got better eating than those she sailed with," Walter grumbled in answer.

Pierre was just entering the galley for another tankard of rum. It was his third, Bert noted in silent count. "And was food all you brought her, mate?" Pierre needled as Walter left the galley, following him onto the main deck.

George, hearing that, laughed, "Aye, given his age. What more?"

Walter ignored them. They were fools to give so much thought to a woman. She would be dead in days.

Dan listened from his place on the quarterdeck, ignoring their raucous talk. They couldn't have her, he had made that clear. If they wanted to get the fire for her out of their bellies by talk, he would let them and force himself to be glad that was all they would do. Though she was only a whore, he would not let them abuse her; she was a woman, fragile and alone on a ship full of men. Even a whore would find such a prospect daunting. She was his, under his protection. No one would touch her.

Tilting his head, beckoning Walter, Dan asked when he was close, "Did she eat?"

"Aye, she ate all that was brought her," Walter answered readily and very truthfully.

Dan dismissed him with a curt nod. He was glad that she had eaten. She must have been hungry after their initial meeting; she would be hungrier still before the dawn broke.

Turning his thoughts from her as swiftly and as purposefully as he would turn the *Serpent*, Dan checked the position of the guiding star. He had sextant and compass and knew how to use them, but he also had learned from an old man in one of the many islands in the Pacific how to navigate from the rising positions of the stars in their courses. Find your guiding star, watch it rise in the night sky, and stay straight on true until the second guiding star rose from the water to guide you the next leg. It was an old system and not often used by those who sailed Northern waters. It was perfect for that reason. Even without sextant and compass, Dan could find his way to port. No other man on board could do that. They knew it. He knew it. It was the knife he held to each and every

50

throat on ship. It was part of what had kept him alive for four years.

He stood at the helm, watching his guiding star rise, waiting for the second star to make its appearance. He would not leave the quarterdeck until the second star rose. He would not go to her until it shone clearly above the watery horizon. He would wait and so would she.

Just as he now set the time for their coming together, he would set the pace in his bed. No plunging orgasm this time; this time, he would drive her before him as the wind drives the sail. She was a mystery, unlike any woman of pleasure he had encountered. Untouchable even as he filled her, mild in her responses even as her eyes ignited passion through him, wanting him but not taking the pleasure of their mating. He could not understand her. She was blatant sexuality in feminine form, from her lush softness to her pliant surrender in his arms to her beckoning eyes. He thought again about her coolness even in the midst of the heat of passion and of his conclusion that it was a part of her game as courtesan. That had to be it. To be honest with himself, it was very effective. But her restraint, her calculated control, was unacceptable to him; she treated him like a dog on a very strong leash, the end of which she held in her fist. Yet he followed her.

Dan grinned ruefully and adjusted the rudder. She was a woman and willing. Nothing else mattered, certainly not whether she found pleasure in their coupling. He had never troubled himself about that before.

But all the others had at least made a pretense of consuming passion, if nothing else. There was never any difficulty in finding a bedmate, just the opposite, in fact. Women had never been a problem to acquire, just to offload. Having a ship on a loose anchor had ended a tedious relationship more than once. This one, this wench, would be different. He could not imagine that she would even glance backward when he dropped her at the dock. For that matter, she did not even know his name. Nor did he know hers.

Dan shifted his feet on the deck and slid his hand over the polished wood of the quarterdeck rail. Named or not, he knew her and would know her again and better. And soon now. Had the stars ever been so slow in rising?

Aye, she had won the first battle of desire and control. He was not such a small man that he could not admit that; he had acknowledged it readily enough. But the next time he was with her, he would best her. He would hold the leash and she would follow where and when he led her. She would pant for him. He would break her professional control; he had the experience to do it. He had played the rutting youth to her jaded sophistication; he would not do so again. No, that image did not sit well.

The first guiding star was well up, but the second had yet to crest the rim of the earth. Not yet, but soon. It wouldn't be more than minutes now before he would leave the quarterdeck and dip his head to enter the low doorway in the bulkhead that led to the captain's cabin. His cabin. Where she waited for him. Was she still lying as he had left her? Naked and unashamed, eager for her own fulfillment?

Was that the star, peeking from the black depths of the sea? No, not yet.

Had she risen? Had she dressed? Had she tamed the thick mane of hair that had tumbled around her shoulders, or was it brushing against her nakedness as it had been when he left her? Did she wonder when he would return?

Let her wonder. The second guiding star, held back by some mysterious and malicious hand, had still not risen.

Out of the blackness, Pierre climbed the ladder to the quarterdeck.

"I'll steer her for you, Dan," he volunteered. "You have better ways to spend this hour than in navigation."

Dan slid Pierre a look of chilly irritation and ignored him, looking again to the horizon.

"Come now, I can hold her steady while you toss the wench about on the straw. She must be bored with only one man to satisfy her and him up here on deck, leaving her down below, alone in the bed."

Dan didn't bother to look at Pierre; he knew he would see a face of sneering cordiality.

"I can point north while you rut on her," Pierre added. "Any fool can do that."

Dan wondered exactly who he was referring to with that comment; somehow, he didn't think Pierre was calling himself a fool. For a first mate, Pierre was getting quite insolent. He must be very sure of attaining control of the *Serpent* to be so open in his disdain. And to be urging the woman on him so ardently; that spoke volumes about his motive in taking her. All of which only alerted him without alarming him. Still, spending hours each day in the arms of the whore below would hardly be wise, given the struggle for power that was most likely taking place on deck whenever he was out of sight. No, he couldn't spend much time with her, much as he would like to. He would just have to make the most of the time he could give her. Damn Pierre. On the positive side, taking care of Pierre and his ambition was becoming an enjoyable prospect rather than just a necessary one.

Knowing that being ignored bothered Pierre more than anything he could have said, Dan did just that. And then he forgot about Pierre. The second guiding star was up, seeming to push the first guiding star to the cap of heaven, chasing it from the sky. The star was up. His time on the quarterdeck was up.

"John, come and take the tiller!" Dan ordered, holding it steady just long enough for John to take hold and no longer. Calmly, Dan left the quarterdeck, scanned the main deck casually, and then ducked and disappeared into the black hole of the bulkhead door.

Pierre, quietly seething, gulped his rum and watched him go.

Chapter Five

Dan swung the door open without knocking. Why should he? It was his cabin and all that was in it belonged to him.

She was in bed, as naked as he had left her, the sheet pulled up to the cover her breasts. Was this how Walter had found her when he delivered her meal? She lifted her arms in silent appeal, beckoning him, inviting him to join her on her couch of pleasure. The sheet fell to her waist. Her hair gleamed in the candlelight, the blond strands shimmering.

"I have waited for you," she said. "I am ready."

Damn if he wasn't ready as well, he chuckled inwardly. This was not a good beginning in taking the leash of control from her hand. She was very, very good at what she did. And that was not such a curse, come to think of it. But again, he was uncomfortable that their roles were topsy-turvy. He was determined to do something about that, no matter her arts.

"So am I, girl, but I would eat first," he laughed. He

was not so small a man that he could not admit that to look at her was to want her; no, not at all.

Slowly, reluctantly, she lowered her outstretched arms.

It was then that there was a knock upon the door.

"Come," Dan barked, his eyes still on her. He saw her eyes widen suddenly and wondered why.

She understood her situation even more clearly with that knock. The captain warranted a knock to ensure his privacy and his control of it; she did not. She was thankful that the pirate did not spare her a glance, though she slid down and buried herself under the thin protection of the sheet.

The captain sat at the table and began his meal of fish stew, watching her as he ate. She showed an insulting lack of eagerness for him to come to her; in fact, she was placidly calm. This was not a good beginning. He fought against the urge to hurry. Conversation would help.

"What's your name, girl?"

She fought the urge to weep. That one question, in the face of all that had befallen her, threatened to destroy her. He had touched her most intimately, more intimately than she had thought possible, and he did not even know the most elemental fact of who she was. He did not know her name.

She didn't know how much time elapsed as she considered his question. She hoped it wasn't minutes, but she had so much to consider. Would giving him her name compromise her family's honor in any way? That she could not do. Her own honor was beyond her, given away at dusk on this very bed, but she would not drag her innocent family into the sewer with her. She did not dare refuse him outright. If she gave him a false name, she could easily forget to answer to it, and that would earn his anger. No, there was a way; she would supply just her given name. That was hers and hers alone. It was her family name, her surname, that she shared.

"Lydia."

"Lydia," he repeated and then he smiled. Rising to his feet, he approached the bed and took her right hand in his. Raising her fingers to his lips, he kissed them in greeting.

"Most honored, Lydia. Your name is as beautiful as the woman it sheaths." He smiled ruefully, still holding her hand. "I have no such name to give you, for my name is as blunt as yours is melodic. I am Dan."

And then, instead of joining her in bed, as she had expected, he returned to his chair.

Lydia's heart sank. This was not a good beginning. He had grown tired of her. So soon. She had not won much of a reprieve after all. The man who brought the food had told her as much. The captain was not happy with the outcome of his bargain. The proof was before her. But her life was at stake; she must not give up without a fight. She might not have any weapons, but she had the worthiest goal of all, life, and she was not going to sit quietly and watch it be snatched out of her hand. Not after having survived this long.

Throwing back the sheet, Lydia slipped from the bed, only her hair hiding her nakedness. Walking toward him, her passage unintentionally slow, she spoke to him from her heart, telling him whatever truths she could find there.

"I have been waiting for you, it seems, forever. The sky is black and the ocean is blacker and I thought of you. I was afraid that you would not come to me again. I was afraid that you would not want me in your bed. I wanted to be ready for you, if you should decide you still want me, and so here I am. Ready for you. Here for you. Wanting only you."

Every word she uttered was the absolute truth.

Dan watched her, heard her, and forced himself to swallow. This was not a good beginning.

"I sat on that bed and remembered your touch. I touched the sheets and remembered your scent. I stood at the window and thought of nothing but you. Waiting, waiting for you to come back to me. To touch me again. To kiss me again. To . . ."

Lydia ran her fingers through his black hair, her breasts dangling before his eyes. Dan released his glass of rum.

"To feel your weight, only yours, press me down against the sheets . . ."

She licked her lips, her eyes calling to him, intensifying the heat of her words, and ran her hands through his shoulder-length hair again. Or at least she tried to; Dan caught her by the wrists and held her away from him, to keep her from touching him.

Caught and held, she could only stare at him; begging him to want her, to take her, so that none else would. Her aqua eyes blazed into his, her invitation all but shouted. Dan licked his lips, suddenly dry, and held on tight. He did not dare let her touch him again. He did not want to hear her words of seduction. He would not be bested by her again, no matter how sweet the defeat. Finally, he let her go.

Rejection was all she saw, all she felt. She did not move away from him but had lost the will to touch him again, and so she stood naked before him, submissive, defeated, desperate.

Dan swallowed heavily, looking past the curve of her waist to the rumpled bed. Not yet, it was too soon. If she touched him again . . .

Dan stood abruptly. She was so close to him that her nipples brushed against his shirt as he stood, dragging, enlarging, darkening. Not yet . . .

"I've come back," he announced with a rogue's smile before sidestepping her, "but we've the whole of the night before us, girl. I'm not going anywhere. And neither are you."

There was a seductive threat to his words, but Lydia didn't hear it. She heard that he would not cast her out, at least for this night. Relief swept through her, followed quickly by mounting anxiety that would not be kept silent. Why did he hesitate? Why had he told the crew that he was not pleased with her if it were not the honest truth? She stood before him, naked and compliant; why would a pirate not grab with both hands at such an offering? He was a pirate and they took what they wanted; none knew that better than she. But why did he stand away from her? He would if he were uninterested. What kind of woman was she that she could stand naked in front of a pirate and not stir his lust? If the matter of her own survival weren't preoccupying her so, she would have been insulted. He had wanted her passionately mere hours ago, teaching her just what it was that made people yearn for coupling. Of course, she wasn't yearning, no, certainly not, but why did he not touch her? Obviously, standing passively wasn't enough; seduction required a little more energy. But what to do?

Dan moved further away from her to stand at the window. The starlight was swallowed by the black and rolling sea. The candlelight reflected her image back to him on the panes of glass. She stood quietly enough, but he sensed dismay in her. Good. He was not so easily tumbled as all that. He could resist her, to a point, and he was a happier man that she understood that. In fact, he felt positively ebullient at his recent victory over her. They would couple when *he* decided and not before.

"So, Lydia," Dan said amiably, "how did you occupy yourself during my turn on deck?" He did not face her as he said this; he was enjoying his victory, there was no sense in compromising it with a foolish act of bravado. Looking at her again would have been such an act.

"Thinking of you," Lydia answered without hesitation, almost without thought.

Dan fought the urge to preen in the murky reflection of the glass, more easily done when he remembered that this sort of talk was her stock in trade.

"Nicely said and very flattering," he answered, bowing his thanks in her direction, showing her how little weight he gave her words, "but not very informative."

At her blank and hopeless look, he prodded, "Did you dress or have you remained in this charming state, awaiting my return?"

Lydia thought furiously at that. Which would please him more? Somehow, her nakedness had not had the desired effect on him. Perhaps he wanted her to disrobe for him again. That made sudden sense; she had not had trouble igniting his lust when he watched her remove her clothes. It was just possible that the act of disrobing whetted his appetite, whereas stark nudity did not. Too late now to change her decision, but if God was merciful to her, she would have another chance. Still, he seemed to like her better dressed, so she answered with the truth, glad that it was the truth.

"I dressed soon after you left," she said quietly. "I removed my gown in anticipation of your arrival."

Dan felt the fires of his lust lick at him. She had anticipated his coming. But that was the problem, she anticipated him. Again and again she anticipated him.

"I hope you did not have long to wait," Dan remarked, smiling, seeing the humor of her position. Lydia did not.

"Waiting is always long," she answered on a whisper, "but waiting for you was especially long. I found myself despairing that you would ever come, and when my despair grew so great that I wondered how I would bear it, you came."

She had walked toward him slowly during this speech of no great length, the appeal in her eyes unmistakable, powerful, familiar.

Dan forced himself to laugh and move away from her, back to his seat and his food. "And so the wait seemed to me, for a man grows hungry on deck, with the wind in his teeth. The dinner hour never comes too soon and never soon enough to a man with appetite."

Lydia watched him raise his spoon, watched him eat heartily of the stew, and considered his words on appetite. The loss of her innocence had opened up a whole new world of meaning to her. The fire that she had felt touching her as he plunged them into the storm had been a hungry fire, set on consuming all tinder in its path. She understood that he had been hungry for her to the point of starving the first time and that now his appetite had been appeased. She must whet his appetite, keeping him hungry for her, or she would lose value in his eyes. A starving man did not share his loaf, particularly if he was a pirate. Could she not slant his words and their meaning to suit her needs? Yes, she could. And would.

"Yes, you are a man with appetite. This I know." She smiled shyly.

Damn if he didn't almost choke on a piece of fish.

"And I am well pleased," she finished with a tender smile.

Actually, her smile was at best tentative, but from where Dan was sitting, tender was the first impression that struck and stuck.

Damn her for a liar.

He knew that she had not been pleased, not in the way of a woman in bed with her legs spread, but she told the lie prettily, sweetly, sincerely. Which made it all the worse. It was damnably hard for a man to turn away from such a lie. And she knew it.

Another mouthful of rum and a swallow of stew before he answered her.

Claudia Dain

"So, you tell me you are pleased." He shrugged in easy humor. "Then you are a woman of mild temperament and easily satisfied, I would hazard? Or would others describe you differently?"

She sensed the danger to her in the question, understood the insult to himself in insisting that she was easily pleased by him because she was easily pleased in all things. He asked her to compare him to others. With anyone, man or woman, this was a dangerous game. With a pirate, it would be murderous.

"I am as you find me," she answered softly, not really answering at all.

"Well pleased?" Dan gritted out with a tight and insincere smile. "Easily pleased?"

Lydia threw the last ounce of her caution and reserve to the winds; Dan was thunderously angry at her for reasons unknown, but she had to turn him toward her, make him want her. She had to survive.

Walking to him quickly, she sat on his lap, her arm encircling his shoulder, caressing him, holding him to her. With gentle and determined ferocity, she kissed his neck, licking a slim path with her tongue to the hollow behind his ear where she murmured in sensual subjection, "I am as you would have me."

She was soft heat against him, pressing her curves against his angles. Enclosing her in his arms, he kissed her, well in control of the kiss, leading her softly into the course of desire. And fulfillment.

She responded, as always.

Aye, he would have her. She had said it well.

The kiss increased in fervor and in hunger and she returned thrust for thrust, nip for nip, wrapping her arms around him with surprising strength for a woman. Raising his hands from her waist, he captured her breasts from below, rubbing her distended nipples with his thumbs. The shiver that shook her frame was most satisfying, and most enlightening. He would go slowly with her, that was the way to break her control. He would drive her before him instead of dragging her behind. He would break her, until she panted for him.

She was not far from panting now.

What he was doing—the kiss, so soft and hungry, the touch of his hands on her reddened nipples, the hot and hard feel of him against her nakedness—was . . . was . . . not repulsive to her. So much less unease than the last time. So much more heat and tenderness in this storm of passion. Why? she wondered distractedly as he lifted her in his arms, not breaking their devouring kiss, and carried her to the bed. Why? Perhaps it was because she knew what was coming. There was no mystery to frighten her, no unknown ahead. Yes, that must be it. There was nothing to frighten her in his bed.

He spread her out beneath him, so pleased with his control that maintaining it became easier with each touch. He would best her in this game of desire. No longer would she hold the leash to his passions; now he would control hers. She looked not far from surrender now, her hair fanned out, her breath catching in her throat, her aqua eyes passion-clouded. But he knew her better than that. She was a woman who looked the part of passion without feeling its fire and without melting at its touch. No, she might have the look of a woman touched by passion, but he knew she had far to go before surrendering to passion's tide. He knew her better now.

She lay beneath him, clutching at his back, pulling him toward her, wanting the weight of him, the hard and solid mass of him to press her down against the sheets. He gave her but half his weight, holding himself back, focusing on her breasts and her ever enlarging nipples. They rose up like twin islands on the horizon, beckoning him, and he happily gave in to their lure. Pressing her breasts together with his hands, Dan licked both at once, like a greedy boy with a handful of sweets, nipping when the moment suited him, gorging himself on her pebbled sweets. Lydia thrashed her head and lifted her breasts to his mouth, eager for his devouring, determined to give him more.

Dan slid his knee between her legs. She opened easily for him. He could feel her wet heat pressing against his leg.

Releasing her breasts from the vise of his hands, Dan kissed her hard, holding her head still with his rope-roughened hands. She would not have moved away from his touch anyway, but the control it gave him was gratifying. Slowly, slowly, he lowered himself onto her, giving her his full weight. She sighed into his mouth, pressing her hips up to his to increase the pressure there.

Dan ended the kiss, smiling.

She placed her hands gently, possessively, on his buttocks, as if to hold him there, next to her.

Dan smiled again.

He released her head, after a light and lingering kiss on her swollen mouth, and ran his hard hands over her shoulders to her breasts, where they lifted instinctively into his palms. Lightly, very lightly, he rubbed his hands against her straining peaks. Lydia bowed her back to increase the pressure that he seemed determined to withhold from her. Finally, satisfied at her response, Dan pinched firmly. She groaned her pleasure. She could not concentrate enough to mirror him, not this time. The waves of passion pummeled her and pulled at her. It was different this time. She knew what was coming and was unafraid. He would not hurt her. He was surprisingly gentle and thoughtful. Had he not sent her food and kept all other men away from her? She trusted him to keep her alive. She trusted him.

When he pulled away, Lydia reached beneath his breeches, breaking off a few buttons in the process, and pinched his buttocks; she had the satisfaction of feeling him buck against her. He would not leave her now, not when she had given so much to keep him with her.

No, he would not leave her. Bucking against her, Dan, so swollen with waiting desire, plunged into her waiting heat without intent. Once there, surrounded by her pulsing heat, he would not, could not, leave.

Pulling out and plunging in again, he noted that Lydia met his thrust with one of her own, matching him like for like. Still holding his buttocks to her, she kept pace with him, breathing hard, flushed across her breasts and throat. Keeping pace, but in the end, Dan outpaced her and finished his race with a grunt. Lydia lay silent and still beneath him, her breathing ragged. But not quite panting.

Still, it was a closer thing than it had been before. And he had all the time in the world with her, if he chose it. He might not have broken her control this time, but perhaps the next, or the next. It would be soon. He was making striding progress.

Keeping her pinned beneath him, his diminished shaft well buried in her, Dan stroked Lydia's face with gentle fingers.

"You would be safe in bargaining that all my appetites are well satisfied now, girl."

Lydia smiled and answered sincerely, "I am glad."

"I believe you," Dan answered, meaning it and wondering why it was so. There was a sincerity about her that puzzled him. Except for her restraint, there was nothing about her that was coy. She was nothing like the other whores he had known. And she was a whore, he reminded himself. "You are very good at what you do; but then, you know that, don't you?"

Having no idea what he was referring to, Lydia answered with a simple, "Thank you."

Dan was seized by a sudden curiosity to know more about the woman in his bed. She was a courtesan, yes, but from where and for whom?

"Where are you from, girl? We snatched you off of Eleuthera, is that your home port?"

She didn't know enough about Eleuthera to dissemble. She had gone there to help her mother's sister, frail since childbed, and had stayed for three months. There was not much to the island, but she had rarely strayed out of doors for the entire time. There was little she could say about Eleuthera.

"No, I am not from Eleuthera," Lydia answered, hoping that would satisfy him.

It did not.

"Where, girl?"

When she bit her lip in indecision, Dan cajoled, "Come, Lydia, I am merely curious about you, which is more than natural, wouldn't you say?" And he pumped his hips into her, making his point. "It is difficult to be at sea for such long stretches, with no female in any direction. I would converse with you. A pleasant way to pass the hours, wouldn't you agree?"

It was embarrassing, the way he talked. She lay beneath him, could feel the hardening length of him inside her. He had only just bothered to find out her name, for mercy's sake, and now he wanted to pass an hour or two in conversation?

It was ridiculous. It had to be a flat lie. She could hardly refuse him.

"I am from the colonies," she said simply and truthfully and, she hoped, finally.

"Which colonies and whose?" was his reasonable response.

"The North American colonies."

"Which are many and very spread about." He smiled, grinding into her again for emphasis. "Which one do you claim?"

This was getting entirely too specific for her comfortable anonymity. The American colonies were indeed spread out, but they were not highly populated. If she gave him much more information, he could find out who she was. As if he would want to.

"I live on the coast," Lydia supplied.

"As does everyone else," he grinned, dipping his head to kiss her lightly.

"Yes, well, we need to be accessible to the ships—"

"Oh, yes, you do," Dan whispered in her ear, his tongue flicking in and out briefly, showing her just how accessible she needed to be and to whom.

Lifting himself away from her, maintaining his connection at one crucial point only, Dan discharged some friendly advice, reminding them both what she was. "Frankly, Lydia, I'm surprised that you aren't more forthcoming with your address. A woman in your profession, one who caters to men and their desires, would want her location well known. If I am pleased with you, I might want to renew our acquaintance, and that could hardly hurt you, don't you see? There can be no remuneration if I can't find you."

More clearly than ever before, Lydia understood what he thought her: a woman who lived off of men's illicit desires, a woman who lived much as other women, except that she didn't have a husband; she had a harbor-full of men who claimed her and paid well for the claiming. Some would call it being a courtesan. By any name, a whore.

And yet, his belief gave her a greater anonymity than anything else because she was not a whore and if he looked for her as such, he would never find her. Not that he was going to look.

"You're right," she conceded. "I suppose I just don't find myself a very interesting subject for extended conversation. I am from the Virginia Colony."

"Are you?" he asked, seeming genuinely interested, even a little surprised. "The place must have changed considerably since I was last there."

"You know Virginia?" Lydia just kept herself from gasping.

"Yes, well, it's been many years . . ."

"But you've been there," she stated flatly, more for herself than for him. A feeling of doom weighing on her more heavily than he did. She did not like the fact that they shared a memory of Virginia. It made him seem too human, as if he had a family and a history of friendship tying him to that place. As she did. It made him seem less the pirate she knew he was. "Do you spend much time there?"

"No, not as much as some would like," he answered evasively. "I am a man of the sea, not the land; there is little there that calls to me. Although that could change." He smiled seductively, his eyes studying her, wondering what her response would be. A clever courtesan would urge him to come. Lydia did not seem very enthusiastic about the idea. He had thought her rather intelligent.

Pray God he remained a man of the sea. It would do her no good if he roamed about Virginia, perhaps finding her. But would he remember her, even if he found her? It seemed unlikely. And why did it matter to her at all? She was just another woman to him, a woman to be used for his pleasure; one woman of many. But for her, he would always be clear in her mind. His face she would not forget. A small thought at the edge of her consciousness whispered that she might not want to forget him. It was a small thought, very weak and easily ignored. But it was too strong a thought to kill.

"I did not think you a man who would change course before reaching his destination." She smiled, encouraging him not to come to Virginia, ever. "Surely there are exotic waters you have yet to sail?"

"Always," he answered simply. "The sea is both familiar and strange; a man loses himself when he seeks to know her, but it is a happy loss, with no regrets."

"I can see that you have no regrets," Lydia said cryptically. He certainly did not look repentant buried deep within her as he was and a smile lighting his dark face. She could not help smiling at him. He was unrepentant, almost adorably so.

Dan smiled broadly, his teeth white against the tan of his skin. "Surely none today." She was a beauty and cultured to boot; not a common occurrence in her trade. What had led her to it? Surely she could have found another way to feed herself. But probably not as well. Who was he to question the means of her survival?

Dan, his lust aroused past the point of comfort, was not going to use his time with Lydia engaged in idle conversation about his travel plans, no matter what he may have said to her to indicate otherwise. Virginia was the last thing on his mind at this moment. Pressing into her, his length full and hard, he gave her his weight while he nuzzled her neck. She turned her head to give him greater access, her questions apparently forgotten.

Not forgotten, but cast adrift. She did not want to know anything more about this pirate than she had to. Whether he knew the Virginia Colony or not, he would never find her there. If he ever wanted to. If he let her go in the first place. Too many ifs, and there were only a few certainties: she had to make him happy so that he would let her live and let her go when he had had his fill of her. Happy enough so that he would keep her, but not so happy that he would never let her go. A very fine line to walk.

But she was being foolish. Pirates were not monogamous. He would never even consider keeping her. That would not be a problem for her. No, her problem was in keeping his passions aroused. After her initial rough start, things seemed to be going well now. In fact, in fact

. . . it was becoming difficult to remember this was all an act. It was not so bad, what he did to her in his bed, and he was not repulsive. No, he was a very handsome man; she could be honest about that, and he was not ungentle with her. Actually, he seemed rather eager to please her.

His kisses followed the line of her throat and down, following the swell of her breasts, stopping at the crest. With gentle bites and nips, he urged her on, feasting on her nipples, his hands lifting the heavy weight of her breasts so that he could feast that much more easily. She helped him by lifting herself toward his mouth, wanting this strange kiss with a fervor she had never known. A line of fire streaked down to between her legs and smoldered there. Her skin felt hot, sensitive to his touch, the feel of the sheets, even the movement of the air. She squirmed against the sensation, increasing it.

It felt . . . good.

She was a fool, but she could not fool herself. What she felt at his hands was unlike anything she had ever known or thought to dream of. Dan had spoken of a storm, and now she understood his metaphor. With his hands he urged her higher and with his mouth he plunged her back again on a violent ride of sensation that rose from some hidden place within her to roar its wild fury.

Dan's mouth raced over her breasts, from peak to peak and around every curve. Her bosom glistened with the sheen of his saliva. He couldn't stop tasting her, gloried as her back arched wildly to give him her breasts, her hands enmeshed in his hair, holding his mouth to her swollen and reddened nipples. She was giving herself to him, holding nothing back; not simply allowing him to have her, as she had before. No, now there was an urgency, an aggression, in her behavior and he reveled in it.

It would not be long at all. Each time he took her, she gave him more of herself. He was not going to be satisfied until he had all of her.

Still firmly anchored inside her, Dan began pumping lightly, his tongue flicking her nipple in like tempo. She rode with him, wrapping her legs around his hips, her arms around his neck. He abandoned her bosom and kissed her deeply, driving into her with more force now, slipping his hands underneath her heaving buttocks, lifting her to accept him, all of him. Allowing her to hold nothing back. Pushing her to the edge.

The kiss deepened. Lydia opened her mouth as far as she could, taking his tongue inside her, his breath, his scent. Dan, his hands sliding down her thighs, lifted and bent her legs until her knees were near her shoulders. And he ground into her. Harder now and faster and deeper than was possible. Yet, he did it, exploding into her with a shudder of violent release. And she accepted him, feeling him touch the very core of her.

But the core remained intact.

She shivered in his arms, heaving against him, holding back nothing of herself, nothing except that final measure of control. He had not broken her, not yet. But he would.

Lowering her legs, he lay atop her for a moment, panting. Sliding out of her, he turned her onto her side and settled himself in the same position so that they both faced the same direction. One arm over her deeply indented waist, he cupped her breast, pulling her to him. She settled placidly against him, her breathing telling him that she was already asleep. Dan grinned against her hair. He had made her earn her bread today, she deserved her rest. She would get little enough later, not when he was this close to breaking her professional control.

In the darkness of the rolling ship, Dan smiled in predatory anticipation.

Chapter Six

"He's been in his cabin for an hour and what do you think he's doing down there in the dark?" Pierre paused for emphasis, eyeing the men who stood clustered in the bow, listening to him talk. "He's laying her well and true, that's what. She hasn't been off her back since she went down there, that's the truth."

"But he's put in his time on deck," Walter objected.

"Aye, while she still lay abed, idle, when she could have been lifting her tail for you 'n' me."

Several of them nodded at the truth of that; there was no good reason that the wench couldn't have been made available to any and all of them when the captain wasn't using her. Such a division of the spoils would have been more than fair; after all, Dan could have her on demand while they had to wait for their proper turn. It would have been a better bargain than the one they'd agreed to.

"Too much talk over a woman," Walter grumbled in

disagreement. "Dan gave up his portion, the largest, remember; why should I complain of that?"

"Because, old fool," Pierre argued, sensing he was losing the disgruntled anger he had so carefully fueled, "we could have had both."

Stark silence met that pronouncement. The wind slid past the ropes, silenced by the slap of the sea against the hull. The bow plunged down, sending up a spray of salt water that wet the back of Pierre's ragged and bloody shirt, and then rose again on the next wave, illuminating him against the night sky: a black silhouette against the blacker night. The eyes of the men gathered around him shifted, the whites showing dully in the dim light, each man thinking the same thought. There was only one way to have both Dan's portion and the woman: kill Dan.

Franco, not immune to Pierre's talk of women and loot, felt the bloodlust rise in him, but he knew Dan better than most on this ship, having sailed with him the longest. Aye, since that first day . . .

"It is not so easy to kill Dan," he said firmly. "Others have tried . . . and died."

Talk of dying did not help Pierre and he quickly quashed it. "What man can kill fifteen?"

Franco growled back, "It's not the fifteen who trouble me, it's the one." He pointed to his chest as he said it.

There was a rumble of agreement. Pirates all, they saw no need to die for nothing; they already had Dan's share. And the woman?

"Who here will die for a woman?" Walter challenged, derision heavy in his voice. "I am no such fool."

His momentum lost, Pierre watched them drift off, shuffling away from the bow and from him. He'd almost had them this time. If not for Franco and Walter, they would have followed him. And Dan would have died. More importantly, the *Serpent* would have been his.

Now, *that* was a prize worth dying for, as he was certain Dan would.

Franco watched as the men drifted off, Pierre the last to go. He had made an enemy in that one by his interference tonight, but he saw no need for a bloodbath with no profit to him and very much risk. He had spoken truly; Dan was no easy man to kill, even at fifteen to one.

Walter stood at the rail, scratching the place where his ear had been, not turning when Franco drew next to him.

"Should we tell Dan what Pierre is about?"

Walter spat into the ocean to punctuate his answer. "Why bother? Pierre is nothing. If Dan cannot kick him to the gates of hell, then he cannot command me."

There was nothing to say to that. It was the truth. If Dan could not defend what he would hold, then he would die in the attempt. Only the strongest and most ruthless led them, and when he stopped being the strongest, he was brought down by tooth and claw. It was a just and fair system and they understood its rules well.

As did Bert, but he did not think it just. He had been listening at the hatchway, hearing enough, though not all. Cook, doctor when needed, he was not quite one of them, though he fought when there was a fight and killed when a sword was raised against him. He had not been born to this life, though no man was. Each of them had chosen this path, bloody and short as it might be.

Dan was a pirate, as was he, but Pierre was a madman. He butchered for the sheer pleasure of it, needing no provocation and no reward. He killed for pleasure, needing no other reason than the act itself.

Bert did not want to serve under Pierre, where he would likely get a pike in the back for stale bread. Also, he did think that it was not quite fair that Dan be kept in the dark about Pierre's methods. For these two reasons, he crept from the galley and into the dark companionway that led to Dan's cabin.

A light knock and Dan appeared, naked and at ease. Bert could just see the girl's pale and reclining form, misty and indistinct in the dim light.

"Is she worth dying for?" Bert asked without preamble, jerking his thumb in her direction. "For that's how Pierre plans to use her."

"No woman's worth dying for," Dan answered good-naturedly. "Pierre knows that as well as anyone."

"Aye, aye, and so I would have said, but he's laying his powder on thick with the others, getting them thinking of having both your share *and* the girl."

"The girl is my portion and it was a bargain openly made and agreed to," Dan declared.

"And he's got them wanting both."

"So I'm to have no share at all? That's a fine justice, and for the captain, too. Let him plot. The captain's entitled to his share, no matter that it's a woman."

"But it's because your share is a woman—"

"Enough!" Dan cut in. "I will not divide my portion with the crew, be it gold or spice or woman, and if Pierre wants to fight the point, he shall find me ready." Smiling, Dan added, "It is not so large a ship that he could fail to find me."

"Aye," Bert conceded on a sigh. "I wonder that I worried."

"Aye and I wonder at it, too." Dan grinned.

"Hearing you, I shouldn't wonder if Pierre will be the one to worry."

Still smiling, but the lightness gone from him to be replaced with deathly grimness, Dan answered, "When the time comes, Pierre won't have time to worry."

Chapter Seven

It was very late in the morning when Lydia awoke. The sun, bright on the water, sent a thousand shooting reflections up from the surface of the sea. She had longed for the sun and now . . . it hurt her eyes.

Dan was gone. She was alone in her bed. His bed. The bed.

Flustered, she slipped free of the sheets, her bare feet touching the floor. Next to the bed, on the bare wood floor, was a tray of food, much like the one brought to her last evening. A glance told her that instead of fish stew, it was bread, cheese, and water. A hearty breakfast. Especially for one who did nothing but lie in bed and dream.

Childish thoughts, she chided herself. She was alive, had survived the night; more than she had dared hope for yesterday. Still, she couldn't help wondering who had entered the room and deposited the tray while she slept. Nude. She hoped it was Dan. It had probably been the other, the old man with the missing ear. Why should she let it bother her, either way? The old man had made it clear that he knew what she was about and he hadn't looked at her with any special interest. That should be comforting. She certainly couldn't say the same thing about Dan. Hardly. Yet, she did hope that he had been the one to bring her breakfast. The thought of him seeing her sleeping, nude, did not bother her much at all.

And that realization, approached from so circuitous a route, frightened her more than anything. When had she become so comfortable with him? She could admit that being disrobed in his presence had assumed a sort of normalcy, but when did she begin to prefer his presence to the old man's? Surely the old man was no physical threat to her, certainly not in the way Dan had been . . . was . . . would be again. And he was a threat. Certainly. Because he used her body for his own pleasure, giving her incredible pleasure as a freakish accident. She had to survive, after all, and should she moan that it was all not as horrible as it could have been? She would not be so ungrateful.

Bending, she retrieved the tray and walked to the table to eat. Today she would not have to force herself to eat over a rolling stomach; today she was ravenous. The bread, fresh, had been out of the fire long enough to lose its warmth, but it was soft and mildly sweet. A good loaf. The cheese was sharp and crumbly, the water clear and unfouled. Eating slowly, enjoying every mouthful, Lydia was finished much more quickly than she would have liked. Shocking herself, she had eaten while naked. Why had she done that? Leaving the tray, she slipped on her clothes, leaving the laces loose, but tied. Knowing that her hair was beyond redemption, she twisted it in a quick braid, snarls and all. Her toilette did not seem to have the importance that it had just yesterday. The bed was a mass of snarled sheets and flattened pillows. Remaining bare-foot, Lydia straightened the bedding, taking an odd pleasure in smoothing out the wrinkles and plumping the pillows. It was in the midst of this housewifely chore that the old man entered. Without a knock.

A small pivot and she faced him, embarrassed to be found near the bed.

"Up are ye?" he grunted, walking to the table to retrieve the tray. Lydia suddenly knew that he was the one who had brought her the meal. "I wouldn't have thought you'd bother. He'll have you in it again soon enough now, won't he? What's the point with making it up, girl?"

Indeed, what was the point? Though his words hurt more than she should have allowed, she would not let him see her pain and humiliation, not this callous murderer, not anyone on this ship. What was a little humiliation when her life was at stake? Let him mock her, deride her; it was the captain who controlled her fate, the captain she must please. And he had seemed well pleased last night. Repeatedly pleased. Holding that armor against her breast, she faced the old criminal.

"Don't know where you get off with your nose up, wench. If you're thinking that you've got Dan in your pocket, more fool ye. He's no man to be captained by a woman. As to that," he added, thinking of the near mutiny last night, "captains come and go on a pirate ship. You'd do well to scout more than one harbor."

Hardly noticing him stomp out with the tray, Lydia considered this new bit of information. Was she wrong in thinking that Dan could protect her against the others? Oh, he had done well so far in that respect, but how long would he be captain of this ship? Would she be forever part of the booty of the *Serpent* or was she Dan's private property?

Wrestling with unanswered questions, Lydia finally decided that there was little she could do about them. She had staked her life on Dan, and on Dan it must remain.

She was dressed, she had eaten, the bed was made; how else to occupy herself until the day waned into night? Or would he come to her in the daylight? What color would his eyes be in warm sunlight instead of flickering lamplight? Her sleep had been long and oddly untroubled. She was full of energy with no means of releasing it. An unlikely position in which to find herself. If she were home, she would be helping with lessons, working in the garden, perhaps helping her father . . . no, it was no good dwelling on the sweetness of her home. A home that was very likely lost to her because of her successful bid for survival aboard a pirate ship. She couldn't think of her family now, couldn't think of them or she would dissolve in tears and self-recrimination and loathing. None of which would hold a pirate's interest.

Dan. He seemed an odd sort of pirate, rather different from what she would have pictured, if she had ever given herself over to imagining a pirate, which she had not. But he was somewhat gentle, in a determined sort of way, and had a lightness of manner that did not seem piratical at all. If she had been at all inclined, he might even have elicited a smile from her, but she had been too preoccupied on firing his lust and getting his full attention, which she had most definitely done. In fact, in some lights, he had been rather kind to her . . .

Oh, God, she could not be thinking such wild, kind thoughts about a pirate!

Leaping up from her chair, she strode purposefully to the window and looked out at the shining water, not so bright now, the sun being closer to its zenith. The window was open and the breeze sneaking in was warm; it felt wonderful against her skin. It reminded her of Dan's breath.

No! He was a means to a very noble end, namely, her survival. She must not paint him in a more flattering light just to make her position easier to bear. No, the brutal

79

facts were that he was a killer, rapist, thief; though, to be honest, he had not raped her. But he would have! Yes, she agreed with herself, he would have and it might have killed her, so she had taken that option away from him by giving herself freely. And freely he had taken, thinking her to be a whore. Which she wasn't.

But . . . why did she spend so much time thinking of him? So much time trying not to think of him?

What did whores think about?

Did they think of black hair, smooth and thick? Did they remember the touch of a hand against a breast? Did they relive the feel of his mouth opening against hers, the weight of him pressing her into the sheets, already damp with their joining?

God, merciful and loving God, help her!

Her own thoughts answered her and none other. She was alone. It seemed to her that the world had shrunk to just this room, this bed, this sea, and Dan. Dan was the only other person in this new creation, and her life revolved around his will.

It was a hellish new world she found herself in.

"Father, heavenly and wonderful Father, forgive me," Lydia prayed, closing her eyes and clasping her hands in front of her. "My soul is troubled and I seek . . ."

But it was not the image of the Lord that rose in her mind. It was Dan's image.

With a cry of mortal alarm, she fell to her knees, the ritualized prayers of the church forgotten in her desperation. Like a panicked child she cried out, the tears building behind her eyes, pleading, "Jesus, help me! *Help me!*"

On the quarterdeck, the sun was hot on Dan's head, the breeze cool as it ruffled his hair and his shirt. They were making good time, the Gulf Stream that swept up the coast of North America running swift and strong. The sun was always hot in the Caribbean, no matter the sea-son, but now, in the North Atlantic, the air was cooling. Still, it was warm for March.

His cabin must be warm this time of day. He wondered if Lydia was overly warm, or even if she was dressed. Perhaps she was where he had left her, naked in his bed, cool despite the warmth of the day because the sheets slid over bared skin.

Perhaps she was napping after having eaten the breakfast he had brought her. He had thought to share it with her, but was loath to wake her, sleeping as deeply as she was. He knew well that she would get little sleep tonight. He would bargain that she knew it, too.

What did courtesans do without a man around? He couldn't imagine a courtesan without a man; she couldn't exist without one. So what would she do to pass the time down in the dark of his cabin during the long hours of sunlight? Did she think of him? She would do well to. Her job was to please him. And she did well enough at it. Damn, better than well enough. Her slow melt for him engaged his interest as nothing else had in years; perhaps it was part and parcel of her package? Did she slowly melt her reserve for her customers, drawing them to her with both the contest and their eventual success at the game?

No, he couldn't believe it. She was too sincere in her responses, too hot in her yielding. She had never melted before, but she would with him. She would pant. And then he would know the woman behind the carefully calm mask she wore. As a courtesan, she was superb, but he had a growing desire to know her as a person, as Lydia. What thoughts did she not give voice to? Why had she been so reluctant to tell him that Virginia was her home? Perhaps she had lied in saying that because he could not imagine her in Virginia.

Still, how did she spend these hours alone? He could easily imagine her well and truly bored, but maybe women were different that way. Theirs was a more sedentary life. He supposed that was by design and preference. A turn on deck wouldn't hurt her; get her blood moving and put color in her cheeks. Oh, but there were other, sweeter ways to accomplish the same thing.

Dan smiled into the wind, tightening his grip on the tiller. Things were quiet on deck today, the mutinous flurry of last night all but gone. Just as well. Pierre had been close to courteous today, seeming to back down from his bid for power. Good and well. He would cast him off in Bath, North Carolina, which they should make by tomorrow evening. By week's end, he would have a new crew to man his ship, all traces of piracy washed from the decks like saltwater sluicing blood. All would be as it should be; all would be as it was. It would be as if the last four years had never been. But that was in the future; as things stood now, keeping the woman out of sight was the safer course to follow.

He didn't once consider putting her off in Bath. He wasn't ready to let her go, not even close to being ready. And that was fine with him. He had all the time he wanted with her, literally, and saw no reason to end their relationship just because they would be in port. As a courtesan, why should she care? She had a protector and provider in him, and that was all that mattered to one of her ilk.

Dan, in idly wondering how Lydia spent her daylight hours, would never have believed that she was on her knees in abject prayer, praying for deliverance . . . from him.

Chapter Eight

Lydia rose from her knees as the first star appeared on the horizon. She was stiff, her knees ached and almost refused to straighten as she stood, but rise she did. Walking to the bed, she quickly unbound her hair from its loose confinement. Pulling back the sheets, she plumped the pillows again.

Dan would be coming soon.

Her stomach heaved at the thought, the knots rolling and twisting with the force of a gale wind. She could hardly breathe. It was dread, rising up to choke her. It was fear of facing him again and being made to debase herself to save her life.

It was desire and anticipation for Dan, because of Dan.

She could not lie to herself any longer. She had been unable to lie to God for a moment. He had not answered her prayers for help, for deliverance, for guidance. Unthinkable, but He had not answered her heartfelt prayer. There was only silence, eternal silence, to guide her. Had she been wrong to choose this path instead of death? Had God turned His back on her for her sin?

She didn't know. She wouldn't have thought that God would ever hold Himself away from her, especially as she needed Him so desperately. To whom else could she turn for protection? In whom else could she put her trust if not in God eternal? He was her rock and her refuge, she had placed her life in His hands and her soul into His keeping. She had. Hadn't she? But who protected her now? Whose favor did she seek and whose pleasure drove her every action, every thought . . .

She couldn't dwell upon that now, not with Dan coming, coming with his quick smile and devilish eyes and hands and mouth and heat . . .

Finally, the second star rose to take the guiding place from the first. He was holding himself to his schedule and it was like holding himself to flotsam in a gale. Never had a woman pulled him with such force; it was almost unnatural, at least unnatural in his experience. But he was controlling it, just as he was controlling her.

"Franco! Come and take the tiller!" Dan called from the quarterdeck.

Franco came quickly enough, Dan supposed, though it seemed as if he were moving through heavy surf.

"You are eager to see your portion? She waits patiently, perhaps more patiently than you," Franco joked.

"I navigate until the sighting of the second star, Franco, tonight is no different," Dan pointed out. "If there is a woman waiting in my bed, who do I have to thank but Pierre, whose idea it was to take her?"

"What you say is true, Dan. I will not argue it," Franco conceded quickly.

"That is good news for both of us, Franco. Enjoy the night."

"As you will enjoy yours."

"Aye"— Dan grinned—"I will."

Sliding down the rails, Dan went into the galley, planning to prepare a tray that would satisfy two appetites. Bert had prepared salted beef, bread and butter, with apples and precious lemons as a garnish. And, of course, rum. Given what he had to work with, the man was an artist.

Dan watched him load the plates, noting the worried look harrying his brow.

Laughing, Dan said, "Are you still not worrying?"

Bert grunted and added another sliced apple to the plate. "I'm still not worrying enough for two."

It was then that Walter entered, ready to do his duty regarding the feeding of the wench.

"I'll take over for you, Walter, as I'm going that way," Dan said.

"I'm just as glad," Walter mumbled, taking a swallow of rum. "Don't much care for uppity, frigid females, no matter if they have all their teeth or not."

"She's cold to you, is she?" Dan laughed, overjoyed to hear it.

"Cold as an Arctic wind."

Dan said nothing to that, delighted to hear that Lydia saved all her warmth for him. Damn, but it must be hard on the girl to be distant with any man, given her line of work. Almost against nature, you could say. He'd be lying if he didn't admit to being pleased at the lengths she went to please him.

Carrying the tray, Dan hurried to his cabin; not obviously hurrying, but just moving with more purpose and speed than he normally did. Throwing open the door with great purpose and speed, his eyes searched the small space for her as he set the tray down on the table. She was at the window, but facing the door, not the sea. Facing him.

85

She was dressed, but casually, her gown not securely fastened, her feet bare, her hair disheveled. She looked glorious, as lush as island fruit and as sweet to the taste.

"Ho, you're up, are you?" he laughed. "When I left you, you were slumbering as deeply as a babe, and as peacefully."

It was true, and guilt nipped at her. She had been peaceful. She felt safe with him, despite all her careful reasoning to the contrary.

"Yes, I'm up and about," she answered with a smile, tentatively given. "Actually, I have been for the better part of the day, believe it or not."

"I believe it well enough. Not much fun being in a bed alone, is there? Much harder to leave when you're leaving someone in it."

Was he speaking of her? Had it been difficult for him to leave her? Of course it had, she scolded herself. He was a pirate and lusty, and she was the nearest woman for a hundred miles. Simple logic. But his eyes hinted at something more than lust when he looked at her; she could almost believe that he liked her.

"I'll have to trust your judgment," she answered, "as I've never left anyone abed."

Dan smiled stiffly and replied, "I don't suppose you have." No, she stayed until her services were rendered and the client was on his way to the door. He knew that well enough.

"No, I haven't," Lydia repeated. She did not want him to think her a whore, even though that was what he clearly wanted and nothing had changed. Nothing had changed. He saw her as a whore and she behaved as a whore; why should he see her as anything less? Or anything more.

"Well, you certainly haven't with me"—he forced himself to grin—"and for that I'll pay you . . ." Dan halted when he saw Lydia's eyes widen in something like pain. Though she was a whore, he saw no need to wound her. He had been about to offer her a gold sovereign or two for her excellence in his bed, but if her strange dignity was offended, he would refrain.

". . . with a new gown," he finished.

Lydia smiled and smoothed her skirts, wrinkled and torn as they were. "You are tired of seeing me in this gown," she charged.

Dan smiled wolfishly, glad to be away from the topic of her profession. "First, I am not tired. Of anything. Second, I like to see you in anything. Or nothing. Third"— he paused—"I didn't come down here to talk about your wardrobe. Or lack of one."

"And what did you come down for?" she teased.

"I came down for something to eat. Shall we?"

"I'd be most pleased." She curtseyed.

"And that is exactly what I want, for you to be pleased." He bowed, gesturing her toward the table.

"Then we are well matched, for what gives me pleasure is giving you what you want."

"We are well matched"—he grinned—"because I very much enjoy getting what I want."

"I'd noticed." She smirked, moving to the table.

Dan kept his distance, setting the plates on the table, pouring the rum. He could feel her desire, but there was more, something else that trailed after, like a skiff to a sloop. There was a lightness to her that he hadn't noticed before, a buoyancy in her teasing remarks and a sparkle in her eyes. He enjoyed her company, which shocked him, and had the impression that she enjoyed his, which didn't shock him at all. It was not vanity that fueled his belief, but reality; she would have starved long ago if she had been unable to convince the men of her acquaintance that she yearned for their presence. And he was one of her men. One of many. But he would make his mark on her, he would not be faceless and nameless in her memory. She would remember him as the one who had broken her professional control. He'd have her panting by dawn. And he had just the method, too. The element of suspense had been missing from their previous encounters, since they both knew what she was here for. But he was going to move slowly tonight and not allow her to take an aggressive stand, as she had last night. Tonight would be played out differently.

"Come and eat, then; or do you have no appetite?"

Lydia looked deeply into his amber eyes. She saw humor there, and something more. He invited her to share in his humor and in the play on words which she had begun; he had access to her body; now he sought access to her mind and her intellect. And she responded to him. Willingly.

"Yes"—she smiled—"I have an appetite, quite a healthy one, in fact. But then, you know that."

"Yes," he agreed, his white teeth gleaming against the bronze of his skin, "you are a woman of healthy appetites and not easily appeased."

"No?" she asked easily, enjoying this verbal foreplay. She walked to the table and picked up a slice of apple. "Perhaps it is the sea air."

"But you get very little sea air below deck."

"That's true," she agreed, biting into the apple crescent. "Then it must be the roll and pitch of the ship. It's quite vigorous at times."

"But the seas have been calm."

"Have they? It does not seem so, especially at night." And she bit again into her apple.

"The nights have been rough for you?" he asked, sipping his rum.

"The nights . . . have been wild," she said, staring into his golden eyes.

"Yes," he whispered, picking up a lemon slice and holding it to her lips from across the table. She hesitated before taking it in her teeth and sucking the juice from it. The juice ran down his hand to his wrist and onto the tabletop. They hardly noticed. "Tonight your appetite will be satisfied. I give you my oath on that, Lydia."

"I believe you," she whispered back, not sure what she believed, but certain that she believed *him*.

She sucked the juice from the lemon and took it from his hand to put on her plate. Picking up a piece of salt beef, she held it to his mouth, feeding him. He took it readily and her fingertips with it, kissing the palm of her hand before he released her. Next, the bread; he buttered it carefully, but did not give it to her as she had expected. Taking a small bite, he pulled her hand across the table and held her hand to his jaw and throat. She felt every muscle move as he chewed his bread, felt the convulsive action of his swallowing, felt the broad and smooth swipe of an old scar just below his jawline.

Dan unbuttoned his shirt and pulled it out of his breeches, leaving it hanging from his shoulders and fluttering around his torso. His stomach was dark brown against the white of his shirt in the light of the single candle in his cabin.

"Feel my appetite, Lydia." He dragged her hand across the table, placing it on his rippled abdomen. He throbbed just below her hand. She could feel its pulsing heat.

"I feel it," she said softly, her eyes captured by his.

"Can you appease my appetite?" he asked, his voice rough.

"Yes," she answered with a smile, "I can."

She fed him another slice of beef.

Dan smiled as he took it from her, chewing slowly, sensually. They were both enjoying this game of dares and denials, each eager to win, eager to lose.

"Is your appetite as easily satisfied?" Dan asked, picking up a piece of meat and holding it before her mouth.

"I would say 'yes,' but it would be a lie," Lydia answered. "My appetite has grown since . . ."

"Since?" he prompted, putting the meat back on the plate.

She could not say it; her convictions warred with her desires, so newly realized, but she could not turn her back on all that she knew to be right. Even though God was silent. And Dan was not.

She would not say it, would not say she wanted him. Her resolve was still strong. Still the professional, Dan thought. But she was close. Her breath came in shallow gasps and her eyes were bright; what would happen when he finally touched her? The table was between them and he blessed the distance; he believed it fired her, to have him so close and not touch her.

He was right.

He was a magnificent looking man, as fit and well muscled as an animal. And with the morals of one. But it was a dimly heard indictment. The vision of him clouded all thought, all reason. She wanted him to touch her. She wanted to touch him. It was all she could think.

Her nipples were turgid peaks pressing against her gown, obvious even two feet distant. She wanted him, her body called to him, even if her voice did not. Dan picked up the meat again, rolling it into a cylinder.

"Do you want this food?"

"Yes," she whispered, her eyes locked to his.

"You will take the meat I give you?" he demanded softly.

Mild confusion clouded her eyes for a moment. To what strange meaning had he twisted those innocent words? "Yes," she answered finally.

Dan came around the table, holding the tightly rolled meat in his fingers. She did not move, watching him come nearer. When he stood so close that her eyes struggled to keep him in focus, he lightly taunted, "Do you want what I have to appease your hunger?"

Lydia could feel his shaft pressing against her belly, hot and alive. He held the rolled meat near her mouth.

"Yes," she whispered, unsure of what he meant to do to her, but willing all the same.

Dan smiled and brushed the meat against her lips, "Then take and eat. And be satisfied."

Lydia bit down on the meat in strange relief. Her stomach was in knots. She could not say that she felt satisfied. She felt sickly alive, her skin touched with a fiery chill, her lungs pressing for air, and her senses awash with sensation. Above all, she wanted him to touch her, needed him to touch her for her very life. She couldn't understand it and was past wanting to. She wanted him. There was nothing else, no other truth but that. She wanted him. She had to have him. And she would.

"I am not satisfied," she breathed when she had swallowed the meat. "My hunger grows."

"Aye," he answered, his voice rough with passion. "I can see that it does. But the table is full of food; you shall be satisfied," he promised, holding her hips in his hands and pressing himself into the softness of her belly.

"I . . . I do not want what is on the table," Lydia softly argued. He was touching her, but it was not enough . . . too many clothes between them, no bed against her back . . . it was not enough.

"No?" Dan challenged. "It has been hours since you broke your fast, hours since your hunger has been appeased. Surely you want what I have brought you."

Lydia looked at the food. It was appetizing and it had been hours since she had last eaten, but she could not eat, could hardly think of food. Not with Dan standing so close, with his chest bare and rippling darkly and his golden eyes holding her gaze, immobilizing her. With his narrow hips pressing their rigid treasure into her, so close, but not nearly close enough.

Lifting her hands to his chest, she pressed against his solid strength, seeking some small part of it for herself. She knew he toyed with her, though she did not know his purpose. She also knew that he was not tired of her, and that sure knowledge gave her confidence. She would play this game out with him, uncaring who won or lost; if only he would touch her.

"Oh, yes." She smiled up at him, her hands slipping under his shirt and sliding it off his shoulders, "I want what you have brought me."

When his shirt lay on the bare floor, Lydia ran her hands through his hair at the nape, loving the feel of its soft blackness. Dan's head arched back, following the tug of her fingers, exposing his throat.

"It has been many, many hours since the last feeding of my hunger," she purred against his throat, rubbing her cloth-covered breasts against his furred chest, getting some slight satisfaction from the friction. Pulling away from him, Lydia kept her grip on his hair and looked into his eyes.

"Feed me again," she commanded.

"You are fierce for a woman." Dan smiled, pleased at the emotion blazing from her eyes, now the stormy blue of the Atlantic. She sought control, but he would not give it to her. Would not, though his passions threatened to swamp him. He would not relinquish the tiller to her; he had ridden through worse than this, or so he would swear on death's bloody point.

"Not fierce," Lydia argued, pulling him down by his hair until his mouth hovered over her own. "Hungry."

The kiss was little more than a taste of the banquet to come, they both knew that, but she gained something from the bite they shared. She knew that he wanted her as fiercely as she now wanted him. The knowledge warmed her. She could wait until the game was through, for she knew now that she would have him. He would touch her and feed this growing hunger that she had not known existed. Until he had touched her, inside and out.

It was Lydia who ended the kiss, using his hair to control him. He allowed it. His strength was so much greater than hers that no simple tug could have controlled him. They both knew that; it was but another facet of the duel they danced together.

"Still hungry?" he asked.

Lydia lowered her hands, brushing them against his swollen flesh as she did so, and then stepped away, putting the table between them again.

"Not as much," she answered casually.

"I don't know whether I should be pleased or concerned," Dan remarked, toying with a slice of meat. "A woman whose appetites swing so wildly . . . it doesn't sound healthy."

"I feel very healthy." Lydia smiled, picking apart a piece of bread. "Don't I look it?"

"The eye can be deceived."

"And the hand?"

"It would depend on the hand," he almost growled.

"Your hand?" she asked innocently, nibbling on her crust of bread.

"Shall we put it to the test?" he challenged.

Lydia looked at him, his eyes wild and hot and challenging; the food dropped from her hand to fall to the floor. "Yes."

Dan came around the small table toward her; she was rooted to the spot. Her breast tingled with heat and her legs were weak. Dan, smiling, placed his right hand over her bosom. It swelled against his hand.

"Heart beats strong," he pronounced.

Running his left hand down her back by slow degrees until he reached her bottom, he squeezed softly. Her knees buckled and she sagged against him.

"Flesh firm, but unsteady on feet," he diagnosed.

Releasing her, he knelt at her feet, his eyes on a level with her hips. One hand holding her from the back, rubbing the globes of her bottom with firm and easy strokes, Dan ran his hand up the line of her leg, from foot to ankle to calf to knee. She trembled when he stopped. She shook when he continued. Up, his hand traveled from her knee to the fullness of her thigh, the action taking her skirt up with it. The single candle cast his upturned face in strange shadow. His eyes glowed like twin suns from beneath the blackness of his sweeping brows. His cheekbones stood in high relief, casting his lower face in deeper shadow. Without a word, he swept his hand higher until his fingers brushed the curls that sheltered her. Cupping her, he dipped his finger into her private well.

"Temperature good." He smiled. She was as hot as melted wax.

She couldn't stand, not without him holding her, but hold her he would not. He remained kneeling, playing with her velvet folds from front and back. When she buckled and fell against him, he stood her against the table, where she leaned precariously. He tickled and prodded and penetrated and flicked and she, legs splayed out and buttocks resting on the edge of the table, let him. She felt sick, was sick; sick with overbearing passion, passion that had her in its teeth and would not let her go.

And then he put his teeth to the core of her passion. His tongue swept over where his hands had been, finding the tiny erection that controlled her, and flicked it into frenzied dimensions.

Lydia cried out in horror and delight, jerking upright and away from that awful mouth that held her. Dan would not allow it. Reaching up, he pushed her down atop the table, scattering their food to the floor. Her torso just fit, leaving her head hanging off at one end, her hair a shimmering falling mass, and her legs, opened to their widest angle, at the other. She was open and completely vulnerable to his mouth, positioned as she was on the edge of the table, and unable to rise as his hand held her down, caressing the tip of her breast as it did so.

She was lost.

Fear warred with desire, leaving no room for guilt. Never had she felt such fire. It consumed even as it fed her. Ate at her, nourished her, sucked the air from her lungs while breathing energy into her blood. And it led her to a place of horror, a place where she had no intellect, no reason. No control. And the most horrible of all was that she followed where it led, not caring if she was destroyed in the process.

This was where Dan led her.

She raced to keep up with him.

The contractions started softly, gently, building in force as they moved down, racing to be free of her. They pounded against her, twisting and rolling, growing, expanding until she felt she was both cannon and shot. Exploding.

Dan's smile was one of pure victory, but he would not yet let her go.

Dropping his breeches and stepping out of them, he stood over her. Her skirts were bunched around her waist, her legs slack and hanging, her delicate feet not reaching the floor. He could not see her face, but he did not need to. He knew what he would find. No composed face with clear eyes now; no, not now.

He ran his hands up her thighs, pressing his unfulfilled flesh against her. She stirred and lifted her head.

"I am hungry, Lydia," he breathed.

She could not look away from him. He had destroyed

her, but she did not hate him for it. No, she did not hate him at all.

"I will feed you," she whispered, sitting up and wrapping her arms around his neck in warm embrace. Dan wrapped her legs around his hips and, still standing, he plunged into her wet and dripping warmth. She welcomed him into her, meeting his thrusts and matching them, holding him to her, breathing his name into his ear.

"Dan."

It was a pant.

When his own explosion had ebbed, Dan wrapped her in his arms and carried her to his bed. With gentle hands, he removed the tangle her dress had become, enjoying the feel of her skin beneath his hand. Her skin was as soft as cream on the tongue and as sweetly smooth. She was quiet and docile in his arms, tired, he supposed. He would let her rest.

He was victorious and could afford to be magnanimous.

Her professional reserve was gone, broken by his hand, as he had sworn it would be. The milk of her passion had flowed over his hands and into his mouth; she had held nothing back. She was his in a way that she had been to no other, though she had known many. Was it enough to keep him pinned in her thoughts, this furious climax that had rocked her? How many men would come after him? How long could he live in her memory against such an onslaught? But there would be no onslaught if he kept her.

And he could keep her. None here would touch her if they wanted life. Lydia wouldn't mind; she would have all her physical needs met in him, and wasn't that what had driven her into whoring? When their relationship cooled, he would leave her a rich woman. Surely it was an agreeable arrangement for both of them. She would likely jump at it.

Lydia felt Dan undressing her, felt him caress her, but

none of it touched her. She was lost. She had no barriers left to put between her and this man, this pirate. He had stripped her of every restraint and every honor, leaving her with nothing but a soreness between her legs and probably bruises on her buttocks. She had been naked before him for most of the time she had been with him, but now she was naked in a completely different way. She was naked to her very heart. He had taken her on a food-covered table. He had taken her with his hand and with his mouth and with his rock-hard manhood. And she had wanted it.

She had wanted him.

Shame, so long absent, now reared up to drown her. What had she become, to want what he had given her? To want taken what he had taken from her? No, she had given it. She had given him her body by necessity; she had given him her blinding passion by choice and therein lay her shame. And worse, she knew that when he looked at her with hunger and reached for her, she would do it again.

God, so long silent, spoke into the tortured whirlings of her mind. He spoke clearly, loudly, and with one word only.

"FLEE!"

Chapter Nine

This night she did not sleep soundly, deeply, peacefully; this night she hardly slept at all. Dan lay silently beside her, heavily asleep, victoriously asleep. Taunting her with the depth of his slumber.

She could not sleep. She napped, and when awake, she could only remember the Lord's command that she flee this ship. No, it was not the ship and it was not the crew; it was Dan whom she must flee. God's word must not be taken lightly, this she knew, but how was she to flee? Should she throw herself over the side and trust the Lord to provide her with a fish, as He had with Jonah?

She was no Jonah.

Mayhap Dan would solve the problem for her by tiring of her and casting her off, either to his men or in some strange port. She no longer cared. Lydia trembled, shaking in her apathy as Dan slept beside her, a solid presence in the blinding dark. No, she no longer gave a thought to Dan's rejection. That was not her fear. But fear rode her now mercilessly, and what she feared now was that she would not be strong enough to leave him when the time came to escape or to be set free. She did not want to be free of him.

She did not want to leave a pirate who used her as his personal whore.

Awful, impossible, and difficult to deny. What had happened to her?

It was revolting.

But Dan was not.

And that was the problem. He didn't seem like a pirate to her; he was clean, cheerful, almost boyish in his manner. He was charming. He had all his teeth.

If only he were more bloodthirsty, more ruthless; it would be easier to fear him. If . . . if . . . there was no soothing "if": she was a pirate's whore. And she liked it.

No, she was certainly no Jonah.

Little by little, the darkness in the room faded; so slowly at first that she did not understand that she could see the door more clearly or the lamp or the table. The table. Lydia looked sideways at Dan. The wide scar that sliced his jaw was shining in the pale light, light too weak to be called the dawn. It was a vicious scar, a battle scar. She wondered how he had acquired it. In truth, it looked exactly the sort of scar a pirate would sport.

But it did not mar his looks or mutilate his charm.

She knew he was awakening by the change in his breathing. So much of him was familiar to her. Two days ago she had not known of his existence; today, today she did not want to face him. She lost a little more of herself with every exchange, every smile, every touch. . . . Closing her eyes and relaxing, forcibly relaxing, Lydia pretended sleep. He had left her yestermorn undisturbed, why not today?

Because he knew she was not asleep. Dan awoke quickly, completely, with no fog to wrap his thoughts.

Lydia lay beside him, curled on her side, the picture of perfect and complete repose.

Except that she was not asleep.

He had seen her asleep. This pretty picture was not Lydia sleeping. Lydia asleep had her mouth slightly open and one hand between her knees. The view now was of a closed mouth and two hands tucked neatly under her head.

Definitely not asleep.

Leaning up on one elbow, Dan very softly, very gently, very deliberately pulled the sheet down until it covered her ankles and nothing else. The blush that stained her breasts and throat gave further proof of her wakefulness, if he had needed any. Yet she did not move.

Her shoulder rose up temptingly. He kissed it. He brushed the hair back from her face and kissed her ear. She showed admirable restraint, and still she feigned sleep. Dan stroked her arm tenderly, drawing circles on the inside of her elbow. She lay entirely too still for one asleep.

"You're a beauty, Lydia," he said quietly into the growing light of the day. "Skin like silk, eyes like jewels, and elbows . . . why, your elbows are worthy of sonnets." And he bent to kiss the angle of her arm.

Lydia smothered a laugh. Who on earth would praise an elbow?

"Oh, no," Dan breathed in mock horror. "She's awake! What will she think, hearing I am enraptured by her elbows?"

Lydia opened her eyes and looked over her "silken" shoulder at the pirate who had captured her. Golden eyes surrounded by black lashes studied her, a smile full upon his mouth. No, he was not at all repulsive to her and hardly piratical.

"She'll think you've been at sea too long," she laughed.

"No one has been at sea *that* long," he rejoined.

100

Dan laughed with her, rolling her on her back so that he could kiss her with tender hunger. She returned his kiss in full, whether from habit or feeling, she could not say. She would not examine herself so closely. Not now, not with him looking at her so tenderly, the laughter still in his eyes.

Maybe not ever.

Wrapping his arms around her torso and one leg over hers, encasing her in a hairy and hard cocoon, Dan hugged her from top to bottom. Lydia nestled into his embrace, enjoying his warmth and his strength. She was safe with him.

"Did you enjoy your meal last night? Was your appetite well and completely satisfied?" he asked, stroking her hair.

She could hear the satisfaction in his voice, and the pure male vanity of it was not going to escape her without a poke or two. "It couldn't have been, for I'm ravenous this morning."

"I did say that your appetites were not easily appeased and thus it is proven," Dan said pleasantly.

"I don't remember denying it," Lydia replied.

"But you did argue it," he announced, his breath brushing her hair.

"Impossible," Lydia argued. "I never argue, I only reason. You must be thinking of someone else."

"Impossible," Dan breathed against her brow.

Lydia snuggled against him in good humor and then said, "Is there anything at all to eat? I really am famished."

"If you can find something to appease your hunger in this bed, then please satisfy yourself," Dan offered lightly.

"It seems I can always find something to satisfy me in this bed," Lydia answered, her voice suddenly husky and low.

"And so it seems to me," he whispered, kissing the soft rise of her cheeks and rubbing his hands down her torso.

"We're making good time," he said into her hair, "and should be in Bath by dusk if the wind holds. If there's a seamstress there, we could buy you a few new dresses to add to your wardrobe. What say you?"

Bath. People. Freedom. The crystalline world of the ship shattered to be replaced by the world outside. God would not let her forget that this small room was not a world unto itself and that Dan was not its god. In trying to please her with a few bits of cloth, Dan had thrust her back out of the cocoon she had sought with him. God would not be mocked, nor would His commands be ignored. She had been told to flee and she must. She must, but . . . Bath, North Carolina, was still a long way from home and she had no money. She was not so naive as to believe that people would hurry to help a wayward girl who had no money to pay for the favor. No, she was not naive at all anymore.

"Lydia?" Dan prompted, noting her diminished mood and wondering at it.

"Oh, perhaps," she answered vaguely.

"What woman does not want new gowns?" he laughed, trying to lighten her mood.

"A woman with no place to wear them?" she answered lightly, trying to cover the true direction of her thoughts.

Dan accepted her words as truth since they echoed his own concerns of yesterday. Lydia must be lonely as hell down here all day while he was up on deck. She was a virtual prisoner in this room. That she was in actuality a prisoner on a pirate ship did not enter his mind. She was Lydia and she was for him: those were the important facts.

The light grew stronger in the room, sending its slanting rays across the floor. The food of last evening was still scattered upon the floor, dried out and unappetizing.

Just looking at it, and the table, Lydia lost the appetite she had confessed. She could see everything in that clear light.

Dan kissed her again with lingering passion, caressing her breast, coaxing the nipple to eager life. Lydia responded warmly and openly, without hesitation. As Lydia always did. It was a pity, but he must get up on deck. Pierre and the rest would be gone by day's end and then he need no longer concern himself about the loyalty of his crew. With Pierre gone, it would be easier to bring Lydia up on deck. He would arrange for some new gowns, surprise her with them. He ought to know her dimensions by now.

Another kiss, another caress, and he leapt out of bed, quickly donning his breeches and shirt of yesterday. In less than a minute he was gone, with another quick and ardent kiss in parting, which Lydia returned with equal ardor.

She almost wondered if she wasn't kissing Dan good-bye.

It was glorious on deck. The wind held more of winter's bite than in days past, but the sun was strong in the sky without a cloud to weaken its force. The sails were full of wind, shining white against the vivid blue of the sky and the gray-blue of the sea. Salt spray was cast up from the action of the bow in foaming droplets to fall back harmlessly, rejoining the body of the sea. It was a glorious, glorious day to be at sea.

"Walter!" Dan called in a moderate and happy voice. " 'Tis time my portion's fast was broken. Bring her food and plenty of it and do not tarry. She will be fair hungry and waiting for your arrival." How could she not when her supper lay in dismal disarray upon the floor?

Walter murmured indistinctly under his breath, too low for Dan to hear, but his meaning was clear enough. He did not relish the job of handmaid to a wench. But his very reluctance, coupled with his advanced age, made him the perfect man for the task. Dan watched him clamber into the galley, his back hunched in displeasure and his brow furrowed as he peered into the relative darkness within. Then thoughts of Walter fled into images of Lydia and the sweet sound of her laughter when he had kissed her elbow. She was a beauty and made for his hand, by his own making made for him, belonging to him as to no other before him and to none after. For when he let her go, when his portion had been met in her, he vowed that she would carry such potent memories of him that she would find all other men ghostly in comparison. And he would let her go, aye, he would; but not yet. Her debt to him still ran high; it might be months before he had been fairly paid for his sacrifice. Months.

Walter also felt that he had sacrificed for Lydia; he had sacrificed his considerable pride and his not so considerable principles. Women did not belong on a ship, even if that woman be a simple whore, and he did not fit as servant to a whore.

"The whore is hungry, so says Dan," he grumbled to Bert, not so careful here to keep his anger still. "Dish up whatever you have. She'll eat it or I will."

Bert refrained from comment. Walter, a surly old salt to all but Dan, whom he respected out of fear, was most clearly at the end of his line. Bert, astutely, saw Pierre's fine hand in this increased animosity. And if Walter had been turned to anger and disgust, then it was a safe guess that more of the crew felt the same. Pierre had been busy while Dan played in his cabin, perhaps busier than Dan realized.

But Bert was not going to worry about it.

By late afternoon a driving wind had kicked up the sea, filling the sails in erratic gusts as the *Serpent* sped north on the Gulf Stream. Dan held the tiller, glad of the cal-

luses that protected the skin of his hands. It was a rough
sea and required a firm hand. He was busily engaged with
keeping her into the wind and with the current that
charged so resolutely northward, but it was an old challenge and one that did not require much thought. His
thoughts were in the cabin below.

How full his day had been. How empty hers must have
been. What to do in a room with a bed, a window, and a
table? Alone. Did she nap to erase a few hours of daylight? Did she press her face to the window for a welcome gust of the wind carrying its load of salt and sea
spray?

Once in Bath, all would change. He would bring her up
on deck, clothed in an unripped gown with perhaps a cap
for her hair. Bath was only hours away, three at most. In
three hours, Pierre, all, would be cast to land, off his ship
for good.

Damn. Why should he wait for Pierre when it was his
ship, his command, his damn portion? He had paid for
her and he could damn well take her out of his cabin on
his own damn ship!

"Franco! Come take the tiller!" Dan called on happy
impulse.

Franco came and readily took the tiller, keeping her on
course in the volatile wind while Dan slid the rails and
charged below to his cabin. His intent was clear. He had
left the deck before the second sighting, before even the
first sighting. Before there was a star in the sky.

It was a happy, happy impulse for Pierre and his plans.

Dan's plans for him in Bath he did not know, but he
had guessed and guessed correctly. His strike for captain
had been too strong and clear for Dan to have missed his
purpose. He must strike and win or be cast off. Or killed.
He did not put much meat to the bone of the latter.

Dan flung open the door, not quite knowing what he
would find. He found his cabin clean and tidy, the floor

free of food, the bed made, and Lydia dressed and standing at the open window looking out to sea.

She looked placid and serene as she studied the heaving sea.

She was plotting the distance to the shore, just visible
as a thin green band. It was very far. She could not swim.

"It is as I feared," Dan jovially scolded, "you are too
idle in the daylight hours."

"And too busy in the darkness?" she countered, turning to face him, happy to see him, God help her.

"What transpires in the darkness had not concerned
me." He smiled.

"You are very much the man in your concerns," Lydia
sighed, her lips twitching against a smile.

"Only in my concerns?" he queried, stalking toward
her. "Am I not the man in other, more flattering ways?"

"What ways does a man find flattering?" She smiled,
watching him come on, eager for his approach.

"Oh, in our strength and cleverness, for a start."

"Very well." Lydia nodded in acquiescence. "Your
strength is very clever or would you prefer, you are
clever in your strength?"

"No," Dan said, reaching her and holding her waist in
his hands, "I do not prefer either. You are not very good
at flattery, I am discovering."

"But . . . ?"

"But . . . I am, and so I tell you that your strengths lie
in other areas entirely, Lydia. You are fair to me.
Exceedingly fair."

"Fair of complexion or fair of face?" she asked in
mock seriousness.

"Um . . . I must confess that I was thinking of your disposition, which is as docile and as agreeable as a favorite
hound—"

With a slap to his shoulder, she stopped him. "So, I am

a hound? A sleepy, hearthside hound to provide nodding companionship to a familiar master?"

"I was thinking more of a playful pup who jumps up in all eagerness when her master calls. Do you not find the image flattering?" He smiled, his amber eyes shining with hidden mirth.

"Flattering?" She smiled regally. "Yes, I suppose it is, or would be to some. And whom had you cast as my master in this fiction?"

"Why, myself, Lydia, and no other."

"How strange . . ." she murmured and lowered her head against his gaze, wanting to prod him out of his composure.

"No, Lydia," Dan said, suddenly serious. "Not strange. You are mine."

For how long? she wondered, unable to voice the question, unsure of the answer she wanted to hear and if that answer would inspire hope or fear in her.

"And you came down to tell me this?" she asked, wanting the lightness of their earlier conversation.

"No." He smiled, his serious mood gone. "I came to fetch you up. You shall watch the sunset with me and stand at my side when we anchor at Bath. The air will do you good."

Lydia nodded passively as he took her arm and led her from the room, eager to reach the openness of the quarterdeck. No longer a prisoner in a small room with an even smaller window, she now had the open height of the quarterdeck on which to contemplate her escape. Had God orchestrated this for her?

Her arrival on the quarterdeck was better than anything Pierre could have planned. Her presence on the *Serpent* had been a real but hidden thing, and men quickly forgot what they did not see. But see her now they did. Dan had put her on the quarterdeck because it was reserved for the man who held the tiller and the captain only; it was not a space for the crew. It was also a wonderful stage on which to show her, Pierre noted with malicious pleasure. They could all look at her now. She was different than she had been two days ago when they had taken her, her look more lush and sensual than he remembered. All the better. Now they all could see what Dan had tasted and what they had not, the money be damned. Dan had taken more than was fair when he took her for himself.

Franco, at the tiller, also noted that the wench looked better than when he had last cast eyes on her. She looked well and truly bedded, that was it, and just one man among them had done the bedding. Damn, but it wasn't right for one man to have it all when others went begging. But he was not such a fool as to challenge Dan; let Pierre have that black honor.

Lydia was not aware of the tension in the crew as they grumbled and stared at her, almost slathering in their greedy lust. She was turned far inward, facing her own tension. The land did not look so far away from up here. She could clearly see the outlines of individual trees, pine and cedar and live oak, and the line of sandy beach that fringed them on the shoreline. Mayhap it was not too far . . .

But she could not swim.

Dan had known that the crew, courtesy of Pierre, was not happy with the division of the spoils, but he had not been prepared for such snarling animosity when Lydia appeared at his side on the deck. No matter, he was prepared for it now. It was not the first time he had fought them off. He was ready should they care to pull knives on him again, though he put his money on Pierre, as the one to do it. The others should know he was not an easy kill.

And so they did. But the girl looked ripe and they meant to pluck her, if Pierre could kill the dog that guarded her. The money meant little to them now; they were at sea and could not spend it. The girl was here, and enjoying what the moment offered was always better than waiting. It was that very philosophy which had propelled them into piracy.

It was when the grumbling rose in volume to a subdued roar that Lydia turned away from the rail and faced the pirate horde. For a moment, it was as if the past two days had not happened. She stood with her back to the rail, the stern rail this time, and felt their eyes roam over her body like ghostly hands and with similar effect. The sun was low on the horizon, it being close to dusk, and the wind pulled at her hair in its confinement. But she was not bound, no, not this time. Dan stood beside her, shielding her from their eyes and their rapacious lust, standing between her and them. She was not bound, not with rope. Dan put his hand to his blade and smiled a chilly greeting to his crew. Again, again she reminded herself, there was nothing tying her to this ship. She turned away from Dan as she thought it.

"You mock us with your portion of the spoils, Dan," Pierre snarled with open hostility, all masks dropped. This would be their final confrontation and they all knew it. "Or did you bring her up to share her with the rest of us? Have you grown tired of her so soon? It must be as you said, she is not worth what you paid for her."

"Worth it or not," Dan answered, his voice pleasant but as cold as the wind that whipped the sea all around them, "I have paid the price. She is mine."

"A good captain would have passed her 'round for all to sample."

"A good captain would have given up his portion of spoils fairly taken?" Dan countered, his smile as wide as his disbelief.

"Aye, when the spoils contain a woman!" Pierre snarled loudly. "Women can be shared easily, with no one losing; money cannot. You should have given her to us."

"I will not share the woman, but is it the woman you want with so much heat, Pierre?" Dan asked quietly, the wind carrying his voice to the far reaches of the ship. They all heard him, had all stopped in their duties: Bert at his cauldron, Walter at his rum, even Franco at his steering. The ship was being driven by wind and sea more than by man and listing hard to port. And land. "Or is it the *Serpent* that sets your blood on fire?"

The crew had known it, in their secret thoughts, but Dan's calling it out so plainly made the truth clear for them all. Pierre wanted the *Serpent* and Dan stood in his way. It was Pierre's fight. If he won, they could have the woman after, but the *Serpent* was a bigger prize. Almost as if they worked under one brain, they cleared the space between Dan and Pierre, their backs against the rail of the main deck. This was not their fight. This was a fight between two wolves, and they would follow the one who lived, not much concerned who that might be.

"You know what I want," Pierre growled, pulling his cutlass free.

Dan laughed, Lydia forgotten, Franco at the tiller forgotten, even the *Serpent* forgotten. Only the coming fight was real, and it might be his last reality.

"Come and get it, then," he taunted on a laugh, pulling his own blade free of restraint.

But Dan did not stand and wait for Pierre to advance on him; no, he jumped to the deck with a loud thud and attacked viciously, catching Pierre on the chin with the tip of his blade at the first blow. Pierre stumbled and saved his head from being separated from his neck with the falter. Dan's blade caught on the binnacle box instead, smashing it. Pierre's blade came up and caught Dan's on a downward slice, the hatred in his eyes blazing as his steel sliced the air, seeking blood. Their blades caught; Dan used that moment of stillness to kick Pierre's knee backward. The sudden lurch of the ship in the trough of a wave saved him his leg.

Lydia watched, spellbound, as the fight continued. It was clearly a fight to the death with no rules except one. Win. Win or die.

The lurching of the ship in that ill-timed trough caused her to look landward. They were much closer now. She could see Spanish moss hanging from the live oaks. A peek showed her that the man at the tiller had abandoned all responsibility to watch the fight that had been brewing for so long. The ship was being driven landward. And no one was stopping her.

Dan and Pierre regained their footing simultaneously; Dan's aggressive lead was gone. Circling the cramped deck, avoiding the cannon that dominated the space, they maneuvered for dominance, for survival. Only one of them would live beyond the next few minutes.

Pierre lunged, his blade low for a slice at Dan's belly. Dan sidestepped and brought his elbow down onto Pierre's nose as he passed, turning and skimming his blade across his back before turning to face him again. Blood ran in thick ropes from Pierre's nose. The blow had blurred his vision. His back hurt. He was getting the worst of this fight and if he didn't strike blood soon, he would die. Dying would not win him the *Serpent*.

Swinging his blade high, Pierre let Dan stop his blade well over his head and with the other hand, pulled loose his dagger and jabbed quickly at Dan's gut.

It was a hit, but not on the mark, the mark that would have given him the *Serpent*.

Turning, the roll of the ship helping him in his evasion, Dan felt the dagger slip into the skin of his waist, missing most of the muscle and all of his organs. While both of Pierre's hands were engaged, Dan punched Pierre with the heel of his hand into his already bleeding nose, driving the bone into his brain. Pierre was dead before he fell to the blood-streaked deck.

Silent, they watched Pierre fall. Silent, they watched Dan pull the knife from his side. Silent, even when Dan began to laugh and hurled the dagger through the air with thumb and forefinger so that it buried itself in the wood of the main mast.

Lydia had thought he was too little a pirate. She had idly wished to see him as more of one. How completely God had given her that wish. How clearly God had answered her prayer.

She could see the bottom now, sand and sea grass waving in the current. The shore was close, very close, and the ship leaning hard to port. She thought she could hear the occasional scrape of sand on the hull. The ship would be beached if someone did not take the tiller soon. Or maybe it was already too late.

Flee.

Yes, she knew it. She had seen enough, even more than enough. Dan was wiping his cutlass on Pierre's breeches, laughing with the crew who patted him on the back, all arguments forgotten. Herself, forgotten.

Flee.

God had done it all for her. She would not drown in water she could walk through. She had heard God's voice. She had seen Dan as the pirate he was. All that was left was for her to obey.

Not allowing herself another look backward, Lydia slipped over the rail and into the cold water of the Atlantic. The water pulled at her skirts and her unbound hair, but she would not allow her fear to control her. This was God's path for her and she would take it, no matter the cost. The sand rose up suddenly in a sand bar, lifting her up and out of the water until she could walk, albeit clumsily. She did not look back, but kept her eyes on the trees, finding comfort in the lazily swinging Spanish moss.

On deck, Dan turned to the quarterdeck, looking for Lydia's approval and pleasure in his having fought for her. She was not there.

Of course, the blood and the fear had been too much for her and she had gone below to the cabin they shared. Laughing, he left the crew, their loyalty no longer in doubt, at least for the moment. It felt good to win, better to be alive. And he had solved the problem of Pierre, permanently.

Throwing open the door to his cabin with a huge smile, Dan stopped in shock. The room was empty. Completely and impossibly empty. There was no place she could be . . . no place . . .

Running back up on deck, just in time to see Walter and Bert throw Pierre's body over the side, Dan asked one question.

"Where?"

Bert didn't answer with words, he pointed to the port rail and beyond. Dan could just make out, in the swiftly falling dusk, a pale shape outlined by black trees, the gently foaming surf ringing her knees.

His boots were off in a trice and he had dropped his cutlass, his eyes never leaving the outline of the girl against the falling night and the forest. When his foot was on the port rail, Bert spoke, both his tone and his words a stark warning.

"You'd leave your ship?"

Slowly, Dan's foot came back down. It would be a fatal and very permanent mistake. He could not leave his ship; without him, it would become *their* ship, or whichever one of them could kill the most effectively for it. His ship was his world, was all that he valued in this world and all he owned. He could not leave her, not even for Lydia. He could not.

As he stood there, knowing he could not leave, that it was damn foolish even to have thought of it, Dan

113

watched Lydia stumble out of the water and almost immediately disappear into the thick growth along the shore. She was gone.

"You just rid yourself of two headaches at once, Dan," Walter muttered in profound wisdom. "She won't survive the night, if you ask me. She'll go of exposure and starvation, if the beasts don't get her first. We're well rid of her, I say."

Dan didn't believe it for a moment. She wouldn't die; others would, but not her. She was gone and he didn't waste precious minutes staring at the hole in the trees where he'd last seen her. Foolish rot. No, the first priority was to get the *Serpent* off the sand bar where she'd lodged in gentle rest; not an easy job but one the rising tide would help with. That done, he'd make for Bath, and put off his crew and pick up a new one; it could be accomplished quickly, with enough money, perhaps even in a day, and with Pierre's death so fresh, he didn't think they'd mind changing ships as long as they took their cut with them. He'd be sailing under full sail by mid-morning and continue north. Virginia Colony, her colony, was north.

Nothing moved as fast as a ship under full sail, and no one was as determined, and as furious, as he was.

Chapter Ten

If he didn't know better, he'd have thought her dead. But she wasn't dead, not her. Any woman who could survive on a pirate ship was more than a match for any bear or wolf . . . or man.

Three months he had searched for Lydia and still had not found her or any trace of her. Not in Bath, where he had assumed she'd gone, where she *should* have gone since it was the closest town to her point of landing. But no one had seen her there. He had traveled north then in stormy fury, skirting Williamsburg carefully but giving considerable time to the Chesapeake Bay. It was then that he wondered if she wasn't avoiding him deliberately. She had told him she was from the Virginia Colony; if he wanted to find her, she would expect him to look for her there. Damned arrogant wench to think that he would spend precious time looking for her in every seaport town in the colonies. But that was what he found himself doing.

After the Chesapeake, he had gone north as far as Newport, but not as far as Boston. She was too ripe for Boston. He could not find her in New York or Annapolis or Baltimore. She had not gone that far north. Swinging out to sea from there, letting the Gulf take him east, he'd looped south again, sighting land at Charleston. She was not in Charleston.

That left him with Virginia again. She had to have gone to her home port; it was the most logical move, and no matter what she was, Lydia was not scatterbrained. She would choose the largest towns because of their larger supply of men, and it seemed likely that she would not travel far from Bath as she was on foot and dressed somewhat shabbily. Well, very shabbily. He couldn't quite remember if she had any shoes or not. Not surprising, as he had seldom seen her with her clothes on. Besides, when a woman looked like she did, a man did not bother to look at her feet.

He had checked every harbor ordinary and every brothel that he had found. No one had seen anyone that matched his detailed description of her. He would not believe that she was dead in the wood somewhere between Bath and hell; it was an image that refused to jell. He could *feel* that she was alive, he was just having more trouble than he should placing her.

Why she had jumped ship plagued him. He had been nothing but kind to her, even seeing that she achieved her own pleasure. Not many a man did that. A woman of her sort ought to know when she had stumbled into a fine and pleasurable bed and make all attempts not to be thrown from it. He knew she wasn't stupid, but her leaving him had been at least that. He'd even wanted to buy her a new wardrobe!

Dan gulped his rum, pushing his plate away from him across the table. He hadn't eaten much since she'd gone. Nothing at all from this damn table.

Bath. He'd start at Bath again and move slowly north to Virginia, covering the area more carefully than he had the first time. He'd find her. He'd be damned if he'd let his portion of the spoils up and jump. He'd be damned.

"But, Patsy, it could hardly be Dandridge," Anna Waters argued. Friends for over forty years, she and Patsy shared a lifetime of memories. Married, widowed, aged, they had shared a life in Williamsburg and a friendship that had withstood all. Patsy Whaley could be rather headstrong when she chose, Anna knew that well, but she had a very large soft spot where Dandridge was concerned and it was for that reason that she trod softly.

"He would certainly have come straight to you if he was back, and yet you say you have heard no word from him. If for only that, it cannot be he."

Patsy was not to be put off as easily as that. She knew Anna had her best interests at heart and so would not say the blunt truth: that Dandridge was most likely dead. Four years was a long time, a very long time, not to have heard any word from him, and they had always been close from the day of his birth.

"Anna, I love you like a sister, but you see that boy in too soft a light," Patsy argued, her eyes shifting as they talked, studying the passersby for his familiar face. "He didn't send word initially because he was having too grand a time, and he doesn't dare begin now because I'll flay him red for having been such a selfish cad."

"But Patsy, it's been four years—"

"Yes, and it's completely logical for the boy to have died. I know. But I also know that there's not much logic in the boy. He's all charm and smiles. Why, he's entirely too charming for anyone to have wanted him dead. And too tough to kill if they tried."

117

"I didn't mean to imply that I thought him dead, Patsy. Of course I don't."

"You're a good friend, Anna, to say so. Not for a minute of these four years have I thought him dead, but if it is the *Serpent* anchored off Williamsburg, Dandridge just may wish himself safely in the grave, if only to escape my tongue."

"I shouldn't say it, but he would deserve a tongue-lashing for putting you through so much worry."

"I've been worried since I first laid eyes on him, he's that kind of boy, you know." Patsy almost smiled. "Nevertheless, it was a blessed day for me when Matthew, God rest him, brought the lad into our home. 'Course, he was close to manhood then, sixteen and already at sea for a year. Matthew, as good an uncle to that scamp as ever was, talked himself blue, but Dandridge would hear none of it. William and Mary could wait, he was back to sea. It was two years he was gone, but then back and as hale as any boy could be; of course, his boyhood was gone. At eighteen, he came back a man. My brother would have been so pleased to see his son so fine a man." She smiled.

"He had his father's carriage," Anna added, remembering.

"And his mother's dark good looks."

"Oh, but he has the Prentis eyes, Patsy, and well you know it," Anna laughed. "Do you want a compliment from me? I've envied you your exotic eyes since we were children, and you know that, too."

Patsy laughed, linking arms with Anna and leading her down the street, her famous eyes not for a moment still in their search for that darkly handsome face she knew so well. She would walk the streets of Williamsburg until she found that darling nephew of hers. She believed what she had heard; the *Serpent* was anchored near, and if the *Serpent* was in port, then so was Dandridge. Patsy understood him well enough to know that he would not come to her home, not for shame but simply because he wouldn't want to face the unpleasantness she would surely pour upon him. So she would walk until she found him or dropped from the effort. She would find him; she was a Prentis by blood, after all.

Dandridge Prentis was at that moment very much in Williamsburg, prowling Marot's Ordinary for his missing portion, though he took a risk as the capitol stood not far off. At the capitol there were lawmakers; he did not particularly want to see a lawmaker.

No one at Marot's seemed to know of her, though his description was lengthy and quite complete. Damn.

Bath had proved more profitable the second time there. It was a farmer, surprisingly, hearing his description as he relayed it to the ordinary owner, who said he'd seen such a girl. Ragtag, she'd been, but modest of manner, and desperate to reach Williamsburg. So Dan had come to Williamsburg.

It was not a comfortable stop for him. Born in the vicinity, reared here, educated at the College of William and Mary just the other end of Duke of Gloucester Street and facing the capitol in symmetrical splendor from one mile distant. Too easy to be recognized in a place of eighteen hundred people, particularly when his father had practiced law and his uncle was a burgess in this very community.

But if Lydia was bound for Williamsburg, then so was he. Damn the girl. It was an unlikely spot for one such as she: a small community of farmers and planters and government officials. Still, it was a growing and prosperous place. She could do worse.

He couldn't.

Of all the places to hide from him, she had picked the worst. He had planned to come home eventually, when the smell of lawlessness had left him. He was not the man he had been, this he knew, and he had planned to spend a few years at sea doing what he had set out to do four years ago: dispatching pirates. In fact, he was a better man now to see to the deed, having spent so long in pirate company. He understood well the pirate mind. In some lights, he was in an ideal position. Once he had found Lydia. Ideally, he would spot her, grab her, and set sail with little fuss to plague him. Ideally, she would not have jumped ship when she did. He would have set her off at some friendly dock when she had met the price of his portion; no need to nearly drown herself. And she had hardly begun to fulfill her debt to him. She had robbed him, that was plain, and he pursued her to force her to make good on the price he had paid for her. It was business that forced him to seek her out in the most dangerous of all places for him. He could not, after all, allow it to be said that he had failed to make a profit. After three months, the litany had gained the strength of truth through sheer repetition. In the beginning, when the loss of Lydia had been fresh, it had been more difficult, much more difficult, but he had learned to believe the lie. And he did.

Leaving Marot's and walking away from the capitol, he kept his head angled to the dirt at his feet and away from curious eyes. Williamsburg had grown, had filled with strangers, in the four years of his absence. This jaunt might not prove too difficult after all.

He had just passed the King's Arms Barber Shop and was preparing to cross the street to visit another ordinary when a flash of aqua blue caught his eye. Just the color of Lydia's eyes; it would be just like a woman to wear a color so perfectly flattering to her face and complexion. Head up, he studied the wench, certain of the face that would appear above that blue faille.

It was not Lydia.

But Lydia walked not far behind her.

It was suddenly and blindingly clear to him why no one in Williamsburg had been able to identify her from his description. He had not been describing the girl who now walked away from him at all. Lydia was lush fruit; she had a wanton's body with a sensual face, all curve and dip with not a straight line to her. This woman, this Lydia who walked in dark brown with her head demurely downcast, was not the woman he remembered.

But she was the woman he knew, no matter her outer deportment.

She walked with purpose, nodding to this one and that in passing, a basket hooked over her arm and filled with small packages. Damn, but she looked like the minister's wife in that garb! She would surely starve to death if that was how she clothed herself. Only a starving man would want to feast on her as she looked now. Or a seaman.

Dan crossed the street on long legs, following her. She either did not see him or was ignoring him, which he couldn't credit. There would never come a day when Lydia would ignore him or the fire he set blazing in her blood. He was the one who had made her pant with desire, desire for him. He was the one who had stripped her professional mask away from her, showing her for the hot wanton that she was. Never, never would she be able to ignore him.

A farmer's wagon passed, blocking his view of her. And she was gone. Damn the girl!

Dan ran with a loping stride to the opposite side of the street. Nothing but dust heated by the June sun met his eyes. There was an ordinary on the corner, his original destination; she might have gone in by a side door. He turned abruptly to climb the wooden steps.

A sharp hand planted square in his chest stopped him cold. It was a vividly familiar gesture and he knew well who had stopped him.

"Well, boy, I've found you," Patsy Whaley said to her

nephew, her amber eyes bright and her smile sharp as a knife. "A four-year wait makes this moment all the sweeter, does it not?"

Dandridge looked down at his aunt. Resigned, he quieted thoughts of Lydia, who could not escape Williamsburg any faster than he could find her, and looked down at his aunt. The years had slackened the skin of her jaw and added gray to her brown hair, but she was the same Aunt Patsy, bold and determined and not to be gainsaid.

"Four years and you're the same spry girl I left behind." Dandridge smiled, bending to kiss the top of her capped head. "Is Uncle Matthew such an old man that he lets you cavort in front of ordinaries now, madam?"

"Your uncle is dead, boy, which you would have known if you'd thought to come home before now," she scolded sadly. "How is it that you've come to Williamsburg but not to the home that is warm for you? I had to hear from near strangers that the *Serpent* is anchored offshore. What are you about, Dandridge?"

Dandridge bent and took Patsy gently in his arms. "I'm sorry. He was a great man and shall be missed by many. When did he go?"

"Two years now," she sniffed, the memories stirred fresh from where she had buried them, "and long years they were. Where were you, boy, and why have you not come home before now?"

Again, Dandridge evaded her question, turning his attention to Anna Waters, who stood in silent solemnity at a polite distance. "Mistress Waters, it is a pleasure to see you again." He kissed her hand with a deep bow. "Now that I am home, will you invite me to dine with you so that I may again taste your sweet potato pone? Nothing has tasted sweet to my tongue since."

Anna blushed prettily and declared, "Why, it's been six years and more since you last ate at my table,

Dandridge. I can't believe that you haven't had a tasty dessert since then."

"Believe it, madam." Dandridge smiled engagingly.

And she found that she did, against all logic. But Dandridge Prentis had that effect on people.

Patsy had listened to Dandridge honey-up to her friend for quite long enough. She had waited four years for the boy to reappear, worried that he was dead during the wait, and she was not going to stand about on the street for another moment. Dandridge was coming home.

"Come, boy, and I'll call you that as I please for you'll always be a boy to me. Come home with me now," she ordered, grabbing his hand and towing him behind her as if he were no more than a six-year-old child caught running the streets. "Anna, I'll see you tomorrow after service and we'll have tea."

Anna waved at their backs and turned to her own home with a beaming smile. Dandridge was back. Williamsburg hadn't been quite the same without him.

"You should be ashamed of yourself, flirting with a woman old enough to be your mother!" Patsy huffed as she charged down the street, her skirts swinging. "But I'll hold my tongue about that; you're fresh home and probably awash with sentiment to see familiar faces again. Though if you'd been to home before now, the matter could have been avoided entirely."

"Should I cut my own switch or do you have one ready?" Dandridge said with a grin, easily keeping stride with his aunt's hurried steps.

Patsy cast him a sideways look and couldn't control the answering grin that raced across her face. "You're a wicked, wicked boy, but I'll not wear myself out reminding you of it. Now, we're here, or have you been away so long that you don't recognize the place?"

Of course he recognized it. Clapboard sheathed a slightly asymmetrical facade with four chimneys rising solidly against the warm June sky and dormers lined up against the cedar shake roof; a solid and respectable home. Matthew had started construction on it just as he had sailed off, but he had studied the architectural drawings and approved all he had seen. Dandridge would know this house anywhere.

"It's beautiful, Aunt Patsy. Uncle Matthew did a fine job," Dandridge praised as she led him up the few steps that served the door.

"He did," she agreed, "though he hardly had the opportunity to enjoy the fruit of his labors."

"What happened?" Dandridge asked softly as she preceded him inside.

"A stroke of some sort. He collapsed on the street and was dead by nightfall," Patsy answered grimly. She still missed her husband. "But that's in the past. I want to know about your venture; has it been a success?"

Patsy had not paused to allow Dandridge to admire her home openly, but admire it he did. The front room where he was now seated was clad from floor to ceiling in paneling, the fireplace was trimmed in fluted pilasters, and the whole was painted in rich butternut. It was an impressive room.

Dandridge sat back in an elaborately carved cane chair and considered her question. The answer lay somewhere four years behind him.

He'd been fresh from the sea and ready for anything. Alexander Spotswood, at Matthew Whaley's prompting, had given him an assignment: take his ship, the newly finished *Serpent*, and hunt pirates. Pirates, the ocean's plague that persistently lapped against the shores of all civilized lands. Spotswood loathed them, not an uncommon perspective, and was determined to exterminate them. Dandridge had eagerly accepted his license and signed on as first mate on the ship that was both gift and inheritance. All that he possessed in the world was represented in that ship. Dandridge grunted in his chair, remembering that day he had first set sail. Red Jack had raised his colors after two days at sea and the crew with him. It had been no mischance, no mistake; someone on shore had arranged it well, except that Dan hadn't died as expected. No, he had lived. Pirates all, they had cared only for profits. And they had wanted him dead. His choice, after he had fought for his life, had been to join them in their trade or die. It was on that day that he earned the slicing scar that marked his jaw; the swipe had been meant to separate his head from his neck. Alone, outnumbered, having already fought and killed and proved he had some worth in their eyes, he had found the choice simple. He had turned from pirate hunter into pirate, to survive. Survival was good. He was not sorry at the choice that he had made, but how to explain such matters to his sheltered aunt? Matthew might have understood, Patsy, never.

And so he chose a carefully constructed truth, to protect her from the harshness of life, he told himself, believing it.

"A success of a sort," he answered. "Pirate ships are difficult to find when you're hunting them, easily found when a ship is near defenseless."

"In four years you have surely dispatched some?" Patsy gasped in outraged disbelief.

Dandridge had a brief and swirling image of all the ships he'd taken in the past months. "Yes, I've taken ships," he said baldly.

"Then you've done what you've set out to do." Patsy nodded in familial pride. "And what does Spotswood think of your venture?"

Spotswood, once friend, now enemy. "I haven't seen him yet," Dandridge admitted mildly.

"But he's been kept apprised of your progress, I would imagine, through dispatch. And if you could keep him notified of your whereabouts, why could you not do the same for your only living kin?" she asked earnestly. Truly, it had hurt deeply that this boy had sailed away with nary a look back for those who loved him. He had changed in the years he had been gone and it was more than just the brutal scar that marked his face. At twenty-eight, he was charming still, but there was something missing in the boy, some emptiness that she could not define. He had passed hard years, if that scar was any testimony. She would never mention it to him; she did not want to be the spark that fired bad memories. She was just so happy to have him home, and safe.

"I have been in far-off places, Aunt," he answered in utter truth. "I suppose I always hoped that I would be back before any note could reach you. It was a false hope, I know, but one I believed in. I never wanted you to worry," he apologized. "Time at sea passes differently, more quickly or more slowly, I know not, but I know that it was never my intent to neglect you, you who have never once neglected me."

It was a moving speech, more so because he was honest in his emotional intent if not his actual words. He had not meant to hurt her, but it was also true that he had hardly thought of her. He loved her, but he had easily left her.

His answer appeased his aunt because she so earnestly wanted to be appeased. They sat together, well content to be in each other's company again, he listening to her tell him of the events that had shaped her life for these four years past. "And what of River Run, Aunt? I will confess to be surprised to find you in Williamsburg."

"I have no doubt of that," she answered with a mild snort. "The truth is that I have become accustomed to traveling to Williamsburg four times a year; even with Matthew gone, I cannot and will not disavow myself of the practice. Mr. McKenzie manages the property quite well. Give an ear now, boy, for this land will be yours when I pass. The land prospers under McKenzie. He dotes on the place like a father with his child, and it is you who will reap the harvest of his care."

Dandridge listened with half an ear; he had no mind to stay landward when he had just now gotten control of his ship. He would not give the *Serpent* up now, not after so many years of battling. But the bulk of his thoughts were of Lydia. Did she live in town or merely visit? Patsy would know, but he did not think it wise to ask her so direct a question. How to explain how he had met the wench? No, a direct attack would not work; something more subtle was required if he was to maintain the image his aunt had of him.

She was a gentle soul, loved and protected all her life. It would be beyond cruel to shake the foundation of her world now, when her life was ebbing slowly out. Let her keep the memory she had of him, he would not topple it; when he sailed away, it would be all she had left. He would not willfully hurt her.

Knowing he had turned pirate would surely kill her.

"And you will surely accompany me to church on the morrow," Patsy was saying, waiting for Dandridge's response.

"I really should get back to my ship," Dandridge began.

"Pah, you can make time for church, dear boy. It is God's holy day, set aside for man to worship and rest." Fixing him with a critical eye, she added, "It's my guess that you did not observe the Sabbath on that ship of yours, did you?"

Dandridge smiled and bit back a laugh at the thought. "No, ma'am."

" 'Tis as I suspected," she harumphed. "We'll begin tomorrow to put you to rights with the good Lord again in regards to the Sabbath."

"I don't think so," Dandridge demurred. "I dare not leave my ship for such a purpose."

"Such a purpose?" Patsy all but sputtered in her outrage. "Now look you, boy, you have not been raised to be a minister but neither are you apostate! In this family we observe the Sabbath and that is the end of it. Will you begin your return to Williamsburg with a day in the stocks for failing to meet your spiritual service? I do not understand your concern for your ship; you are the owner of her! She will not sail away without you, I'll warrant."

Dandridge made no comment as to that, but in the end he did agree to accompany his aunt to church on the morrow. It was a small enough gift to give her while he anchored at Williamsburg, because when he found his portion, he would be swiftly gone.

Chapter Eleven

Not yet dawn and she lay awake, straining toward sleep with no hope of reaching it. It was ever so, at least in the last three months it had been so. Her life had changed irrevocably since . . . since . . . him. She would not name him or the things he had done to her. She would not give any of it the permanence of a name. But it was a game that had no purpose, for even without voicing his name, she could still see his extraordinary eyes and sometimes, half asleep, she could almost feel his mouth pressing down on hers.

She had escaped him. She had not left him.

The days were better than the nights. During the day, she was busy in productive business and the house and streets were full of people and noise and activity. She could easily subdue him in such a row. But in the darkness of the night, he was a much more formidable adversary. In the quiet and darkness of her room, she had only her own strength with which to fight him. It was painfully obvious how very weak she was.

She was only thankful that her mother and father could not witness her nightly struggle . . . and defeat. Coming home, helped by many in her journey, she had told them all, eager for forgiveness, eager to share the burden of her sin. In this, she was not disappointed. Anna and Robert McIntyre had embraced her fiercely and with more love than any prodigal had ever received. In a few days she was again blessed with the arrival of her monthly flow.

All was at it should be, as it had been. She had survived.

But not intact.

Her body was the same as it had ever been, her family as warmly loving, her life as full, but she was not intact. Now, her mind was a storehouse full of images and sensations and feelings that had not been there before, and they clamored for release. Each night her memories beset her and each night she battled against them. Each night she lay awake, waiting for the sunrise, defeated.

Dan was with her, in her, a part of her. Now, there was nowhere to flee. She carried him with her.

How freely she had confessed her loss of innocence to her mother and how certain she had been of welcome and loving care. How different *this* confession, for this she could not confess, this branding was more shameful. She could not admit it.

And that knowledge tore at her peace.

She could not imagine admitting to anyone that Dan washed over every thought and that she sometimes yearned for him. She could hardly admit it to herself. There . . . she had named him, after refusing to. There was no surprise in that; she was accustomed to defeat at his hands.

Her thoughts revolved in this way, in this increasingly familiar way, until the dawn broke. It was a gentle breaking, the roosters heralding it first in competitive chorus as the sky lightened to day. Lydia's two youngest sisters, Ruth and Hannah, did not break their slumber as gently. This was also familiar. She could hear Miriam, her younger sister by three years, chastening the girls to hurry and dress for the Sabbath. It was enough to propel her from her bed, leaving the musings of the night behind. The day awaited and she was eager to meet it.

"Lydia! Have you arisen?" Ruth, aged ten, did not wait for an answer. She opened the door to the attic room and bounced in to see for herself.

"Of course I have. Would I be late for service, did you imagine?" Lydia answered, smiling at her sister as she quickly made up the bed. "But where is your other stocking?"

"I'm going to tuck this foot up beneath my skirts and stand outside Bruton Parish and beg for alms as was done in old Jerusalem and so remind everyone that Jesus loved even the beggars."

"She lost the other one," Hannah, aged eight, said drily, peeking around the door jamb.

"Out you go now." Lydia shooed them toward the hall with her hands. "I'll help you find your stocking when I am finished here."

"But I am going to be a beggar—"

"You can be a beggar with a good wool stocking covering your tucked-up limb. No one will see it anyway, and it would please Mother if you were well clothed in your beggary," Lydia argued logically.

"As you say," Ruth sighed. It was impossible to argue with Lydia, she was so logical and calm in all events.

"I think that you left your stocking by the well, Ruth," Hannah offered, "when you used it as a flag to signal the ships on College Creek."

"Ruth, you did not flail your undergarments about for all to see, did you?" asked Miriam, coming into the room.

131

Claudia Dain

"No," Ruth answered indignantly. "No one saw my flag, er, my stocking."

Lydia looked at her expectantly, her brows raised in inquiry.

"Though I did wave it for near an hour," Ruth finished glumly.

"Oh, Ruth," Miriam sighed; it was too horrible for her timid fifteen-year-old soul to bear.

Lydia, at just eighteen, smiled at them all. How she loved her sisters in all their differences. Miriam, the closest to her in age, was the most like her in temperament. Calm, reasonable, affable, she liked to think, but Miriam possessed a brimming sweetness of spirit that she did not. Lydia did not view herself as sweetly docile; she was practical and calmly stable in her manner. Or she had been, until Dan. Now Ruth, Ruth was not timid, could not be taught to be timid, though no one in the family would have thought to try. Ruth was gay impetuosity and humor, making her own amusements and not hurting anyone in the endeavor. She was a burning light, and Lydia loved her for her brightness. Hannah was always just a step from Ruth's shadow; she was a person in her own right, but she played well against Ruth's gaiety. Hannah was never one to accept a stated fact as truth until she had tested it for herself or unless she trusted devotedly the one who spoke it to her. Lydia liked to think that Hannah was developing a very good mind.

"Out, the lot of you"—Lydia grinned—"or I shall be late and defeat your purpose, Ruth, for didn't you come to make certain that I was well ahead of the day's events?"

"Yes, but hurry, Lydia," Ruth answered.

"I can smell spoon bread," Hannah mumbled before running out of Lydia's small room. Ruth was right behind her and they clattered down the wooden stairs together at a near run.

132

"Shall I stay and help you with your laces, Lydia?" Miriam offered.

A memory of being on the *Serpent* where she had had to cope with her own laces washed over Lydia. By necessity, she had learned to do without feminine help.

"No, thank you," she answered quietly. "You go on. I'll be down directly."

Miriam hesitated for just a moment and then smiled gently and left. Lydia had not been herself since her return from Eleuthera; she seemed almost invalid with suppressed pain. Surely, she had cause, but it grieved Miriam sorely that her sister carried such a burden.

Lydia was not far behind Miriam in her descent to the room in which they ate their meals. Though they had only lived in this house for three years, it was more home to her than any other. There were only two rooms on the ground floor, not including her father's apothecary which fronted the street, and two rooms above, omitting the attic where she now slept, but it was lovely in its proportions and appointments. A fine gateleg table with six banister-back chairs at which to take meals dominated the space, and the fireplace had a wonderful paneled surround. The walls were whitewashed scrupulously twice a year and the woodwork painted a cheery mustard yellow. A lovely room in which to both start and end the day. The front room, reached first by the stair and which abutted the dining area, was equally welcoming. One wing-back chair upholstered in colorful needlework, which was her father's especial favorite, sat near the hearth. A handsome walnut table stood not far off near the window; it was a fine place to do needlework. The fireplace wall was symmetrical, an arrangement which suited her mother to perfection, and even had a single row of Dutch tiles to frame the fireplace. Graceful chairs of local wood, fashioned by local hands, provided seating for them all. It was a warm room of love and companionship. This house, so new to them all, was home.

Crossing through the front room to reach the dining room, Lydia was just in time to eat the last of the spoon bread; washed down with buttermilk, it was a warm feast. She ate quickly, not wanting to be the one to cause a delay in their departure for Bruton Parish. There was small chance of their being late as Bruton Parish stood just half a block up, on the corner of Duke of Gloucester Street and Palace Green. It was a quick walk in even the worst of weather; the only excuse for being late on such a lovely June day as this would be sheer dawdling for the very beauty of the day.

But they would not dawdle and they would not be hindered in their progress, for Ruth and Hannah, being too young to attend service, would stay at home and receive their instruction from their mother. Swallowing the last of her milk and wiping a smudge from the corner of her mouth with the tip of her thumb, Lydia declared herself ready. Her father and Miriam were waiting by the door, in no distress at the hour, and off they went together, enjoying each other's companionship as readily as they enjoyed the weather.

They were not alone in their progress. All of Williamsburg attended Bruton Parish and all walked together to their joint destination. Smiles and nods of greeting were passed between them all, everyone known to her, not one a stranger after three years of living among them. Lydia was serene and calm, politely greeting those she knew best, but her efforts could not conceal the tired eyes she turned to friends and the lack of color in her cheeks. Lydia had not looked well since her recent trip abroad. The common consensus was that travel did not agree with her. There was much to be said for the benefits of staying at home. Robert McIntyre, hearing the well-meaning murmurs, smiled in silent agreement, but, wisely, said nothing.

Though they were not late, they were also not early, and obtained a pew near the rear. No matter, the acoustics were good and the pulpit high; they would hear all very well.

The reverend mounted the steps to the pulpit, ready to begin the worship service which was their privilege and duty to God. All eyes turned to him, expectantly, waiting. And then he began to speak.

"Our text today is from the book of Genesis, Chapter Thirty-nine: 'So he left everything he owned in Joseph's charge; and with him at hand he did not concern himself with anything except the bread which he ate. Now Joseph was handsome in form and appearance. And it came about after these events that his master's wife looked with desire at Joseph, and she said, "Lie with me." But he refused and said to his master's wife, "Behold, with me at hand, my master does not concern himself with anything in the house, and he has put all that he owns in my charge. There is no greater one in this house than I, and he has withheld nothing from me except you, because you are his wife. How then could I do this great evil, and sin against God?" And it came about as she spoke to Joseph day after day, that he did not listen to her to lie beside her, or be with her. Now it happened one day that he went into the house to do his work, and none of the men of the household was there inside. And she caught him by his garment, saying, "Lie with me!" And he left his garment in her hand and fled, and went outside.'

"Joseph was a goodly man of God," the reverend continued, his voice sonorous and solemn. "He was a man, fully a man, yet he did not give in to the lust of the flesh. No! He turned and ran from temptation, from Potipher's wife, and the lust that consumed her; he fled before it could consume him and God delivered him. Yes, God delivered him as He will always do when we turn away from sin and toward righteousness."

Lydia could feel a blush rising from below the high collar of her gown. This talk of lust and desire seemed directed at her and her alone. Casting a sideways glance at her father, she was relieved to note that he looked in no way different. He was not even looking at her. Raising her eyes to the pulpit, half expecting the good reverend to be pointing a long finger at her exact location, she expelled a quick breath when she saw that he was paying her no special attention. In fact, no one in the entire congregation seemed to be in any way sensitive to the topic of today's sermon.

But she was, extremely so.

This passage of scripture was suddenly too familiar to her. She had known the story of Potipher's wife, but now it rang with a different and clanging note. She had been that wife, nameless now for all time; she had hungered for the touch, the intimate possession, of one man and she had made that hunger known to him. But she had also been Joseph. She had fled. Not for the first time she wondered if she had fled too late.

But she had survived.

Was God as satisfied with her survival as she was? She was afraid to submit the matter to prayer, at least afraid in such a public forum. No, just afraid.

Lydia was a bit startled at the rising of the congregation, more startled to realize that the service had concluded. How deeply entrenched in her thoughts she had been. Miriam smiled next to her and waited for her to exit the pew. Recalling herself, Lydia walked from the enclosure of the pew to the wide aisle that bisected the church, her family following close behind her. It was a perfectly ordinary sermon, she rationalized, nothing to be so consumed over; they would walk home, engage in pleasant conversation, and eat their Sunday meal. There was nothing unusual in this day. No one knew. It was all behind her. She had survived.

A strange commotion tumbled toward her from the altar and she, along with many others, turned to look at the cause before leaving the church. No, it was not the altar, but the governor's pew. Governor Spotswood, along with his council members, were gathered round some gentleman. Who, she could not see. Black hair, catching the light from the large windows that graced the building, suddenly gleamed as the stranger stepped forward toward Governor Spotswood. But he could not be a stranger; she knew everyone in Williamsburg. He did seem familiar. Miriam, pushing gently from behind, forced her to turn and continue on, but that dark head nagged at her. So familiar. So out of place.

A chill raced up her spine to spin around the top of her head. Lydia turned sharply in the very portal of the church, unmindful of the crush she was creating. That dark head turned serenely, calmly, unerringly and amber eyes locked with hers.

"No," Lydia breathed, denying the truth of him in Bruton Parish, talking with the governor and watching her with too-knowing eyes. *"No!"* she said again, even more softly, willing him away.

When had Dan ever bowed to her will?

Having been pressed so often from behind, Lydia gave Miriam a shock when she all but bolted from the church. In fact, Miriam and her father were almost at a trot to keep up with her. Lydia did not wait for them at the door of the house, did not greet her mother and sisters, did not pause in her rush up two flights of stairs to reach her small attic room. Nor did she pause in falling to her knees and beseeching God for deliverance. Again. From the same man. In the midst of her prayers for herself, worthy and necessary prayers, to be sure, Lydia found herself

137

praying that Dan even now was not under arrest and in gaol. Piracy was a hanging crime and the execution of sentence was almost always immediate. Williamsburg was the center of government for all of Virginia Colony. Why had he come here of all places?

The possible answer sent a thrill through her. Whether a thrill of fear or excitement, she could not be certain, and she was too busy in her prayers to reason it out.

At first he had not seen her. Sitting in the front as he was with his aunt, there were few people to see and he could hardly squirm around for a look. Of the service, he heard none; his thoughts were all on Lydia and finding her, taking her, having her. It was unfortunate that Spotswood had seen him before he could take his leave, having done his duty to Patsy and to the laws of Virginia. He had not considered it a duty to God.

He had turned then, as the governor first greeted him with reserved goodwill, knowing somehow that she was there for his eyes to catch. And she had been. She was as beautiful as he remembered her and looked just as exhausted as she had after a sleepless night of passion. He smiled at her in lethal anticipation, reading the "no" on her lips and seeing the unwelcome in her luminous eyes. He did not know who was keeping her awake these warm spring nights, but it would continue no longer. He was here and she was his. She had but barely begun to pay her debt to him.

For a moment, his anger flared more brightly than his lust. What game was she playing in that solemn fabric and severe cut? She was a wanton. She should be dressed as such, declaring herself for what she was. He hated her for her duplicity in that brief moment.

It was then that Spotswood commanded his full attention.

"I had thought you lost, Prentis," he said. "It has been

many months, nay, how many years since last you notified me of your progress?"

Patsy muffled a gasp of surprise at that statement. It
was surely derelict of Dandridge to have neglected to
notify the governor. What could the boy have been
thinking?

"Near on four, Governor," Dandridge answered
smoothly with a slight bow. "It is surprisingly difficult,
sir, to post a letter from the deck of a ship," he added
drily.

"And no port made in all that time, sir?" Spotswood
asked half comically.

"Governor," Dandridge said seriously, "the places
where I let my anchor fall seldom have any need or desire
for postal service."

"And so you have returned to give me information on
your assignment," Spotswood surmised. "Very nicely
done, Prentis, but better done if done the sooner and more
often. Come to the capitol tomorrow at ten. We shall talk
then. I look forward, sir, to what you will tell me."

"I am at your command, sir." Dandridge bowed in
acquiescence before taking Aunt Patsy's arm and escort-
ing her from the church.

Alexander Spotswood watched him leave with great
intent. Dandridge Prentis had been at sea for many years
with an able crew and a fast and well-armed ship. It
would not be the first time a man had turned to pirating.
Or been hanged for it.

Dandridge, once he had turned away from Spotswood,
spared him not a thought. His thoughts were all of Lydia,
finding her, finding out what he could of her. His plans
were more complicated now; he could hardly lift her and
run with Spotswood watching him. He was not deceived
by Spotswood's courtesy; the man would be a fool not to
have a question as to what he'd been about the past years.
Spotswood was no fool. But then, neither was he.

Descending the short steps from the door of Bruton Parish, Dandridge and Patsy were met by a full gaggle of women of Patsy's acquaintance. Patsy Whaley rose to her full stature and proudly presented her nephew, Dandridge Prentis. Eyes of every color, wreathed in finely lined skin, sparkled up at him; Dandridge, it seemed, was the hero of the hour.

"Ladies." He bowed deeply, his smile wide and white. He looked every inch the aristocrat he was in his damask coat and satin breeches, and Patsy was well founded in her pride.

"Welcome home, Mr. Prentis," said one, her eyes gray-blue and cheery. "It is both a pleasure and an honor, sir, to meet a gentleman who has been engaged so valiantly in service to his sovereign."

"Thank you, mistress, but I am hardly comfortable with your description." Dandridge smiled with charming reluctance. "I had rather thought I was having a high time on a good ship, and perhaps accomplishing some small good to my country in the bargain."

"Mr. Prentis," said one woman with dark brown eyes and a crimson bonnet, "is it terribly dangerous, searching for pirates?"

"Heaven help us, Alice, what a question," Patsy barked, clenching her elegant walking stick.

"Terribly." Dandridge smiled, his eyes for her alone, "Why, madam, between one sea battle and the next, I hardly have time for my supper."

"He asked specifically for my sweet potato pone," Anna Waters whispered in an aside that included everyone.

"And have you found many? Pirates, that is?" another asked, this one with pale blue eyes and a dark blue bonnet.

"Unfortunately, yes, madam; the seas swarm with the vermin and I am ever among them."

Their eyes widened in horror and disgust. To be among pirates, even for the honor and protection of

England, was a terrible sacrifice for any young man to make. And one so good-looking, too.

"Surely you must be pleased to be back in Williamsburg where you can ease your mind and attempt to erase its vile associations." This from a lady who had once been quite handsome if he could judge by her lively green eyes surmounted by a wine red bonnet.

"Surely I am," he answered, "for you will not forget that while there are battles aplenty aboard a seagoing vessel, there are no ladies. I am certain you will not be surprised to learn that I have most heartily missed the gentle companionship of God's softer creation. It is my fear that I have grown quite the beast having been in the company of only men for so long."

Heartfelt cries of "certainly not!" mingled equally with "yes, it's true; men are better for having women around them." Dandridge watched them flutter, knowing he had achieved his objective in part. They were now thinking of women and his companionship. He would have them thinking of one woman only and he would have any news they had of her. Be she saint or whore, these ladies would know all.

Patsy was equally delighted with the turn in the conversation. It was better entirely for Dandridge to end his fascination with the sea and take up an equally riveting fascination with the land that would become his with her death. River Run was a large and prosperous plantation; she would not see it go to strangers. If he took a wife while on shore, he would be less disposed to run to the sea. Yes, it was not a bad thing, this talk of female companionship. It would suit.

"My nephew, Thomas," Anna Waters inserted into the general conversation regarding the incivility of men, "has been a widower for near two years now and has quite lost the shine on his manners. I have reason to believe that he sometimes takes his meals in his shirt sleeves!"

This proclamation brought a general round of horror and served to bring an element of competition into the group.

"That is quite awful, of course," the wine-colored bonnet, Mistress Campbell, agreed, "but Mr. Campbell's youngest brother, who as you well know has never married, has not purchased a new pair of shoes for at least three years; in point of fact, he has only the one pair and wears them every day!"

"Have they never been cobbled?"

"How can they be, my dear?" Mistress Campbell answered. "He has not even a pair of slippers to see him through."

Patsy cast a speculative look at Dandridge. Though he had been in the exclusive company of men, and seamen at that, he had turned himself out quite well; his apparel and his manners were impeccable. She thanked the good Lord that he had not lost the training of proper breeding during his heroic service to England.

"Horrid," breathed Mistress Griffin into the temporary lull, her dark eyes wide to give emphasis to her words. "It was much the same with my father when my mother passed on; he did not so much as order a change of linen or a new waistcoat on his own initiative. I spent the greater part of my days in making certain that he was properly affixed."

"But, certainly, that is a daughter's duty," Mistress Whaley argued gently, "and he must have been most pleased with your care."

"Of course, I would never begrudge my father one instant of my time," Mistress Griffin defended, her bonnet almost bristling, "but the truth of the matter is that he was most annoyed with me for my efforts. I believe I heard him mumble that a mosquito served more purpose and with less irritation." This last was said with some embarrassment, but she felt driven to defend herself.

"Inexplicable," someone murmured, and fashionably capped heads nodded in sagacious agreement.

Dandridge was beginning to wonder how to bring them back on course, but Aunt Patsy was well ahead of him.

"I hardly think that this is an appropriate conversation for either the location, the time, or the company," and she looked archly in Dandridge's direction.

At least one blush was raised at that remark, but no arguments.

"You must come 'round, Mr. Prentis," Mistress Waters began, "perhaps this Tuesday? I shall prepare a sampling of sweets for you to enjoy at your leisure."

"Sweet potato pone?" he asked with a grin.

"Sweet potato pone and more." She smiled in answer.

"I cannot hope to compete with Anna's desserts," Mistress Parks said, "but I do have a daughter, recently widowed, and a son attending William and Mary College; we would be most pleased to entertain you."

Dandridge studied her pale blue eyes, looking for a trace of Lydia in them. He did not see one, but then she could have taken after her father . . . but no, he had known Mistress Parks as a boy. Her daughter could not be the one he sought.

"Thank you, ma'am, for your graciousness." He bowed, neither accepting nor declining.

"My daughter, Mary, would have attended today," Mistress Parks continued, "but she is taken ill. If she does not improve by morning, I fear I shall call Mr. McIntyre and hear what he prescribes."

"He is a good man, Mr. McIntyre," Mistress Waters put in.

Yes, thought Patsy, and he has two comely daughters of marriageable age. They had attended service, of course; she had seen them leave, had even noted that the eldest, Lydia, looked for a moment at Dandridge, now that she recollected it. A fine-looking girl and her sister,

Miriam, as well; just the sort to turn a man's thoughts to marriage and family. If she introduced Dandridge to the family, he could look them over and take his pick, if they appealed. They had one other advantage, besides superior appearance, over the other girls of Williamsburg; they were new to the area, been here not over three years. Dandridge would like that. Dandridge liked what was new, different, challenging. The other girls, most of whom he had known in varying degrees of intimacy since childhood, would not interest him as these late arrivals would. Of course, it would have been more desirable if a local girl of good property had been available, but they were safely at home on their plantations. She did not dare wait more than a moment. Dandridge's affections must be snared soon or she would lose him to the sea again. It was not such a large sacrifice, offering him the McIntyre girls; they were a fine family and well respected in the community. It would be a fine match, once settled.

"Yes," Patsy agreed, "a good man, honest and diligent in his profession, and with four sweet girls and a loving wife to keep him civilized. Four daughters, Dandridge," she added, with a happy gleam in her eyes, "and beauties every one, though the two youngest are mere children and still at their chalk work."

"The name is not familiar to me," Dandridge admitted.

"No, it would not be," Mistress Waters explained, "for they came over from England two—"

"Three," Patsy corrected.

"Three years ago," Anna continued. "Mr. McIntyre is an apothecary of superior training, and what your aunt declares is true; his daughters are lovely girls in both appearance and character." Anna did not mind agreeing with Patsy; she had no female relation to offer Dandridge and so had little to lose. Not so the other women, and they would not accept the proclamation without resistance.

"I wouldn't think of saying a word against the skills of

Mr. McIntyre," Mistress Griffin declared righteously, "but surely beauty, or the appreciation of it, is not so firmly set that it cannot be argued." She had an aging cousin of bad complexion but good teeth who was in need of a husband. The McIntyre girls would not get Dandridge Prentis for free!

"You can't mean that you don't find them quite above ordinary in looks?" Patsy argued sternly.

"In that I agree with you, but being out of the ordinary can hardly be termed a desirable quality," Mistress Griffin returned.

"I must agree," Mistress Parks added, determined to protect her daughter's interests in the matter before Dandridge was auctioned clear away. "If one prefers a rather . . . overblown shall we say? quality, then the McIntyre girls fit the bill. For my own tastes, a more subdued beauty is preferable."

"I fail to see how your tastes in beauty are pertinent," Patsy snipped.

Dandridge smiled and slipped his arm behind Patsy's back in an effort to calm her and show her that he was not being swayed to stand against her opinion. In fact, the more he heard, the greater his curiosity.

"Speaking from the masculine perspective," he said, "beauty is a gift to the eyes, whether as a daisy or a rose, and any man is a fool who does not appreciate the gift."

"How very gracious," Mistress Campbell replied, frantically trying to determine how she could get word to her sister to bring her girl to Williamsburg before Dandridge Prentis found himself wed to another.

"How very kind," Patsy added. "I suppose you must make the acquaintance of the family and form your own judgment, Dandridge, though I can hardly imagine that you will find fault with their beauty, unless you have developed an aversion to light-colored hair?"

"No, ma'am," he answered, his curiosity heightened.

Lydia's hair was most definitely light in color. "Pray, madam, what can I hope to win as a prize for judging the comparative beauty of these women? Like doomed Paris of Greek fame, will I be cursed in bestowing the apple of highest praise? Tell me"—he smiled, all gaiety, though his motive was solemn—"they are not named Aphrodite and Athena, perchance?"

"No, boy, no such heathen names as that but good Christian names," Patsy answered. "Miriam is the younger and Lydia the elder."

Lydia the elder.

So he had her, and so easily done.

He admitted to being momentarily stunned that she was a respectable daughter of good family. It was hardly what he had expected. But then, who knew how she had spent her time in England? It was no innocent who had lain with him on the *Serpent* and it was no innocent whom he had found in Williamsburg. He knew her. He knew her for the sensual wanton she was. Lydia McIntyre was no prim maid. Lydia McIntyre was his, by fair means or foul.

Chapter Twelve

Sally walked through the open doorway, her arms laden with a tray of mutton seared brown and steaming fragrantly. Lydia placed the last silver fork beside the last plate in distracted silence. In unbroken silence, she took the platter of meat from the tray and set it on the table.

Sally frowned at the girl intently for a moment and then swung out the door and back to the kitchen; something was not right with the girl. Something had been "not right" with her ever since she came home from that ocean trip, but she seemed worse now than she ever had. Sally didn't care for ocean passages herself, had been sick most of the way from England and had a sick headache for the first few days of her arrival. It was a blessed thing that Mr. McIntyre, the man to whom she was indentured, was an apothecary and had the knowledge to see that she carried no disease or she would have been not only in debt but homeless. A few days on shore had set her right and she had expected much the same for

Claudia Dain

Lydia, but it had been months now and instead of show-ing signs of improvement, she looked suddenly worse.

Dear Lord, but she hoped that Lydia was not carrying some disease! Dishing up the greens, she considered it. Lydia had lost the strength that had set her apart from the rest; her sleep was disturbed and her attention slack.

Wasn't there a fever that began that way? Hadn't her older brother died of some such thing? The more she thought on it, the more it seemed so.

Dear Lord, but she was bound to a house that had sick-ness running rampant through it! She was tied to this house as if by a chain, such was indenture, and doomed to die before her debt was paid. She had not crossed the ocean, sick every inch of the way, to die! Loading the dishes on the tray, Sally reluctantly left the kitchen. There was naught she could do about it. Stay and die, that was her lot. But she would stay as far away from them all as she possibly could for the remaining two years, or until she determined that the sickness had passed.

Thank heaven, it had not seemed to have spread beyond Lydia. It was most likely a slow-moving sick-ness. They were always the worst, she reasoned.

It was a test of her resolve to find that Lydia was still in the dining room when she returned; circling wide of the disease that Lydia certainly carried, Sally set the bowl of greens down on the opposite side of the table and hurried back to the safety of the kitchen.

Miriam entered as Sally was leaving. Miriam also noted that Lydia was not as she had been and that she seemed to be getting worse every day. Miriam did not attribute Lydia's malaise to a sickness of body; she and Sally, if they had cared to compare speculations, would have differed sharply. Miriam believed Lydia to be suf-fering from a sickness of spirit. Lydia was not the vital, resolute, peaceful woman she had been when she had departed for Eleuthera to help Aunt Jane. Lydia had returned from her travels, her ordeal, a distracted, anxious woman. A woman out of step with herself. A woman of no peace. Surely she had cause; to be aboard a ship taken by pirates was no peaceful event, but she had come through unscathed. They had released her almost immediately upon reaching shore. Lydia had stated plainly that they had no wish for captives and so had released her without ceremony as she was of no profit to them. And so she had made her way home, helped by many, and welcomed warmly. Still, these past months, there was something very different about her. Lydia had no peace.

Anna came into the dining room bearing a pitcher of water fresh from the well. It was time to dine and the younger girls, Ruth and Hannah, were nowhere about. Robert had gone to find them and bring them to the table. Wiping the condensation from the bottom of the crockery, Anna set it on the table near her own seat. Miriam and Lydia stood behind their chairs, waiting for all to assemble before they sat.

For all the homeyness of the scene, the atmosphere was one of suppressed worry. They all had worried over Lydia since the moment of her departure to the Bahama Islands. But her safe return had not ended the worry, and therein lay the problem. Lydia had shared with them her pirate capture and, to save her composure, they had all agreed to keep the knowledge within the walls of their family. Lydia didn't doubt that Ruth and Hannah had all but forgotten it by now.

Later, in the quiet of the night and in complete privacy, Lydia had revealed to her parents the full extent of her capture: she had been raped. Oh, she had not fought for her virginal honor, she had been clear about that, but she had fought with all her resolve for her life and had succeeded. Of course, the girls were told none of this, being too young and innocent. Anna knew that her eldest daughter had lain with a man not her husband, knew that she had done it to survive, and so knew the source and the moment of the change in her daughter. Lydia had paid a high price for her survival; she had been forced to endure much.

As the months passed, Anna's prayers had been increasingly that God would heal her daughter, because Lydia was not the girl she had been. At first she had watched her closely, exceedingly closely, and her surveillance had little abated in the weeks that followed her return. Lydia was not sleeping and so they had hastily provided a small room for her in the attic, hoping that the solitude would ease her. Lydia could not follow a conversation for more than a few minutes before her mind would wander while she stared with unfocused eyes at her feet or her hands. Lydia hardly ate what was set before her and showed an odd reluctance to sit at table with the rest of the family. Lydia was bruised to her very soul.

Robert entered then, a small feminine hand in each of his, and a wide smile on his face.

"I've found them, Anna, and let us sit and begin before they are off again," he declared.

"And what were you doing while the meat is cooling on the table?" Anna asked as she sat in her place.

"We crept to Bruton Parish," Hannah answered.

"And why would you creep to church?" Anna wondered.

"We crept so that no one would see us coming," Ruth volunteered.

"Yes, that part seemed obvious," Anna murmured with a smile.

"We'll continue this after prayer, shall we?" Robert suggested and they all bowed their heads to thank God for His providence, His generosity, His goodness, and His holy day.

They lifted their heads, and the food was passed and

distributed. Hannah and Ruth ate generously. Miriam ate moderately. Lydia ate sparingly.

"Now," Anna continued, "for what purpose did you creep to Burton Parish?"

"Miriam told us," Ruth said when she had swallowed her meat, "that there was a stranger there today, a man, young and good-looking."

Lydia paled and sipped her water.

Miriam blushed and argued, "That is not exactly what I said, Ruth! I only said that there was a man in church whom I did not recognize."

"You did say he was young," Hannah put in.

"I may have," Miriam hedged, "but I most certainly did not say that he was good-looking!"

"You said that he was tall and that his hair was dark and that his clothes were fine," Hannah said, pushing the greens around on her plate.

"Good-looking," Ruth pronounced in summation.

"Nevertheless," Robert cut in, hoping to save some of Miriam's tender dignity, "that does not explain why you were skulking your way to your very own church."

"Why, because we did not want him to see us! We wanted to see *him!*" Ruth explained in slight exasperation. "We couldn't very well study him plainly if he knew we were there. That would have been rude, wouldn't it?"

"And sneaking up behind him and peering at him from around the corner was not rude?" Robert asked, controlling his smile.

"How could it be if he did not see us? We caused him no discomfort, and is that not what rudeness is?"

Anna and Robert exchanged an exasperated look of their own. Ruth was not wrong, yet she was hardly correct.

"There were so many ladies around him that he could hardly have seen us even if we were not being sly," Hannah offered, hoping to soothe her parents.

Lydia twisted the napkin in her lap until she thought she heard the linen fibers start to break apart.

"Ladies?" Miriam asked in dismayed disappointment.

"Yes, scores of them," Ruth answered around her mouthful of meat.

"There aren't scores of ladies in all of Williamsburg," Miriam delicately snorted.

"Well, perhaps one score," Ruth modified.

"There were six," Hannah supplied as she reached for a biscuit.

"They were introduced by Mistress Whaley and fluttered about him like ducks over corn," Ruth said.

"Ruth! That is hardly a kind description!" Anna pointed out.

"Perhaps we could have been introduced as well, if we hadn't left the church so abruptly," Miriam said softly, suddenly slightly irritated with Lydia.

"We didn't leave abruptly, Miriam," Robert gently corrected, "we left promptly."

"Yes, Father," she admitted, remembering her own nudging of Lydia from behind.

"Anyway," Ruth continued, "Mistress Whaley introduced him to all of her friends—"

"Do you mean that the ladies of whom you spoke were of an age with Widow Whaley?" Miriam asked.

"Of course, what did you imagine?" Ruth asked, unhappy at the interruption.

Miriam breathed a soft sigh of relief, which was echoed even more softly by Lydia.

"Anyway," Ruth repeated, "he was introduced, and greeted them all very gallantly, answering their questions and conversing, and wait until I tell you what their conversation came round to!"

"Ruth, that is quite enough," Robert said rather severely. "It is mere childishness that has you creeping about the streets, but it is odious in the extreme to repeat a conversation that you are not privy to. I will not hear one word of what was said; what they spoke of was not for our ears."

"But, Father, I heard nothing evil!"

"Then I can praise God for that, but I will not encourage eavesdropping in my home. It is dishonest and deceitful. How will you feel when you are eventually introduced to this man, having already listened to a private conversation in which he was a party?"

Ruth secretly thought that she would feel very secure since he had been told that the McIntyre girls were very nice-looking.

"Can't I even tell you his name?" she asked, close to whining. What was the good of listening if you couldn't even repeat what you had heard?

"No," Robert answered firmly. "I will gain his name when we are introduced and not before. Now," he said, changing the subject, "let us discuss what was for our ears and for our edification. What did you think, Miriam, of the message this morning?"

Lydia knew his name. His name was Dan. He was a pirate. He was not someone to whom her father should be introduced.

"I found it provoking," Miriam answered slowly, thinking carefully. "I suppose I had not thought before that lust was something that a woman battled."

"The sermon was on lust?" Ruth asked, her mouth open.

"Yes, on the lust a married woman felt for a man of God and how that lust would have destroyed him had he given in to its call," Robert answered calmly. He felt no shame or embarrassment in discussing this topic with his daughters; if the Lord could speak of it in His inspired word, then he could speak of it to his family.

"When will I be old enough to go to service?" Ruth asked eagerly.

"Little girls who eavesdrop are clearly not old enough," Anna remarked with studied solemnity.

"Miriam," Robert returned, "so before today, you had not thought that a woman could desire a man. Had you acknowledged that lust was battled against by man?"

"Yes," she answered softly.

"And do you see that Joseph did what was right in running from this woman, this woman who sought to assuage her lust with him?"

"Yes," she said, looking into her father's eyes, "there was no other way. Christ has taught us to flee temptation and here was such a case. Perhaps Potipher's wife would have been wise to flee from Joseph's presence when the lust for him first came to her."

"Yes," he agreed, "that would have been wise and she had more freedom to flee than he. Joseph was a slave and he risked death by his refusal of her. I believe he understood, because he put his faith in God, that sin, though promising satisfaction, does not satisfy and leaves a man more parched for whatever it is he desires than before."

"I truly believe that I am old enough to attend," Ruth put in, trying to sound more serious than eager.

"And I," added Hannah quickly.

"Your mother shall decide when you are old enough and then we shall all attend together." Robert smiled. "You have many years to attend; enjoy the instruction you receive from your mother. This is a special time in your life; it will end soon enough."

Lydia listened to all with half an ear. How easy it was to talk of lust and desire and temptation at the warm sanctuary of their table, how difficult to face it in all its ribald strength. She, too, believed that it was right to run from temptation, she believed that giving in to the lust of the flesh was wrong, she believed that only God could truly satisfy the spirit. But she had been touched by a man and his passions and she had burned.

She yearned to burn again.

She hated herself for feeling so, yet she had no power to fight against it. Instead, she had fled. She had listened to God's voice and she had run from her lust and the man who inspired it. She had escaped to save herself, but her flight had accomplished little.

Her lust she had taken with her.

The man who ignited it had followed her.

She had spent three months battling against her thoughts and desires and memories. She had battled the memory of Dan until she was weak with it. Her father did not know this. He did not know that she ran from the lust in her thoughts; how well could she run from memories she carried with her every step of every day?

Her father did not know. He did not know that Dan was here, in the flesh, now. And Dan was a more formidable adversary than her thoughts.

But he might not seek her out. He might not care, even if he did see her in Bruton Parish, he might not care, he might not come. She felt her cheeks pinken in shame, in confusion, at how the mere thought of that rejection wounded her.

Why was he in Williamsburg?

Who was he?

Chapter Thirteen

Under the guise of a Sunday afternoon stroll, Dan walked
the mile or so to College Creek where the *Serpent* was
moored. He'd left her the day before and was uncomfortable in the absence. The *Serpent* was his escape if matters
in Williamsburg became too heated. If Spotswood discovered how he'd spent the last four years, he'd have a
rope around his neck within twenty-four hours, that is, if
he couldn't make it to the *Serpent* ahead of the authori-
ties. He was more comfortable aboard her than anywhere
else, and he couldn't quite remember when that had come
to be. In the early days, when the role of pirate had been
forced upon him, he had longed for the shore and for civ-
ilization and for the just order that ruled there. He had
longed for the warm security of family and the ease of
friendship. But as the years had silently passed, he had
ceased to yearn. He had learned to live the life he had
chosen, learned to appreciate the freedom of lawlessness
and the naturalness of self-indulgence. Virtue and vice

156

had clasped arms as comrades and bellowed, "Survival!" He realized, dimly, that he had come to long for little else. Except Lydia. He longed for her in a way that matched his thirst for survival at any cost. Once he had Lydia in his bunk, all the longings that he now felt would be fed by her.

Dan had just sighted the mast and was quickening his step when a familiar voice confronted him.

"I'd heard the talk and had to come see for myself. It's good to see you again, Prentis."

Dandridge bowed slightly and stiffly and said nothing. Ben Charlton had never been a friend, though he should have been; same school, same background, same upbringing, the ingredients had been there but not the temperament. Was it possible that Charlton had arranged for Dan's lawless crew? Dan frowned and considered the possibility. Motive and opportunity both seemed lacking; Charlton was wealthy and had as much opportunity for contact with the lawless of the world as he had had four years ago: none. Added to that was the matter of his character. Such an act of treachery and deviousness seemed beyond him. In college, Charlton had been called "the Lawgiver." Dan smiled grimly, his mind settled, Charlton removed from consideration. But they had not been a match four years ago and were even less likely to be so now; his heart did not warm to see the face of this old companion from his naive past. Charlton would never understand the world in which he lived and he most certainly would never have survived.

"I've been upriver and just returned," Ben continued in the face of such a cool greeting. "Couldn't believe the talk that you'd returned at last and had to appease my own curiosity. And here you are, sir," he finished, his brown eyes speculative.

"And here I am, sir," Dandridge echoed.

"It's been many years, sir,"

"It's been four years, sir," Dandridge clarified.

"Four years and no word. I imagine, sir, your family was worried."

"My aunt, sir, worries no longer," Dandridge said stiffly.

"How nice for her," Ben replied with the smallest bite. "And what of the governor? Are his concerns regarding you at an end as well?"

"I imagine his concern for my welfare," Dandridge answered, changing the wording enough to imply a compliment when none had been intended, "is eased. I saw him at Bruton Parish this morning. He seemed glad to see me."

"I imagine he would be," Ben said pleasantly, his speculative gleam undiminished.

"Perhaps even more interested in my return than you seem to be, sir," Dandridge added.

"Perhaps he is," Charlton agreed easily. "It *is* good to see you again, though, Prentis. You were given a Herculean task, fraught with danger and potential disaster; I had wondered at the time whether you would survive it."

"And so you have come to see that I have, in fact, survived," Dandridge said coldly, insulted by Charlton's implied doubt as to his capability. "I hope I haven't disappointed you?"

Ben laughed briefly, saying, "Hardly. You've been missed, Dandridge. Williamsburg is of a size that when someone of your stature and family leaves, a considerable ripple is sent out in all directions." Looking deeply into the amber eyes that stared into his, Ben said earnestly, "I wish you a most warm welcome back."

Feeling just a small finger of Charlton's sincerity, Dandridge said, "Thank you, Ben." He had remembered Charlton as stiff, unbending, serious; perhaps a better word would have been disciplined. Time, and maybe experience, had changed his impressions of this man he had known since boyhood; or mayhap the man himself had changed. It was not impossible, though he would not have thought it likely ten years ago.

"Now that you stand before me, hale as ever," Ben continued, "I wonder that I ever doubted you would succeed. If there ever was a man born to hunt pirates, it was you, Dandridge. The thrill of it must fire the blood to boiling. The four years must have passed in the blink of an eye for you."

Oddly, he spoke the truth and Dandridge nodded in agreement, saying nothing. It had been thrilling in the beginning, when he had been ignorant of the merits of the captain and crew, and when he had believed that none could hinder him in attaining his goals.

Ben was also correct about the four years passing in the blink of an eye. He had told Patsy truly; he did not know where the time had gone. It had simply passed, carrying him along with it. Strange, how being on land again brought that into sharper focus.

"Still," Ben continued, "four years is four years, and Governor Spotswood has had no word of you in all that time. It was understandable that we thought you dead or . . ." Ben let the sentence hang. He knew full well that Dandridge Prentis, descendant of one of the finest families in the colony, could have, might have, turned pirate. The evidence, though circumstantial, was damning. Dandridge had always been impulsive, bordering on reckless; it was one of the reasons that he had been approached in the first place. Now it was that very recklessness which might have propelled him into a life of lawlessness. He hoped it wasn't so, but if it was, he would pull the trap himself that set Dandridge swinging by the neck. Peer or not, piracy was an abomination, and those who practiced it should be exterminated. But looking at Prentis, the strength of him, the scar that marked him telling its own tale of the past four years, he hoped with all his heart that Dandridge had remained true to his upbringing and his oath.

"Or what?" Prentis prodded aggressively. If Charlton had doubts about him, let him state them openly so that they could be openly dealt with.

"Or shipwrecked," Charlton finished safely and somewhat truthfully. It had been a possibility speculated upon in the early days of Dandridge's absence.

"The *Serpent* is too fine a vessel to cast me off," Dandridge replied. "She would not let the fury and caprice of the sea defeat her, or me."

"You sound fair smitten."

"I am, sir," he truthfully replied. "And now I must be off. Farewell, Charlton." Dandridge nodded and continued on his way to his ship, leaving Ben Charlton behind him.

But not forgotten. Charlton was no fool, never had been. Dan doubted that time had changed that. Ben would wonder if he had turned pirate, had alluded to it with his delayed "shipwrecked" remark; but Ben was not a hasty man. He was methodical and given to detail; details required time, time that Dan was not prepared to give him. He had come for Lydia, had found her, knew her name and her family; he would not be here long enough for Charlton to do anything about any information he could find, if he found any at all. Charlton was a problem only if he tarried. Lydia was a problem only if she balked at boarding the *Serpent*. That wasn't likely to happen.

Dan boarded his ship absentmindedly, his mind on Lydia. A brief nod to his new first mate, John, and then he paced the quarterdeck, the breeze playing with the tail of his hair. The crew watched him and kept about their duties quietly; their captain was possessed of an uncertain temper.

Dan had no thoughts for his crew, they were all for

Lydia. She would come back. She must be as hungry for release as he was. She wanted him, had always wanted him; she had made that abundantly clear from the first. He was here now. She would find him and find her gratification in him, but he would not share her while he pleasured her, pleasured her as no other had done. No, she would have to leave Williamsburg because he would have to be sure of her fidelity, and he could only be sure of that on his ship, where his word was law. He also had to leave Williamsburg to avoid the noose that would surely find him here.

Soon, he would have her. Soon, he would sail away to far-off seas and back to the life he'd known for so many years. For four years.

Dan stopped, startled at the thought. He was in Williamsburg again, in firm command of honest men, and he wanted nothing so much as to be at sea.

That was not how it had started.

Four years ago he had survived his first beating, a fight to the death, and accepted the unfamiliar role of pirate. To survive. To survive until he reached a safe port and could escape. But there had been no safe port for pirates anchored in pirate ports. He'd been willing to leave the *Serpent* then. He'd been playing at pirate to escape a bloody and torturous death. He could walk away from it now, at this moment. He could leave his ship and resume his life in Williamsburg, the plantation, Aunt Patsy. Lydia.

Why did he not leave the past, bloody as it was, behind and reach for a new, clean life?

He had no answer.

Frighteningly, he had no answer.

Chapter Fourteen

The tea was fresh and strong, that much could be said for it. Dandridge longed for his accustomed rum, but Patsy would have been shocked had he suggested it: no spirits on the Sabbath.

There was no Sabbath at sea.

She sat opposite him, her seat near the fire which crackled gently. It was June and warm, even though the sun had set, but she insisted that the walls and floor held the chill of winter still. Dandridge had not argued it. He was comfortable, though he sat as far from the fire as he could without appearing rude. In fact, they were well situated physically, like opposing royals on a chessboard. He knew what was on her mind. The same matter that was on his.

Lydia McIntyre.

She wanted him to meet her. To find favor in her. To marry her.

Aunt Patsy had wanted him to marry from the moment

he left William and Mary College. In her mind, marrying
would have discouraged him from going to sea. He knew
that nothing would have kept him from it, certainly no
woman. And now, more than ever, she would want him
landward. Safe. Being a woman, she would use a woman
to achieve her ends.

And because she had been so warm on the subject of the
McIntyre girls, he would encourage her attempt in every
way possible. Without her knowing it. Because Patsy
Whaley was of all things shrewd. If he, after years of
reluctance to dally with respectable women, suddenly
strained at the leash to receive an introduction to one
woman, she would know that something was seriously
amiss. That must not happen. And so he would feign lack
of interest, reluctance, boredom, and finally, acquiescence.

Lydia would be presented to him like a turkey on a
platter.

There would be no suspicion, nothing untoward to
indicate that he sought her out. Too many eyes watched
him in Williamsburg, Patsy's not the least; he had to be
the Dandridge they remembered. A man above reproach.
And when he had her, he would fly over the waves like a
gull and be gone. It had to happen quickly because time
was his enemy. Time would help Charlton in his search
for facts. Time would erode the facade he wore with his
elegant aunt. Time would loosen Lydia's tongue to reveal
what he did with himself when not in Williamsburg. He
was half convinced that shock at seeing him and a desire
to keep her own true vocation a secret from the people of
Williamsburg had kept her silent until now. They could
not know what she was; they would have thrown her out
of town at the knowledge, no matter her father's worth to
the community. No, time was not his ally, but no striving
energy must mark his outward appearance, though it
roared through him like a storm. He must wait for Patsy
to move the first pawn in this game of matchmaking, and

she must not know that her king had been lost until the wind filled the sails of the *Serpent*.

Watching her, sipping his tea, Dandridge waited, poised and ready. He would allow her the first move.

"It's fine to see you sitting there, boy, sharing this hour with me," Patsy said warmly, wistfully. "It's many years I've waited for your companionship."

"It's good to be home, Aunt." Dandridge smiled, sipping from the porcelain cup.

"You'll see Spotswood tomorrow, is that correct? That's fine," she continued at her nephew's nod, "then we can put this episode behind us. River Run needs your youth and strength, Dandridge."

"Meeting with Spotswood," he murmured; "does that preclude my returning to sea? Would you have me desert my duty?"

"Pah! Let him find someone else. You have given enough," she argued.

"A man can never give enough in his country's service, Aunt. I have no plan to leave the *Serpent*," Dandridge argued calmly and sweetly, sipping again of his drink.

Patsy, after years of reasoning with Matthew, abandoned her current tack. Argue a man into a corner, especially where loyalty and honor were concerned, and he would invariably strike out in exactly the wrong direction.

Setting her cup and saucer down, she began gently. "I've worried about you, Dandridge. The sea is such a lonely place and must be especially so to a man of your vigor."

Dandridge smiled broadly and set his own cup down. They were moving closer to the center of the board now.

"Hardly lonely. I have a score of comrades and many responsibilities. No, Aunt, I have not been lonely once."

"I was not speaking of your crew, boy," she said a trifle sharply. "They can hardly satisfy your social needs. I was, in fact, wondering if you did not miss the sweet solace of female companionship."

"You have a complaint against my manners, madam? Are my buckles tarnished? Is the damask of my coat spotted with yesterday's breakfast?" he softly demanded, alluding to the conversation of the ladies outside Bruton Parish earlier that day.

Patsy sat up straighter in her chair and smoothed her bodice. The boy was impossible. She almost suspected that he was being deliberately obtuse.

"You are adequately turned out and well you know it," she argued, more irritated with him at each phrase he uttered. How could she have forgotten what upheavals he had caused in her orderly life? Could the boy never do as he was directed? "You are in the prime of your manhood, Dandridge, and nicely situated. Have you never thought to wife?"

"Never," he answered in truth. "It is not a thought that one contemplates at sea."

"That is exactly my point!" Patsy exclaimed forcibly and then immediately regretted it. She had moved too boldly and too quickly. She did not dare alert him to her cause.

"Is it?" he replied amiably. "Then we are in perfect accord."

She took a deep breath, gathering her composure, rethinking her position. She was so angry with him that she could think of nothing.

Dandridge could.

"Do you plan to entertain while you are in town, Aunt Patsy?" he asked casually, stretching his legs out in front of him.

The amber of her eyes kindled and she smiled to herself before answering, "Yes, I thought I would." With all the nonchalance she could muster, she added, "Perhaps I will invite Mr. and Mistress McIntyre to dine with us. He is an educated gentleman, recently from London; a pleasure to converse with. I think you would enjoy him."

"Is he the man you mentioned earlier? The apothecary?" he prompted, allowing her to see that he was not alarmed, encouraging her to proceed along the route they both so ardently desired.

"Yes, I believe so," Patsy said mildly. "He is a man of good repute . . . with many daughters."

"A man much blessed," Dandridge replied with equal mildness.

"He would agree with you. He is a man most devoted to his family, and his daughters show the fruit of his care."

"Then his daughters are blessed as well."

A speculative silence grew between them. It was going well, extremely well, from Patsy's perspective. Too well? It was unlike Dandridge to be so mild. Dandridge, for his part, did not know how to propel her into making a bolder move, unless he moved a few of his pieces out of the way, allowing her to see his king clearly.

"Blessed with both beauty and a loving father; fortunate girls," he added. He did not think of what he was saying, he did not think of Lydia having a father who loved her devotedly; he only thought of how to achieve his end. They were but words on his lips for a moment and then gone.

Patsy considered Dandridge carefully. He was being exceptionally agreeable; it was exceptionally unlike him. Knowing him as she did, it seemed clear that he was open to the idea of meeting the McIntyre girls; perhaps he was not so opposed to marriage as he declared.

"I daresay that an invitation to dine would be well received by them," she said, "and they could bring the two eldest, Lydia and Miriam, with them. Six at table would be quite a treat for me," Patsy added, endeavoring to arouse Dandridge's pity in the event that she had misread him. "I haven't had that much company at supper since before Matthew passed."

Dandridge recrossed his ankles, the image of ease, showing his aunt that he was not alarmed by this turn in their social plans. "Then now is the perfect time to change that. By all means, invite them to dine. I must confess, I find myself eager to meet such paragons of beauty."

Patsy's eyes snapped at that. She would arrange this supper before Dandridge could rethink himself of this compliance. Such docility was surely not a permanent feature of his character.

"I shall send an invitation 'round to them for Wednesday evening, then," she declared. "They live not far from here, just behind his shop, which is located on Palace Green. I tell you, at my age, it is a comfort to have an apothecary near."

"One can never be too young to have good neighbors," Dandridge said smoothly, quietly exulting in the knowledge that he knew Lydia's exact whereabouts and that she was so close to his hand. The knowledge sent his pulse racing through him.

He was just planning an evening walk toward the apothecary's shop to find the cure for his throbbing when a servant announced the arrival of a messenger, from Spotswood, reminding him of his appointment for ten on the morrow. With chill civility, Dandridge acknowledged his receipt of the reminder. It was an order and nothing less. Spotswood was reminding him that questions would be asked and answers given. While Dandridge felt sure of the questions, he was less sure of his answers.

The servant left the house, but did not leave. From the parlor window, Dandridge watched him move to the shadowed corner of the house, in full sight of both street and garden doors, and stop. A sentinel had been placed. Dandridge would go nowhere that night without

Spotswood's knowing. The unwelcome knowledge did nothing to stop the pounding of his blood.

Lydia would have to wait. After three months of waiting, one more night was hardly worth mentioning, but he could not help mentioning it to himself. One more night. One more endless night.

He could wait. Tomorrow would come soon enough and bring with it the meeting with the governor of Virginia Colony, the king's representative.

Patsy stirred in her chair behind him and he turned to sit again with her in companionable quiet. There was little conversation; Patsy was too busy exulting in her maneuvers and trying to suppress that exultation, and Dandridge was taking a cold look at his situation.

He had hardly thought to find himself in such a one. In the morning, Spotswood would demand answers. If his answers were not good enough, he would find himself in gaol for the short period of time that it would take to try and execute him. He was suddenly and extremely motivated to come up with some very good answers.

Sipping his freshened tea with his aunt in such calm civility, Dandridge could not stop himself from thinking what an odd spot he found himself in. Alexander Spotswood was a friend, or had been one, and a good one. Now, it was imperative to his survival that he hide the fact that he had played pirate from the premier legal authority in the land. And he understood Alexander well enough to know that he was holding his hand regarding him, holding his hand when the evidence of four years' silence urged him not to. He did this in the name of an old friendship.

Or did he? Dandridge shifted his weight in his chair and turned glittering eyes to the window. Spotswood had arranged for his license to hunt pirates. How much had he arranged in regard to the *Serpent*'s crew? How could a shipful of pirates have burrowed in the seat of government for all of Virginia Colony without the king's representative being aware of it? If he was to be accused as a pirate, he might have some accusations of his own to voice and a saber with which to underline the point.

He had never thought of himself as a pirate these past years; he had simply thought himself alive and was quite happy with the accomplishment. It was only now, here at home, that the truth of his identity was suddenly and blazingly clear. He had done piratical deeds, deeds that would guarantee a hanging, deeds for which he must find cover. Spotswood, once a friend, must not know what he had become. Patsy, for all her love of him, would turn away from him in disgust if she knew what he had been about. Pirates were an abomination, he remembered thinking that, remembered believing it. He had even acted on that belief.

Look where it had brought him.

Old friends, beloved family, would turn away from him, wishing that they had never known him if they discovered his acts of piracy. New friends . . . he had no new friends. The men he had associated with were ruled by fist and club.

One person in Williamsburg knew the truth. Lydia. Lydia, who had sought out his caress; Lydia, who had run from him. Lydia held his life in her hands.

Chapter Fifteen

If he was as ruthless as he should be, he would kill her. If four years of pirating had taught him anything, it was "kill or be killed," but he couldn't kill her. It had taken him most of the night and half a bottle of rum to decide that, but he couldn't kill her. Despite everything else he had done, he couldn't kill her.

After Aunt Patsy had retired for the night, he had left the house and made a round of the ordinaries, uncaring if Spotswood's man followed him. There was nothing illegal in drinking rum. He had much thinking, much planning to do, and it was better done with a pint of something stronger than tea. Drinking was somewhat frowned upon on the Sabbath, but it was the rare man who turned down coin. Dandridge had been able to drink his fill. And while he was drinking, he had cautiously asked about the McIntyres, about Lydia McIntyre. What he had found out had spiked his thirst and given him nightmares.

She was a good girl from a good family; it was a universal judgment. They had emigrated from England three years previous and made a valued place for themselves in the community. She had traveled to the Bahama Islands to care for her mother's sister in her confinement. She had returned looking the worse for wear; the common belief was that travel apparently hadn't agreed with her. He had felt like laughing when he heard that, but hadn't been able force any sound past the bile in his throat.

The facts, and he knew they were facts because he'd checked them three times over from three different sources, were ranged against him with the cold and lethal precision of opposing gunports. He saw no mercy for himself nor did he expect any. She had been an innocent when he had cut her bonds and hauled her off to his cabin, but she had not stayed an innocent long. Those brief glimpses of uncertainty and vulnerability that had troubled him then were now explained, and the vision he now had of her facing him with her arms crossed against her chest and her chin held high in precious dignity burned like flaring powder in his mind. She had been a virgin and he had taken her; but would he have done any differently if he had known?

That was the worst question of all because he knew the answer, the bile rising higher in his throat to confirm it.

Pirates did not respect virginal women or seasoned whores.

He remembered again how she had looked to him, a prisoner trussed up on a pirate ship: wanton sensuality and feminine vulnerability. He grew hard at the memory, as hard as he had been then. His body answered him; pirates followed their own inclinations on every point.

Knowing her for a virgin, he would have taken her still.

Dan swallowed hard, forcing down the truth so it was hidden in the dark of his gut.

And really, she had not behaved like a woman hard used. He had taken time with her, made certain of her pleasure, conversed with her, laughed with her. Fed her.

Dan swallowed again, forcing the bitterness out of his mouth and into the dark.

If she had pleaded, explained her position, he would have listened. He was no ravisher of innocents. All she would have had to do was be honest with him. She had hidden the truth of what she was by wearing a mask of sexuality, and she had obliged him to act on her facade. It was even possible that she had wanted it that way. She did, after all, have a wanton's heart.

He had been her first, and she had burned hot for him.

No, he would not kill her. And he would not let her go.

Dan swallowed heavily. All trace of his shame and guilt lay quietly in the dark of his gut, held there by will alone. There it would stay; he had done much in the last four years by will alone.

The night had not been a total loss; he had determined on a plan to thwart the governor and had spent most of the night polishing it. The light of day hadn't dimmed it, much. Besides, it was all he could devise. The beauty of it was that much of it would be the truth.

Dandridge straightened his waistcoat and squared his chin. He left Patsy's house with an easy step and confident mien, as was his way when things were blackest. The capitol was not far; he would be in good time for his "appointment," neither late nor early. It would work. He had no experience with failure. He would be victorious in this encounter. His definition of victory was very simple: victory was survival.

His timing was perfect, the first victory, but it was with unwelcome surprise that he found Ben Charlton awaited him as escort into the governor's presence in the very formal and very official Council Chamber.

"I'm surprised to see you here, Charlton," Dandridge admitted. "What keeps you in Williamsburg?"

Dandridge did not stop and allow Ben to lead him to his interview, so Ben was obliged to follow a step behind.

"I've been named a burgess and so spend June in Williamsburg, Prentis."

Dandridge did not pause or show any reaction, but he couldn't help thinking that *he* might have been elected burgess instead, if he'd been here; he and Charlton were of the same county and so would have been in competition. No matter, he had no yearning to be so tied to the land or to Williamsburg, the legal heart of Virginia Colony.

The door was open. Dandridge did not pause, but walked right in. Spotswood was not seated at his chair, a thronelike affair of intricate carving, but stood with his back to one of the five windows in the oval room, his face partially hidden by shadow. As he was not invited to sit, Dandridge stood as well, facing his opponent. Ben Charlton stopped behind and to the left of him. Dandridge instinctively moved to the side, keeping both men in his sight. He did not like a man at his back. Both Spotswood and Charlton noted the maneuvering. And understood its implications.

"Strange behavior for a man who is among friends," Charlton remarked.

There was to be no polite and civilized discourse, Dan saw; they would start on him and finish him quickly, if they could. He had played such games before, and won.

"I haven't been among friends in four years," he answered bluntly, holding first Charlton's and then Spotswood's eyes. "The reason I'm here today, sir, is that I don't leave my back open, to anyone."

"You insult us, sir," Spotswood said coldly, "and I do not pretend to understand you."

173

"Then allow me to make myself clear," Dan replied with a tight smile.

But would he? They were moving in rapidly for the kill, these civilized men. Charlton he had already absolved as being of incompatible temperament for the sort of arrangements which would have been necessary for manning his vessel with pirates. Spotswood, a man accustomed to power and the pursuit of it, was more likely. Pirates made a keen profit; was Spotswood the sort of man to turn from such a lure?

Dandridge eyed them both with a flinty expression, weighing for a final time how much of the truth to tell and how much of the truth Spotswood spoke. Their expressions were equally hard and equally closed. Perhaps the friendship he had counted on was not as strong as he had thought. But this was a game he had often played and with the same outcome for the loser: death. He was very good at this game.

"The *Serpent*'s crew, which I did not pick but was picked for me, were not of the highest caliber. In fact, they were the dregs of every dock for miles in any direction. The captain, Red Jack, was of the same ilk. Unfortunately, this fact did not become apparent until we were some miles from shore. By then, it was too late."

Dandridge watched shock register on Spotswood's face to mingle with pity until suspicion surfaced. And remained.

"But you live," Spotswood stated. Did he hear disappointment?

"I live," Dan affirmed. "And I am here to ask you, Governor, who it was that made the arrangements regarding the *Serpent*? I was young and eager, seeing little but the chance to be away upon the sea in glorious duty to my country." Dan's voice hardened though his smile remained intact. "You gave me license, sir. Who picked my crew?"

Spotswood did not pale beneath the unspoken indictment, which told Dan something of the man's character. Without a quiver of discomfort, he answered, "The arrangements were left to your uncle, sir, the appointment was left to me. The killing of pirates was left to you. Tell me, sir, how it is that, while surrounded by pirates, you live?"

In all the years he had known him, Dan had never known Spotswood to act beyond the normal routines of government, so his answer had the ring of truth or, at the very least, policy. As to Uncle Matthew, never would he submit to the belief that his uncle had betrayed him. They had been as father and son. Matthew Whaley had been a wealthy, influential, and honorable man and he had loved Dan unstintingly, even in the issue of his passion for the sea. Dan's father had left him his fortune with Matthew as executor; it was Dan's wish that all be invested in a ship, his ship. It was for love of Dan that his uncle had agreed, despite Patsy's complaining. Matthew would never have plotted Dan's murder. In the simplest terms, he had nothing whatsoever to gain.

Spotswood had answered his charge and returned fire; it was now Dan's turn to answer the charge of piracy. He would be walking a thin rope in a high wind. But he had never fallen yet.

"I live because I convinced them that I would rather turn pirate than be killed." Dan smiled easily. "Not a difficult point to make, gentlemen." If Spotswood wanted him dead, he had just given him the knife. Dan watched and waited, his smile wide, his instincts for survival whispering that he had chosen a wise course.

Spotswood's expression hardened at that. "Is there a difference, then, between acting a pirate and being a pirate?"

Dan had always believed so, but he couldn't stop the image of Lydia that came to him then, standing tied in the bow of his ship, waiting to be ravished by them all. Lydia knew the truth. He would lie. Victory was survival.

"Yes, Governor, there is. I have taken ships, pirate ships, and turned their crews over to whatever governor in whichever port was nearest. The ships the *Serpent* has taken have met their just fate." It was what he had been sent to do. It was what Spotswood wanted to hear. It was true enough to keep him from the noose. Unless Spotswood was looking for a reason to hang him.

Spotswood frowned. "Which ships?"

"The *Sea Maiden*, the *Sprite*, the *Golden Goose*," he returned. "All pirate ships and all taken by the *Serpent*." The two French ships and the three Spanish that had been lawful vessels, he did not mention. He had not been captain; he was not responsible for all those deaths, had even argued against them, at his peril.

Still, Dandridge clasped his hands behind his back, hiding remembered blood.

"I wanted them tried and hanged in Virginia," Spotswood said.

Spotswood spoke as if he had had a choice. Dan smiled ruefully and lifted his shoulders in an expressive gesture. "Dead is dead, Governor. And Red Jack didn't answer to me."

"Yes, the captain of your ship. The pirate. Where is he now?"

"Dead," Dan answered without blinking.

Spotswood studied him and Dan returned the service. The question as to how the captain of the *Serpent* had met his death and by whose hand did not need to be asked or answered. Charlton was a silent shadow in the room, a room full of doubts and speculations and broken trust. And lies.

"Why did you not simply leave the vipers who nested on your ship?"

"My first thought, Governor, but pirate ships anchor in

pirate ports. Leaving the *Serpent* would have gained me nothing and lost me a way home. With Red Jack dead, I was free to follow my own course."

It went without saying that Red Jack had died recently. None need know of Lydia and the vital part she had played in his return.

"I had expected to hear something of your progress, Prentis. Four years is a long time to hear nothing," Spotswood pointed out.

Dan laughed gently, the sunlight from the open window lighting his amber eyes to gleaming gold and sparking the blue lights in his black hair. "So my aunt has informed me, often, since my return. And I have told her that time aboard ship passes quickly. The sea is an alluring mistress, gentlemen; she consumes a man without his protest. Still"—he held up a hand when Spotswood would have argued—"I have sent missives. In fact, I sent a report some six months ago from Madras, but I am not surprised that you have not received it. The pirate trade is flourishing. And, gentlemen, a taken ship transports no mail."

It was a lie. He had sent no missives. In the beginning, it had been because he was not trusted and he would do nothing to feed that mistrust. In the end . . . in the end it had been because the memory of Williamsburg had become as dim as a dream.

Both men smiled in response, their posture relaxed. His answers had the ring of truth, yet there was something . . . perhaps it was that he was too easy in his manner. Perhaps they merely suspected a man who had survived treachery. His honor would have been without question if he had died.

"You have given your report, Prentis," Spotswood said in dismissal. "I would hazard that you will now seek to discover the one who betrayed you?" When Dandridge only smiled, Spotswood continued, "Have a care. You must not run wild throughout the colony, tossing accusations into the wind to watch where they will land." It was a rebuke and they all knew it.

"I *will* find the man who plotted against my life."

"Of that I have no doubt," Spotswood answered calmly. "When you have sufficient proof, come to me with it and he will be lawfully tried in open court. You seek justice, sir, and there is no justice outside the law."

The only justice on a pirate ship was swift death, and he had become the pirate in his desires. Dan said nothing in response to Spotswood's warning.

"You have been foully betrayed, Dandridge," Alexander Spotswood said, his voice gentling. "That you seek the culprit under every stone I well understand, but, sir, a lawful man seeks lawful redress."

Spotswood's meaning was clear to Dan; if he sought pirate justice, he would be pirate proved. It was upon this action that Alexander would lay his guilt or innocence.

If Alexander was the man who had wanted him dead, he would hardly instruct him in his own survival.

If Dan wanted to live, he could not deal with the man in his own fashion. At least, not in Virginia Colony.

Chapter Sixteen

"Didn't you notice how silent she was during supper yesterday?" Anna McIntyre questioned her husband as they worked picking herbs and medicinals from their garden.

"Her silence was no more pronounced than at any other time of late," Robert answered, less willing than his wife to look for trouble. Trouble pursued quickly enough without aid.

"Of late," Anna repeated. "Husband, our daughter is not well and has not been well since her tribulation."

"Some sicknesses take much time to heal. Give her more time, Anna."

"I am not impatient," Anna argued, knowing what she wanted to say but unable to find the proper words. "I would give her all eternity, but can't you see that she is worsening? Yesterday it was more pronounced than ever."

Robert fingered the leaf between his fingers gently and slowly rose from his knees to his feet. How completely he cared for each of his patients, selecting the freshest plants, grinding the most potent potions, monitoring the progress of everyone who came to him for help. How very little he could do for his eldest daughter. She had come home bruised and starved and tangled, her soul a ragged thing she carried behind her like a weed caught in her skirts. He had cleansed her wounds, fed her, loved her, and given her a full measure of healing forgiveness. He was so very thankful that she was alive. And still she sickened. A clean body and well-mended clothing could not cure the putrefaction that seemed to be consuming her from within. He had no potions to heal what ate at her. It was a loving father's grief he felt, arms outstretched to a beloved child he could not quite reach. Every day she fell further from his grasp, and he could only pray to the Father whose grasp she could not escape, and love her more fiercely in her struggles.

"Yes," he admitted, "I saw."

"Oh, Robert, I knew you had," she whispered, leaning her head against his shoulder for an instant in communal love and misery. "I watched her carefully because she seemed different somehow and I wanted to see some small sign that would show me how to help her."

Anna stopped, uncomfortable and uneasy, turning away from her husband to face the rear of their garden.

"And what did you see, Anna? What sign was there?" Robert prompted.

What she had seen was impossible, she knew that. Absurd. But it weighed heavily on her mind and she would have it off her shoulders. Perhaps Robert would have a logical interpretation, because hers had nothing of logic in it.

"The man in church," she blurted out. "The man whom Miriam wished an introduction to and the younger girls had spied upon." Anna turned to face Robert, her blue eyes penetrating. "She reacted badly, Robert, awfully, when he was spoken of."

Robert waited, unsure of what to make of that statement, or what she wanted him to make of it.

"I believe . . . I wondered if . . . perhaps he is the man who raped her."

"Impossible," Robert uttered, his first thought.

"Why impossible?" Anna argued. "Did you watch her as I did? Did you see that she turned white as chalk whenever he was mentioned, scarcely breathing at first and then panting like a field hand? Did you know that she ripped a long tear in her napkin? She did not eat, Robert. She almost ran from Bruton Parish and up to her room well ahead of you and Miriam, and she did not come out until it was time to prepare the table for the meal. Yes, she has been silent. Yes, she has been withdrawn. But, Robert, when has she ever behaved like this?"

Robert could not refute her observations; he simply could not believe that it was possible for a pirate to roam the streets of Williamsburg and attend service at Bruton Parish. It was impossible!

"Does it seem likely to you that a pirate would dress himself in good fashion and attend church services? For what purpose, Anna?"

"I do not pretend to know the mind of a pirate," Anna said somewhat proudly.

"And didn't Ruth state that he was being introduced by Widow Whaley to her circle of friends? Would she be on such close acquaintance with a pirate? No, Anna, it is impossible that this man is the same man who . . . who . . ." He could not finish, the images were too clear.

Anna stroked his cheek comfortingly. "Of course it is impossible. I had forgotten about Mistress Whaley's introduction. You are quite right, Robert. He is not the

181

man. Perhaps . . . perhaps they share a likeness and that is what put our daughter off."

"Yes," Robert agreed, "that is a logical assumption. She saw him and was frightened, remembering. . . . No, he cannot be the man."

"No, he cannot be," Anna agreed, still troubled.

Leaving Robert to his plants, Anna returned to the house through the garden door. The girls were in the sitting room, the windows open to the warm early summer air. The sound of their voices, soft and feminine, soothed her. It was a good life here in the colonies; she was most thankful they had come. It was a peaceful, good life . . .

"I just don't understand it!" Hannah exclaimed, throwing down her chalk, scattering tiny shards of white over the table.

"But, Hannah," Lydia argued softly, picking up the chalk, "multiplication is the easy way to do addition. Instead of having to add all those numbers, multiply them. It is much quicker."

"Not for me," Hannah replied sullenly, tears pooling in her blue eyes. "I don't see why I have to learn to multiply when I only want to draw."

"To draw well, you must understand mathematics, Hannah," Lydia pointed out, wiping clean the slate. "Have you forgotten proportion, perspective, and angles? You'll find mathematics rooted there. Think of learning your multiplication as a means to improve your drawing, perhaps that will help."

Hannah's eyes welled over with her tears of frustration. Mathematics and drawing? Would she never escape those terrible numbers?

Ruth stopped practicing her handwriting to gaze at her sister in commiseration. Mathematics was hardly her favorite subject, but because of that, she rushed through it, eager to put it behind her. Hannah just wanted to ignore it.

"Oh, Hannah," she said, "once you learn the tables you'll never have to learn them again. I did it. You can, too."

"Perhaps I'm just not trying hard enough," Hannah murmured.

"And perhaps you're trying too hard," Anna offered, entering the room fully. "Come with me. We'll go to the kitchen and help Sally with the biscuits, forgetting multiplication for the time and focusing on fractions and their sweet results instead. Ruth, you can come as well, if you promise to finish your letters before the day's end."

"I promise," Ruth said quickly, rising to her feet. Anna put an arm around them both and led them out of the room, but not before casting a meaningful look at Miriam. Anna would not pry into Lydia's thoughts; she was available if Lydia opened the door, but she would not even presume to knock. But if Lydia opened her heart and mind to her sister?

Lydia was a grown woman. She should have been long married, with children of her own under her tutelage. But Lydia was responsible, perhaps too responsible. When she had suffered an unexplained bout of fatigue, Lydia had remained close to home, taking on all the duties of a mother toward her own sisters. It was a time in her life when she should have been courted and wed. Though one or two men had made initial overtures, nothing had come of them. Anna suspected that Lydia had given them no hope; she believed her duties lay elsewhere. Lydia, who had been taking care of her family during her most marriageable years, was now in danger of becoming a spinster daughter, maiden aunt to her sister's children.

Now, of course, it would be a more difficult thing. Many men, maybe most, would not have a forgiving enough nature to give their name to a wife who was not a virgin. Circumstances had not been kind to her eldest daughter, but with God, there was hope. It was this that she clung to when she watched Lydia fade before her eyes. Perhaps she would open up to Miriam. It was this thought that Anna communicated to Miriam before she left them alone. And Miriam understood.

Alone together, Lydia and Miriam silently put away the books of learning and the tablets on which to practice that knowledge. The silence between them seemed all the heavier for the warm sunshine slanting across the pine floorboards and the resonantly cheerful chirping of the birds in the fruit orchard. The air was warm, but not heavy. The sun was bright without being blinding. The silence between the sisters was empty. The room tidied, Lydia stood absently, her hands at her sides, her gaze on the dust motes swirling in the sunlit air before her. She did not move. She did not speak. She behaved as one asleep.

Miriam was frightened for her.

Hannah's laugh caused Lydia to start just a little. She looked up and smiled abstractedly at Miriam and then collected her garden hat and scissors. Miriam, watchfully, did the same and followed her through the length of their property, passing the well, kitchen, smokehouse, dairy, and orchard on a path lined with crushed seashells before reaching the kitchen garden at the rear of their land. Kneeling side by side, they worked the soil between the plants, creating an unwelcoming environment for weeds.

Lydia, her hands fully in the dirt, was not thinking about weeds. Her sole purpose in coming to the kitchen garden was to keep busy, but no matter how busy she kept her body, her mind returned to Dan. Dan, praising her elbows and making her laugh. Dan, feeding her from his fingertips. Dan, showing her a civility, a consideration, that was far above pirate fare. Dan, bursting through the door of his cabin, his eyes only for her. Dan, finding her and holding her gaze in Bruton Parish Church. Yesterday.

Now she had new memories to add to the old. Memories of how he had looked, clean-shaven and clothed in shining damask. Memories of how his golden eyes had sought hers, holding her, wanting her. Even from that distance, with all those people in between them, she had felt his wanting. And it had warmed her. It was not only him she had run from yesterday; she had run from that desire. Desire she had felt and returned. He wanted her. She wanted him. And he was here.

This battle of desire, of the desire that had been born the moment she had willed her own survival, was the greatest battle of her life and she knew it, but she couldn't tell anyone about it. It was too humiliating. If she was honest with herself, she would admit that she lacked the courage. Being honest with herself was becoming more and more difficult.

There was also the worry about what he was doing here in Williamsburg. Second to her irrational concern that he would get himself hung was the worry that he would tell what he knew about her. It was bad enough, what he had done, what she had let him do, but for everyone else to know. . . . She wouldn't do that to her family, she would leave first. And run where? But she was worrying herself needlessly; he wouldn't tell because it would reveal too much about him and that would be putting the noose around his own neck. No, he wouldn't tell, couldn't tell that she had melted against him, laughing in his embrace. But why was he here? Who was he, really?

Miriam worked alongside her, but Lydia scarcely noticed. Miriam saw that she scarcely noticed. It was becoming increasingly clear that Lydia would not open up on her own, so Miriam, with uncharacteristic boldness, opened the subject herself. She did it for Lydia's good; an unlanced boil spreads its infection. She did it out of love.

"You're thinking about your ordeal, aren't you?"

"What?" Lydia asked, her eyes clouded with her own thoughts.

Miriam swallowed and began again, "You're thinking about being on the pirate ship, aren't you?"

"What?" Lydia repeated, startled and mildly shocked. This was something which was never discussed. "Am I thinking about . . . the pirates?"

Miriam clapped the dirt from her gloved hands and adjusted her woven hat, determined to handle this coolly and well. "Yes. You are, aren't you? You think about that time quite a lot, I think."

"Well, perhaps," Lydia answered awkwardly, unbearably uncomfortable. "It was an unusual event. I am unlikely to forget it."

"Share it with me, Lydia. Perhaps that will help."

Lydia considered that. She was surprised to discover that she wanted to; she wanted to talk about Dan with someone. But her sister . . . Miriam was an innocent, as she herself had once been. There was only so much she could tell without damaging that innocence. Still, there were certain things she could tell.

"Yes," she agreed softly, uncertainly.

Miriam paused for a moment, choosing her words carefully. "You must have been very frightened."

"I was," Lydia agreed quietly, somberly. "I expected to die at any moment."

"Did they . . . was there anyone else . . . ?"

"No. Many were killed," Lydia whispered, looking down at her gloved hands. The barrister and his assistant, just past boyhood with curly black hair. The planter with his gold brocade waistcoat and pipe. Each gone in a gush of blood. Each killed without the humanity of hesitation. She would never forget, and when she dreamed of Dan reaching for her, sometimes his hands were blood red and it was not lust that pursued her, but fear. And then she awoke in the quiet of night not in the heat of unfulfilled passion, but in the chill of remembered fear. "The decks were covered in blood and entrails and pieces of . . . I was the only one left." Lydia stopped and looked deep into Miriam's eyes. "I was alone."

"Oh, Lydia . . ." Miriam murmured, her eyes glistening with sympathetic tears. "It was God's mercy that they spared you."

Lydia looked down again at her hands; the dirt clung to her gloves. She had but to remove them and she would be clean. God's mercy? Dan had cut her ropes. Dan had led her away from the carnage of the deck. Dan had protected her from the killers.

She was a fool! Dan was one of them! Dan's hands had been red with the kill. Dan had been one of them, was one of them. Mercy? He was a pirate.

"Yes. It was," Lydia agreed, holding her thoughts in tight.

"How did it come to pass that you were spared?"

"The captain, it was his decision."

"And they agreed?"

"He forced them to."

She remembered well that he had fought for her life so that she could serve his lust. Lust that she had ignited. Intentionally.

"He must be a strong man and have some good left in him to do so."

"Yes," Lydia agreed, her eyes lifting to her sister, seeing the innocence there. "He protected me."

"Is it him you think of when you think on those days?"

"Yes. I think of him. I remember him. He . . . he—" she struggled. He was a pirate and she could not purge him from her thoughts.

"He saved your life and you remember him without

187

malice," Miriam finished, a little aghast at her own conclusion.

"That's right. I bear him no malice," Lydia agreed, surprised at the open mind with which Miriam was prepared to hear her tale. "He was kind to me when he had no need to be. He took a great risk when he took me from the rest of them, keeping me safe from them all. I was given privacy and good food and . . . and a bed to sleep in. He was charming in his speech, treating me with more civility than I ever expected. He made me laugh, Miriam," Lydia finished, her cheeks slightly flushed. Dan's hands had not been red when he touched her.

Miriam had passed through mild astonishment to something near horror. She had not forgotten that they were speaking about a pirate, a pirate who had attacked a vulnerable ship, killing most onboard. Lydia seemed to have forgotten that. Lydia seemed unaccountably warm in her regard for this pirate captain.

"He made you laugh?" Miriam asked stiffly.

"Yes," Lydia confessed, "and that is why I am so preoccupied. I think about this captain and my thoughts grow more fond with each passing day." Seeing the expression on Miriam's face, Lydia added heatedly, "Do you think I do not know that he is a pirate with blood covering his hands? Do you think I *want* to remember him? This is my struggle, sister! I remember a man and a time that I want to forget! The battle waging in my own thoughts is a hundred times more brutal than the battle in taking a ship at sea, and there is no escape from thoughts. Do you see? I cannot escape!"

Miriam did see, and her heart broke for a second time for her sister. Wanting to ease her pain, she looked for a way to justify the cause of Lydia's fascination. With a pirate. Lydia needed to talk more than she needed to be censored. Miriam could only pray that God and the passage of time would take care of the rest.

"He must have been an extraordinary man," she offered quietly.

Lydia stared again at the dirt on her gloves, her passion abated. "He was."

He is, she wanted to shout. *He is in Williamsburg. He is the man in the church. He is unabated in his desire for me.*

She did not want to shout, *He is a pirate.*

A little stunned by their conversation, and now struggling with her own thoughts, Miriam quietly left the garden. She sensed that Lydia needed time to herself; she knew that she herself did. To imagine Lydia the practical, Lydia the logical, Lydia the cool, consumed with memories of a lawless pirate . . . well, she couldn't imagine it at all.

Alone, Lydia continued her digging. The ground was soft from frequent turnings. They had had so little rain that there were few weeds. Still, she kept at it, if only to keep busy. Talking with Miriam had not helped weaken Dan's hold on her mind; Dan filled her thoughts as much as he ever did, perhaps more. She had opened the door to him more fully in talking about him with her sister. He was a more real presence now, not just a lone memory but one that had been given voice and one that she could share.

Worst of all, she was beginning to enjoy her memories. But how could they harm her? They had no substance. They were ghosts of the past and could not touch her any more than they already had. Maybe, like Hannah at her multiplication, she had been trying too hard. Maybe if she just let her mind wander at will, she would tire of his image and he would fade away to indistinction. Perhaps it was the fight that kept him alive in her. She chose not to consider that he was in Williamsburg, that he was of no ghostlike substance but very physically present. She did not want to consider that. She also did not want to forget it.

Having given herself, by this very logical route, permission to indulge in thoughts of Dan, she dug more contentedly in the dirt. Loosening the top two buttons of her shirt in response to the rising June heat, Lydia looked up from her task.

Dan stood on the other side of the fence, not twenty feet from her. The heat of his staring golden eyes made the summer sun cool in comparison.

For all her memories, she realized that she had forgotten how formidable a presence he really was.

She was rooted to the spot, on her knees in the dirt, looking up at him.

His memories had not exaggerated her sensuality. She looked now like a primal goddess of ancient origin, pure and lusty at once. She was worthy of a sacrifice. He would have killed for her in a moment and considered it well done, but he did not want to worship her. He wanted to tumble her, there, in the dirt.

Running children, girls, interrupted the image. They ran toward her, around her, playing tag, shrieking joyfully. Dan watched as Lydia turned from him to watch the girls in their play.

"Ruth, Hannah, you know you're not supposed to run in the garden," she said. She had meant to say it firmly, authoritatively. She only managed audibly.

They ignored her, running right to her, using her as both base and barrier, laughing constantly. Lydia, still on her knees, put an arm around each of their waists and held them still. She was grateful for their interruption, grateful for their physical closeness. This was an embrace that was pure. This embrace of sister to sister would not haunt her, and with Dan so near, she felt the need to hold and be held.

But the girls were not still, they reached around her, tagging each other and squirming in her arms. She held them fast, more for her sake than for theirs.

Dan could not take his eyes from her. Even on her

knees in the dirt, her arms full of boisterous children, she exuded sensuality.

"You will drive your sister into the ground like a peg if you do not give her ease," he said loudly, loudly enough to be heard over their shrieks of excitement.

Ruth and Hannah stopped, noticing the man for the first time, seeing him clearly. Then their small bodies began to rattle with excitement; this was the man on the steps of Bruton Parish! This was the man who had been told of the McIntyre beauty! This was a man to hold still for! Three pairs of blue eyes turned to look at the man by the fence. Lydia couldn't help thinking what an insignificant-looking fence it seemed, hardly able to keep out a cow or a pig or a . . . pirate.

"I know you," Ruth said excitedly.

"Do you?" Dan asked, looking sharply at Lydia.

"Ruth," she admonished, "mind your manners."

"Excuse me," Ruth mumbled. "Good day, sir." She curtseyed, Hannah copying her. That courtesy dispensed with, she repeated, "I know you."

"So you've said, little miss," Dandridge answered calmly. "How do you know me?"

"I saw you at Bruton Parish with Widow Whaley," she said, beaming.

Dan relaxed and smiled charmingly, "Did you? I didn't see you."

Ruth beamed a huge, gap-toothed smile at him, "I know."

"We hid from you," Hannah supplied, her own smile more gum than tooth.

"Did you?" he asked, his face registering great surprise. "You must be prodigiously good at it, because I'm very difficult to hide from and yet you accomplished it without my ever knowing. I can only think that I must have been very preoccupied not to have noticed two such very pretty girls."

They increased the power of their smiles at that well-deserved compliment: They did not overly care that he had called them pretty; it was the hiding part that was of true value.

"Tell me," he asked somewhat piteously, "did you get very close to me?"

The rules of civility demanded their response and they were not unhappy to give it. He was a very nice man. "No," answered Ruth, "we were not very close at all, just close enough to see your face." It did not seem a very good idea to reveal that they had heard every word; he might not be so nice then.

It was disconcerting in the extreme for Lydia to watch Dan being so civil, so courteous, to her younger sisters. He was not the sort they should have acquaintance with, no matter his current charm and civility. She had seen this man with blood on his hands; she had not forgotten that. Had he?

"Ruth, Hannah, go in to your lessons now. I will be in when I have washed the dirt from my hands. We cannot keep this . . . gentleman from his appointments."

Ruth considered it and Hannah with her. He was fun to talk with; handwriting exercises and multiplication drills were not nearly as interesting as he was.

"It has been a pleasure, ladies." Dan bowed. "May I come again? Perhaps then I shall have the honor of your names."

Lydia stood, pushing the girls behind her and away from Dan. She did not want him near her sisters. How could she have forgotten how dangerous he was?

"Go on now," she urged. "Go to the house and tell Mother that I am on my way."

They left reluctantly, more concerned with making a pleasing impression on the stranger than with anything Lydia said. When they were well on their way up the path to the house, Lydia felt an easing on her heart.

When she looked at Dan, the easing ceased abruptly.

"Is that a warning for me, Lydia?" Dan smiled warmly, his eyes glowing. "Did you think that I would snatch you over the fence and make off with you?"

She had wondered. She had also wondered how much she would mind. He was before her again, when she had never hoped to see him. He stood just there and if she ran into his arms he would lift her over that sorry piece of fencing and keep her safe from the whole world. But who would keep her safe from him?

"I was just speaking to hurry them off; there was nothing hidden in my meaning," she answered.

"Pardon me?" Dan held one hand up to an ear, cupping it like one who is hard of hearing. "Did you speak? I cannot hear you, you are so distant."

"I think that you can hear me very well," she answered, taking a step or two nearer just the same. She had to get just a bit closer to him. She just had to.

"I'm so sorry, would you repeat that? This distance is a damnable nuisance and with this fence between us, too."

"I don't see what the fence has to do with your hearing," she answered, suppressing a smile, walking nearer.

"It keeps us apart, Lydia," Dan answered, his smile growing hotter, "as does the distance and so I damn them both."

Those words stopped her. She was six feet from the fence. She would go no closer. She would not yield to his warmth. She could not. Not here. Not now. Not ever.

"Have you seen Spotswood?" she asked, both changing the subject and appeasing her worry, no, her curiosity.

"Earlier today," Dan answered easily. "In fact, I just left him."

Though she could not imagine what Dan had said to Spotswood that had left him walking free, she was relieved, ashamedly so. Who was Dan that he could circumvent English law?

"He . . ." she stammered uncertainly, "he saw no reason to detain you?"

"No, Lydia, did you think he would?"

"No, well, I wondered . . ."

"Come closer, Lydia, my hearing is not what it should be," he cajoled, his eyes bright with laughter. "I would read the message of your luminous eyes to aid the weakness of my ears."

She did not want to laugh, but he was so winsome and she was so relieved that he had not been cast in gaol. She closed the distance between them to four feet, out of his arm's reach, but close enough to see the dark line of his shaved beard. His black lashes radiated like the spokes of a wheel from his amber-colored eyes. Black brows, like the wings of a raven, swept low over his bright eyes. She had remembered, but she had forgotten. The physical presence of the man was nothing like the memory; Dan was a primal force, his memory was a shadow, manageable, just.

"Is that better?"

"Better," he whispered, "but not good enough."

The sudden blazing heat in his eyes sent her a step backward. He raised his brows in silent condemnation; she had never yet retreated from him. She understood his mocking and steeled herself to do better. She would not be mocked by him; besides, there was the fence, feeble thing that it was.

"Are you related to Mistress Whaley?" she asked, determined to find her own answers about him and set at least that part of her mind at rest.

Dan lost his smile, but she did not rejoice, she became wary.

He could see no reason for her question, unless she planned to turn him in; she would gather all the facts of his identity, convincing Spotswood that she knew exactly whom she was indicting. There would be no plea of mis-

taken identity, she would be certain of that. A word from
her and his web of truth and lies would be ripped from
him, exposing him to Spotswood. But he would not quail
before her. Never. Even with her hand full of weapons,
he would defeat her.

"Yes," he answered coldly.

She could not understand his coldness, unless he
feared for Mistress Whaley's reputation at her hands.
Small fear when she had her own reputation to guard.

"Is your family name Whaley?" she asked.

"No," he answered brutally, "it is Prentis." He did not
recommend himself for valor; it was information that she
could have acquired from anyone, innocently. Best tell
her from his own lips.

Lydia stopped, stunned. Prentis—his family name was
Prentis. They were well known and well respected. It was
an old name in this place, a name of wealth and responsibility and duty. It was Dan's name. Wait, she had heard
of a son, a son in service to his country and gone many
years. Dandridge Prentis.

Dan.

Impossible!

But the evidence was irrefutable. He was nephew to
Patsy Whaley, had been introduced to her peers on the
steps of Bruton Parish. He had been greeted warmly by
the governor himself. He was heir to a vast fortune. He
owned his own ship and was an able seaman. He was a
graduate of William and Mary. All this she knew, it was
common knowledge, but she and her family had never
seen him. They had arrived in the colony a year after he
had sailed away. Dandridge Prentis, agent of the king.

Dandridge Prentis, pirate.

She could not reconcile the two images in her mind;
she knew him as pirate all too well and as landed aristocrat not at all. He could not be both, yet he stood before
her, behind an ineffectual fence, glaring at her. He was a

pirate, there was no doubt. But Dandridge Prentis had attended church with his widowed aunt.

Confused beyond redemption, Lydia whispered her dilemma.

"Who are you really? Pirate or aristocrat? To me, you are the pirate."

It was a question that struck too close to the heart and Dan struck back in like form.

"And I wonder who you really are. Whore or prim daughter? To me, you are the . . ."

She blanched before he could finish and backed away from him, crushing the tender plants beneath her feet as she stumbled over the rows.

"You *are* a pirate," she whispered hoarsely, her aqua eyes filled with revulsion and shame before she turned to run into the sanctuary of her home.

Dan watched her go, angry with her for provoking him and with himself for losing his temper with her. Next time he would have a better hold on himself. Next time it would be easier because he would be accustomed to seeing her again. It had been a shock, a pleasant shock, to feel the effect she had on him again. His memory had been a dim thing compared to the reality. Next time . . .

Ruth had watched them from the corner of the necessary house. She had heard nothing, but what she had seen had not looked good.

Chapter Seventeen

A tall man with black hair, dressed in burgundy silk faille, strode with angry purpose past their shop window in the direction of Duke of Gloucester Street. He did not carry his cane elegantly; he carried it like a club. Anna, arranging pots of herbs in the display window, watched him pass with avid interest. She knew who he was. He was the man who had been engaged in conversation with Lydia while she worked in the garden.

Ruth was not the only one of the McIntyre household who had seen the stranger and his effect on Lydia.

They had stood not close, not chillingly distant, but a few polite feet apart, yet even at that distance, the emotion that swelled between them had buffeted Anna at her accidental observation post near the well. Like Ruth, she had heard nothing. Like Ruth, she had been disturbed by what she had seen.

Theirs was not the meeting of strangers, nor was it the meeting of friends.

Anna, after a quick conversation with Ruth, had learned what she had already strongly suspected—that this dark man was the stranger in church and also Dandridge Prentis. Eavesdropping was wrong, she had made that point repeatedly to Ruth even as she asked for a repetition of what she had heard outside of Bruton Parish. Eavesdropping was wrong, but Lydia needed help, and Anna would stoop to eavesdropping if it would help her daughter.

Of course, knowing now who he was, she could see that Robert had been right: this man who had so upset Lydia could not be the pirate who had robbed her of her virtue. That was flatly impossible. Yet he did have an unusual effect on her, one that Anna could not interpret intelligently. He was handsome, surely, but he was not alone in that state, and Lydia was not the sort of woman to be moved by simple and transient comeliness. And Lydia was most definitely moved by him.

There was no explaining the surge of emotion that had swept over them as they stood in the garden. Robert needed to be apprised of this.

"Robert," she began, turning away from the window and facing him at his counter, "I happened to see Lydia talking with a man in our garden, the man from church yesterday."

Robert looked up from his grinding to show his wife that he was listening and then promptly went back to what he had been doing. Lydia being sociable was hardly worth comment.

Anna waited for his response, found that he had none, and continued on, "I have learned that the man's name is Dandridge Prentis, nephew to Widow Whaley."

Robert stopped his grinding and looked at his wife with greater attention. Whereas his wife had found, upon the knowledge of the stranger's name, a decreased inclination to think him the robber of their daughter's virginity, Robert found that he was being moved toward belief. A simple pirate would not walk the streets of Williamsburg; Dandridge Prentis would. Dandridge Prentis owned a ship. Dandridge Prentis had been away, without word, for many years. And now Dandridge Prentis had spoken to his daughter in the seclusion of their garden. Why?

"And how did this conversation progress?" he asked simply, intently.

Anna played with the edge of her apron, running the folds through her fingers, searching for the words that would accurately describe what she had seen.

"They did not behave toward one another in quite the way of strangers, yet there was nothing intimate in their posture," she began. "I would say that what was most apparent was the depth of emotion that each displayed. Odd, for so casual a meeting between two strangers, don't you think?"

"Yes," he answered, pondering her words, "I would have thought so."

A foot scraping the sill of their shop terminated the conversation before it had a chance to really begin. They turned to face the prospective client and found themselves face to face with a servant of Patsy Whaley's.

"Excuse me, ma'am, sir." The boy bowed quickly. "I have a letter of invitation from my mistress. I am to wait for a reply, if you please."

Anna reached forth her hand to take the heavy and costly paper, folded twice and sealed with blue wax. Opening it, she read it quickly and without a word, speechless in fact, handed it to Robert.

It was an invitation to dine with her, and her nephew, this coming Wednesday. Lydia and Miriam would round out the party. Robert considered the facts he was in possession of: Lydia, rushing from church where Prentis was in attendance; Lydia, so highly wrought that he had considered giving her a sedative to ease her mind; Lydia and Dandridge Prentis in the garden in heated conversation; and now the invitation to dine from a woman they had been passing friendly with for three years. Why an invitation now, when her nephew had just returned? Was the nephew the reason, the instigator, of the invitation? It was a likely assumption.

"Thank you," Robert said, looking up from the missive to face the boy. "Will you wait for a written response or will my verbal affirmation of our intention to attend be sufficient?"

"Your word is sufficient, sir. I'll relay your response to Mistress Whaley. Thank you, sir." He bowed and was gone.

Anna stared at her husband, dumbfounded. After their earlier conversation, after the episode in the garden, after all the unspoken speculation that swirled between them, he had accepted the invitation?

"We're going?" she asked.

"We're going," he replied.

"But should we? Lydia has not been herself for months, and this man, somehow, has set her back even further. I know he cannot be . . . be . . . him, but he clearly has an unnerving effect upon her. I don't know if it is a good idea to place them in such close proximity, Robert."

"Lydia has had three months in which to recover. I believe it is time that she faced her demons."

Anna did not argue; she understood that her husband could only see things from a man's point of view, a view distinctly different from her own, obviously. God had placed man on earth as protector and provider, two very aggressive roles. He would want to face his fears and his demons, besting them, defeating them, even destroying them. Her goals were not so grand.

Quietly, from the doorway that connected shop and

home, Anna said, "Robert, some demons are better run from."

Robert looked at her eloquently; he could find no argument against that truth, nor did he try.

It was at the afternoon meal that the family was told of the invitation. Ruth and Hannah sulked at being excluded. Miriam glowed with expectation. Anna, watching Lydia carefully for her response, was not encouraged. Lydia took the news badly—quietly, but badly. She did not eat the rest of her meal. She did not speak. She tore another napkin.

Anna was heartsick at Lydia's response to their plan to dine with Mistress Whaley and her nephew. She felt that Lydia could not help but be better if she would only open her heart to her family so that their love and acceptance could heal her. She did not know why Lydia reacted so very strongly to Dandridge Prentis; she was almost afraid to know. She did know that she wanted her daughter back, the same daughter she had allowed to travel to her sister; this shadowed and haunted girl was not the Lydia she had loved from the cradle.

"It was kind of Mistress Whaley to invite us, was it not, Lydia?" she asked, wanting to draw her out on this tender subject.

"Yes, very kind," Lydia answered.

"And so unexpected," Miriam added.

"That, too," Lydia agreed.

"I wonder what precipitated it," Miriam said, looking at her mother.

"She has a much-loved nephew home from the sea," Robert remarked, looking at Lydia as he said it. "She most likely wants him to be entertained and to show us how well deserved is her pride in him."

"She seemed very proud of him at church," Ruth added.

"Is that who you spied upon yesterday? Dandridge Prentis?" Robert asked.

"Yes, Father," Ruth answered meekly. Hannah looked on with wide eyes, uncertain of the way this would blow.

"When you meet this gentleman, if you ever do, you must apologize for disturbing his privacy," Robert instructed most seriously, "both of you."

"Yes, Father," Ruth and Hannah said in unison and then Ruth added, "But we have already—"

"*Ruth!*" Lydia interjected loudly. "There's a fly in your water! Run outside and spill it out!"

Ruth jumped in her seat at the first words and then inspected her water. "That's not a fly, Lydia, that's my acorn. I'm soaking it."

"Oh," Lydia said dejectedly.

"*Anyway,*" Ruth continued, "Mr. Prentis has—"

"*Ruth!*" Lydia said again with slightly less volume. "Why . . . why are you soaking an acorn?"

"Really, Lydia, do you have to shout?" Ruth asked before answering, "I'm soaking it so that I can carve it. I'm going to make a necklace."

"That's wonderful, Ruth," Anna said, wanting to keep Ruth from her favorite topic of Dandridge Prentis almost as much as Lydia. Obviously, Lydia did not want the family to know that Dandridge Prentis had visited her, however informally. "Now, I don't want you to say another word until you have completely finished your meal. You see that the rest of us are nearly finished and you have but barely begun. It is not polite to keep the rest of us at table while you dawdle. Eat now."

Ruth obeyed, eating her meal with frowning determination. She had so much to say about Mr. Prentis and so little opportunity to say it!

"Mother," Lydia said softly, "I don't feel very well. If you'll excuse me, I'll lie down for a while and rest."

"Certainly," Anna said quickly, eager for Lydia to leave while Ruth still had a mouthful of food.

Climbing the stairs to her room, Lydia felt as weary as a woman thrice her age. The blood pounded in her temples and in the pit of her stomach. Her heart was racing. Her muscles were as weak as damp straw. She wanted nothing so much as to fall into her bed and never rise from it again.

And Dan was responsible for all of it.

In the three years that they had known Mistress Whaley, not once had they mixed with her socially, and for good reason. They were not in the same social sphere at all. But Patsy Whaley's nephew, her closest living relative, was a ruthless pirate; perhaps their social spheres were closer than she had thought.

Lydia laughed weakly and fell to her bed, throwing her arm over her eyes to block the June light. The darkness felt soothing and restful, easing the vise on her skull.

Why had he come to Williamsburg? Because his aunt was here, the rational part of her mind answered.

He has not come before. Why now?

Because . . . she answered herself . . . because . . . he was a pirate and answered to his own whims and nothing else.

Yes, he was a pirate. She knew that. Better than anyone, she knew that.

He was a pirate and she was a . . . No! She was not what he had almost named her, what he had always thought her. He should know that, now that he knew who she was and what she came from. She was no whore!

But he was Dandridge Prentis. Did that make him not a pirate?

No, he was a pirate. He had attacked her ship, killing, brutalizing, raping . . . but he had not raped her. He had not used force against her. She had gone willingly, warmly, frequently.

And she still went to him, in her dreams.

Lydia rolled onto her side, her knees pulled up to press against the knot in her stomach. Could it be true? Was she a wanton? A whore? Her doubts tormented her with as much vengeance as her memories of Dan. She remembered his easy laughter and she smiled. Sometimes she awoke in the night, pressing her hands to the soft seat of her passions, aching for his hardness against her softness. Aching for him in the deep well of her womanhood.

Was she a whore? Who better than Dan to know: a pirate with experience at whoring.

A pirate and a whore . . .

Her head pounding, Lydia pressed her hands to her skull and forced sleep to take her. Sleep and nothing, or no one, else.

Chapter Eighteen

It was amazing how much better she felt after a good, long nap. Gone was the headache, gone thoughts of Dan, gone the pounding and rolling in her stomach: she obviously just needed sleep. Obviously. She did feel a little woolen behind the eyes and decided that a long walk in the gentle early evening light would be just the thing to get her blood flowing again. A long walk just for the sake of moving. It sounded like a wonderful idea.

Lydia left with her parents' goodwill; they were happy to see her take the initiative and leave their home for a reason that had nothing to do with duty. In the three months that she had been home, Lydia had left her yard to go to church and to run an errand for her mother or father: otherwise, she had not left.

She enjoyed the verdant width of Palace Green, which fronted their dwelling, before reaching Duke of Gloucester Street. There, though it was late in the day, she saw many people she knew. She knew all of them, in fact, to one degree or another. Though a small establishment, Williamsburg swelled in numbers for the four times each year that the general court met. June was just such a time for meeting, but she had been here for so many sessions that all the additional faces now in town were familiar to her, too. It was a lovely place, quiet and domestic in a way that London had never been. She had been eager to emigrate, eager to come to a new place in the world. Even after her recent tribulation, she was glad that they had come, glad that Williamsburg was home.

Her cheerfulness and her true pleasure at seeing each and every familiar face radiated from her and was clear in each melodic greeting and graceful wave. No matter what had befallen her, she was content with her home and with all who dwelled there with her. She was greeted warmly by all she met and could not see a person without being stopped and questioned and entreated and cajoled to "Come for tea next week. How is your mother? Are you on an errand for your father? My eyes have stopped running, be sure to tell Mr. McIntyre that his tonic worked. You're looking well, Lydia. Bring Hannah and Ruth to visit with my Anne, she's pining for them."

Finally, realizing that she was doing more visiting than walking, when walking had been her earnest desire, Lydia turned aside from the main thoroughfares and took a road not regularly traveled. It was a narrow road that led to a plantation some six miles distant and there was not much else in between. The planter maintained it for his own convenience and, except for a small farmer or two, it was not much used. It was perfect for her plans. She would be able to walk unstopped, unobserved, and unmolested.

Dan, having followed her since she first left her house, watched her take the little-used road and smiled. It was not a cheerful smile, not the sort that she had passed out like so many glass beads to everyone on the street.

He was not angry with her, not as he had been. That anger had passed by dint of will alone, but he had not spent three months looking for Lydia to leave her alone now. Nay. Especially when he saw this side of her, this sweet and warm girl with the ready smile and tender demeanor. It was a manner she had never shared with him; nay, with him she had been just slightly remote and guarded in her responses, even when at her warmest and most playful. He had thought her guard and her reserve to be the studied allure of a practiced courtesan. He'd discovered last night how wrong he had been in that conclusion. It galled him now to realize that she had been guarded with him because her guard had been up, nothing more complicated than that! Never had he seen this side of her; never would he have thought it possible that the woman who calmly stripped herself naked and lay with such cool self-possession on the damp sheets of his bed could greet a milliner with more warmth than she had ever shown him.

But she was leaving the town behind, walking into the uninhabited farmland that surrounded Williamsburg. That much hadn't changed in four years. He knew where she was headed, where this road led, and he smiled in anticipatory delight, following her.

Alone on the road, Lydia increased the length of her stride, liking the way her muscles moved and stretched beyond their normal range. It was good to be out of the house with no demand upon her time. The sun was low but off to her left and so did not blind her. In the distance, she heard birdsong and smiled to herself, focusing on that sound and on the feeling of the sun on her cheek and the feel of the dirt beneath her shoes. She focused on these innocent and earthly sensations to shut out the memory of Dan.

She blushed now to think of the things she had admitted to Miriam; sweet and loving sister that she was, what must she think of such confession? She would apologize and explain when she returned. She felt so much better now, more herself; the need for sleep could drive a person into quite erratic behavior. Miriam would understand. Lydia felt blessed in her sisters. Ruth and Hannah, almost always conjured in the same thought, were as sweet as Miriam, though more wildly so. She saw them again running through the garden and hanging on to her like a maypole ribbon. It was not a great leap from thinking of them at that moment to thinking of Dan.

He had watched her with a fire burning in his eyes, a look she both remembered and understood; she had seen the same look in her own eyes once in a looking glass, remembering him in that instant, living a moment in time with him again. She had turned away at what she had seen there, that strange emotion in eyes once so familiar. She had not looked away when Dan had stood and stared at her today.

Like a compass, her thoughts swung to Dan.

Just as a compass would ever point north no matter which way it was turned, she had no control.

She did not want to hear the voice that named her liar for such an unchristian thought and so turned away from it. No control? A person's life was based on choice and the accompanying result. She was no mindless puppet to be controlled by fate. But it was wearying to try so diligently not to think of him. She was prodigiously tired of it.

Perhaps thinking of him was not so very bad; she had been engulfed by thoughts of him for three months and nothing horrible had come of it. Thinking wasn't actually *doing* anything . . . but she thought there was a verse in Scripture which read, "As a man thinks, so is he."

Unfortunately, there was nothing difficult to understand about that.

Was it true? Maybe she was a wanton. A whore. Her thoughts were consumed by lustful acts and torrid memories involving a man of no honor and no morality. Did her thoughts reveal the truth about her? Dan had said that she was a whore; he hadn't quite finished the thought, but his intention had been clear. Dan would know, wouldn't he? Just the way that she knew he was a pirate.

The facts were piling up against her and she wrestled with their conclusion.

So deep in thought was she that Dan knew there was little chance of her hearing his step, not that he cared. They were well out of the hub of Williamsburg, well beyond human interference. Since his interview with Spotswood, he had been left alone, though he had made a trip to the *Serpent* and seen a man standing idly there. He had understood; why watch the man, who moves, when you can watch the ship, which does not? The change in tactic suited his purpose quite well. Lydia was alone, with no sisters, no house, and no damn fence to delay the inevitable.

The birds skimmed the ground, seeking their nests before dusk overtook them. The air was warm without being hot, and the insects that plagued Williamsburg in the summer had not reached their full force. It was a quiet and peaceful evening to spend walking placidly along a country road, the sun so low on the horizon that it had grown to huge proportions and lay glowing like molten gold. A peaceful and tranquil setting in which to enact a seduction and abduction.

"Lydia," he called softly, and she turned abruptly to face him, her dark blue skirt billowing around her at the movement before twisting around her knees. The dark indigo of her bodice darkened her eyes to blue, killing all trace of the sea green that he remembered. There was none of the desire that he had always associated with her eyes; that too was gone. What he saw in its place was anxiety and . . . fear.

Lydia had been unable to drive him from her thoughts

209

and now she was discovering that she could not escape his presence. He was everywhere she turned. How could she conquer this mad and unholy passion for him if he would not give her the distance to do so? How could she escape him if he would not let her go?

He would not let her go. There was a thrill of pleasure in that thought. She suddenly knew beyond any doubt that he had not come to Williamsburg at such great personal risk to see his aunt. Dan had come for her. She had admitted to living in the Virginia Colony and here he was.

Golden eyes watched her, studied her . . . appraised her. Lydia fought the rush of desire that surged through her vitals at the sight of him and forced herself to see him truly. He had come for her because his pride had been pricked. There was no tenderness in his gaze; he was a man bent on having his selfish way. A pirate who had lost his portion and was determined to have it back again.

See him, she ordered herself, *not as you wish him to be, but as he is*. He did not need her. He only meant to have her.

"Lydia," Dan repeated, closing the distance between them.

The birds had all flown to the safety of their nests and the air around them was still, silent even of the hum and vibration of insects. The sky was streaked with a continuous and unbroken veil of cloud thinly stretched to span from horizon to horizon where it seemed to meet the sandy soil. Not far from them, a young and orderly orchard broke the horizontal lines of the scene with vigorous vertical energy. Dan and Lydia stood facing each other on the sandy road, the only two of God's highest creation to be seen in any direction.

Lydia felt an uneasy sense of destiny about their meeting before pushing the sensation away as dangerous nonsense. There was more of lust and anger in this meeting than destiny. In fact, as Dan advanced upon her, she had a renewed and heightened sense of how dangerous he truly was. She had not remembered him this way.

"You have walked far from home," he said. "I would say that I did not know you for a woman of so athletic a nature, but that would be a lie."

Lydia's eyes widened and she clutched the folds of her skirt. No, she had not remembered him this way. "You came to Williamsburg for me, didn't you?" she charged more than she asked. "But how did you know? How did you find me?"

"The land is wide, but the ocean wider," he mocked. "If I could find you in the midst of all the blue Atlantic, did you truly believe I would not find you in this scattering of colonies?"

The sense of destiny swept through her again at his words, and it was with greater effort that she fought its implications: was Dan to be in her future even as he had been in her past? Was there something of God in this pursuit of her and in his endless victories?

She could not answer. She could not even step away from this assault both verbal and imminently physical. He was so close to her now that she could see the blood pulsing beneath his scar and the fringe of his black lashes. She was afraid. She was afraid because he frightened her with his ferocity and because he attracted her in spite of it.

"I never thought that you would want to find me." She did not admit that she had hoped he would more than once. Perhaps there was more than pride in his motives, for who would go to such lengths for pride's sake? Perhaps, if there was a divine destiny at work, perhaps there was the smallest breath of love in the storm they had shared.

"You cannot be surprised that I have come for you." He smiled gently. Lydia now saw for herself what his crew understood: there was nothing of goodwill or humor in Dan's smile. "I've killed for you, Lydia. Pierre was killed because he wanted to take you, my rightful portion, from me. How much less will I allow you to walk away from me?"

They were hardly words of love, and she chided herself again for seeing something in him that had no basis in reality. Where was the logic she prided herself on? Ah, pride, how powerful and insidious a vice; Dan could have been the father of pride, so determined was he to protect his own.

Was it true? Had a man been killed because of her? And was that not what she had striven for from the moment she found herself among them? No, she had not purposely plotted a man's death, but she had wanted to tie the captain to her so firmly that he would not let her go to his men, at any cost. And that was what had happened. And death had been the result. She was no Lady Macbeth to scrub hands stained by symbolic blood, but she scraped her palms against her skirt just the same.

The woman who faced him was not the woman who had met his lust with equal passion. Lydia was not as he remembered her, and not as he wanted her to be. She was fearful of him, that much was obvious; perhaps it was her fear that was killing the passion he knew she felt for him. She had been a virgin, aye, but she was a virgin no more. The damage had been done because she had not confessed who and what she was. Just as she would now not confess that she was his and that her passion was all for him. There was no soft and melting passion in her eyes, and that passion was what he had come so far to find. Never mind that he could have found such well-paid passion in any half dozen ports, it was Lydia's face he wanted to caress and Lydia's mouth he wanted to taste and Lydia's laughter he wanted to fill his hours. She dared to deny him now, when he had combed the continent for her?

He was angry with her for killing the image he had of her, an image he knew firsthand to be true, and as his anger crested, Dan determined to transform her from this frigid girl into the sensual woman she had been. Into the wanton he wanted her to be.

Dan's desire outpaced his anger, and now Lydia was truly afraid.

He had reached her. Reaching out his hand, Dan traced the arc of her cheek to the corner of her mouth with a gentle fingertip. Lydia stood rooted to the spot.

"Did you believe that I would not come for you?" he breathed, his amber eyes serious. "Did you believe that the ocean itself could weaken the bond we forged together? Oh, Lydia," he sighed, lifting her unresisting chin with his fingertips, "where is the heat that forged that bond? Where is your fire?"

Now she could speak, now, because this was the Dan she feared the most. Not the pirate who killed without remorse, but the man who could kindle in her a passion raging unrestrained. This was the Dan whom she had fled.

"I have no fire," she denied, jerking her head away from his touch.

Cupping her face in his hands, holding her still to endure his touch, Dan forced her to look into his eyes.

"No fire? No one knows that for a lie as well as I do," he mocked tenderly, moving his hands into her hair and mapping the contours of her skull. "Your fire for me burns still, but has been banked by distance and time." He leaned down to her and kissed her softly on the mouth, his breath warm. "What smolders can be stoked, Lydia. You will burn for me again."

No pirate ship and no rapacious crew now. No liquid eyes begging to be taken and possessed. No willing response and no easy acquiescence. No whore. But he wanted her, his wanting a fire that scorched and blistered

213

where his soul had been. He would not be alone in his torment. Lydia must share his desire, by whatever means; he had to have her. He would not burn alone.

She backed away from him, desperate to put distance between his body and hers, desperate not to press her length against his and feel his sinewy arms hold her to him. She took a wobbly step backward and he released her.

There was nowhere to run.

"I did not burn," she argued, lying.

Dan smiled and slipped an arm around her slender waist, pulling her up against his chest. Her liquid eyes revealed the depth of her deception. "You lie," he charged softly, molding her to the length of him. "I bear the marks of your burning, Lydia, in my memory. Do not swear to me that you are not equally branded; I know you better."

His thumb beneath her chin, he kissed her deeply, searchingly, and she forgot for a moment that her survival no longer depended on submitting to this man. His taste was familiar and sweet, like a long-remembered and yearned-for treat that one had thought never to taste again. She had been hungry for him. He held her as she wanted to be held, tight and firm, as if forever would pass away into dust and he still would not let her go. And for all her talk of logic and pride, she thought that in his kiss she breathed lightly of love.

A fire flicked at her loins and she squirmed against him for relief.

Dan deepened his kiss and pulled her hips against his in possessive authority.

How easily he had proved her a liar.

As always, from the moment when he had first locked eyes with her on the deck of his ship, the passion that raged between them was as palpable as a storm at sea. Tossed, bruised, they clung to each other, need feeding need as hunger for something as simple as physical touch rained down upon their souls to drench their hearts. She pulled at something, this wanton innocent with the passion of a practiced whore; she tugged at strings of conscience he had thought burned away by four long years of brutality. He felt the yank of pride and guilt tangle with the thick rope of his desire for her. She did not deserve to be so used. She had been pure. She had not plotted her course to this place. As he had not. But he had survived, as had she. Survival was all that mattered. Survival now meant having her. Guilt would not deliver Lydia into his arms. Possessing Lydia was survival, survival in any world in which he found himself.

The creak of wagon wheels called her back from passion's abyss and she pulled out of his grasp in panicked relief. He read the thought easily on her face. She believed she had been granted reprieve by the arrival of an outsider; he would enjoy disabusing her of the notion.

"You must doubt your appeal, Miss McIntyre, if you believe that a lone wagon with a single driver will stop this seduction. I'm the man who took you off a ship full of witnesses, remember? How think you this farmer will fare if he steps between you and me?"

It was a false threat. The man who could have made good on it was dead, buried the day he took on an honest crew, leaving his pirate identity behind. But Lydia did not know that.

Lydia knew that he held her hand in both of his because she could see it. She could see that he caressed her palm and the delicate inside of her wrist, but she could feel none of it. Her skin was as cold as marble and her blood icy. What was he not capable of? How had she pretended to see love in such a man?

"I will have you," he declared, his eyes flaring gold. "Nothing and no one will keep you from me. Pray with all your strength for those who try," he charged, his voice husky with promise.

She read the truth in his eyes. She heard the squeaking wood of the wagon more distinctly now and also felt the faint vibration of the plodding horse beneath her feet. Lydia took Dan's threat seriously, but his words had an unintended effect. She thought of her parents and of what they would have to face in terms of scandal if word was brought to them that their eldest daughter, so recently home from abroad, was found to have been embracing a man in the middle of a public road at dusk. She wouldn't do that to them. Her thoughts were not of Dan now and they were not of her; they were of her parents and their good name. She would not be the cause of its loss.

Turning away from the sound of the approaching wagon and its driver, Lydia faced Dan. The sun had set, but the day was still bright in the way of summer nights. Full dark came slowly. All the pain of her position was in her aqua eyes as she faced him and whispered one word, "Please."

Please. She had never asked him for anything. It was little she asked of him now. He had taken her innocence with rough pirate lust and she had not cried foul. He had threatened to shame her, to name her whore. He had blamed her for Pierre's death and she had not buckled against the false charge. The strength of her, the steel which seemed to form her core, charmed something from him other than lust. In that moment, respect was born.

The pain in her eyes pulled at something deep inside of him, something so long smothered that he had forgotten its existence, and he found himself wanting to give her what would bring her pleasure, with no thought to his own. It had been years since he had felt such an impulse. But he would not have her see such suicidal weakness in him.

Dan released her and stepped back to a respectable distance, but warned, "Your release is but temporary, Lydia, do not be misled on that. You are mine."

Lydia hardly listened, her whole attention on the imminent arrival of the farmer in his wagon. Dan must disappear; she must not be found with him.

"Never run from me again," he commanded, holding her chin in his hands, golden eyes slicing into blue, repeating his message with their glistening intensity. He could not lose her again. Her rejection had cut him with as much lethal skill as a sword; he bled still from her running. "As you were on the *Serpent,* that is how I want you. That is how it will be between us again."

The wagon was almost upon them, a scant hundred yards off. Dan had to leave her, now, or he would be seen and her parents' respectability lost. "Yes, I understand," she murmured absently and was immediately relieved when he let her go and moved off to the orchard. It was a young orchard, but not sparse. In the fading light, he would not be seen, God willing.

Lydia waited in the road with her hands clasped in front of her and then wondered if it would seem more natural if she were found walking in the direction of the town. She took a few steps in that direction and then considered that it would seem more odd to be walking when a ride was clearly on the approach. She stopped again and waited.

The driver, a farmer by the name of Jackson, pulled up just behind her position on the road so as not to cake her with dust. With a demure "thank you" Lydia climbed up to sit beside him. The horse plodded on at a word from its master, and Lydia sat as straight as her spine would allow on the wooden seat. She did not look in the direction of the orchard.

"Out late, Miss McIntyre," he commented amiably.

"I didn't intend to stray so far, Mr. Jackson. The night overtook me," she offered in explanation.

"Fine night for walking," he said.

"Yes," she agreed, hoping for a normal tone, "the weather is delightful."

"The man you were talking with decided to continue on, I take it?"

Lydia froze and then struggled mightily not to appear nervous. Of course, it had been too much to hope that he hadn't seen Dan; with miles of flat land in every direction, a squirrel would scarce pass unnoticed.

"Yes," she said casually, "he is just off ship and is walking to shed his sea legs."

"Know him?" Jackson asked curiously.

"He's a stranger to Williamsburg," she answered a trifle stiffly. "I don't know him."

Jackson looked at Lydia's profile and then shrugged slightly. Stranger or no, the man looked like Dandridge Prentis. What would Prentis be doing more than a mile from town on a farm road?

Chapter Nineteen

"Where have you been and what have you done to be covered in dust and your fine breeches ripped?" Patsy shrilly questioned Dandridge when he returned. "Your clothing is ruined! When a gentleman plans to walk in uncivilized byways, he should wear the appropriate clothing, Dandridge. The correct attire must be chosen for each occasion, and you have known that since wearing leading strings!" Her hands on her slender waist, she pronounced in solemn finale, "Consorting with pirates has completely eroded your fine upbringing."

Dandridge listened to his aunt politely, as he had been taught to do from birth, controlling his wry laughter with effort. If she only knew.

But was there truth in her charge? Had pirating changed him? He had never thought so, but he also had never given the matter any thought. Surviving had taken all of his time and attention. Now was not the moment to consider the lightly given accusation because Aunt Patsy was demanding his full attention. He was not at all disappointed at the interruption and diversion of his thoughts, which were threatening to become entirely too somber.

"Really, Dandridge, what were you thinking?"

"I thought of walking, Aunt, not of my wardrobe."

"The streets of Williamsburg are not as rough as all that, to so ruin a gentleman's breeches."

"Ah, but I have not been walking in town; I walked a country road, little more than a path really, to enjoy the solitude. Williamsburg is rather more crowded than the deck of my ship, you know," he prodded, sure of the result.

Patsy's eyes flared with alarm. Home two days and already yearning to quit decent company and the social congress of an elegant multitude? Impossible boy.

"If you require solitude, I suggest a trip to River Run. It's quiet enough there, I assure you," she suggested, sensing he would decline. "Mr. McKenzie has not stopped inquiring about your welfare since the day you sailed four years ago; he would most assuredly be delighted to show you how well he has managed River Run in the interim. In fact, I sent off a note informing him of your return. I'm certain he will be most pleased." Dandridge *would* decline. He must. The McIntyre girls would not be coming for two days, and he must not go anywhere before that.

He had no intention of it. Cannon shot couldn't have blasted him from Williamsburg as long as Lydia was in it.

"And miss your first dinner party in months?" he asked in exaggerated alarm. "I am no such nephew to desert you in your social need." Dandridge paused to study his aunt's face. "They are coming, aren't they?"

His obvious interest appeased her as nothing else could. He wanted to meet them, that was clear.

"I am pleased to say," she said smugly, "that they are.

We dine on Wednesday. I was just going over the menu when you returned; have you a preference?"

"As long as it is not salt beef and hardtack, I will be more than content," he said, smiling in answer.

Patsy nodded her understanding, silently wondering what his preference would be in regards to the girls. They were both lovely, though different. Lydia was more exotic in her looks, and that might appeal to Dandridge's daring nature, but she was a very serious girl and old for a maiden. Miriam was sweeter in both temperament and appearance, and younger in the bargain. Still, she would not choose for him, as long as he chose one of them.

"Mr. and Mistress McIntyre are charming people, of a godly bent, and their conversation is most refined," Patsy supplied, not wanting Dandridge to face the evening without a frame of reference.

"And the girls?" he prompted after a few moments.

"Lovely." She smiled, glad of his interest. "Gracious adornments to any social intercourse. Lydia is the elder, you understand, and of a responsible and serious nature, as is often the case in an older daughter. Miriam is a delight, affable and calm-spirited."

"You prefer the younger," he stated, amused.

"I have no preference," she sniffed. "We are speaking of dinner companions, after all."

Dandridge raised his black brows to an exaggerated degree. "I certainly hope so."

Impossible boy. "I just thought that you might be interested in our dinner guests; there is no reason to become so agitated."

"Agitated? Are these girls likely to agitate me, Aunt Patsy?" he asked playfully.

"Don't be ridiculous," she rejoined. "This is a simple dinner. Do not make more of it than that."

"I can assure you that I will not," he answered seriously, teasing her. "A simple dinner then, with the apothecary and his wife and daughters elder. I suppose that I need not wear a coat to such a homey and insignificant dinner as you are planning. Is it to be in the artless style of a picnic supper?"

"Dandridge! If I have to come up and dress you myself, you will come to this dinner properly attired!" Patsy shrilled. "In fact, you should march yourself to your wardrobe right now and mend your wayward appearance—"

Patsy was interrupted by a knock at the door, to their mutual disappointment. Patsy had not finished in her harangue on personal deportment, and Dandridge had a devilish desire to tell his aunt that far more than his appearance had gone wayward.

The arrival of Benjamin Charlton put an end to their mutual fun. Patsy, though surprised, was glad to see this schoolmate of her nephew's. Any tie or connection to Dandridge's past was to be strengthened at every opportunity, and Ben was just such a tie. Four years was quite long enough to have given to Mother England in dangerous, sacrificial service. Patriotism, after all, must have limits.

Dandridge was not at all glad to see Charlton. His feelings ran strongly against this distant acquaintance who had such close fellowship with the governor.

Unknowingly, Ben had come for reasons Patsy would approve of heartily: he had come to remind Dandridge of his identity. He did not believe, did not want to believe, that Dandridge Prentis had gone lawless, but he was not so sentimental that he could not see how much Prentis had changed. There was a tough exterior to him that lay over him like armor, dulling the good humor that had always marked the man. He looked and acted like a man on the edge of raw-toothed survival. Of course, Prentis's story to them would account for that, but his explanation of his untrusting behavior with both Spotswood and himself, old friends, did not have the ring of truth. It seemed more likely that he would have dropped his armor with relief at being among friends again, and Prentis acted not at all like a man among friends. That led Charlton to the conclusion that perhaps he was not among friends after all. A most distressing conclusion.

"I hope I am not interrupting, madam," he began as Patsy led him into the sitting room.

"No, not at all, Mr. Charlton," she assured him. This was a perfect opportunity for the two men to reminisce, tying Dandridge to shore. "Though I had just been encouraging my nephew to change his attire," she said by way of both explanation and apology.

Ben sat in a gracefully worked Windsor chair and smiled at Dandridge. "Been out walking, Prentis? Not to the millers?" he asked, looking at the dust and tears on his breeches.

"No, I walked briefly on Wheeler's Road."

"Not all the way to Wheeler's Folly?"

"Hardly, sir," Dan answered coldly and succinctly.

Ben rubbed his hands against the fabric of his breeches. They were damp with the perspiration of social graces ignored. "Just a stretch, then, to lose your sea legs?"

"If you will," Dan responded.

Patsy was completely mortified. If she needed any more proof that going off to sea had ruined her beloved boy, this was it.

"Mr. Charlton," she interjected to the relief of all parties, "are you enjoying your position in colonial government? My husband, God rest him, found it satisfying."

"And his good name is still honored by those who knew him, ma'am," Ben responded politely. "Yes, I do enjoy being of service to the community."

Patsy tensed. She did not want to hear another young

223

man declare his determination to serve his country, and she most assuredly did not want Dandridge to hear it. "You feel that you are shaping the destiny of Virginia Colony, creating stability for all who live here," she rephrased, adding her own emphasis and praying quickly that he would not interfere.

"Yes, that is my desire," he affirmed.

"And you communicate with Governor Spotswood regularly? He is a most able administrator, is he not, sir?"

"Mistress Whaley, Alexander Spotswood was well chosen for his position; he is accomplishing much in this colony."

"He has most able help," she replied, gazing at both Charlton and her silent nephew.

"Yes, ma'am." Ben smiled. "Dandridge, much more than I, has given his energy and his time to ensure the safety of all Englishmen in his scourging of the pirate trade. My part is small and of no personal danger."

"You know," she mused excitedly, "I have been saying much the same to him in our private conversations. He has been engaged in a dangerous occupation, an honorable occupation, in self-sacrificing service to his country; there are less calamitous ways to serve, wouldn't you agree, Mr. Charlton?"

"Obviously, I would." He smiled, looking over at Dandridge.

Dandridge, the unhappy object of their conversation, said nothing. His participation was not needed, and he felt sure that if he spoke his mind, it would not be appreciated.

Into the uncomfortable pause, Patsy spoke of what was next on her mind: the McIntyre dinner. Surely Dandridge was interested in that?

"This is quite the busiest social week I've had in a great many months," she began. "First with Dandridge's return after such a lengthy absence and now with your kind visit this evening."

"I hope I have not inconvenienced you," Ben repeated, "in being a burden to an already full social agenda."

"Not at all, Mr. Charlton." She smiled. "I am sincerely delighted that you came by; I was about to add that we are to be entertaining in a more formal manner"—she cast a meaningful look at Dandridge—"in two days' time. We are having the McIntyres to dine and their two eldest girls, Lydia and Miriam."

Ben's eyes lit with genuine pleasure. "Lovely girls both, you will have a delightful evening without doubt. I must confess that I have seen them both, somewhat infrequently since I am required to travel often, and have been quite intrigued. They are lovely young women. I'm a bit jealous of your good fortune, Prentis, at having two such beauties to yourself for an evening. As a bachelor, who has no relations in town, it is almost impossible for me to entertain as I would like . . ."

His remarks, intended with all goodwill, were met with instant and near lethal animosity. Ben could not fathom it at all.

Patsy was violently alarmed. This interloper would not be allowed to compete with her dear nephew, though it was without doubt that Dandridge would win any such competition handily. Dandridge was to be given an unimpeded field from which to make his selection! Mr. Charlton could find his own wife!

Dan did not like at all Ben's warm enthusiasm over the beauty of the McIntyre girls. Not at all. Lydia had lived here for three years, Ben for all his life; just what sort of connection was between them? What was this man's history with his wild wanton? Dan sat forward in his seat, his amber eyes glowing with feral intensity. He hadn't felt such pulsing aggression since Pierre had tried to steal the *Serpent*. And Lydia.

Patsy, wanting Ben out of her house before he could manipulate an invitation out of her in the name of friendship, rose from her upholstered seat. "If you will excuse my bad manners, Mr. Charlton, I must retire. I have a sick headache that is threatening to topple me. It is late," she added pointedly.

It was not yet eight o'clock.

Ben rose and excused himself. "You are a most kind hostess to welcome me so warmly when I was so unexpected a guest. Good night, ma'am."

"Good night," she said firmly and walked to the stairs, leaving Dandridge the duty of seeing their guest, no matter how unwelcome, to the door.

"Before I go," Ben said to Dandridge, "I thought we could meet for a midday meal at Marot's Ordinary tomorrow. Say, one o'clock?"

"Certainly," Dan answered. He would meet with Ben, if only to keep an eye on him.

"Good. Good night, then," Ben said as he walked through the portal.

Dan did not reply other than with the firm closing of the door upon his old acquaintance.

"What brass!" Patsy exclaimed from her position on the stairway. "I do believe he wanted an invitation to our dinner!"

"I agree with you. Quite intolerable," Dandridge responded. "We were never close."

Raising her skirts primly to ascend the stairs, Patsy sniffed, "I can certainly see why."

Her mind was not on the game. Her chessmen were scattered over the board. She had no defense except movement, pointless movement. It was a situation that bore too many similarities to her relationship with Dan. She couldn't stop thinking of him, remembering his advance upon her in the road. He had touched her again, touched her as she remembered. Her memory had not played her false. All she had wanted in the world at that moment was to be touched by him, consumed by his passion, devoured in his mouth. What would have happened if the wagon had not come? She shivered violently in physical response. Smiling apologetically at Miriam, Lydia conceded the game.

Anna, standing behind Miriam and watching Lydia, asked, "You do not seem yourself, Lydia. I wonder, are you well? I note that you shiver."

"A sudden chill," she answered quickly. "I have no other explanation for it."

"A chill, a pounding head earlier today, and a long nap," Anna recounted. "Together, they indicate something is amiss. Or am I reading too much into it?"

Lydia's mind whirled. How well her mother read her. How easily she could turn this to her aid. She could not go to the Whaley house to dine if she was ill in bed. What a liar she had become.

"No," she answered quickly, "I think you have seen the truth while I have not. I do not feel well. In fact, I feel quite horrid." Rising to her feet, she placed cold hands against her flushed cheeks. "I'll go to bed, don't you agree? Sleep and solitude are the best first step, aren't they, Mother?"

Anna saw the desperation in her daughter's eyes, the yearning to escape, and she commiserated with her. "Yes, Lydia. You hurry up and bundle in. I'll bring you a pot of tea shortly."

"Yes, I'll just go up . . ." and she hurried from the room.

Once in her attic solitude, Lydia disrobed with an abstracted air. Her thoughts were dominated by Dan; how he had looked when he faced her in the road, how he had sworn that he was bound to find her and that nothing was strong enough or large enough to separate them, how he had kissed her and held her in his roughened hands. Uneasy thoughts, dim and indistinct, came with the

Claudia Dain

memory. She could never think of Dan without seeing
the blood on his hands, smelling the death in which he
was covered. He had killed, an act which God forbade.
As God forbade adultery. She was hardly sinless herself.
But what other way had there been for her to survive?
Empty, rambling, pointless thoughts; she could not
change the past. She could not change Dan. What had he
said about her not running away? Had he said that he
wanted her to want him, as she had on the *Serpent*? He
might have. She couldn't be sure, she had been so eager
for him to go, so willing to appease him to get his agreement to leave her.

Of course she wanted him to leave her. And to leave
her alone. Oh, yes, what a liar.

Her clothes fell from her body with languid grace.
She let them lie upon the floor. She did not feel well
enough to do as she had been taught and hang them
away in the wardrobe. It was a warm night. Lydia
decided that she needed a quick rinse to wipe the perspiration of the day off of her skin. Pouring water into
the bowl, she dipped the cloth in and wrung it out partially. Standing near her bed, she ran the cloth, wet and
cool, over the skin of her throat. Water ran in a thin
stream down the center of her chest and over the mound
of her belly before it splattered onto the wooden floor. It
felt good. She moved the cloth slowly over first one
breast and then the other in a caressing gesture, her
mind registering the fact that her nipples rose against
the friction of the cloth that covered her hand.

Dan had touched her this way. Dan had caused her
body to respond to his touch. Dan had somehow made
her very skin vibrate to his nearness. Dan had laughed
and made her laugh. Dan had . . .

She felt hot. The air of this room was suddenly too
still, too warm. Her skin was alive with nervous tension,
her sense of touch more acute than was normal.

Perhaps she was sick!

Heartsick. Lovesick.

No, she argued, her reason battling for supremacy against this onslaught of memory and sensation.

Lydia tossed the cloth aside, missing the bowl and not caring. Lifting her arms and sliding into her bed gown, she tumbled into bed. She would rest. All would be well with her again.

Dan followed her into bed. She felt again the power of his thrusts inside her, the hot jolt of his mouth over hers, and the roll of the sea as he rolled with her in his bed.

From below, the sound of Hannah's laughter rose to her, finding its way past her closed door. Following it was the warm rumble of her father's answer. She was home, she was safe, and the sounds of her family were sweet and cozy and wholesome.

And upstairs, away from them all, she lay in her bed, sick. Sick with lust. She was not a part of them anymore.

Lust held her in its teeth. Lust kept her in her bed, away from those who loved her. And, God help her, she was beginning to like the disease.

Chapter Twenty

"Dandridge Prentis? Are you home, then? Welcome, lad, welcome home from the seas. I'd given you up a full year ago and my wife with me, but my son, Bradford—you remember him from William and Mary?—he said that you would come back again. He told me and his mother both that if anyone could chase pirates and return to tell the wild tale of it, it was Dandridge Prentis. I'm glad to see that he was right and I was wrong, though I'll deny it if you repeat that to him! But why are you standing here, lad, in front of the apothecary shop? You're not ill, not after surviving such danger for these three or is it four years? Not ill? I'm glad to hear it, as I'm certain your aunt is as well. Have you the time now to come with me? Bradford is just down the street, having a pair of shoes made. He'll burst with pleasure to see you again. No? Perhaps another occasion. I'll send him 'round to see you and soon. He won't believe it when I tell, but then, he might. He never lost faith in you, you see. The optimism of the young and all that. Well, I'm off and welcome home, lad. It's glad we all are that you're back."

Dan watched Mr. Boyle amble off, his step light and energetic for a man so past his prime. He hadn't remembered the older man as such a talker, but then Boyle hadn't been alone in his effusive greeting. He'd been standing, walking, pacing, striding, in the vicinity of McIntyre's Apothecary for the bulk of the morning and had received an abundance of welcome from anyone and everyone who passed. He had forgotten most of them in his battle for survival, forgotten them until one by one they had approached with smiles warming their faces and their words. He had been missed. They considered him friend, as he had once, in the dim past, considered them. Family friends, school friends, hunting friends, all a part of the web of his Williamsburg life.

There had been no such web of cordiality aboard the *Serpent*. On the *Serpent* there had been only domination and survival. On the *Serpent* if a man came close, with hand outstretched, Dan had looked for the knife that was sure to be clenched there. Still they came on, these faces from his youth, greeting him as one returned from the dead. And had he? Dandridge Prentis, as they knew him, had died so that a new man, a more ruthless one, could be born in the blood of raw survival. But who was he now? The man they remembered or the man he had become? He was not certain he knew himself anymore. The only thing certain in his mind was that he could not leave Lydia or tolerate her leaving him again, even if he risked death to be near her. And in his desire to be near her, he had not left the vicinity of the apothecary shop, a fact he was having increasing difficulty in explaining.

Lydia was the reason, but he had no justification in naming her so, and so he remained silently mysterious on the subject. Mr. McIntyre, or a man he assumed was Mr. McIntyre, had peered at him from his open doorway on more than one occasion, clearly expecting him to either enter his building or go on about his business.

Dan chose, suddenly and impulsively, to enter.

Robert, who'd been watching him all morning, watched him come.

"Good morning, sir," Robert greeted civilly, glad for the opportunity to observe this young man at closer quarters.

"Good morning," Dan responded, looking not at the man behind the wooden counter, but at the bottles lining the shelves behind him. This man was Lydia's father; he would prefer not to look the man in the eye.

"Is there something I can help you with, sir?"

"I'm uncertain, sir," Dan answered, still not looking at the man who was the father to Lydia.

Robert straightened behind his counter and, placing his hands upon it, leaned forward. "Then why are you here?"

Dan looked at him at that. He was a forceful-looking man with light brown hair and deep blue eyes. Those blue eyes had a very knowledgeable gleam, which Dan could hardly fathom.

"To be honest, sir," Dan began, being anything but honest, "I don't know what I need. I am not sick; no fever, no stomach ailments, but I am not myself." Noting again the astute look in McIntyre's eyes, Dan added, "I have been walking, sir, back and forth in front of your shop, hesitating between coming in and going off."

"Yes, I noticed," Robert said.

"So, here I am. Perhaps you could prescribe a general tonic?"

"Yes, I could do that," Robert answered calmly and meditatively. "I think that what you suffer from, going only from your symptoms as you describe them and judging from the time of the year, is a general malaise that strikes often in the spring. Here, sir—" and he held up a bag wrapped with string at the top—"is a tonic of Urtica dioica." Robert smiled at Dan's look of inquiry.

"Stinging nettle is the common name for it. It works as a circulatory stimulant and a general restorative. It is taken by infusion," he explained.

"Thank you, sir," Dan said perfunctorily, handing his money over the counter. Money, coin money, was a rare thing in the colonies; Robert McIntyre was glad to take it. "I probably should have begun our conversation differently, Mr. McIntyre," Dan said with more charm than he had thus far shown, "as we will be dining together at my aunt's home tomorrow evening. I am Dandridge Prentis."

"It is a pleasure, sir," Robert responded. He did not tell Prentis that he knew who he was, that he had heard half of the conversations that Prentis had been engaged in while loitering outside his shop. That would have been rude.

"I'm glad that we met ahead of our appointment, sir, if only for the added pleasure," Dan said smoothly. "How fares your family?"

It was not an uncommon question, indeed it was almost trite, but there was nothing casual in the way that Dandridge Prentis asked after his family, and Robert knew it. He watched carefully for Prentis's reaction when he gave his response.

"My family fares well. All except my eldest; she lies abed, ill with a malady that bears striking resemblance to yours, sir. We pray that she will be recovered enough to join us when we dine with your good aunt tomorrow."

"I am most sorry to hear of her indisposition," Dan murmured, adding, "If you will excuse me, I must go. I have an appointment which cannot wait. Good day, Mr. McIntyre."

"Good day, Mr. Prentis."

Dan left promptly, but he did not go far. Never beyond sight of her house. Damn Lydia for a liar! She was not ill! She was a coward! He had touched her yesterday, kissed her and held her, and now she was hiding in her bed. Hiding from him.

He was so furious with her for thwarting his desire to see her that he wanted to strangle her with her own shimmering hair.

He was so delighted at the effect he so obviously had on her that he wanted to laugh out loud. What a little liar she was. How little she knew him to think him so easily thwarted in his plans for her.

Down the street he saw a woman he recognized, some acquaintance of his aunt's. Not wanting to be the recipient of another warm welcome, Dan walked briskly to Marot's Ordinary. He was going to be late for his appointment with Charlton. He was hardly looking forward to it, but was eager to get it behind him. He had more enjoyable plans for his day, plans for tormenting his delicious portion.

Marot's Ordinary, near the capitol building, was doing a good business. Ben Charlton was there waiting for him; if he hadn't been, Dan would have walked right back to Lydia's. Seeing him across the room, Dan walked over to his table and sat down without any preamble or preliminaries. He was eager to get this meeting behind him.

"Good afternoon, Dandridge," Ben welcomed.

It was one welcome which Dan did not feel bound to acknowledge. A man in a leather apron hurried over to take his order.

"Rum."

"The beef is good here," Ben tried again at sociability.

"Rum," Dan repeated, ignoring him.

The waiter departed hurriedly.

"How is your aunt feeling today?" Ben inquired. "Improved, I hope."

"She's fine," he grunted.

"You've been to McIntyre's, I hear. He should fix her up handily. A good man."

"You hear a lot, maybe too much," Dan almost snarled, angry with this man for his constant interference

234

in the business of his life. Charlton had been in Williamsburg for the same three years that Lydia had been. There were not many women of Lydia's caliber. In fact, there were none, and Charlton must have shared at least a portion of her attentions. Even an innocent portion was too damned much. "Keep to your own affairs," he ordered, taking the rum from the tray before the waiter could put it on the table.

Charlton, his suspicions not in the least appeased by this hostile display, lost his patience, quietly. There were many ears in an ordinary, and he did not want to put Dandridge's head in the noose unnecessarily.

"My affairs are to see to justice in this district. I think that puts you well in my path, Prentis."

"I have broken no laws here."

"No? Have you not broken an oath which you took not a hundred yards from this very spot? Have you not broken faith with all you knew and all you were? I would hear your assurances that you have not, Dandridge. I would prefer not to charge you with piracy."

Dan looked across the oaken table at the man he had known for so long, his eyes bright and hot. "I am no pirate," he said, "I did what I had to do to survive; it's that simple. And that brutal. But I wouldn't expect you to understand," he finished derisively. No, Ben wouldn't understand. He had been safe in Williamsburg. With Lydia.

"Still no answer," Ben pressed, leaning across the table and keeping his voice just above a hoarse whisper. "I ask you; have you taken innocent vessels? Have you killed for profit? Have you led pirates in acts of brutal piracy?"

"I am no pirate," Dan repeated, finishing his rum in a long swallow.

"And I am no fool," Ben charged. "I would ask you one thing more and I would like as honest an answer as you can give. You have said to me and to the governor that you had to act the pirate in order to survive; how can you act the pirate and not become one, Dandridge? Are we not judged by our acts?"

"I survived," he gritted out, his hand a solid fist on the water-stained table.

"As what?" Ben whispered back.

The question reverberated eerily to the depths of his soul. He did not want to answer; he did not even want to consider. What had he become in feeding his thirst for life? What had he done to Lydia in feeding his thirst for her? Dan stared into the eyes of his one-time schoolmate and now opponent. He would survive this newest battle. All else was secondary and could be forced down; he knew this to be so from years of experience.

"I, too, am no fool." He smiled coolly.

Ben smiled in return and answered, "This I knew."

"Then let us part with that in agreement between us," Dan said, rising. Ben rose with him. "One more thing," Dan said, "my aunt is giving a dinner for six. There is not room for seven."

Ben, taken off guard by that unexpected remark, had no response. The two men did not shake hands upon parting company.

Dan avoided Duke of Gloucester Street on his return back to Lydia's; he was heartily sick of warm-hearted welcomes. He approached her house from the rear, as he had once before, and was rewarded a second time. He was just in time to see her stepping out of the necessary house, which was hidden from the house proper by the dairy.

"Feeling better?" he called softly, a scant fifteen feet from her.

Lydia whirled to face him, turning white before flushing pink.

"Coward," he taunted with a gentle smile, enjoying

catching her at such a clear disadvantage. "I can assure you that a privy door won't stop me from seeing you, Lydia, nor all the wagging tongues in Williamsburg. When I want to see you, I will."

Despite his recent conversation with Charlton, Dan felt almost euphoric. He was safe: at least no harm would come to him at her hand. If she had wanted to tell the world of his pirate identity, she would have done so by now. Since she hadn't told anyone yet, evidenced by the fact that he was not in gaol, she never would.

For the first time in years, he felt again what it was to have the gift of trust given and received. He had trusted her and she had not betrayed that trust. She had nothing to gain by keeping his identity a secret, yet she had done it. As a gift. Gratitude, warm and alien, flooded him, to be followed by pure admiration. These were feelings for Lydia which were unclouded by passion and they shocked him with their strangeness. They frightened him with their prostrate vulnerability. Vulnerability was weakness and weakness was death, quick and bloody. These emotions had no place in him because they were not the emotions that fostered survival. His skill at survival was all he had to hold on to; Lydia had fled him, and someone had set him on a ship full of pirates. No, he could not abandon survival for the uncertain warmth of trust.

Lydia watched him, caught like a deer by a hunter that had crept too close. She wanted to run, but had the insane notion that if she kept still enough, quiet enough, he would not see her and she could escape his grasp. She should have known better by now.

What she feared more than anything—a fear that was rising like the tide and which she was as powerless to stop—was that she was losing her moral compass. Her thoughts no longer gravitated to honor and family and God. No, her thoughts were all of Dan. She didn't think of doing right, she thought of holding Dan. She didn't seek out her family, she sought solitude in which to re-create Dan's smile. The needle of focus always swung to Dan.

And he had an almost supernatural ability to come upon her at will.

Ridiculous! He was not supernatural, just persistent and determined and stubborn and . . . always there. She didn't understand why. He had been with many women. She was but one more. It would have been easy for him to let her go. He should have let her go. But he hadn't. He was here, he was not going away, and he wanted her. She did not understand it, but she was coming to accept it. Expect it. Want it. Believe in it.

With desperate resolve, Lydia turned her face away from his and marched along the seashell path to the house. She would not feed this hunger that roared through her. She would ignore him and he would go away.

"Would you run, Lydia?" he laughed lightly, following her alongside the fence. "You have run before and where has it got you? Did you think I would forget the softness of your arms around my neck as you rose to meet my thrusts? Did you forget what it was like to have me deep inside you, pulling out only to plunge in again? And have you forgotten that we dine together tomorrow?"

Yes. She had forgotten. Never, never could she sit at table with him, her mother, her father, and her sister; sit with him as if they had shared nothing more than a smile. She couldn't do it. She wouldn't do it!

Dan read her easily. She would reject him, again. She would run, denying that they had shared anything more than a chaste greeting. He had risked everything in coming here to find her and he was heartily sick of her repeated rejections. "Do not think to thwart me, Lydia.

Remember your promise yesterday to be the wanton that we both know you are, at least for me. Wear your garment of purity and chastity for the world to see if you please, but don't forget that I know who you really are. It's the wanton I want."

She was not a wanton! It was not true and she would tell him so, she would tell him from a safe distance, in the daylight hours, and in assured privacy.

"I am not as you describe me," she said haughtily, her anger rising as she carefully kept her distance from him.

It was her desire, not her anger, that he wanted to fire within her. Even as he struggled to define himself, he stumbled over his images of her. He, remembered a wanton; he had learned she was no wanton. He remembered warmth and laughter; she gave him now only wariness and lies. He could not do as he wished. It would have been simpler if she was the woman he remembered, eager and warm and hungry for him. It was for such a woman he had come searching. But no matter how he found her, he was not leaving her. She was Lydia, his portion, and that was all he needed her to be.

"No?" he answered, smiling, trying to put her at her ease. "You are not the woman who waited for me in my bed, telling me that you despaired of my return? Telling me that you longed for my weight upon you and between your legs? You are not the woman who offered herself to me while I tried to eat my stew? The woman who could not wait another moment for me to take her and mark her as mine? You are not this woman?"

His words brought the memories fresh before her eyes. She remembered it all, and she remembered it with less loathing and more longing with each day that passed. She was that woman. She was.

Lydia looked frantically at the rear windows of her home, afraid someone was watching them. More afraid

239

that someone would hear the words he said and know her for the deceiver she was.

"Are you not the woman who lay on my table, offering herself as a banquet to me? And did I not eat fully of that offering? And, Lydia, are we not to dine again on the morrow? I can hardly wait," he chuckled softly.

Chapter Twenty-one

It began normally. The sun was shining; the Duke of Gloucester Street was busy with shopkeepers, travelers, politicians, wives, and children. She walked among them, in the midst of them all, but no one spoke to her or acknowledged her in any way. She found that odd. A sudden sensation of extreme anxiety caused her to stop and look down at herself. She was naked! Her hands flew up to cover herself, a hopeless and futile task, and she ran to hide behind a barrel next to an open doorway. Where was she? Was there a shop where she could beg clothes? Did anyone she knew live near so that she could run to them for shelter and concealment? No one seemed to be noticing her; they did not see her in her nakedness, but that would soon change. It could not last.

Someone did see her. Dan. He walked toward her unerringly and unsympathetically. Raising her shivering form, he kissed her on the mouth, his hands running the length of her curves, molding her to him. And people began to watch, to see her and to know that she was without clothing, naked amongst the properly covered. For some strange reason, though their awareness of her was extremely embarrassing, she did not push Dan away. No, impossibly, she was holding him to her, caressing him in return. The crowd multiplied around them.

And then they were gone.

She and Dan were on the *Serpent*, in the place she knew best, his cabin. His hands were light and seductive as they played over her naked breasts; she arched into his hands, moaning. The kiss she gave him, the kiss he accepted, was full of passionate longing and promise. It was a kiss from memory. He pressed her onto his bed and spread her legs with gentle hands. She could feel the calluses on his palms. With a sudden lunge, he filled her and she gasped at the quickness of it, holding him to her, wanting this domination. Her release began, the pulses starting at the center of her and moving outward, cresting, like waves when they reach shore. She could feel Dan's release and looked into his eyes. He smiled at her, his eyes glowing and tender, and she smiled in return.

Her smile froze.

She was perched on the bow of the *Serpent*, smiling woodenly in her nakedness, the waves breaking against the prow below her. She was the ship's figurehead and she would remain brazenly naked until she rotted to dust.

Lydia awoke with a start, her hands pressed between her legs against a dull throbbing. She was trembling from her head to her feet. Did not God speak to His people through their dreams? Had not God given Daniel the power to interpret dreams? She knew the interpretation of this dream: if she surrendered to this passion that was hounding her, it would kill her spirit as surely as a sword and leave her as lifeless and empty of thought and feeling as a piece of carved wood, however prettily rendered.

Dan would destroy her if she succumbed to his lure.

She had not needed a dream to tell her that.

She would not go to the Whaley dinner and that was that. She could not go. But how to demur without alerting and worrying her parents?

By noon of Wednesday, after many hours of no symptoms beyond an odd nervousness, Anna insisted that Lydia rise from her sickbed. She was edgy with Ruth and Hannah when helping them with their lessons; Hannah actually came close to crying when she was sharply rebuked for mismanaging her sums. Anna thought that working in the garden might give her daughter some ease in her mind and spirit. Lydia was adamant in refusing to leave the house. It was most unlike her. She was frantically fussing with her clothing, settling it about her repeatedly and obsessively and checking the laces every few minutes. When Sally opened the door and it chanced to bang against the wall, Lydia jumped half a foot into the air. Anna was confronted by a daughter she scarcely knew.

Lydia scarcely knew herself. She couldn't seem to breathe. She had to get out of this house, but she couldn't think of a method. She had to get out because Dan knew this was where he could find her; she would not venture into the garden, a place where she was both on display and bound by a restricting fence. Given the events of the past few days, she wondered if she'd ever go there again.

She doubted it.

Her father, heard through the door that opened onto his shop, gave her the solution, temporary but workable.

"He is to have a tincture of this twice a day, perhaps three times if the symptoms are very bad, but not more than that, do you understand?"

"Yes, I think so, sir," the boy answered uncertainly. He was an indentured servant and very young; he did not know about medicinals.

"It is only agrimony, chamomile, clove, and cinnamon," Robert assured. "You've heard of those, I'd wager. Nothing to be fearful of, but the dosage must not exceed thrice daily. This is most important."

"I don't see Mr. Wharton often, sir, I mostly work outdoors. I don't think that—"

"I think I should go and supervise the administration of Mr. Wharton's medicinal, Father," Lydia offered boldly, already tying on her bonnet.

"Would you, ma'am?" the boy pleaded, obviously relieved not to have the burden of it.

"I don't think that's necessary," Robert objected.

Lydia, puffing the bow of her hat ribbons, sidled close to her father and spoke softly, "The boy is young and nervous, the gentleman is old and ill, and the housekeeper has a reputation for being unreasonably ill-humored. I believe Mr. Wharton would be more at ease if I went. I am happy to do it," she finished. She only hoped he didn't see quite how happy she was to leave her house and hide where Dan would have no way of finding her.

"A reasonable argument, Lydia," Robert conceded. "You may go and attend Mr. Wharton."

"Thank you," she murmured and then hustled the boy before her like a wayward goose, slamming the door behind her in her haste.

Robert could only stare at the place where she'd been. Peculiar behavior for Lydia; more typical of Ruth, actually.

Hours later, he was reminded even more strongly of Ruth. Lydia wasn't home. It was inexplicable. He sought an explanation.

Miriam was sent the short distance to Mr. Wharton's home on Nicholson Street to find the reason for this delay. They were expected to dine and waited only upon the arrival of their daughter to depart for Widow Whaley's.

It took repeated knocking before the green-painted door of Mr. Wharton's home was opened. If Miriam hadn't known that Lydia was within, she would have given the house up for empty long ago.

"Yes and what is it?"

Miriam backed up a small step at receiving such a greeting and in such a shrill tone, but she returned with, "Good day to you."

"Good day? Little chance of it; the day is near done and it has been a day of sweaty work and nothing else. You're the second one who has disturbed me with your knocking today and I'll hardly thank you for it. Now, what will you?"

"I have come to inquire after my sister, Miss McIntyre."

"And she was the first to disturb me, so I should not be surprised that the same clan is set to work its mischief upon me. The reason you're here, you've said, is to fetch her, but can you answer why she is here? Mr. Wharton has no need of a nurse, not while I am breathing and sweating out my days in ceaseless labor. One and now two have come; will your mother be sending any more of her brood for me to take charge of in the name of charity, I ask you?"

"I have come alone," Miriam answered with soft dignity, "and I have come to speak with my sister. My sister only," she added for clarification.

"And so I'm to hobble up the most crooked stairs a carpenter ever banged together and fetch her for you? Is that how you have determined I am to be used?"

"If you will allow, I would be happy to find her myself—"

"And let you trail the dust of the road all over my fine and newly scrubbed floors? Fine pride I would take in my work to allow you to ruin hours of hard effort at keeping this drafty place clean. Why, there are so many cracks in

245

the walls and gaps around the windows that the dust blows as freely as it would upon the open road. *No,*" she charged shrilly, "you stay on the step and make no move to enter. I'll fetch your sister. And I suspect it's what you wanted all along."

Miriam let out a shaky breath when the door was closed firmly in her face. She turned to face the street and cleansed her mind by watching the clouds race peacefully across the blue of the sky. In the distance, she could hear geese honking and the answering quack of a determined duck. A horse and rider walked slowly past her, the soft sound of the hooves a pleasant sedative. There was so much of beauty and peace in the world; although she didn't guess much of it dwelt in the house behind her.

She whirled around at the sound of the door opening. Miriam was immensely relieved and gladdened to find herself facing Lydia.

"I'm glad to see you," Miriam said with complete sincerity. "How is Mr. Wharton? Improving? We thought you would be home before now."

"I would have been, but the old dear is so very in need of care; I couldn't leave him and still be in possession of my good conscience," Lydia answered, forcing herself to lie with the glibness of a practitioner, which she was fast becoming.

Miriam's brows drew together in lines of consternation. "I was under the impression that he suffered from a condition of the bowel. In what manner are you helping him? Has he refused his medication?"

"No, nothing like that," Lydia answered quickly, her eyes scanning the street as she stood in the doorway, using the door as a partial shield. "He is very unstable on his feet, very feeble, and needs . . . well, the necessary house is not near."

"He is not walking that far!" Miriam cried. Why wouldn't he be using a more portable solution?

"Well, no," Lydia admitted, "but it is difficult for him to see to his own needs, and his housekeeper is very busy with her normal duties . . ." Lydia straightened her spine and firmly declared, "It is my Christian duty, Miriam."

"Of course," Miriam quietly agreed. "Then you will not be joining us at Mistress Whaley's?"

"I don't see how I can," Lydia answered truthfully, deceiving her sister as to her meaning.

"Good-bye then, for now, and I'll tell Father of your efforts here. Do you know when you will feel free to return home?"

Relaxing, Lydia answered, "I'll be home by the time you return from your dinner. Have no care for me."

"Very well," Miriam said.

Lydia had closed the door behind her before Miriam had stepped off the stoop.

Home again, Miriam relayed her conversation with Lydia. The news that she would not be joining them for their dinner at Widow Whaley's was met with sincere disappointment. Anna dashed off a quick note to inform their hostess of the unavoidable change in number; they delayed their departure until she would have had the time to make the necessary adjustments. Anna silently speculated that it might have been providential that Lydia was not to be thrown in such close quarters with Dandridge Prentis. Whatever the reason, she did not do well with the man. Anna quietly shared her thoughts with Robert.

Robert listened to his wife in silence, deep in thought. He agreed with her observations but found himself differing in his conclusion. He had ardently hoped to watch Lydia and Dandridge interact, knowing their emotionally charged proximity would tell him much. Nevertheless, tonight he would be watching Dandridge Prentis very closely and very carefully.

Chapter Twenty-two

Patsy read the note with disappointment. Signaling a servant, she motioned for one of the place settings to be removed and then shifted the plates to fill in the gap. Lydia McIntyre would not be attending. It was a hard blow.

Dandridge had been at his ship for most of the day, doing what Patsy did not care to guess, but he had returned in a buoyant mood. She did not know whether to attribute his high spirits to having been on the *Serpent* or to the dinner tonight. What she hoped was plain enough, but she had years of experience with the boy's love of all things nautical to sober her. She had counted on tonight's company to keep him riveted to land; it was a bitter pill to swallow, losing one prospect of only two. Still, Miriam was the younger and she was especially comely . . .

Dandridge was descending the stairs, looking devilishly handsome in his dark way, when Patsy's guests knocked upon the door. Patsy paused to look at

Dandridge before turning to greet their guests. She had hoped to tell him of the change in their guest list, but he had dawdled upstairs for so long that it was no longer possible. Chewing her lip for a moment, she decided that a hurried and whispered explanation was her worst possible course of action. He would know when the door opened, and it was not such a calamity; he would be able to give his full attention to Miriam. Yes, there could be advantages in this sudden change of plan. She only hoped the girl could hold up her end of a conversation without help. Dandridge would have no tolerance, nor interest, for a quiet miss.

Admitted by a servant, the McIntyres entered somewhat hesitantly, until Patsy hurried over to welcome them to her home.

"Good evening, Mr. McIntyre, Mistress McIntyre," she said smiling. "It was so good of you to come."

"Thank you, Mistress Whaley, for your kind invitation," Robert answered with a bow. "May I introduce my daughter Miriam."

"Good evening, ma'am." Miriam curtseyed.

Patsy looked the young girl over quickly while her head was lowered; a fine-looking girl with delicate coloring and classical features. A fine, full bosom, too. Dandridge could hardly find anything lacking in her appearance. What on earth was he frowning about?

"This is my nephew, Dandridge Prentis," Patsy began, "of whom I am most fond. Dandridge, Mr. and Mistress McIntyre and their daughter Miriam."

"Sir,"—he bowed—"Madam." Taking Miriam's gloved hand in his, he kissed the back of her hand lightly. "Miss McIntyre," he murmured politely.

It was the closest thing to a caress that Miriam had yet experienced in her sheltered life. Mr. Prentis had her full attention and was little likely to lose it.

"Aunt, I was of the knowledge that you had extended

Claudia Dain

your prodigious hospitality to four of the McIntyre household. Is not a daughter gone missing?" he questioned politely, his voice a heavy rumble.

Of them all, only Robert heard the suppressed rage in the man's voice. Why should this man, this stranger, care if Lydia did not keep her appointment in this house?

"Very true," Patsy answered, "but as you have only just arrived home, I had little opportunity to tell you that there was an unexpected change in plan. Miss Lydia McIntyre was forced to cancel at the last possible moment, to the regret of all."

"She is ill?" Dan asked curtly.

"No, sir," answered Robert, "she is not, but she is tending one who is."

"Not another of your daughters, I hope," Dan prodded, furiously determined to know just what hole Lydia had scurried into this time.

"Happily, no," Robert responded. "An elderly gentleman with no living relations and suffering from a painful malady has need of a caring hand. Lydia offered to go and soothe him."

"Do you speak of William Wharton, Mr. McIntyre?" Patsy asked. At Robert's nod, she continued, "She is much needed in that household, for his housekeeper is a slattern and a scold. You have reared a fine daughter to be so charitable," she complimented.

Dan snorted and turned his face away from their guests. Damn her! So she wore the mantle of charity now? He would strip it from her, as well as all the others: duty, chastity, purity. . . . She donned masks like a stage player, but not with him. He would strip her bare. Damn her!

"Please," Patsy said, interrupting his silent fury, "I am being a poor hostess to keep you standing when the food is hot and ready upon the table. I can only confess my fault and say that it has been many months since I last entertained and my manners are stiff from ill-use. Come

250

in and sit and we shall continue our discussion while we dine."

The table was beautiful, of shining walnut, glowing with hand-rubbed wax and sparkling with crystal stemware. Miriam had never seen anything as elegant. The chairs were ornately carved and perfectly matched, the seats covered in pale green damask that matched the cornices on the windows. Candles flickered from wall sconces and from an enormous silver candlestick in the center of the table. Eating pork stew in such a setting would have been a delight.

They were not served pork stew, however. Chicken smothered with oysters, duckling with apple stuffing, baked striped bass with stuffed clams, fried eels, black-eyed peas, mashed carrots and parsnips, collard greens, and bourbon sweet potatoes comprised the bulk of the menu as it sat steaming upon the table. It was a feast for the eyes as well as the stomach. With studied and determined nonchalance, Miriam sat, Dandridge holding her chair for her before moving to assist his aunt. As he leaned over the back of Patsy's chair, she hissed a whispered warning, "You must have thrown every social grace you ever learned overboard every time you dropped anchor! Mind your manners and converse with our guests!"

He did not trouble himself to answer—it would have been awkward in any event—and sat himself down at the table. But he would fulfill his social obligations to please his aunt; and to keep them all ignorant of his rage and disappointment. He had no appetite for the banquet spread before him. He had no desire to engage in idle chatter with strangers. He wanted Lydia, here and now, and she had denied him. His desire was for her. His appetite was for her.

Damn her.

"Mr. Prentis," Robert opened, "I understand that you

have been engaged in service to Governor Spotswood. How is life aboard ship? Do you find it agrees with you?"

"Yes, sir, it does," Dan answered bluntly, reining in his anger.

Patsy clattered her fork against her plate and murmured a soft apology while throwing a killing look at her nephew. Incompetent boy! Had he forgotten how to speak?

"Some men are made for the sea, my father used to say," Robert continued. "It is an affection that will brook no pretense. Do you, sir, find that this is so?"

Dan looked at his aunt and wanted to laugh at the look in her eyes; if she could have spoken for him, she would have. It would cause him little effort to please her. Lydia, who doubtless thought herself very clever for avoiding him, would wait. He knew where she was. She had only delayed their meeting, not deleted it.

Turning to face Robert McIntyre, Dan answered, "Yes, sir, I do. The sea has called to me for as long as I can remember, and sailing across her has always been my firmest desire. I was not tutored to this desire, as my aunt will attest, but was born to it."

"You are fortunate in that you have found a method by which you can be of great service to your country and fulfill your heart's wish at one and the same occupation. Not many men are as privileged," Robert commended. Pausing for some moments, measuring the truth of Dandridge's words, Robert said, "My daughter Lydia is one who lacks such desire. She has recently returned from a sea voyage and found that the experience did not suit."

Dan stiffened and stared at McIntyre until Patsy broke the somewhat awkward silence, a silence which Robert found both compelling and illuminating.

"How well I remember her return," she agreed. "A most unhappy looking female. Although I am aware that she traveled to be of service to your family, I cannot help but say that she would have been better served if she had stayed safely at home."

"We would all agree with that sentiment," Anna said, "as would Lydia herself."

"For some, perhaps, it is an acquired taste," Dan said softly.

Patsy knew that this talk of loving the sea was diametrically opposed to her purpose and, gracious hostess or not, she would not tolerate it for another breath.

"I have no difficulty in believing her," she huffed, lifting a forkful of greens to her mouth. "Nasty, lonely life with poor food and worse company," she pronounced. "Let me hear no romantic nonsense about the 'call of the sea,' for it is gibberish invented by investors to lure men to the docks. A merchant's trick and nothing more."

"Yet it was no merchant who called to your nephew," Robert politely argued. "England needs men who will sail for her, protecting her interests on the sea. Mr. Prentis has, I believe, scourged pirates from our sea lanes. Do I speak the truth when I speculate that there are fewer pirates preying on innocent vessels today than there were when you began your mission?" Pausing, he added with intensity, "Or are there more?"

Dan smiled in answer and sipped of his wine. "There are always more. 'Tis what keeps me so busy," he laughed lightly.

Robert ate a few bites of duckling, measuring this man who sat with such ease at such a fine table. He was a gentleman in deportment and in bearing, but he was something else in pure ruthless strength. Power emanated from him in pulsing waves, power resolute and lethal. Robert gazed at his wife and daughter, eating peacefully, chatting with each other and Mistress Whaley in inconsequential conversation. It was clear to him that they did not perceive the man as he did, and he could but wonder at their blindness.

"You have chosen a hard and dangerous path, Mr. Prentis," he said suddenly, seriously, gauging the man's response. He was disappointed.

The ladies stopped their chat.

Dan smiled again and lifted his glass of wine, holding it to the candleflame so that it glowed deep red in his hand. "It is a way familiar to me after so many years, Mr. McIntyre. The danger has dimmed. I do not find my path hard."

"Danger perceived dimly is danger magnified, for then a man becomes careless," Robert answered. "A path well worn is not always a safe path."

Dan studied his guest, understanding the suspicion that flavored his words, but not the cause. Suspicion without proof was groundless. And Lydia would never supply the proof. Without doubt, he trusted her and did not so much as pause to question his trust.

"I could be charged with much," Dan admitted, "but carelessness would be absent from the list, sir. A man who spends his days as I do cannot afford it."

"Have you seen many pirates, Mr. Prentis?" Miriam asked, intrigued by this handsome and charming gentleman who selflessly spent his days in such dangerous pursuit for the good of his country.

Dan laughed easily and sipped his wine. He had indulged freely of his wine and little of his meal, as had been his way for the past three months. "Many upon many, Miss Prentis, and they are a gruesome lot to a man. I much prefer my present company." He smiled.

Miriam glowed with shy pleasure, as did Patsy, though her pleasure was not at all shy.

"Are they truly as bloodthirsty and unrepentant as rumored?" Miriam persisted, glad of his attention and not eager to have it pass from her.

Dan smiled again and this time sent a sidelong glance to the father of such a beautiful daughter before answering, "I hesitate to tell you . . . I should not tell you, innocent that you are, but pirates are violent creatures who kill without remorse and with very little provocation."

"They feel no shame in their acts of cruelty? No contrition?" she asked in shock.

"I have never seen a pirate show even the smallest hint of remorse, Miss Prentis. It is perhaps this quality which makes them piratical."

"But any man may be turned from his sinful acts, Mr. Prentis, by a loving and just God," Robert McIntyre stated, joining the conversation and removing his daughter from it. She understood so little, as he was coming to understand so much; still, he was not certain . . .

"Do you argue that God loves the pirate, Mr. McIntyre?" Dan challenged arrogantly. "It seems hardly likely."

Now Robert smiled in answer. "It is beyond human comprehension, I readily admit, yet a man must take God Almighty at His word. All have sinned and all fall short, both pirate and apothecary."

"Please, Mr. McIntyre," Patsy cut in, "do not compare your profession to that of the pirate's! They hardly compare! I must admit, though I would deny it to our pastor, that I find myself agreeing with Dandridge, who has had such vast experience with the pirates of our age. It is beyond me to believe that a pirate could be redeemed; they are the lowest of humanity and deserving of our most severe judgment."

Studying Dan's hard expression, the burning glow of his amber eyes, Robert said, "But human still, madam, and if human, then not beyond the power of redemption, a power that defeated death itself."

"Your argument is logical," Patsy admitted, "but I

would find it easier to accept if I could but see an example of such spectacular redemption."

Robert smiled and said nothing; it was easy to believe, having seen: to believe without seeing was the act of a man of faith. He had to admit to himself that his faith was being stretched to the utmost.

The dinner was concluded with blueberry crisp and wild blackberry pie and pound cake. Dandridge ate sparingly, no more than a mouthful of each. Patsy eyed him closely; for a boy who loved sweets as he did, he ate of them strangely.

Robert and Anna paid Mistress Whaley ardent and sincere compliments on the beauty of the table, the delicacy of the dishes, and the joy of their conversation; it had been a truly enjoyable evening and they thanked her for it. Miriam, quietly watching Dandridge, had enjoyed herself immensely. Dandridge, knowing the effect he had had on the girl, was amused at his easy conquest of her; how different she was from Lydia. But of them all, Patsy was the most pleased with how the dinner had evolved. Miriam McIntyre was clearly impressed with Dandridge, as well she should be; Dandridge had stoked the fires of his slumbering etiquette and presented himself admirably, though the talk had been too much of the sea for her liking. It was unfortunate that he could not have met Lydia, but he seemed to have taken a liking to Miriam. One or the other, it did not matter much to her, as long as Dandridge was happy. And away from the sea.

Walking home, Anna slipped her hand through her husband's arm, contented with the world in general, though sorry that Lydia had missed an enjoyable evening. Dandridge Prentis was such a well-mannered gentleman; her worries had obviously been groundless. She was relieved that Robert loved her enough not to think her a fool for her suspicions.

Robert was thinking anything but that his wife was a

fool. He had gone to Widow Whaley's home to delve into the character of her nephew, and he had not come away empty. One thing more was needed to set the picture straight in his mind, for he was not a man to act rashly. One thing more, and he spun the wheel at that moment to set it in motion.

"Mistress Whaley is a fine hostess, but lonely since her husband's passing, according to her speech. I suggest that we reciprocate her generous invitation and invite her to dine with us, Anna."

"Of course, what a fine idea," she agreed. "Perhaps next month—"

"No, Anna," he corrected softly, holding her hand close to his heart, "next month is too long for a lonely woman to wait for companionship. Let us return her courtesy as soon as we are able."

He wanted to reach out a kind and sociable hand to the widow, that was true enough, but he also wanted to see Lydia and Dandridge Prentis together; that was all the proof he would need that Prentis was the pirate who had so thoughtlessly robbed his beloved daughter of her virginity and her peace of mind. And this time, Lydia *would* be there.

Chapter Twenty-three

"It would be no trouble at all to stay with you through the night, Mr. Wharton," Lydia repeated as he escorted her down the darkened stairway, the candle he held in his shaky hand the only light in the black house.

"And I say no again, miss, and it's on your way. I don't need help. I don't want help. I sent the lad to McIntyre's for medication, not for nursing."

"But you're weak on your feet, Mr. Wharton, and should you need a strong shoulder—"

"I've two shoulders of my own, Miss McIntyre, and have been able to find my way to the privy for longer than you've been on this earth. Now, I'll hear no more. It's home with you and past time for it."

They had reached the door and he grasped the knob like a man reaching for a life rope. Before she could think of another argument in favor of her staying with him the night, she was on the walk in front of his house and the door was closed tight behind her.

Still, it had worked. She had successfully avoided dinner at Mistress Whaley's. She had avoided Dan and his leering and his insinuations and his hands. And she had helped an elderly man in need of succor, no matter his ingratitude. All in all, she was quite cheerful. Home was a short walk, the night was warm and soft, and the roads were dry. Swinging her arms in an unconscious mood of bonhomie, Lydia walked happily homeward, feeling that she had accomplished something of note for the first time in months. Three months, to be exact.

Her mood would have been instantly crushed if she had known that Dan, having waited in the shadows near Wharton's house, was following her now, closing the gap between them with each step. He, too, was smiling. But it was not a smile of genial accord. Not at all.

Dan could almost smell the reek of self-satisfaction coming off her, she was that pleased with her little scheme to elude him. Her success had been temporary, though she did not know that yet. But soon. He enjoyed trailing after her in this way, with her so unsuspecting and joyous. Joyous because she thought she had outmaneuvered him. Her plan would have succeeded if she were properly chaperoned now. But she was not. She should have been. Her parents were entirely too trusting of the general population to let her travel about so freely; if she were his responsibility, he would make damn certain . . . but she was not his responsibility. He had no responsibilities beyond his ship, fought for these past four years. He could not give that up, not after so much struggle. Neither could he give up Lydia, though she ran from him at every opportunity. If he could only be convinced that she wanted him, wanted him as constantly as he wanted her . . .

Lydia jumped a small but very energetic hop into the air when she felt a hand pressing against the curve of her waist. Turning, she felt warm lips pressed against the hair above her left ear and heard a familiar voice lowered in whisper, "You missed our appointed meeting." Curving his arm around her and pulling her up against his chest, he taunted, "I've scheduled another."

It was the hand sliding up to her breast that broke through the shock and instant longing his touch infused within.

"Can't you stop touching me?" she choked out, lurching ahead of him into the darkness.

Dan smiled as he let her put a few scant feet between them. "I've done without my portion for three full months, Lydia. Why should I not partake now?"

Lydia backed away from him, praying that the darkness would make a hiding place for her.

"I am not a 'portion,' " she whispered, glancing sideways at the darkened houses and shops lining the street. "I am a person, with a name, with feelings of my own—"

"Oh, Lydia," he breathed, his voice a warm caress in the night, "I know your feelings. I share them." He willed it to be so; she had to want him as much as he yearned for her.

No, he could not. If he could read her as he claimed, that would leave her too vulnerable. She turned from him, ready to run if she had to.

A candle flickered in the front room of the gunsmith's; he must be working late. Lydia was thankful that she was not alone in this dark world with only Dan as companion. From across the street, the thin door of a necessary slammed; another human soul occupied this shadowed avenue. Her house was but a half a block away and across the Palace Green. She would make it. Dan was being unusually passive. Perhaps, God let it be so, he feared making a scene on a public street. She walked as closely as was possible to the erratic and feeble human lights as she could, instinctively knowing that in light lay her best safety, as in darkness lay Dan's. But there was so much darkness and so little light.

Dan stepped directly in her path, blocking her, touching her with his hands on her shoulders. Stopping her. A door slammed and Lydia lurched around her pursuer, lifting her skirts and trotting to the light beckoning from the corner. She was almost to the Palace Green, the broad sweep before the governor's own residence; surely, surely she would be safe from him there.

She was not safe from him anywhere, surely she should know that by now.

He caught her from behind, his hands encasing her waist. Even that small touch fired her desire for him. It took so little to initiate the melting of her resolve. He held her against him, pressed against his chest; she could feel his breathing and found that her own breath matched his.

"Don't touch me," she commanded in whisper.

Dan smiled and whispered against her hair, "You want me to. Almost as much as I want to."

"I don't."

"You are such a liar, Lydia," he said, his hands moving down to cup her hips. He prayed to a God he had forgotten that he spoke the truth.

"And you're not?" she flared, angry that he named her what she was becoming, what he had always been. "I suppose your aunt knows how you spend your days when not in Williamsburg?"

"And does your honorable father know how hot you are in a man's bed? Have you told him that?" he snarled softly, pulling her back against the bulging length of him.

She gasped at the contact and told herself that she had to put distance between them, that distance was the only cure for the throbbing ache that twisted through her. She told herself repeatedly . . . and did not move.

His hand moved to the front of her skirts and pressed

against the heat of her, the fabric instantly wet with her aching. And she let him. Slowly, his hand slid from her shoulder to her arm to her heaving ribcage and so, to encase and caress her bosom. And she let him.

She let him.

There were no more lights to run to for sanctuary; they were all behind her. Ahead spread the leafy darkness of Palace Green and beyond that, her house. But she could not see her house from here. She could not see it.

He turned her in his arms until she faced him, the black silhouette of him blocking out even the feeble light of the stars. There was no moon. Why was there never a moon?

"No lies between us, Lydia," he breathed. "We are beyond lies and deceit. I know you . . . as you are. And I want you. I need you."

His kiss was gentle, more gentle than even her dreams of him. His lips pressed and nibbled softly against hers until she opened her mouth to his, sharing his breath. It was like coming home. He did not hold her harshly, he did not demand a response from her; he gave. He gave her his strength and his passion and the struggling flicker that she had timidly named love. It was not love, she knew it was not; mayhap tenderness or compassion, but never love. It could not be love. He was a pirate.

The response she gave him was all her own. Her tongue met his and they swirled together as wet and joyous as dolphins at play to be reunited after so long an abstinence. Her hands swept up the ridges of his muscular arms to entangle themselves in the black glory of his hair, sweeping away the unhappy restriction of his binding ribbon. Freed, his hair fell in loose waves about his shoulders. She pressed herself against him, against the hard and familiar feel of him, standing on tiptoe as she hugged him to her. One of his hands held her, pressing her rounded derriere against the lean length of him, the other rubbed rhythmically over her turgid nipple.

A sweet ache throbbed through her, throbbed from the very center of her to touch every nerve and every thought and every desire. He did know her, as she knew him; intimately, possessively, passionately. There was no room for any other; he consumed her completely. And she gave herself to him willingly, her past reluctance and guilt fading away like fog in bright sunlight. He was all she needed, and she did need him. Now.

Now.

A door slammed a few yards away and she spasmed as if coming suddenly awake.

Pulling out of his arms, Lydia jerked away, gasping for breath and the will to subjugate her passion. She was ashamed. And she was angry.

"Would you take me here, in the dirt?" she accused, her blue eyes hostile, condemning, passionate.

Dan did not even have to think.

"Would you let me?" he rejoined.

They both knew the answer. Yes.

She hated him for that, for showing her what she had become, what she was.

He was furious with her for accusing him and leaving herself blameless of all responsibility. For showing him what he had become with her: a beggar, unworthy and unwanted.

This time, when she turned from him and stalked off into the night, he let her go. The darkness swallowed her slight form quickly enough, but he let her go. He could find her at will, especially in the night. The night held no fears for him.

Would you let me?

She couldn't shut it out, the sound of his voice, accusing her, demeaning her, revealing her in a way that she hated.

Would you let me?

His face, his beautiful face, suffused with passion, passion for her, because of her, was before her eyes, whether open or shut.

Would you let me?

His hands on her body, where she wanted them to be. His mouth on hers, breathing his breath into her. The cursed fabric of their clothing keeping his skin from hers.

Would you let me?

If he had raised her skirts. . . . If she had lifted them to her waist, would he have plunged himself into her, feeding the painful ache of her longing for him with his pulsing shaft?

Would you let me?

Whores lifted their skirts and took their coin where they could. Whores did it. He had treated her like a common whore tonight! But when had he treated her as anything else? He was despicable and insulting, his behavior hideous. He was a pirate. And she . . . she was kissing him in the open street, leaning into his hands and cursing the fabric that stood between them, wanting to be naked under his hands and feeling the weight of him between her legs.

She was walking to her own destruction—no, she was running to it. The prophecy of her dream cried hoarsely in her mind. It was an irritating cry. Why would that inner voice not be still?

Was she a whore, a wanton, for wanting him?

Chapter Twenty-four

She got very little sleep in it, but she could not seem to leave it. It was here that Dan was with her more than any other place. Here, she could lie still and let her mind wander at will without having to make a pretense of worthwhile activity or conversation. Here, though she could not sleep, she could dream. And remember.

When she hadn't arisen by eight o'clock, Miriam came up to check on her. She had known someone would come eventually. Someone always did, interrupting her thoughts and forcing her to give them some small part of her attentive energy. She found these interruptions more of an intrusion with each passing day. Before, she had welcomed them as much-needed diversions. Now, she resented them with jealous intensity. She wanted to be left alone, and they would not leave her alone.

"Lydia?" Miriam opened the door quietly, slipping her head inside the small attic room.

"Mmmmm," Lydia answered, her eyes open and staring at the ceiling beams.

"Are you not feeling well?"

"Not entirely," Lydia answered dispassionately.

"Shall I fetch Mother?"

"Mmmmm . . . no."

Miriam came fully into the room and carefully sat on the edge of Lydia's rumpled bed. "I haven't had an opportunity to tell you about dinner last night. Oh, Lydia, I so wish you had been able to attend. I'm sorry," she said, interrupting herself, "I should have asked how Mr. Wharton is doing. It was so kind of you to take care of him and consider his welfare over your own." Lydia fussed agitatedly with her sheet and turned her face to the wall, away from her sister's concerned expression. "Is he suffering?"

"He assured me as I was leaving that he felt much improved," Lydia answered honestly.

"How fortunate that you were able to help him," Miriam murmured, feeling a little guilty at her own self-centeredness.

"Yes. I was glad to do what I could," Lydia said.

"Next time, I shall be the one to do the nursing and you shall be able to pursue your own interests. You are such an example to me, Lydia. I so often pray to have your strength of purpose and your selfless charity."

Lydia sat bolt upright, tugging the sheet nervously around her legs. "Do not make me your example, Miriam; I am hardly a worthy one."

Miriam smiled and reached out to take her sister's hand. "How very like you to say so, and it only works my point to a sharper edge; you are a unique woman, Lydia. Anyone can see that. I admit to being a little glad that you did not accompany us to Widow Whaley's last night for that very reason. I am certain that Mr. Prentis would have had no conversation for me if you had been present. He

would surely have seen your worth and disvalued mine in
its glow."

Lydia's dreams of Dan fled at her sister's words; here
was a reality far firmer. She understood that Miriam was
not belittling herself or speaking as she did to gain pity;
she was merely delivering a sincere, though inaccurate,
compliment. But what Lydia heard was that Miriam had
conversed with Dan and found the event so enjoyable
that she guarded it like a goose with a gosling. Alarm
rushed through her veins to race with her blood.

"You enjoyed your evening, then?" Lydia asked.

"Oh, yes, Lydia." She smiled, her blue eyes dancing
with remembered delight. "He . . . it was a lovely
evening. Mistress Whaley's home is lovely and fashionable and elegant. She is a fine hostess, though lonely
since her husband passed. We ate like the governor himself with imported wine and a wide and varied menu
from which to choose."

It was not the menu that interested her. "And Mr.
Prentis?"

Miriam sat upon Lydia's bed, hugging her knees to her
chest and grinning like an infant. "He is a most fine gentleman; courteous to his aunt, gracious to his guests, and
so courageous in his pursuit of pirates! I dared to ask him
about his exploits and he was kind enough to answer my
questions without a trace of condescension. It is really
quite horrible what he has seen, Lydia. He must be a very
brave and noble man to have given so many years in
service to his country, don't you agree?"

Lydia could hardly think to answer. She gave a weak
nod and sat wrestling with her thoughts, trying to pin
them down before they subdued her. First and obviously,
Miriam had been favorably impressed with Dandridge
Prentis and not by accident. That was bad enough, but
what was exploding within her was the knowledge that
these people all believed that Dan pursued pirates to

bring them to justice! It was suddenly very clear to her why Governor Spotswood had greeted him warmly and not arrested him on the spot. What a colossal charade he was playing! And he had the brass to call her a liar?

Her fury and indignation frothed like an angry sea in the tumult of her mind, until she remembered the scar upon his jaw and the delicate upbringing he must have received as Dandridge Prentis. He had obviously begun with good intentions, as an agent of the crown and a respected member of this community, but somehow it had all gone wrong. That wide white scar that sliced his jawline rose again in her mind. A man did not get a scar like that pursuing pirates with a lawful crew. Something had gone badly wrong. And Dan with it.

He was a pirate, and that was the flat truth.

It was a truth she would never share with anyone.

"So," Miriam was saying, her recitation having continued despite Lydia's unusual silent preoccupation, "you must be well, because we have invited Mistress Whaley and Mr. Prentis to dine with us on Friday. Mother has just received a reply and we have so much to do before tomorrow to prepare . . . Lydia! You're as white as a lamb! I'm going for Mother!"

Dan, here? Never! It could not be! It must not happen! Or else she must not be here to see it. To see him.

Lydia lay down upon her bed, dizzy, nausea rising in her throat. That was how her mother found her, and it played well to her cause.

"Lydia? Poor child," Anna crooned, stroking her daughter's forehead, feeling for fever. "You do not look well."

"I do not feel well," Lydia agreed.

"It may be that you did too much yesterday, exerting yourself beyond wisdom. I should not have allowed you to go to Mr. Wharton's last evening, especially when you felt poorly yourself so recently. Is it possible that you have contracted his ailment?"

It was an excuse, a logical one, and she jumped at it. "I believe it may be so," Lydia said weakly, licking her dry lips. "My bowels are unsettled and the idea of food is repugnant."

"That doesn't sound good," Anna said, smoothing her daughter's crumpled bedding and folding back the sheet neatly. "Miriam, will you run down to your father and ask him to come up? Perhaps he will prescribe for you what you were so kind as to administer to Mr. Wharton yesterday."

Robert, Hannah, and Ruth had watched the comings and goings up and down the stairs with interest, though for different reasons. Hannah because it was unusual, Ruth because she wanted to know what was happening up there, and Robert because he knew that he would have a part to play in this bedroom drama before the morning was gone. Miriam's urgent summons to Lydia's bedside confirmed his belief. He ascended the stair with an almost morbid desire to see his eldest child; what prompted her strange behavior? Or whom?

She was the picture of invalidism and she had been in the blush of health so recently; it was a disturbing picture, for she was in actuality not looking well. No amount of drama could have achieved her pallor and haunted eyes. Poor Lydia. What net was she struggling against?

"What ails you, Lydia?" he asked, standing beside his wife as she sat with their daughter.

"She believes that she may have contracted Mr. Wharton's disorder, Robert," Anna supplied.

Robert looked at Lydia long and searchingly before saying, "Leave us, Anna, so that I may be alone with Lydia for a moment. Please."

"Of course," she murmured, leaving. She had rarely seen Robert looking so severe.

"Do *you* believe that you have what Mr. Wharton has, Lydia?"

"I *do* have an uncomfortable sensation in the bowel and an irritable stomach, Father," she answered. "Also, at the thought of food, I feel mounting nausea."

These were Wharton's symptoms and she recited them well; she should, after listening to him complain about them for so many hours.

Robert studied Lydia, his hands behind his back in contemplation. He loved her. He loved her with all his strength, and she was lying to him. Her eyes were bright and alert; not the eyes of a woman with a stomach ailment. Her posture was all, wrong; her shoulders were tense and her abdomen relaxed. Still, she looked terrible. The result of her lie? Or of something else?

"Lydia," he said, his voice very serious, "it is not possible that you should have contracted the same ailment as Mr. Wharton. In the first place, if he were contagious, I would hardly have allowed you to go to him, no matter how great his need, which was not great at all. Secondly, and I must ask you to keep this confidence strictly, Mr. Wharton has an illness for which there is no cure. It is fatal. I am only making him more comfortable until the Lord takes him home. Even Mr. Wharton does not know of his condition; in an effort to be merciful, I did not tell him what I suspect. After all, God may decide to heal him and I did not want to interfere in His divine will for Mr. Wharton."

Lydia had been growing whiter under this revelation and now was as white as the bleached sheets at her back. To be caught in a lie! Revealed as a liar! What could be worse?

To be revealed as a whore.

She did not want him to know that about her; better a liar than a whore.

"I do not dispute what you say," she said calmly, her voice quivering in spite of it, "but I say that I do not feel well."

"You felt well enough a few days ago," he said, thinking of the arrival of Dandridge Prentis and how neatly the two events coincided.

But Lydia was thinking of the months of hidden longing, the shameful dreams of her passion for a brutal pirate, and the growing acceptance with which she viewed her desires. She answered from the heart, her voice choked with emotion, "I was not well. I have not been well since I returned from my journey. It is only that as each day passes, I lose the strength to hide my malady from your eyes."

He had never seen her so distraught, so hopeless. He could not ignore the ring of truth to her words, nor did he have any desire to. He wanted to help his daughter to heal.

"Would a change of scene be beneficial?"

A swirl of memories of her last attempt at a change of scene and all that it had wrought flooded her heart, spilling over with such ache that the tears tumbled soundlessly from her eyes. Hiding her salt-washed eyes from her father, Lydia shook her head at his suggestion.

His girl was battered and bruised, not physically but spiritually. Perhaps she had chosen the wisest route, that of solitude and prayer. God could heal her. He could only pray that she would be healed.

"Stay in bed, Lydia, and nurse your ills," he advised, stroking her hair with a large hand. "But I caution you to walk about sometime today or you will have trouble sleeping tonight after a day of such inactivity."

"Thank you, Father," she whispered, her heart breaking under the burden of her hideous secret sin and thankful that she would not have to face Dan tomorrow.

"You must pace yourself so that you are at your best and strongest when we entertain tomorrow evening."

He read the shock and disbelief in her eyes. She thought she had won a reprieve for herself, but he would not allow it. Lydia would face her demons, she would face them before they swarmed over her and pushed her under. Once she faced them, they would run. It was time, past time, that Lydia stopped running.

"I do not think . . . I had thought," she stammered, her eyes casting about the room. "I do not think that I will be well enough to entertain—"

"It is a quiet, at-home affair, Lydia, and it would be unspeakably rude for you to miss two dinners with the same family. I would not so ill-use Mistress Whaley. Or her nephew," he added as an afterthought.

"Of course," she said. What he said was true, she couldn't deny it. She also couldn't do it.

Left alone, Lydia sank down into her mattress and pulled the blanket up to her chin. The sheet beneath her was wrinkled and irritated her skin. The blanket was too warm. The pillow was too flat. Everything about the bed bothered her. Why was it that she couldn't seem to leave it?

Forcing herself with the mightiest force she had ever summoned, Lydia slid to her knees next to the bed. She would pray as she had never prayed before. God would hear her, He would deliver her miraculously from this coil of desire and deception, and she would be herself again.

But God was silent.

She had never felt more alone in her life. Even on the *Serpent* she had had more of a sense of God's presence, but here, in her own room, in a home she loved completely, within the loving embrace of her mother and father and sisters, she felt as emotionally isolated as a stranger.

And that was the problem; she was a stranger. Did God know her anymore? Did her family? Did she even know herself?

She had changed, irreversibly, and was continuing to change. She had changed, and no one seemed to see it.

Except Dan.

Chapter Twenty-five

A breeze from the east played with the ropes that criss-crossed the *Serpent* as she lay at anchor. The wind seemed to want to tease her from her mooring and entice her out to play on the great wide sea. She had been at anchor far too long, as had her crew. The mood aboard ship was far from pleasant. That was fine with Dan as his own foul mood was more than a match for his crew's. They hadn't picked up any cargo, they hadn't taken any pirate ships: they hadn't made any profit.

"Let's up 'n'away, Cap'n," John grumbled. "There's no profit hangin' from an anchor chain."

Dan swung his face away from shore where he had been spying the tower of Bruton Parish; Lydia was but half a block from there. He was on his ship to keep the crew in line and in sharp remembrance as to who was captain here, but he wanted to be in town, closer to her.

It was the first time he could remember wanting something more than the *Serpent*. He had never imagined such could happen. The *Serpent* was all he had ever dreamed of, and being at sea was all that had consumed him as a youth. His only love had been ships and the sea, and he had willed himself to hurry and grow so that he could be upon her the sooner. Everything else, the plantation, colonial government, college, had been a pastime; the sea had been his only passion.

Lydia, somehow, had usurped his first love. Lydia was the passion that consumed his thoughts and his dreams. Lydia, who kept running, denying that she felt anything for him, even passion.

It had to be a lie. He could not have had his life turned over like a skiff in a trough while she felt nothing. It was a storm shared, certainly.

But she certainly had never admitted it.

She was lying. She had lied before. She could lie again. All he had to do was prove her for a liar.

"Goin' ashore again?"

Dan forced his eyes from the tower of Bruton Parish and his thoughts from Lydia to face a member of his hastily recruited crew.

"Later," he answered.

"You go ashore a lot. More than most captains," the man said. His name was Will. He had red hair and a surly disposition.

"I do what I please on my own ship," Dan answered pleasantly. Only his pirate crew would have understood the danger in his smile.

"Not much profit in port. I signed on to go to sea, not sit on College Creek and be bitten to death," Will pressed.

"You signed on to the *Serpent*. You stay on her no matter where she goes," Dan said, his back to the rail and his sword within easy reach. "John," he called with a wide smile to his first mate, "see that Will cleans the hold. It will get him away from the insects who torment him up on deck."

Will sulked in the ugly way of an adult, his hands clenching in irresolute anger. "Didn't think a pirate would care about the way his hold smells."

Dan felt the stillness of battle readiness settle over him; it was familiar, welcome. The men had formed a loose half circle around him, indecisive but still threatening. It was fifteen-to-one odds. He had survived those odds before and he understood better now how to play the game.

"I'm no pirate," he said almost on a laugh. It was on just such a laugh that he had killed Pierre.

"That's not what Franco said in Bath," Will pressed.

"It's what I say now that should concern you." Dan smiled coldly.

"I've heard of you before," Will said. "A few of us have. We're no fools. We want a cut of your profit, else we'll tell what we know of you to the law." When Dan did nothing, said nothing, Will added, "You were a fool to come here and sit, waiting for the noose."

He was a fool to come for Lydia, a woman who had fled him at risk to her own life. That was the charge that plagued him in the night when the moon shone in to show him how alone he was in the dark.

"Was I?" he asked with a wide smile, patience gone. When he grabbed Will's shirtfront, the man did not respond except by the accelerated beating of the pulse in his throat. "Would you say that your captain is a fool?" he demanded, clasping him by the throat with one hand. "Come, what say you?" he demanded loudly, tightening his grip. Will did not answer, could not; he was clawing at the hand that held him, the hand that was slowly crushing his windpipe. Only when the man began to lose consciousness did Dan release his grip and let him fall to the wooden boards.

And then, for the first time in a long time, Dan was disgusted with himself.

How had he become this . . . pirate? He had only

wanted to survive, a lamb among wolves. Now he was the lead wolf, ready and willing to tear the throat out of any man who challenged his authority. More than ready, more than willing: enjoying it. Wanting it.

The breeze ruffled his black hair and he pushed the silky waves away from his face with a callused hand. How many men had this hand killed? Ten? Dan laughed inside himself at that deception. Twenty? Yes, he had fought in the name of self-preservation, killing mostly men the king would have cheerfully hanged. Still, he had killed many and done so without remorse.

What had he become?

Dan turned from them, his revulsion rising like bile in his throat, and looked again at Bruton Parish tower rising like an ancient battlement over the flat peninsula. He knew this place; he knew who he had been when he lived here. He knew civility and companionship in his memory; he could know it again. He was *not* a pirate.

He owned the *Serpent* and could do with her as he liked. There was nothing piratical about his ship or his crew. None here could name the deeds he had done, the lives he had taken to keep his own. Lydia alone could bear witness against him in this place, and he trusted her as he had trusted no other in four long years. Lydia had run from him, but she would not betray him.

Dan's eyes grew dark with inner shadows as he plotted a new course for himself. He was captain of a trim ship. He was the heir to River Run. He was the son of a respected man and the nephew of the formidable Patsy Prentis Whaley. He could do as he wished. The sea would wait for him; he could return to her at any time. Lydia was much more elusive. The past few years could be erased, except that he bore a wide scar on his jaw. And he had met Lydia McIntyre.

And by staying, he would find the man who had given him over to pirates.

* * *

Hours later, Dan and Charlton sat in the semi-gloom of Marot's Ordinary, drinking. Drinking, but not drunk. At least, not very.

Dan, who had been drinking steadily for many hours, was not drunk by anyone's definition. To be drunk in a pirate port with pirate companions was a good way to find yourself dead. He did not get drunk. He would not get drunk. Old habits died hard.

But the drinking and the lateness of the hour and the subdued lighting of the room did work together to relax him in a way that he had not relaxed in years. Ben, his voice husky and soft, told Dandridge what he had been doing since they had last seen each other; he was enough of a gentleman and a diplomat not to ask the question of Prentis.

"So when Gordon died, with no living children, his wife went back to England, Shropshire, I believe. I bought his fields, at a good and fair price. Almost doubled my land. Of course, it doubled the work, and then I took on this position as representative . . . makes it deucedly hard to get the best yield when I'm so often preoccupied with colony affairs . . . no woman to see to things when I'm gone." Ben took a long swallow of his brandy and pronounced, "I need a wife."

"You need a manager," Dandridge contradicted pleasantly. "A wife is more difficult to discharge if you find your expectations aren't being met."

"Can't get heirs off a manager."

"True, but I hadn't been thinking of heirs, just profits. Always profits," Dan countered.

Ben looked at Prentis over the candleflame. "What sort of man doesn't think of heirs?"

"A man who has spent the last years of his life fighting and sailing and fighting again," Dan answered softly, staring blindly into the shadowed corners of the room.

"Every day a battle, a fight to the death in the seafaring game I've learned to play. Every night, still alive, I know I have won."

Ben, his drink forgotten, was immobilized by the look on Dan's face and the harsh sound of his voice. Shadows cast his face in black planes and hollows. His eyes, gleaming gold from beneath the heavy shadow of his black brows, were the only spark of life in the stillness of his face. He looked a man haunted.

"A harsh life, Prentis," Ben offered haltingly. "I'm sorry."

Dan laughed softly from his gut, his wide shoulders shaking with ragged mirth. "Life is only harsh if you're dead, Charlton." Taking a deep drink, the candle lighting the brandy so that it resembled thick honey, he added sardonically, "Living is sweet on any terms."

"But how has it . . . I mean to say, that is not what—"

"Not what it should have been?" Dandridge smiled and took a deep swallow of the rich liquid. "True. And I intend to find out who arranged the last four years of my life for me. I can wager with confidence that he did not have my best interests at heart."

"You spoke of having to fight your crew . . ."

Dandridge studied his glass, hesitating, considering how much to disclose to Charlton. He was absolved; Spotswood had seen to that. He had nothing to fear from Charlton, nothing except personal shame. He had sat down with pirates, living with them as one of them . . . but he was Dandridge Prentis first and foremost. And he had survived. Shame could not shadow him because he had made choices by necessity. There was no shame in survival.

"Pirates all, including the captain," he finally said, having absolved himself of the weight of personal guilt. "Obviously, no accident. Just as obviously, I was not intended to live to tell the tale." Dan gestured to his wide scar, visible even in the dim light of the ordinary.

"No accident . . . then someone, here—" Ben began.

"Prepared very nicely for my death aboard my own ship."

"Any hazards as to who?"

"Not yet," he said heavily, "but I will find him." As he had found Lydia. If he could only stop thinking of her, he might be able to find the man who had plotted against his life. But all thoughts swirled around Lydia until he was pulled into a whirlpool consisting only of her. Even drink couldn't drown her.

Their conversation was interrupted, perhaps mercifully, by the arrival of two men. They were not gentlemen. They were not tradesmen. They were not even farmers. They were from the *Serpent*. Dan, seeing them, set down his drink and stiffened his shoulders. Seeing their captain in the room girded their defiance at leaving the ship against orders. Dan knew that they would not leave the ordinary except by force now that they had bearded him. They were counting on his determination to keep his past business in the past to keep him in check; it was subtle extortion boldly played. It was his survival they dallied with. They had to go. He had to do it. The local citizens were even now becoming distressed at the frothing tension of these two men who had invaded their placid environment.

But he did not want such a confrontation in the place of his birth and education and so he hesitated. In his hesitation, the men, Joe and Barto, grew bolder, taking his inaction as license. Which he had known they would.

With all the care of a gentleman, Dan excused himself from Ben's company and walked deliberately toward the two who had disobeyed him. Each step in their direction left the gentleman in him further behind so that by the time he was standing directly in front of them, he was the captain of the *Serpent* and nothing more.

"Get back to the ship," he ordered, his voice not rising

from a conversational tone but containing much more authority.

Joe and Barto exchanged a look. They had gambled much to come here and drink. They had gambled that Dan would not find out. They had gambled that he would not be able to stop them if he did. For a moment, that hope had been kindled, and it would not die easily. For a moment, Dan had seemed unsure and unwilling to confront them, and perhaps this was a good sign? Perhaps they could defy him and he would do nothing. They were gambling on that.

"No," Joe truculently announced. "We're here and we're stayin', same as you."

It was not their lucky day.

Dan smiled, his teeth white in the darkness of the room. Dan smiled and unleashed his fury.

His right hand fisted, he backhanded Joe across the mouth and then reversed his swing to strike him a rounding blow to the temple. Joe tumbled to the floor, not even conscious enough to moan. Barto, knowing he could not back down now, gave Dan his all, which was scarcely enough. Breaking a bottle on a table, Barto lunged at Dan, the jagged points of glass catching the dim light of the candles. Dan did not avoid the lunge; he anticipated it, smiling in predatory satisfaction. Jabbing the bottle with a stiff hand, Barto was off-balance. Dan grabbed Barto by the wrist and pulled. Barto landed on the ground with a grunt, the bottle skidding out of his hand and across the floor to crash into the wall. A few kicks from his captain and he was as unconscious as his friend.

Ben could only watch. In that whole room, there were only watchers. True, there had been time for little else, but in that time Dandridge Prentis had beaten two men into unconsciousness. Brutally and efficiently he had done his work. Day upon day until the days numbered more than a thousand, Dan had fought and won.

Hoisting Joe over his shoulder like a sea bag and grabbing Barto by the belt, Dan left Marot's. He did not speak to anyone. No one spoke to him.

But Ben decided that whatever profit Dandridge had managed to keep out of the treasury was well deserved.

Chapter Twenty-six

It was quite a nice millinery. It was the only millinery. Even so, Patsy Whaley was almost positive that she would never frequent it again. Not after what she had heard, or overheard.

It was hardly the sort of conversation one expected to overhear in a respectable shop on a Friday morning, but heard it she had and on hearing that vindictive, jealous, malicious gossip, she had promptly marched out of the store and into the street, slamming the door with angry effect behind her. No one would utter such nonsense, such outright lies, about her nephew and not feel the weight of her displeasure. It was slander and nothing less, and if she were not such a charitable soul, she would sue whoever was responsible for this tale and assure herself of the culprit's penury.

But she didn't know who had started the tale—though, thinking it through as she marched with military rigidity down the street to her home, Ben Charlton seemed a likely source. Wasn't he in competition with Dandridge for the McIntyre girls? Hadn't he fished for an invitation to their very private dinner? Patsy pressed her lips together and tightened her hands in her fashionable muff, her golden brown eyes shooting emotional gunpowder as she paraded home. If she were the gambling sort, which she most certainly was not, she would place a sizable wager on Charlton's malignant imagination as being the source of the whispered tale she had overheard while shopping.

A tale of Dandridge being involved in a brawl at Marot's! Dandridge! Brawling! Why, it was absurd! No gentleman of Dandridge's social position would show such lack of restraint, and in a public house, of all places. Dandridge was a superlative boy. Dandridge had sacrificed four years of his life to the king's business and the empire's welfare. Dandridge was of the finest family, and who should know better than she? Dandridge was her nephew!

What more was there to know?

Much more, apparently.

"Oh, Patsy," Lucie Smith gushed, almost barreling her down in her enthusiasm. "How is poor Dandridge today after his awful experience last night? Did the poor boy sleep at all? What can have happened to provoke such a display, my dear? The way I heard it—"

Holding herself as regally erect as was possible and as stiff as a stick, Patsy snarled politely, "I'm quite sure I don't know what you're referring to, Lucie. Dandridge is as fit and healthy and as dignified as he ever was. Now. If you will excuse me, I have other things to do that do not include standing about on the street to exchange idle and fanciful dialogue with every person with whom I have a passing acquaintance. Good day."

Vile woman. She never should have invited her to her wedding all those years ago; a moment's kindness and a lifetime to manage the unfortunate results. One must be so careful when issuing invitations.

She was half a block from home, just half a block, when Mary and Elizabeth Harrison scurried to catch up with her. It was past reasonable for her to run to her door, and she would hardly give them the pleasure of thinking that they had run her off the public roadway.

"Patsy, dear, we were just coming to pay our condolences and are frankly startled—"

"Yes, shocked—"

"To see you on the street. It's obvious that you—"

"Yes, as clear as rain—"

"That you don't know what has befallen Dandridge just last night," Mary said over Elizabeth's interruptions. They had been like this since children, breaking into each other's sentences. Patsy found it highly irritating and never more so than today.

"I can assure you," Patsy declared, clutching her muff like a weapon, "that nothing has befallen Dandridge. He is as fine—"

"Oh, it is clear to me that you have not heard about Marot's and the fight he was engaged in there. Why, nothing like it has ever happened before in Williamsburg history!"

"Are you a frequent customer at Marot's to know what happens there with such certainty?"

"Patsy, you are understandably upset," Mary soothed so sweetly and so falsely. "Why, he could have been killed! The one man, a rugged and ill-kempt sort, had fashioned a weapon out of a bottle—"

"A broken bottle," added Elizabeth.

"Though no one can understand why Dandridge approached the men when they did nothing to arouse his attention and, according to what I heard, did not make an aggressive move against him—"

"Until he struck them first," supplied Elizabeth.

"And when they both lay as unconscious as stones, he picked them up and carted them off—"

"Like sacks of grain—"

"And they haven't been seen since!"

Malicious brown eyes waited for her response, glittering in the morning light. Patsy had played with the Harrison girls as a child, never happily. She had taken dancing lessons with them, at her mother's insistence. She had invited them to her wedding, because her father had demanded it. Oh, the sacrifices she had made to please her parents as a dutiful daughter! Why had her mother thrown her in with these two superficial and spiteful girls? Thinking back on it, Patsy remembered that their mother had had something of the same look about her that these women did now. Poor Mother, trying to placate a false and hostile woman. But Patsy was not her mother. Placating was not in her nature.

"Dandridge Prentis, my nephew, is one of the finest men this colony has ever produced," she announced in ringing tones. "He was chosen by the governor himself to scour the seas of pirates and he has been diligently about his task, though he has sacrificed much to do so and with not one word of complaint. But others are not as noble as my nephew," Patsy continued, warming to her oratory. "Some would slander him, jealous of the fine work he has done for his country, jealous of his nobility of spirit, jealous of his position in the high regard of others. And there are those who would spread lies about him, slandering him—"

"Excuse me, Patsy," Mary interrupted, her color high, "I do not lie! I know that this information has been upheld by Benjamin Charlton—"

"Yes, he was there when it all happened—"

"Benjamin Charlton!" Patsy burst out, given all the proof she needed. "Benjamin Charlton is more jealous of Dandridge than anyone! Why, he considers himself in competition with Dandridge for the attentions of . . . well, for the attentions of certain young ladies of marriageable age. He even tried to invite himself to my home when he discovered that one of these young ladies would be coming to dinner. I would not trust *anything* that Mr. Charlton said, and I encourage you to do the same."

"But, Patsy—"

"Come, Mary, can you honestly imagine Dandridge engaging in such rough behavior? It's the cut of a field hand, not a Prentis! Isn't he always immaculately groomed? Isn't he always courteous? Isn't he dignified in his deportment? Such a man as that, throwing his fists about in a public house? You are not such a fool as to believe such a monstrous lie. Are you?"

Mary, drawing herself up and fighting to keep her blush under control, stood shoulder to shoulder with her sister Elizabeth for solidarity. "Of course not!" she exclaimed. No one was going to imply that she was a fool! If what Patsy said about Charlton's jealousy was true, and why wouldn't it be? then it cast the whole tale in a different light. Lies had been told for lesser reasons than jealousy. Dandridge was the image of elegance and refined aristocracy. It was approaching impossible to imagine him engaging in such behavior as a public brawl; she was most irritated with Elizabeth for convincing her of it.

"I'm glad to hear it," Patsy affirmed, satisfied that she had put out at least this fire. "If you will excuse me, I must get home."

"Of course," Mary said, Elizabeth nodding at her elbow, "and if I hear anyone disparage Dandridge, I shall be certain to tell them the truth of Mr. Charlton's involvement in the whole affair."

"I'm sure you will." Patsy smiled coldly, looking remarkably like Dandridge at that moment. His crew would have recognized the look. The Harrison sisters did not.

* * *

"I don't believe it."

"I don't know why you don't believe it, because it's the truth. I overheard Mistress Harrison telling—"

"You shouldn't listen to other people's conversations and you know it, Ruth!" Miriam objected.

"I couldn't help it!" Ruth protested. "They were right next to our fence and I was under the bush pretending to be—"

"You should have alerted them to your presence."

"In my own yard? Miriam, just listen to me," Ruth argued. She had *never* had such an incredible piece of information and Miriam was just ruining it! "Dandridge Prentis knocked a man down with his own hands!"

"You already said that and I told you that I don't believe it," Miriam said primly.

"I *know* I told you about the first man," Ruth huffed, "this is the second man! He knocked down two men in Marot's! Two men with his own hands and no one helped him do it either! Have you ever heard of such a thing?"

"No, I haven't," Miriam pronounced coldly, "and I don't believe a single word of it. It's malicious gossip and nothing else. It has to be. Though I can't think of a reason why Mistress Harrison would lie—"

"*Lie?* Why would anyone tell a lie about such a thing as that? Of course it's the truth! I *wish* I had been able to go with you to Widow Whaley's on Wednesday. Was he terribly ruthless, Miriam?"

"Of course not!"

"Not even the tiniest bit?" Ruth whined pleadingly. It would be just like Miriam to keep something like that from her. Sometimes it was just terrible to be so young.

"Ruth! I will not dignify these lies about Mr. Prentis by discussing them, and I strongly encourage you to do the same."

"Fine," Ruth agreed, thoroughly disgusted with

Miriam's lack of participation in this tantalizing tale about a man she already found very compelling. He was a mysterious man and very good-looking. This story only made him more appealing; couldn't Miriam see that? "Do you know where Lydia is?"

"You are *not* going to upset Lydia with this package of lies! She has enough on her mind—"

"Not so much that I wouldn't appreciate a rousing tale from my sister," Lydia interrupted. Having spent most of Thursday in bed, hiding from her family and from Dan, she was grimly set to face the coming dinner with Dan and his aunt. But she didn't like to think that her inner battles were impacting her family, especially her sisters. Dan had enough of her life, she was not going to give him the girls, too.

"Lydia," Miriam argued, "you don't want to hear what—"

"Stop speaking for Lydia," Ruth interrupted. "She can make up her own mind, and I don't believe that *she* will call me a liar!"

"I didn't call *you* a liar, Ruth, I just don't believe what can only be slanderous and malicious gossip."

"Someone tell me the story so that I can decide for myself," Lydia chuckled, glad to be down among the normal turbulence of her family again. She had adopted the role of recluse for too long. It wasn't healthy, it couldn't be; though she enjoyed the hours spent alone with memories of Dan. Dan laughing, his shoulders shaking with it. Dan coming through the door, his eyes lit with hot expectation. Dan standing on the quarterdeck, the wind tangling his black and shining hair. Dan folding her in his arms, lowering his head to hers, his mouth pressed . . .

"Lydia! Are you listening?" Ruth asked eagerly.

"Yes"—she smiled, redirecting her thoughts—"I'm listening."

"So there I was, under a bush, pretending to be—"

"Does she have to hear all this, too?" Miriam asked.

Ruth sighed dramatically. "I suppose not." Gathering her breath, her blue eyes wide with excitement, she began again. "I heard that Dandridge Prentis was in a fight last night in Marot's Ordinary and that he attacked two strangers for no reason at all and that he struck them both unconscious with nothing but his bare hands and that he carried them out of the ordinary all by himself and that no one has seen any of them since!" Gulping another fast breath, she breathed excitedly, "Do you think they're dead?"

A vision of a man with black eyes dying by Dan's hand flashed before her eyes as if it were happening again before her. Dan in a fight. Could Dan kill in a fight? Yes, he could.

"Ruth! You're not saying that you wonder if Mr. Prentis has killed?" Miriam objected loudly, past all indulgence with her sister. "Lydia, you don't believe one word of that gossip, do you? Someone is clearly endeavoring to slander Mr. Prentis . . ."

Lydia knew he could kill and that he had killed. She had seen him do it. The memory of seeing him fight to the death had sent her running to the privy more than once, had jolted her from her sleep, had compelled her to choke down her screams in the dark of night. Had left her sobbing into her fists that this man she wanted to love had tumbled so low. And now he was unleashing his violence on the people of Williamsburg, the very seat of the legal structure for Virginia Colony. He had held his piratical personality in check until now, but now the bloodthirsty rapacity which so marked all pirates was surfacing like a shark. He could not be the man she knew he was and survive in Williamsburg. He had to leave. Leave or be hanged as the pirate he was.

But he would not leave, and she knew, she knew, it was because he was here for her.

The thrill that realization caused was very difficult to overcome. Very difficult. With great effort, she suppressed it. For now, she had to think of a way to get Dan to leave this place. Dan could not die.

Lydia commanded her mind to function, much as she had when standing bound in the bow of the *Serpent*. The difference was that now she thought not of her own survival, but of Dan's. He was here for her, she knew that. The answering surge of her heart was most difficult to ignore, but she did. She had to. She had to find a way for Dan to survive. If he was here for her, and he was, then . . . if she left, would he leave as well?

Possibly.

Probably.

She very much wanted it to be probable that Williamsburg would lose its appeal with her out of it.

"Lydia, you believe me, don't you? You don't think someone is lying about Mr. Prentis, do you?" Ruth asked, tugging at her hand.

Lydia looked down into the lovely blue eyes of her sister and answered truthfully and from the bottom of her heart. "I believe you."

Ruth, satisfied, scampered off to tell Hannah. But not her parents; she had learned they did not want to hear such interesting conversations.

Miriam was aghast.

"You don't," she whispered.

"I do," Lydia contradicted.

"Why do you believe this story?"

Looking at Miriam and smiling sadly, Lydia asked, "Why do you not?"

"That I can answer easily. He is a gentleman of good family and of good reputation in our community. His manners are genteel and his words well chosen. He is a good nephew to Widow Whaley. And . . ."

"And?" Lydia prompted.

"And"—Miriam blushed and looked down at the floor—"he is of very fine form and figure."

"You find him attractive," Lydia stated bluntly, masking her alarm.

Miriam looked up at Lydia and smiled. "Very." It was the smile of a lovesick child. Lydia knew the look well; she had a mirror in her room.

It was not jealousy she felt. She was not jealous because her sister found Dan attractive. She did not feel sick to her stomach because Dan had clearly shown Miriam a gentlemanly civility and attention that he had certainly never shown her. She would not allow herself to sink so low as to be jealous of her dear sister over a filthy pirate. So he had been charming and gracious. To Miriam; never to her. It did not change what he was. Dan was no gentleman, he was a murdering pirate, a thief, a killer. Dan's manners were charming, but in a predatory way; they were the manners of the bedroom, not the front room. If Dan was interested in Miriam . . . why did it hurt to breathe? . . . it was an attraction of the moment and full of pain—for Miriam. He was fickle, this pirate captain; had he not sworn that she belonged to him and that no ocean or continent could stand between them? Had he not said that he could not forget her and would not let her go?

But she did not deceive herself that he would always think of her. She could imagine him engaging in many behaviors, but fidelity was not one of them. She was concerned for Miriam, who was obviously attracted to the genteel mask that he had worn for her. He was a pirate, none knew that better than she, and she knew what pirates did: they took what they wanted, damning the consequences and their own souls as well.

And if . . . when . . . Dan tired of her, would he then come back to Williamsburg and pluck the flower that was now opening just for him? Would Miriam be the next woman to lie in his bed aboard the *Serpent*? And after

Miriam, Ruth? And then Hannah? Would he work his way through her family like a storm, conveniently picking up a new face and a fresh body when the old one became stale to his jaded eyes? How very, very convenient for him. It was just possible that he would do it; he was a pirate, after all, and they were ruthless to the bone. Yes, she could imagine it; Dan sweeping in to feast off her sisters, using them to feed his sexual hunger and then discarding them at his discretion in any port that met his whim.

He could do it. He was capable of it. He had planned to do just that with her.

Anger fired by jealousy flooded through her as passion had so often done. She had experienced a myriad of emotions in connection with Dan: fear, panic, passion, despair, hopelessness. Anger was new. And strong. She surprised herself by enjoying it.

He was coming tonight, to eat at their table and partake of their food. And look over the crop of McIntyre girls. Tonight, she would begin her campaign against him, revealing him for what he was to Miriam first so that she would not fall into his charming lure. Oh, yes, he could be very charming when the mood suited him. The mood seemed to suit him whenever there was a bed at hand. But not with Miriam, she vowed.

For the first time in a very long time, in three months exactly, Lydia breathlessly and enthusiastically awaited the arrival of Dan at her door.

Dandridge was just about to knock on the door when Patsy laid a proprietary hand upon his arm. He halted his action, reluctantly. He was pantingly eager to open the door and find Lydia on the other side of it.

"Don't forget to give at least half of your attention to the older girl, Lydia," Patsy admonished. "You've met Miriam, so conversation with her will flow more easily, but that's no excuse to ignore the older girl, Lydia. And don't forget her name, it's—"

"Lydia," Dandridge supplied sharply. "I can assure you that there is no possibility of my forgetting her name."

"Don't get sharp with me, boy," she snapped, adjusting her gloves. "You're not off to a good beginning with such mulishness. I'm not so old that I did not notice how well you and Miriam got on together. It would unforgivably rude if—"

"Lydia."

"Lydia were excluded. Give the girl a chance. Give them both a thorough going over. She may be the elder, but then she may also be the better. I won't hold her age against her, and neither should you."

"There is no chance of that happening," Dan assured his aunt, his frustration mounting with each syllable.

"So you say, but your manners have been as unsteady as a lace cuff; put some starch in them, boy. Don't disgrace yourself tonight."

"I have every confidence that I can handle myself with Lydia. There is not the slightest possibility that I will not give her my express attention." Dan smiled down at Patsy, suddenly amused by her worries. "I do know how to behave with women."

Patsy snorted under her breath, unimpressed. "There is certainly no evidence of it, is there? You haven't managed to get yourself married, now, have you?"

Dan smiled widely and said, "There are other measures of success with women."

Patsy narrowed her brilliant eyes upon her nephew and asked, "Which are?"

Dan bit back his defense of himself and gallantly replied, "Not worth mentioning."

Patsy's delicate sniff indicated her satisfaction. His manners were not in complete disarray.

Ruth and Hannah, peeking out of the window over the

door, might not have agreed. What was taking them so long? Would they never knock for admittance? And what were they talking about? Couldn't they have talked at home? Now was the time to eat and they were ridiculously slow about entering. It was beyond their comprehension and they were whispering furiously about it when Lydia came up behind them.

"What are you doing?"

"Just sitting. And talking. It's cool here by the open window and I can see at least a hundred lightning bugs on the Green," Ruth answered.

When Lydia just stared at them expectantly, Hannah said, "We're spying."

"On?" she questioned.

"Mr. Prentis and Widow Whaley," Hannah supplied.

"Ruth!"

"It's just that I wanted to see if he was all bloody from his fight last night and if he looked any different after having knocked two men down until they couldn't get up, but he doesn't look any different than he did before and they've been out there for at least thirty minutes and they're not coming in. Do you think they are going to change their minds about dining with us?"

"How long have they been standing there?" Lydia asked with a smile.

"It may have been only fifteen minutes, but I'm very uncomfortable, my legs are stiff and I can't feel my feet so it seems as if it's been longer."

"Fifteen minutes?" Lydia questioned again, enjoying herself very much.

"It's been five," said Hannah in her no-nonsense fashion.

"Five minutes," Lydia repeated. "You must know that Widow Whaley is too fine a woman to renege on her social obligations at this late hour; that would be unspeakably rude, wouldn't it?"

"But what do you think they're talking about?" Ruth persisted. "Do you wonder that perhaps Mr. Prentis is trying to convince her not to enter? Perhaps he does not want to come in."

Lydia smiled in full confidence and said, "I am certain that Mr. Prentis is very eager to dine with us and that they will be in shortly. Now, off you go and straight to bed. Sally will be up to check on you soon. And if you're very, very quiet, you just might be able to hear what we say at the table. So be very quiet."

Like two little rabbits they scampered off to bed, eagerly anticipating a glorious episode of eavesdropping. Lydia had told them the truth. Dan would never miss this opportunity to come into her home, her last remaining sanctuary against him. He would derive great and sadistic pleasure in taunting her in front of her family. He was a pirate, and they found great fun in cruelty.

The knock on the front door could be heard in every corner of the house.

Lydia seemed to feel its pounding on her heart. It was Dan. He was here and she was waiting for him. Swallowing heavily, Lydia walked to the small staircase and forced her feet to descend. Dan was downstairs and she was going to him.

She had to. She had to protect her sisters.

Robert and Anna greeted their guests warmly as Sally opened the door to admit them. It was a group in which all present eagerly anticipated an evening of great excitement and personal progress. Robert wanted to observe his daughter with this man who had so affected her. Miriam was beyond thrilled to be with Mr. Prentis again and so soon, and she was quietly determined to show him that she did not believe a word of the evil lie that was being spread about him. Patsy hoped for the best tonight; Dandridge would be able to view both of the girls together and make a thorough comparison. It was not impossible that he might be married in a few weeks' time and off that ship of his permanently. Dan visually searched the shop for Lydia as he entered her home and then the small front room where Miriam and only Miriam waited. Lydia was near, he could almost feel her, but she was not where she should be, waiting for him when he came through the door. It was a bad beginning, but he was accustomed to such in dealing with her.

Lydia was not present in this foyer of anticipation. Lydia was lingering on the stair.

The ladies were talking, Sally taking Widow Whaley's light wrap, and Miriam rising to her feet to join them if they did not soon come to her, when Lydia's feet came into view on the stair.

Dan stood as stock still as a deer caught in an open field, every sense alert and ready and heightened by the presence of man. Or woman.

The hem of her skirt followed, dark green and richly embellished with needlework. Robert knew that dress; it was her richest and best. She hadn't worn it in months, but she chose to wear it tonight. For Prentis.

Dan watched her come. She looked glorious. Her hair was a golden swirl, the rich green of her gown accentuating its yellow shine. She wore no gems. Her eyes, looking as green as her gown, were her only adornment and they suited admirably. White lace frothed around her forearms and at her throat like the surging surf. She was to him as compelling as the sea itself. And infinitely more attainable. Lydia he could possess. Lydia belonged to him. She was his. If only he could convince her of it.

As amber eyes met aqua green and held, the connection between them as clear and as strong as a rope, the others in that small space sensed this possession, this oneness, too, but did not know what to name it.

Robert was afraid he did.

Lydia stood at the bottom of the steps, staring into

297

Dan's eyes, assaulted by memories of his coming to her on the *Serpent* and the inevitable result. Dan also remembered and he shared the memory with her. The compounded result was that she couldn't move, could hardly breathe; she fought the impulse to walk straight into his arms and wrap herself around him like a cloak. She couldn't do that. She mustn't ever do that.

Dan smiled at the battle so clearly reflected in her eyes. She wanted him still; he had known it, but she fought against her desires. He would have to teach her the foolishness of that. What she needed to learn and what she did not yet know was that he cared for her. Desire he had felt with the first look and now desire had fused with tenderness. It was more than desire that had driven him to find her in Williamsburg where she could but breathe out of rhythm and he would be hanged as a pirate. He wanted her with a wanting that was beyond the physical and did not know just when that line had been crossed. But he had crossed it. He cared for Lydia and would care for her, beyond the tangled sheets of his cabin. He had only to explain that she need not fear him, he was not a pirate, indeed never had been. Then she would be free to return his regard and she could cease this foolish struggle to deny what she felt for him. What she surely must feel for him.

It must stand without argument that she loved him. For he was no pirate.

"And this must be your eldest daughter—" He grinned in greeting. "Please introduce us, that I may know her."

Robert and Anna stood in momentary shock. So, he would pretend that he did not know her when they knew that he had spoken with her in the garden. Anna could not understand his motivation, unless it was that he did not wish to appear to be on socially unacceptable terms of familiarity with a woman to whom he had not been formally introduced. Patsy puffed with pleasure; Dandridge had not forsaken all of his manners while skimming over the waters for these past four years.

Lydia was also pleased by his words, though for an entirely different reason; the spell his coming had cast over her was broken, broken by her anger at his deviousness and his duplicity. He had spoken with her here, on this very plot of land, just a few days ago and half of her family had witnessed it. To pretend otherwise now, when faced with her father, was a low act, even for a pirate. Still, she was glad of the anger that now swept through her. Better anger than desire.

"Of course," Robert said into the silence that had followed Dandridge's request. "Mr. Prentis, my daughter Lydia. Lydia, may I introduce you to Mr. Dandridge Prentis."

Dan bowed at the waist, his smile bright and charming . . . and expectant. She knew him too well to doubt what he expected of her, the only thing he had ever expected or wanted from her. The only reason a pirate would ever want a woman. Holding her hand out stiffly, her eyes never leaving his, Lydia accepted his polite kiss of greeting.

It was hardly that. Miriam could certainly have received no such kiss as this! Holding her hand to his lips, he kissed her demurely. But not before he had licked the tight space between her fingers.

Lydia flinched and tried to jerk her hand away from his mouth.

Dan grinned in pleasure at her high reaction and held her fast.

Her anger fired the higher at his arrogance in seducing her in front of all these people, family to them both. He was shameless, unrepentant, and wallowing in guile. Never would she allow him to pillage her home for the women in it. Miriam must see what he was! And she must remember it. Why could she not seem to grasp that he was a worthless, unregenerate pirate?

"I am charmed to meet you, Miss McIntyre," he breathed softly. "It was with profound disappointment that I learned of your inability to dine with us on Wednesday evening, though your sister Miriam was a delightful dinner companion." Dan cast a fond smile at Miriam for added emphasis, but Lydia did not need the reminder. If he thought to add Miriam to his collection of women, he was mistaken. She had no illusions that she could ever get Dan to change his plotted course, but she could, she had to, get Miriam to hide herself away from him. Tonight, she would cast all of her natural caution to the wind. Let Dan play his games, let him use her as he wanted, if only Miriam would *see*. She would gladly be the parable if only Miriam would understand the message and protect herself.

Yanking her hand from his clasp, Lydia stood her ground, her eyes sparkling like the sun reflected a thousand times on the sea, ready and eager to use Dan's seduction of her to Miriam's gain. Keeping him firmly to herself was an unpleasant variable in the equation, but familial love demanded no less. She would do whatever was required to keep Dan as far away from her sister as possible, so great was her love . . . for Miriam.

Dan had never seen her like this. He had seen the practiced courtesan; he had enjoyed her. He had seen the trembling and blushing maid; he had respected her. He now saw an opponent, for Lydia was almost martial in her agitation. Her sails were unfurled and she was coming down on him under a full wind. She was not out of control, not her, but only highly focused in her energy. And all that energy was directed at him. To say the least, he was intrigued.

"Thank you, Mr. Prentis," Miriam said, having joined them fully. "I had a delightful time."

"And we shall hope for the same tonight," Anna said graciously. "Shall we sit? Dinner is on the table, though it cannot compare in elegance to the meal which you bestowed upon us."

"I'll not believe it," Patsy said. "Food always tastes better at someone else's table, that's what I've found, and I lay all compliments at that door. I have been looking forward to this evening, when we all could be together, for a long while." Truer words she had never spoken.

Anna, escorted by Dan, entered the dining room, followed by Robert and Patsy and Miriam and Lydia.

"Do you still believe him capable of brawling?" Miriam whispered as they lagged behind.

"Completely," Lydia responded. "And before the night is over, I hope that you will agree with me."

Miriam did not have time to reply to that strange challenge, but she wondered at it as they sat to table. Lydia was behaving very strangely. Perhaps she was not feeling completely well and should have remained in bed; her health had been quite unsteady lately.

The meal, as Anna had predicted, was not as grand as that which the Widow Whaley had served, but it was a fine meal. Chicken chowder, raised cornmeal rolls, ham, wild duck, fried soft shell crabs, young greens with bacon dressing, and wilted salad comprised the fare. None who sat at the table were disappointed, though all there were little interested in the food; it was the company which had drawn them and the company which detained them.

"Lydia," Patsy said, trying to draw the girl out so that Dandridge could make a fair assessment, "I do hope that Mr. Wharton has improved in health under your ministrations. It was most kind and thoughtful of you to attend him."

Resisting the urge to slide a glance at her father, Lydia answered, "He did seem somewhat improved, though I would not lay claim to having been the cause."

"Nonsense," Patsy declared, seeing no need for false modesty, "a gentle hand and a strong shoulder in time of need is never wasted. Of course you aided him. You did say that he felt improved when you left him?"

"I would have better said that he felt much improved on my leaving him," Lydia said sardonically, remembering how eager Mr. Wharton had been to get her out of his house.

"Surely not." Dan smiled softly, swirling the wine in his glass. It was of a color with his burgundy coat and the deep reds glowed in the soft candlelight. His black hair and dark skin set off his light amber eyes so that they seemed almost to glow like the fire itself. He was a study in ebony and crimson, both sinister and warm, intimidating and compelling, arousing both fear and desire. Lydia watched him as he watched her, hating the destruction he had brought to her life. But not hating him. Not fearing him. Her fear was for Miriam. Her desire was for Dan. Still.

The double weight fired her anger even higher.

"Surely yes," she argued. "Mr. Wharton was ready for me to leave long before I was ready to leave him," she said pointedly, knowing Dan would understand that she had been looking for any reason to avoid him.

"The ill often don't know what is best for them," Anna said soothingly.

"Ill or not," Dan said, sipping his wine, "I would never hasten you from my dwelling, Miss McIntyre, and never, ever, in the dead of night."

"I should say not!" Patsy added. "It's hardly fitting for a girl to walk the streets at night; any number of mishaps might befall her."

"I might have disputed the point with you in the past, madam," Lydia said coolly, pushing the food around on her plate, "but no longer. I am convinced that you are correct and I shall never do so again."

"And you shall never have to"— Dan smiled enchantingly—"for I shall be at your disposal, miss, should you ever need an escort. I wouldn't be able to rest knowing you walked about all alone in the dark. The darkness can be dangerous to those unaccustomed to it."

"And you are accustomed to it?" Lydia bit out.

Dan shrugged, the fabric of his coat straining through the shoulders with the action. "I am."

"Is that by practice or design?" she purred caustically.

"More cornbread, Lydia?" Anna asked, thrusting the bowl in her daughter's direction. Whatever she had thought of Dandridge Prentis before, she was at a complete loss as to what to think now. She had never seen Lydia behave in such a way. If Lydia were a man, she might think a duel would be called to settle the tension between them. But Lydia wasn't a man.

Dan smiled fully before taking another swallow of what was very mediocre wine. He loved her like this, like a ship bringing her guns round and lighting off her powder. There was a lot of excitement in taking a ship like that.

But he would come about and let her wonder. Let her roll in the swells and watch him skim just out of range. Soon enough he would fire his own guns, but when she thought the danger past. He had to get past her firing; she would never listen to a declaration of love from him now.

"By practice, I'm afraid," he admitted mildly, turning to Miriam, speaking now to her. "I sail by plotting the stars and they are best seen at night," he explained.

"How wonderful, sir, to be able to read the stars," Miriam murmured, her eyes shining.

"You've said it well," he complimented. "It is much the same as plotting a course through London. You have but to know the language to read the signs."

"Except, sir, that the signs move," Robert commented.

"True, sir," Dan agreed, "but that just makes it more of a challenge."

"Men also plot by the sun, do they not?" Robert asked.

"Yes, and that is part of the skill, but I prefer the night and the stars. To see the stars rising in their paths, arcing across the sky, racing each other across the heavens and with nothing but the shining surface of the sea to anchor a man to the earth . . . it's been years and I haven't tired of it yet."

"How fortunate for the stars," Lydia muttered, frustrated at Miriam's blindness and furious at Dan's . . . everything.

"Pass the butter, Lydia?" Anna asked with odd urgency.

Lydia passed the butter dish to her mother, but her eyes never left Dan, leaning toward Miriam in his conversation with her. Such intimate conversation for two near strangers; couldn't Miriam see that he was a rogue? Did a proper gentleman smile in whispered conversation with a woman gently bred? Did respectable men have eyes that glittered and gleamed like minted gold? Did worthy suitors have skin that was sun-darkened and hair the color of polished onyx? Could Miriam not see what she had seen from the start? That this man was danger and peril and seduction in human form. That this man, this pirate, would destroy even as he protected. That to be joined with him was to lose yourself.

It was clear that Miriam could not see. She listened in open animation to his words, laughing lightly on occasion to some softly spoken phrase. Miriam did not see the danger of the man; she did not feel it.

Dan's danger was only for her.

But Robert sensed it and could only wonder that the women at the table, with the obvious exception of Lydia, could sit so placidly when a wolf was in their midst. For a wolf, a predator, he surely was. Clothing mattered not, bearing mattered little; could not the devil assume many forms and most of them pleasing to the human eye? It was the essence of the man that shouted what he was. He was a predator.

But was he a pirate?

Lydia watched the pirate at their table. She wanted Dan to get away from her sister, to keep away from her sister, and to stay away from her sister. Her thoughts were in no way confused or uncertain. Dan, talking to Miriam, laughing with Miriam, flirting with Miriam, was completely unacceptable. Intolerable. Unbearable.

Was he truly so fickle? Even for a pirate . . .

The thought drew her up short. Did she want the attentions of a pirate? No, she adamantly maintained, drawing her chest up in indignant dignity, but she also did not want a pirate's attentions for her sister.

Dan watched her. He directed but a small fraction of his energy to entertaining Miriam; it was Lydia who consumed him. She was angry with him. Jealous? He hoped so. Perhaps she could see the truth in its glow. Miriam was a sweet girl and comely, but she could not compare to the banked fire of Lydia. Lydia needed but a match to set her ablaze, and he wanted her to understand he was the only match that would ignite her. Lydia had no cause for jealousy. But he was just as glad that she did not know it. Watching her, judging the spark in her sea-colored eyes and the irritated jut of her jaw, he decided to bring his guns round on her now, as she wallowed in her own angry sea.

"But, excuse me, miss"—he smiled warmly at Miriam—"I fear that we are neglecting our dinner partners. You have caused me to forget myself, Miss McIntyre," he murmured seductively.

Miriam simply smiled in response before blushing and dropping her eyes to her lap in flattered embarrassment.

Lydia was either going to retch all over the table or throw something hard and heavy at Dan's face. Her hand reached for the pewter water goblet in front of her. Dan raised his eyebrows and smiled expectantly at her, challenging her to do it, to lose face in front of his aunt and her parents. She wouldn't give him the satisfaction. Smiling sweetly at him, she dropped her hand back on the table, not so terribly far from the goblet.

Dan smiled back, laughing at her.

"Thirsty, Miss McIntyre?" he asked.

"No," she answered bluntly, "why do you ask?"

"You have a hungry look about you. Not enjoying the meal?"

It was true, she hadn't eaten much, but neither had he.

"I always enjoy dining with my family," she said, explicitly excluding anyone not of her family.

Dan smiled again in acknowledgment of her point in this battle in which they were so civilly engaged. Then he made his own point. "You are a woman of small appetite then? Easily satisfied? I would not have thought so."

Lydia blanched to hear those words, so familiar to her heart and so foreign to this environment. That he could repeat, here, in this company . . . that he could speak again what had been said between them . . . how could he be so casual . . . ? Because, she answered herself ruthlessly, he is a pirate and they are cruel. Did she expect mercy? Kindness? Compassion?

She never had before. Why did she now?

Because she had hoped for love from him.

"My appetite is healthy," she answered, refusing to let him see the wounds he inflicted on her. "When I am hungry, I eat and eat until satisfied."

"Then you are satisfied now?"

She stared into eyes of golden fire sheltered beneath boughs of black sable and gave her answer, the only answer she could give and the one answer she must. "I am."

"I envy you, Miss McIntyre," he said softly, his eyes going molten in intensity, "for my appetite is not satisfied. This table is heavy with offering and yet I am not satisfied. I am hungry. I am so hungry that it seems I have been empty forever," he finished, his voice husky and private, though they were hardly private.

"If you're hungry," Patsy interjected, mortified by her nephew's appalling lack of manners, first with Miriam and now with Lydia, so clearly playing one sister against the other, and insulting the offering of their hosts, "there is a table full of food to satisfy you, Dandridge. A man would be a fool to complain of hunger with such a generous repast."

"Then I am a fool, madam"—he smiled, still looking only at Lydia—"for though the table is full, there is something which I do not see sitting upon it which would satisfy my deepest hunger. Something which I had once before and have not forgotten . . ."

She had seen that look before and knew what it boded. She knew that he was aroused completely and that soon he would touch her, take her, possess her in the way that only he could. She remembered everything and so clearly, so vividly. How could he fire such hunger in her? How could her memories be so alive? That little window showing a square of starlight, the dampened sheets, the gentle roll of the ship, the sight of him, tanned and magnificently windblown, in the portal of his cabin, the fire in his amber eyes, the table. A table just like this one . . .

"Excuse me! Please!" Lydia choked out, rising rapidly to her feet and leaving the dining room before anyone could grant her request.

Robert and Anna and Miriam and Patsy watched her bolt from the room and into the garden. They wore quizzical and worried expressions. Dan watched also. He wore a knowing smile.

"Please excuse her," Anna said to all, "she has been of uncertain health these past few days."

"Of course," Patsy was quick to say. "And to have

helped poor Mr. Wharton in spite of it . . . you have a dutiful and generous daughter, Mistress McIntyre."

"Yes, Mistress Whaley," Anna agreed quietly.

"Now, what was it you were saying about a special dish that you once had, Dandridge?" Patsy asked.

Dan turned from facing the open doorway to face his aunt and then the rest of the table. "It was something exotic and from a far off port-of-call. Unusual. Distinctive. I haven't been able to forget it."

"That's fine, but you certainly can't expect to find such an item in Williamsburg, can you?" Patsy demanded.

Dan did not answer. He smiled. Patsy assumed it was in agreement.

"Will you also excuse me?" he asked, placing his napkin next to his plate.

"Certainly," Anna responded politely.

Robert said nothing. He watched as Prentis went out to the garden, following Lydia's route. He was glad that the door had been left open to the night air. It was not such a large garden. Lydia would be fine, though he was glad that the door was open.

She walked the crushed shell path that led to the rear of the garden and the necessary house, but she was not going there, though her stomach was in knots and she had the sheen of perspiration that comes before nausea. She knew enough about herself now to know that it was not nausea she was suffering from, it was desire. His words, his seductive words, had caused images and sensations that she could not kill to rise up and flood her. She had been on his table, naked but for her passion for him, spread before him like a banquet from which he could partake at his discretion. Shaking in her passion and her need. Trembling at his touch. Throbbing and aching for his hard possession. Wanting him and growing wet with the knowledge that she would soon have him. As he would have her. Hunger appeased. Appetite satisfied. Until he touched her again.

Lydia reached the end of the walk, a pale thread of white in a dark world, and turned to walk back the way she had come. The night was soft with sound and motion. Insects hummed and clicked, lightning bugs flashing through the night with delicate unpredictability. A breeze, moist and warm, brushed against her skin and moved loosened strands of her upswept hair. In the sky, a crescent moon hung midway to the cap of heaven and the stars were bright beacons of light in a dark night.

It was a night to be in love, but she was not in love. She could not be in love. She was bound in desire and unfulfilled lust. It was lust. It was not love. They were not the same. To be filled with lust for a pirate was repulsive enough, but to be in love . . . Impossible.

And he had more than proved that he did not love her.

Lydia smiled up at the stars, feeling the moist night air on her skin. It was not so terrible a thing, to admit she desired him. In fact, the more she said it to herself, the easier it became. *I want you, Dan; I want you.* Yes, it was simple.

And natural. They had been intimate, more than intimate; how could it be any more wrong to couple again? It couldn't. It was done, and not doing it would not change that. So . . . being with him, wanting him, did not really matter. Not really.

I want you.

Halfway to the house, a dark shape blocked her path. It was a very narrow path, she could not go around. She knew who it was, who it had to be. She did not stop walking.

He waited for her. She would come and he would touch her and in touching her, he would reach her. She was near helpless against his touch. She would know he loved her by his touch.

Dan wrapped her tenderly in his arms, holding her to him, pressing his lips against her throat. Lydia leaned into his strength and his welcome length, feeling small and safe against him. His lips moved up, caressing her, until they reached her mouth and then they joined and the joining was hot and wet and so very welcome. Dan's hands slid down to her derriere sheathed in that fine green cloth and gripped her with heart-wrenching familiarity, pressing her against his rigid length, rocking her against his narrow hips in mock rhythm of a deeper joining as his mouth moved over hers and his tongue plunged in to taste of her again.

I want you.

He lifted his mouth from hers to kiss the tip of her nose and her brow and her throat and he breathed, "Sail with me again, Lydia. Remember how I filled you aboard the *Serpent*. Come with me and I will satisfy your every hunger. I can feed your appetites," he whispered, his breath soft and urgent against her skin. "We will feast upon each other, a love feast upon the endless ocean," he promised before plunging his tongue into the open warmth of her mouth.

It was true. She was hungry for him. So hungry that she thought she would die of it, starve to death for want of tasting him again. Had he spoken of love?

If she was back on the *Serpent*, he would leave Williamsburg. He would be safe. She would be with him. She was lost anyway, she tried to reason as his lips moved to the lace-covered swells of her breasts. Worse than lost, fast approaching unredeemable, and it would keep Miriam away from him. Miriam, who was far too comely. Miriam, who could not see the danger in him. Could not see him as she saw him, with his eyes glowing gold in the June night and the feel of his hands molding her to fit his form and the wet heat of his mouth devouring her . . .

As she devoured him. No more was she passive beneath his caress, accepting what he would give her. No, she wanted this, wanted him, and would give as well as take, devouring him eagerly. She did, truly, have an appetite and he would feed it.

She was not thinking of Miriam. This had nothing to do with Miriam, though the lie of self-sacrifice was a comfortable one and one grown easy through repetition.

"Take me away from here, aboard your ship," she softly commanded against his mouth. "Let us have done with groping against our clothes."

"You want me, then? You will admit it?"

"I want you." It was so easy to say. It seemed as if her life had begun with those words. There was no life without Dan; it was the only truth left. God was mute in the dark of her passion.

She had always wanted him, he had known it from the first moment. It had always been so and so it would always be. Dan felt the flush of victory as he wrapped her in his arms, cradling her almost tenderly. She would stay with him now; she would run from him no more.

"You will stay with me?"

He needed to hear her say it, he who had pursued her only to have her run from him again and again until he thought he would lose his reason. She had to choose him, to want him and to cling to him. If she, Lydia of good family and impeccable respectability, chose him, it meant that he was certainly no pirate. Lydia McIntyre would not give herself over to a pirate. And he was no pirate, he was Dandridge Prentis and nothing less. Certainly nothing more. Not a pirate. He had never been a pirate; he had been seeing to his survival and there was nothing blameworthy in that. He knew he was no pirate, but he needed her to know it, too. If Lydia, of all people, could choose him, seeing him as he knew himself to be, then he would be truly no pirate.

He could not be a pirate.

"Will you?" he repeated, hearing the tinge of desperation in his voice and despising it. "I love you, you know. You must know how much I love you, want you . . ."

Need you. He could not say it. There was too much weakness in saying it. He did need her. He needed the freedom from guilt that her acceptance would give him.

She was still in his arms, so very still. He raised her face with his fingertips and searched her eyes for the absolution he needed from her, willing to say anything to attain it. Lydia's eyes glimmered in the darkness, her long lashes casting deep shadows onto her cheeks.

"You love me?" she whispered, the very timbre of her voice shouting her disbelief.

"Do not doubt," he said, rubbing his thumb under the angle of her jaw, so smooth when compared to the ridges of his scar. "Have not my actions spoken for me before now? Have I not behaved in all ways like a man in love? Do not doubt your appeal, Lydia."

Perhaps it was as simple as that she did not understand the ways of a man in love. Perhaps he had shown her all along in his desire for her. Perhaps his pursuit of her had been driven by love and not lust; she had wanted many times to believe just that. And now he had declared himself; he was in love with her. She wanted to believe him because the words poured through her like warm honey, covering and sweetening old and bitter wounds inflicted by this very man. This man she wanted to love.

Oh, God, please let him love her.

"You . . . you want to marry me?"

The question, as blunt as a fist to the belly, caught him unprepared. He had not been thinking of marriage. Lydia was sex and laughter, desire and conquest; he had never imagined her as hostess or mother or wife. Ever. He had wanted her, but not as wife. That truth showed clearly in his expression. It was a truth that shouted to the distant moon, though silence reigned between them.

Lydia stepped back from the false security of his embrace. From the lie he could not tell.

Lies, it was always lies between them. It had been lies from the start, from the first look and the first touch and the first word. She could not breathe for the lie her life had become. And she wanted to hurt him as he had hurt her, wounding her in the very taking, rejecting her in the act of declaring his love, hurting her with the truth. She had truths of her own. She would lie to him no more.

She would not lie to herself.

"I don't want you." She said it loudly, firmly, and could see the rejection mold itself to his features. It was surely sin to feel such satisfaction.

Dan regained some of his composure and laughed gently, "Liar."

He was right to laugh. Had she just not sworn to leave off lying? "I will not go," she repeated with greater intensity.

"And if I take you?" he asked with a rough intensity to equal hers.

Lydia looked straight into his molten eyes and declared, "I can still leap a ship's rail."

Dan didn't like being reminded that she had risked her life to escape him. Damn her for her obstinacy and her lies. Didn't want him? She had to want him!

"Everything has changed," she added, seeing his anger.

"Nothing has changed," he snarled savagely before he attacked her.

It was an attack of hands and mouth and heated passion. His hands scored her body from hip to shoulder and back again, pulling her against him and holding her pinned within his determined embrace. A hot mouth lashed over hers in ruthless entry, plunging in where she had no strength to keep him out. He was a pirate, attacking, bent on victory. But this time, the victory was not in keeping her beneath his hand and bent to his will, it was that he wanted her arousal to flare up and burn her will to deny him what he knew they both wanted. Her breasts were full and soft beneath his fingers as he cupped her, relishing the heavy weight of her bosom in his hand. He knew every inch of her and every pore, but something was wrong. She was not responding to his touch. Lydia always responded, even against her spoken will. This woman was cold beneath his hand.

Dan's anger raged unremittingly.

"You gave yourself to me freely enough on the *Serpent*," he charged. "You want me now as you wanted me then. You wanted me with the first look," Dan hissed angrily.

She thought of the first time she had seen him on his ship and of the first time he had touched her. She had not wanted him; she had wanted to live.

"No," she answered softly, "I did not."

She had not wanted him? When her eyes had pleaded for him to take her from the moment he had first looked upon her? She lied.

"Then you are a whore," he spit out, "who gives her body to any man who grabs for it and pretends her passion as part of her trade."

His accusation was a painfully familiar one; was it not what she had charged against herself? Had she not examined the evidence which mounted against her in greater height every hour and found herself guilty? He had called her a whore. But his words, equal to her own, struck her differently. Was she a whore?

Did whores love?

She had vowed to leave all lies behind, and the truth she faced now blazed with the light of the sun. He was a pirate and she could not love a pirate. He was Dandridge Prentis and she could not love a man so far above her social sphere. He had taken her virginity like a spoiled child, not cherishing the gift she had made. She had deceived him, run from him, submitted to him, and rebelled against him.

She loved him.

It explained much.

It comforted little.

"No," Lydia answered firmly, her mind resolved and at peace. Finally. "I was . . . I am . . . no wanton."

The moonlight, so faint, lit her pale eyes with cool and luminous light. She looked ethereal and chaste as she stood before him. He wanted the impression to be a lie because if it was the truth, guilt would drown him as no ocean had yet done.

"I was a woman taken by pirates," she continued, her voice rising in confidence. "I knew what would be done to me. I chose the man and the method. To survive."

Her dress was black in the dim moonlight, her lace white as foam, her skin pearly and her eyes pale reflections of the moon; she was as he had never seen her. And he knew she lied.

"You chose me?" he barked angrily, damned sick of her deceptions and her lies.

She saw his pain, revealed in anger, and was ashamed at the pleasure it gave her. He had hurt her so much and so often and with so little effort; it could not be wrong to hurt him just a little. But she would not lie to him. He must see her as she was and know what was true of her and what was deception. She would not be the whore for him any longer.

"I chose the one who could best protect me against the mob," she said simply.

"The captain," he stated coldly, understanding at last just what she had done to survive.

"Yes"—she nodded—"the captain."

Dan could find no argument against her, no matter which course he pursued. She had not wanted him, she had wanted the captain. If Pierre had challenged and killed him the day before the taking of her ship, if Red Jack had not died minutes before he had seen her, if mangy old Walter had been captain of the *Serpent* . . . she would have turned her lustrous aqua eyes on any one of them, seducing him, convincing him of her exclusive desire. It had been the captain she had turned to, wanted, given herself to; it had not been to him.

"Any port in a storm," he breathed, his anger icy, deadly, his eyes chips of age-old amber.

"Yes," she whispered, understanding the loss of personal worth he now bore; had she not borne the same? But she was unable to lift the truth from him. They had deceived each other from the beginning; it would stop now.

"Then we're more alike than you pretend, Lydia," he growled. "You did what you had to do to survive. As did I. The only truth is survival. And you did want me, still want me."

It had been the truth, then, and they were speaking of then. But now . . . now . . . now the essentials were still true. She did not want him, not the way he meant it; a whore and a pirate, an outcast and an outlaw. She could not be that, as he could not. He would go on being Dandridge Prentis and she would go on being . . . ruined. How well had she survived? How well had he?

"Sail away from here," she urged, laying a hand upon his arm in entreaty. It was a mistake. She had touched him and they both were lashed by it.

Pulling her to him, Dan held her fast, his hands encircling her narrow waist, his breath warm upon her brow. She raised her hands to hold him apart from her, but all she succeeded in doing was feeling the ridge of muscle that banded his arms. He was a black outline against the slash of the moon. Black figure against a black night; she did not fear him or the darkness.

It was her best proof that he must leave Williamsburg if she was to survive her impossible and sinful love for him.

Robert stepped out into the night, his silhouette against the warmly lit doorway a solid and steady thing. He had heard enough. He could see his daughter and the man who had taken her virginity clearly as they stood in the path, though they were at a distance.

A pirate stood in his yard, a pirate who had raped his daughter. He was most certainly justified in his actions. He would not be prosecuted for killing such vermin.

"Lydia!"

His daughter jerked as if struck. He did not want such a response from her. She was not the target of his rage, nor would he foul her with it. Lydia, to the best of his ability, would be protected from further harm. The one who had tried to corrupt her stood with his arm around her waist. Robert's rage pulsed with life.

"Go into the house and to your room; lock the doors if it gives you ease. I will deal with what remains behind." He would not call him a man; he did not deserve the honor.

The pirate held her tightly to his side for a moment and then slowly released her, an act which seemed to pain him. The impression was obviously a lie. His daughter rushed past him, avoiding his healing touch of comfort, and into the house. She wore shame like a cloak. It was unnecessary; the man who deserved the shame and the censure stood before him, looking brutally unrepentant.

Robert was not surprised. In fact, he was almost pleased. It made what he was determined to do so much easier.

With awkwardness born of fury, Robert pulled his pistol free and aimed it at the renegade in his garden.

"You raped my Lydia, my eldest and most treasured, and you were reared to understand the horror of it."

Dandridge jerked under that indictment and snarled like a cornered wolf, "It was not rape."

"It was," Robert charged in an instant. "It was nothing less. You took from her what belonged to her husband."

"She gave—"

"She opened her fist before you broke her hand to pry loose what she protected. You are educated enough to understand the difference."

"It wasn't that way," Dan argued, fighting for the image he had carried of himself for four long years. Dandridge Prentis did not rape innocent girls, no matter how tempting. "She offered herself, proclaiming herself a wh—"

"You lie!" Robert charged, the gun shaking in his hand, his knuckles white. "Lydia would never have said that! You tell me what you *wanted* to hear. You took her and then made her what you wanted her to be."

"It is no lie!" Dan flashed back, his bloodlust high. He fought for his very life, for if what McIntyre said was true, then he was depraved, debased . . . a pirate. "I did not know what or who she was, only what she seemed to be. If she had only—"

"You lay this at her feet? You are the pirate still, no matter the coat you wear or the polish of your table manners, for you will take no responsibility for your own actions. Listen to yourself! Who did you 'seem to be' on that pirate ship?"

Dan shivered in the warm night air, a shiver that had nothing at all to do with the weather. He shivered from the center of his bones, the chill shaking his very soul, for the truth that cracked against him. It all fell away then, the deceptions he had spun around himself to keep his sanity in the past four years. He had been tricked and manipulated and almost murdered four years ago and he had made a choice: turn pirate or die. He had not died.

Dan swallowed against the pain that rose up in waves to swamp him. Visions long smothered rose up in ghostly horror: the people he had killed, the women he had bedded, the ships he had taken. He had pushed them away from him, sailing on to the next encounter, cherishing the memory of Dandridge Prentis of Williamsburg. Dandridge Prentis had died four years ago; he had killed him to survive. It had been his first murder and the one he had worked the hardest to forget. Standing here, in this honest man's garden, he was forced to remember. Remember how he had used an innocent girl, a girl who had found herself among pirates and merely sought a method to survive. Everything that she had endured, had suffered, he had done to her. Sweet, sweet Lydia to be so used and for such an end. She had merely fed his lust. He had just now tried to steal her soul and crush her spirit . . . in the name of love. It had been a lie.

Dan stood beaten, beaten for the first time in years, and not a welt or a cut or a bruise stood bloody upon his skin; no, the blows had been to his heart, and his heart lay broken within his chest.

"Kill me, then," he commanded Lydia's father, his arms open wide and his voice hoarse with the horror of memory. "Kill me. I deserve it and more."

Lydia bound, her gown ripped, her eyes wide with panic, stood with him in that garden. Lydia gulping her brandy, her eyes mutely seeking mercy, hovered at his elbow. Lydia watching him kill Pierre in a fight of no rules and no honor wrapped herself around his knees and kept him bound in place to face her father's vengeance. Lydia's pain and struggle for survival in the world he had forced her to inhabit choked him. He had done nothing but hurt her screamed the shrill voice of guilt that had somehow survived, though he had done his best to kill it. As he had killed Dandridge Prentis.

"Kill me!" he shouted, advancing on Robert McIntyre, the visions of Lydia clinging to his steps. "You have the right!"

Robert McIntyre lowered his pistol slowly, silently.

"*Kill me!* It will be less than I have done! Take your vengeance, for it is just!"

"No," Robert said softly, though his voice was strong with resolve.

"Yes! Do it!" Dan commanded, a mere arm's length from the man he urged to be his executioner.

"Still the pirate, urging others to follow a lawless path."

Dan slumped in defeat. Was he truly so lost in sin that he did not understand his own motives?

"I'll not kill you," Robert said. "If I did, I'd be the same as you." He turned and walked back into the house.

Dan was left in the darkness. Alone.

Chapter Twenty-seven

Patsy, having made whatever excuses she could think up to explain her nephew's outlandish behavior in deserting his dinner companions, left the McIntyre house. Dandridge she could not find, and she could not help thinking that it was in his best interests to make himself scarce; she would flay him red when she got her hands on him. What had the boy been thinking to bait the eldest girl so? And to demean the culinary efforts of their hosts! Dandridge had been at sea quite too long; settling at River Run would serve them all better. In order to rest easily in the hereafter, she needed to know that her nephew would be running the estate she and her husband had built with so much effort. Mr. McKenzie was a capable man, but he was not family, and River Run must stay in the family. Dandridge would be convinced of that fact if he did not already see it. She would make sure of it. As soon as she found him.

In typical contradictory fashion, she found him as soon as she arrived home. He was in the parlor and Mr. McKenzie, of all people, was with him. Who, if not Mr. McKenzie, was seeing to her interests in River Run?

Mr. McKenzie was seeing to his own interests in Williamsburg. In the person of Mr. Dandridge Prentis.

". . . and when the word came that you had returned, sir, I could not wait to see for myself . . . er, I could not wait to see you again myself."

Dandridge, his emotions raw and bleeding, was in the ideal frame of mind to deal with a man who had come to Williamsburg for the express purpose of "seeing for himself." McKenzie, the man, he barely remembered, but seeing him again brought certain memories from the darkness into the light of recollection; McKenzie, thin and balding, had wheedled the job of manager from his uncle through the time-honored method of favors owed. Only it had been a favor owed to a friend upriver that had spurred his uncle to grant McKenzie the job. Dandridge had a difficult time believing that anyone would ever owe McKenzie a favor. Enoch McKenzie had no friends or relations. And McKenzie had overseen the outfitting of the *Serpent* all those years ago.

McKenzie was ambitious.

Dandridge was suspicious.

"Good heavens, Mr. McKenzie," Patsy huffed, removing her gloves and her light summer shawl, "why have you left River Run? And who is monitoring activities there while you traipse to Williamsburg?"

"He had something to see to in Williamsburg," Dandridge said with chill civility. "Isn't that right, McKenzie?"

"Well, yes, I . . . I . . . as I was saying to your nephew, Mistress Whaley, I heard that Mr. Prentis had returned and I was most eager to welcome him back."

322

A hired man traveling rough country miles to welcome home his master?

"Nonsense!" Patsy said, summing up the situation nicely. "What are you about, man, to leave your situation untended? And don't bore me with faddle about this boy's return, for I'll not believe it. You scarcely know the boy!"

"He knows me better than you believe, Aunt, and has great interest in my welfare. Isn't that right, McKenzie?"

Dandridge knew he was right. McKenzie, trusted by Uncle Matthew, had overseen the bulk of the arrangements for Dan's outbound voyage on the *Serpent*. McKenzie had hired the crew. McKenzie had found the captain, assuring Dan personally that Red Jack was an able captain and honest. Dandridge, eager to be off, had listened to his assurances with half an ear. Matthew, more interested in River Run, had trusted his overseer to deal well with the details for the *Serpent*'s maiden voyage. McKenzie had betrayed them all.

McKenzie chewed his lower lip in obvious anxiety. He had miscalculated badly in anticipating the response to his arrival in Williamsburg.

Dan smiled coldly. The man had also miscalculated badly in arranging for pirate profit and Dan's death.

"Whatever do you mean, Dandridge?" Patsy said. "Your manner tonight has been completely incomprehensible and I am at a loss—"

"Excuse me, Aunt Patsy, let me be clear. McKenzie had quite naturally assumed that I had died at sea. He had arranged it all so thoroughly, you see."

For once, Patsy Whaley had nothing to say.

McKenzie damned himself with his response: he turned as white as a sheet and bolted for the door. But Dandridge, charming boy that he had always been, had changed in his four years abroad; Dandridge Prentis knocked him to the ground with one blow and held him in place with a hand about his throat.

Again McKenzie had badly miscalculated.

"You did it," Dandridge charged, his fingers digging into the pulse points on the man's throat. "You hired the crew. You arranged something with the captain."

He was feeling his way to the truth, watching the eyes of the man he held captive. This was the man who had stolen his life, leaving him marked with more than just a scar on the throat. This was the man who had murdered Dandridge Prentis. If not for this man, he would not have become a pirate. If not for this man, he would not have hurt Lydia. If not for this man, he would have . . . honor.

"What was it? Did you want pirate profit? Did you think that, by giving Red Jack a ship, he would share his plunder with you?"

McKenzie's eyes bulged from the pressure on his throat.

"Tell me!" Dan commanded.

McKenzie nodded frantically. Patsy sputtered her outrage, clarity coming with each syllable.

"Fool!" Dan almost laughed. "No pirate gives away profit. Who was he to you? How did you know of him?"

Dan eased off the pressure, allowing the man to breathe a full breath and gain the air to answer.

"Mates," he gasped. "Childhood mates."

"You are a double fool," Dan said softly. "Pirates have no mates."

"Don't kill me!" McKenzie rasped, his throat constricted. "I didn't mean for you to go! I didn't think you would go! Your aunt railed that she wouldn't let you sail and I took her at her word. I only wanted to be rich," he finished pitifully.

Dan tightened his fist. His life had been destroyed for money. The man deserved to die. He had taken a promising life and turned it to dust, and for what? To serve his own ends, feed his own desires, his self-serving lust for money.

McKenzie choked, ". . . kill me!"

It wasn't what he had meant to say, but it was all he could get out past the fist holding him down. Dan knew that. But the words struck a chord, haunting and painful.

He was a pirate still.

How different was he from this man?

No different at all.

Again he heard Robert McIntyre's voice in his head, the indictments damning, his own arguments weak. He was blaming another for the choices he had made. Again he proved himself empty of mercy and long on selfishness. He had rejected Lydia because she was not good enough for him to marry, and he was the one who had destroyed her worth in the marriage mart. He had lived with lies about himself for so long that the truth was as uncomfortable as bright sun on water.

He loosened his grip, allowing McKenzie to breathe easily. It was his first act of mercy and compassion in four years.

"Get up," he growled. "You I shall not kill. Mercy you shall have of me, because mercy was shown me."

The words were spit out of his mouth like pebbles, each one heavy and awkward and dry. Foreign. He was learning compassion and it was uncomfortable.

"But you have betrayed me, the Whaleys, and the crown. Get out of Virginia Colony and do not return. That is all the mercy I can give you."

It was more than McKenzie had dared to hope for. He scrambled noisily to his feet, cast a frantic glance at Patsy, who looked ready to kill him herself, and stumbled out of the door. The darkness swallowed him.

Patsy turned her scowl on Dandridge. "We have much to discuss, boy," she declared. "I'm going to assume that you didn't want to shock me with your tale and that is the reason for your deception. I'm less inclined to fits and faints than you would think, and would hear the whole of it. Now."

Dandridge studied his aunt, taking in her glowing amber eyes and her rigid posture. A hurricane would run from his Aunt Patsy. Smiling slowly, he answered in the only way he could.

"Yes, ma'am."

It was a solemn and subdued group who found their way to their beds, leaving Sally to clean up the disarray of their entertaining. Could anyone clean up such havoc? Robert and Anna attempted to try.

Knocking, they entered Lydia's attic room. Their daughter sat on the edge of her bed, staring into the candleflame on the table. In this world of darkness, she needed the light, even such a little light as this.

Anna sat next to her daughter on the bed, ready to comfort. Robert faced his daughter. She was in misery, clearly, but she also possessed a sense of calm that he had not seen in her in months.

"What will you tell us?" he asked her.

Raising her eyes to him, she sighed tremulously. She would lose nothing by telling them what they must already suspect. "Dandridge Prentis is a pirate, the pirate . . ." Her voice quivered and she took a breath to steady it. "I knew him as Dan. He is the one . . . the one," she said shakily, her voice rising. "I never thought to see him again. I didn't know who he was or who he had been, but when he came . . . when I saw him . . ."

"He came looking for you," Robert said, stating a fact.

"Yes, that is what he told me," she answered, looking down at her hands clutched in her lap.

"He wants you." When Lydia looked up at her father in shame, he added, "That is what he told me."

"He is angry, that is all. He is angry that I escaped

from him. He paid for me," she explained, blushing deeply. "I was his portion of the spoils."

"Oh, Lydia, my poor girl," Anna breathed, taking her daughter in her arms. Her daughter resisted her embrace.

"You don't understand . . . I can't . . . I want . . ."

"I understand," Robert said, his expression grim. "You love him."

Lydia's shame was complete. She wanted to die under the weight of it, letting it bury her, hiding her from the horrified expressions on her parents' faces. What was wrong with her that she could believe herself to be in love with Dan? He had done nothing to earn her love and everything to win her violent hatred. Where was the logic on which her pride rested?

Tumbled down in the dirt with her sinful pride, she answered herself. Was it any wonder she found herself in such a position with so much pride paving the path to destruction?

"Do you have any reason to believe that he loves you?" Robert asked, his voice remarkably controlled.

Only that he had said so, she silently answered. But then, she knew it was a lie. He always lied. And his lies were so sweet and so hard to resist. But when a man loved, he wanted to marry; everyone knew that. Dan did not want to marry her and she knew why, because of what he had done to her himself. *No*, she chided herself, *what you gave him permission to do*. He had not taken anything that she refused to give. Except her heart. *That* he had taken by chance.

"No," she answered her father slowly, "I do not."

"Do you have any reason to believe that he will leave you alone?"

Every word they had spoken, every touch shared, every kiss tasted swam through her memory. Not for a moment had Dan ever left her alone, and with every breath he had promised that he would always want her.

327

How could she stand against such determination, such passion?

She couldn't. They both knew that quite well enough. And he did not love her, no matter the lie on his lips.

"No," she said with a tremor, "I do not."

"Well," Robert said with impressive calm, "I would say that the best course of action would be for you to leave Williamsburg for a few months, until his blood cools. It will, in time," he prodded, not taking his eyes from her troubled ones. "This frustrated anger of his, rooted in pride, cannot burn for long without tinder. He'll sail off when you are no longer here for him to plague."

So she had concluded. It was reassuring to hear it from another. He would sail away with her gone, wouldn't he? Would he also forget her?

"Then I'll go," she said, reaching out to hold her mother's hand for comfort and support. "But where?"

"To my sister's home in Charlestown. Margaret has been lonely since your cousin Mary has wed. She will welcome an unexpected guest."

"When?" Lydia asked somewhat bleakly. She knew what they planned was right, but she would be leaving Dan and it would be a permanent leave-taking. He would never find her. She would never see him again, no matter what false destiny she imagined for them.

"Tomorrow morning," her father answered.

"Tomorrow," she repeated. It was so soon. But perhaps it was already too late.

The weather was fine, clear and warm, and the wind steady. The Virginia coast slipped past, the trees losing their individuality to become a green blur and then just a dark line upon the horizon as the ship moved relentlessly out to sea.

Lydia thought she was going to be sick.

She was sailing under her mother's maiden name on an

unremarkable ship to one southern port of many on the itinerary.

He would never find her. Never.

It was difficult to see the shore now, difficult even to see the rail at which she stood. God help her, she was crying! Crying from the center of her soul so that her pain tumbled in monstrous waves up from her stomach to crash against her throat and eyes, shaking her with its strength, bruising her and twisting against her ribs. Was it animal lust that tortured her? Never; surely lust was not so strong as this. Lust did not seek what was best for Dan against her own longings.

Only love was sacrificial.

In her pain, pain physical, emotional, and spiritual, she cried out to God for help and release and comfort. She cried out the truth. No more lies, not even to God.

"I love him," she whispered, the tears running down her face like heavy rain. "I want him," she confessed, her heart turning with the words. "I love him, but . . . I will not have him unless You will it." Wiping her tears with her fingers, she choked out, "Please will it. I want him so much that I'm breaking apart. I have no peace, no rest. He is a part of me and that part is being torn away." Clutching the rail, she begged in a ragged whisper, "There is no life without him."

The ship continued on. No miraculous abating of the wind, no fish to open its mouth and carry her back to the Virginia coast, no sign that she had been heard and given what she most wanted.

She loved Dan. She wanted him. But she would not defy God. She would have him with God's blessing or not at all.

"I will know," she whispered in her resolve, "I will know that You want him for me if he finds me today. Not tomorrow," she added forcefully, needing to hear herself say the words, "today only, before the sun has set. And he must not only find me today," she continued, "he must ask me to marry him."

If Dan was her destiny, then she would know it without doubt.

She said it for herself; she knew that God would never give her over to be any man's whore, especially a pirate's. Still, feeling calmer having laid it all at the feet of God, she knew how God would answer.

Fresh tears erupted and she buried her face in her hands as the sobs roared through her.

"You *saw* her at the rail?" Dan demanded roughly.

"Yes, I did," Ben answered in surprise at his friend's obvious agitation. He had meant it only as a casual remark; Lydia McIntyre had clearly been cured of her fear of sailing since her last disastrous trip.

"What ship?" Dan shouted at him.

Ben blinked in surprise. It must have been an extraordinary dinner party for them to have formed such an attachment in so short a span of time. "I believe it was the *Constant*."

"Bound for?" Dan shouted again. Could the man offer nothing? Did it have to be pried out?

"I have no idea," Ben said, "though I believe it may be making stops up and down the coast."

"North and south both?"

"I'm afraid I don't know," he confessed.

Dan groaned, thinking of all the places he must search for her. Again. He must find her. He must. An incredible sense of urgency was driving him, far greater than the last time she had slipped his net. A hundredfold greater. He had never felt anything like this force that gripped him. He could not rest until he had her.

Ben was a waste of time and he could not waste any time; that he knew above all. Ben didn't know her destination. But Robert McIntyre would.

Chapter Twenty-eight

The door was closed, unaccountably. Dan pounded on it with his fist, causing the wood to rattle where it had been joined, threatening to break the joints. Sally, irritated, opened the door, ready to give as good as she got. She had never faced a pirate before. It was a pirate she faced now. Gone was the veneer of respectability and decorum; he didn't have time for it. The sun was straight overhead, the day half gone, and he was still anchor out. He had to find her!

"Yes?" Sally asked coldly, her body blocking the opening.

Dan ignored such a feeble defense and pushed past her. "Where's Mr. McIntyre?"

"Excuse me, sir," she bit out, "but Mr. McIntyre is not available—"

"He will be," Dan snarled, crossing the floor of the apothecary shop to the door which led to the family and private portion of the house.

Miriam had been sitting with Hannah and Ruth in the front room, working with them on their needlework. At the commotion coming from the other room, she had stepped into the doorway and was met with the startling image of Dandridge Prentis striding through the house, looking more like a wolf on the hunt than a man paying a social call. His manner was anything but sociable.

"Where is she?" he demanded.

"She?" Miriam stammered, overwhelmed by his fury, so clear to see in his burning yellow eyes.

"Lydia," he forced out, sick unto death of so much ignorance, feigned or genuine.

"She's gone," Hannah said.

"Where?" he retorted, closing on her like a wild beast.

"Uh, uh," Hannah babbled, unused to such anger aimed in her direction.

Even Ruth, so vocal and so fluent, was speechless. This was a far different man from the one who had charmed her in the garden and charmed the ladies at the church door; this man was not charming at all. This was a man who could most definitely trounce two men in an ordinary. Miriam was silently thinking the same thing. As was Hannah.

And so was Robert. He had come in from the garden, where he had been gathering herbs, after hearing a man's voice raised in anger. He had known who it must be. He was not surprised to find Dandridge Prentis in his house, demanding to know of Lydia's whereabouts. Rather, he would have been shocked if he had not made an appearance.

So he was here and acting like a beast with his foot in a trap; a beast set on freedom from his pain and, perhaps, on inflicting a little pain of his own in retaliation. Robert watched him froth and pace, unafraid.

"Where is she?" Dan demanded, rounding on her father. This man would know all. And he would tell all.

Robert took a moment to gaze at his three daughters and at his wife, who was coming up the path from the dairy. "I presume," he said with irritating calm, "that you speak of Lydia? Gone," he said succinctly.

"Damnation!" Dan roared, bunching his hands into threatening fists. "I know she's gone! Where?"

Robert waited until Anna had arrived. Without a word, she took the two younger girls in hand and, with Miriam following like a new calf, led them outside and away from the pirate in their midst.

When they were well gone, Robert answered, "Away from you, sir."

Dan reconsidered his approach. He had to calm down; this man, this father, would likely not tell him anything if antagonized. He had to appear calm and reasonable if he was to get what he wanted, though he felt as far from calm as he ever had. This urgency to find her, reach her, hold her again in his arms was crushing him down to the dust. He was suffocating with it.

"I would know her destination," Dan requested, his voice carefully modulated. He could not know the anguish and desperation that wept through his words.

"That you will not have. She is well away from you."

"I understand you, sir. I know you believe you are in the right," Dan all but panted, "but I must find her. I must!"

Robert felt uneasiness settle on him like a damp fog. This encounter, it was becoming too much like the dream. He had dreamed a dream last night after much tossing, and it had been a dream like no other. He was afraid it had been a dream sent to him from God. He did not discount such supernatural things; if Daniel of Babylon could find interpretation in a dream, so could he. And this dream had left him shaking and awake until the dawn.

"You will not," Robert repeated, uneasily aware that those had been his words in the dream.

Dandridge turned away from him and ran his hands through his hair, anguish apparent in his every movement. Why would a pirate care so much about his daughter?

"Please, listen to me," Dandridge said softly, his eyes alight. "I don't know what to say to you to make you understand that what I feel for Lydia is . . . that is to say, what I want from her . . . I don't . . . there is no *time* for me to explain! I must reach her! I must find her! By sundown, I must find her!" He paused, his face a mask of pain and longing. Just as it had been in Robert's dream. And then he said the words Robert had known he would say: "Survival is the same as death without her."

Dandridge had never thought to say such words, nor feel the truth of them to his very soul.

Robert felt the weight of God's hand upon him. Even with the prophecy of dreaming, he struggled to obey, for God had told him in his dream to give Dandridge Prentis what he asked for. He asked for his daughter. Had Abraham suffered so when asked by God to give up Isaac? The weight of fatherhood struggled with holy conviction within Robert McIntyre's soul; conviction won. He would obey, though he understood nothing.

Dandridge faced Lydia's father and met his gaze squarely. "I want her as I have never wanted anything before. I want to give her . . . everything . . . my wealth, my children, my name . . . even my life. Gladly, my life. There is no life without her. I will do anything, if only she can forgive me," he said haltingly, the depth of his pain and longing for Lydia choking him.

"You need to ask it of her," Robert said, giving to Dandridge Prentis what God said he must.

Dan's panic at the passing of every minute threatened to choke him, but he swallowed it down and said, "I will, when I find her."

"She is bound for Charlestown on the *Constant*."

Chapter Twenty-nine

The wind had carried them steadily all day without so much as an erratic gust; they were making eight knots sailing away from Williamsburg. Not a cloud all day to mar her view of the sun as it made its way across the sky and down, down, to the wet horizon. It would not be long now. The sun was nearly set. She had not left the deck all day, but had searched the water for what she knew she would not see: a sail. The sea had been an unbroken and unmarred expanse of darkest blue in every direction. There had been no sail.

The passengers, of whom there were many, crowded the deck and grouped around her, talking and laughing, pointing out to sea in animated pleasure. She wanted no part of crowds. She wanted to be alone when her dream died and destiny mocked her. She wanted to be alone when the sun set and God showed her the answer to her heart-rending prayer. Dan would not come. She would live out her life without him. How many days in forty years? How many thousands of days spent in bare and brutal survival without him, for her life would be an empty cage without Dan in her world. She would survive, but she did not believe she would live.

She finally understood the difference.

She moved to the bow and set her face into the wind, wanting it to dry her pregnant tears and hide her misery from herself.

The commotion on the deck increased in volume and activity. Lydia turned from her solitude and saw what they all saw and what had aroused their interest in the middle of an ocean: a sail. A sail white as a cloud and flying just as swiftly. A ship cutting the waves like a sword and bearing down on them. A ship in pursuit.

Just like before.

Now she saw, they all saw, a ship well gunned. This was not a passenger ship, nor a merchant; this ship was rigged for battle. Heaving in the seas she was, her course true and swift, slicing for them. She could not miss.

And then she fired a shot across their bow.

Shrieks and shouts met that blast. The mystery ship flew no colors; all knew what that meant. A pirate ship had targeted them. The *Constant* was outmatched in gunnery. The captain had no choice but to order, "Lay to."

She watched from her place in the bow as the ships were grappled together. It was the *Serpent* and Dan was at the tiller. His black hair was loose and whipping about his head like frayed rope gone wild in the wind. Black breeches were molded tightly to his muscled legs. His shirt was bleached linen, the lace fine where it brushed his throat and cascaded over his gold brocade waistcoat. It was his voice that had commanded the cannon to be sounded. It was he who leapt from the quarterdeck, shunning ladder altogether, and now jumped the distance between their rocking ships.

Just like before. Only this time, he had not come for plunder. He had come for her. And this time, God had sent him.

He did not have to search for her; he knew exactly where she was. He had been watching her through the glass for half an hour, but he knew that his blood would have told him even if his eyes could not. She was in the bow, waiting for him.

His crew held the crew of the *Constant* at bay, their swords drawn and ready. But they would not fight; their purpose was to give him time to face her and to win her.

Among the cluster of frightened passengers were two elderly women, sisters, who had been on their way to visit a niece in Charlestown. Mary and Elizabeth Harrison knew that they were breathing their last breaths. Nevertheless, they could not stop the pattering chatter which had marked their lives to this point.

"I knew it was a mistake to sail in such lovely weather," Mary groaned. "All the rodents of the world come out when the weather is fair. Only honest men venture to sea when the storms—"

"Rage," her sister, Elizabeth, finished.

"And so now we face the worst," she moaned. "Death at the—"

"Hands of pirates."

"A diseased-looking bunch of criminals, I can't help but notice. Look at that one, burned brown as a—"

"Nut."

"And as well dressed as an earl. The captain, I suppose," Mary concluded. But as Dan passed near her in his pursuit of Lydia, Mary squinted her eyes, which were never reliable in the twilight of the day, and took a closer look. "He has a familiar look, sister, don't you think?"

"No, how could he? . . . But he does have a way about him."

"Yes, the angle of the jaw and the eyes . . . Heaven help us! It's Dandridge—"

"Prentis!" Elizabeth finished on a collective gasp of horror, disbelief, and morbid glee.

Dan, hearing them without difficulty as they had not even the presence of mind to whisper, stopped and turned to face them. Friends of Aunt Patsy's clearly and, if so, then the formalities would be observed and with sardonic pleasure. Bowing deeply and flashing them a rakish smile, Dandridge greeted them as a gentlemen ought, "Ladies, please forgive the delay I have caused in your social calendar, but I must speak with Miss McIntyre. A matter of the heart, you see. Love is impulsive and reckless, as your memories will attest. Have I a chance with her at all, do you believe?"

"Oh, yes, I do believe that she'll be quite—"

"Receptive."

"She has been forlorn all day—"

"And staring out to sea—"

"And crying."

"Then I'd best hurry," he said. "I have a handkerchief."

Dandridge hurried to the bow and to Lydia.

"Such a romantic," Elizabeth whispered wistfully.

"And so dashing, too."

The light of mischief flared within them both at the same moment, as was their way.

"Do you think Patsy knows?"

"Or should we tell her?"

It was so much like their first encounter. She could hardly breathe for the memories. He came toward her, his face set with firm purpose and his amber eyes glinting in the warm and weakening light as she awaited his coming, standing in the narrow bow of the ship. Everything the same. Everything different.

God had been so merciful in answering her impossible

prayer. Dan had come and he had come before the sun had set. But would he ask her to marry? Did he love her even a little?

He closed the distance between them, but stopped six feet off. A strange reversal, but he did not trust himself if he drew nearer. He would not lose control with her again, that he vowed, for he would not have her answer with her mind clouded by passion, and her passion was assured if he but touched her. It was a clear and reasoned response that he was after; she would know exactly what she did. There would be no regretting later.

She waited, her eyes eager and expectant, for him to ask her the one question she wanted to hear. Two words and two words only and she would be complete. *Marry me*, she whispered in her heart, sending him the message with her eyes.

"Forgive me," he said in a harsh whisper. He had meant it as a fervent request; it came out nearer a command.

They were not the two words she needed. A wave of despair and pain crashed against her. He would not ask for her. He did not want her; no, he wanted cleansing forgiveness from her. He did not even want to touch her.

Her pain was a blaze that nearly blinded him. She did not speak. He could not blame her. She was not going to forgive him; he was beyond forgiveness. She was beyond his reach because he had cast her that far from him with his treatment of her. What had he done to deserve her love? He deserved her hate and nothing less. He had abused her at every turn, exposed her to depravity and danger with every moment he exposed her to himself. He had nothing to offer her beyond his name and his love, and what counted they in the face of his identity? He was a pirate. It was all he had been with her. But the pirate had loved her. And so did Dandridge Prentis. No matter what he did or who he thought himself to be, he always loved her. Lydia was all that mattered of survival.

Dan took a step back. He had come to ask this of her; if she could not forgive, then she could hardly love. He would not bruise her further, no matter what it cost him. He would not demand from her what she could not give because of his own acts. This truth lay at no one's feet but his own.

Lydia saw clearly, poetically, that Dan had just taken the first step of many that would lead him out of her life—if she let him. This time, it was Dan who was fleeing. God had brought him across the sea to stand before her. Couldn't she even open her mouth to encourage him to stay? Was he not worth one word, one sentence? How much was she willing to lose to keep him?

Everything.

"I forgive you . . ." she said softly, delicately, "for interrupting my sleep on so many nights."

Dan stopped in his retreat from her, studying her changeable eyes for a sign of her meaning. "We were only together on the *Serpent* for two," he gently protested.

"I know." She smiled, thinking of all the nights she had lain awake in Williamsburg, surrounded and harried by him.

Dan took a step closer to her.

"I forgive you"—she paused to contemplate—"for paying so much attention to Miriam."

Dan smiled and stepped closer. "I was hardly more than civil."

"I know." She shrugged helplessly.

"And . . . ?" he prompted, enjoying the gentle fire of her eyes and the golden shimmer of her hair in the slanting light.

"I forgive you for sending the one-eared man with my food."

Now it was Dan's turn to shrug. "He was the oldest."

Lydia smiled and said, "I know."

Taking a step toward him, her first, Lydia closed the

distance between them to a handsbreadth. "I even forgive you for treating me like . . . for mistaking me . . . for a whore."

Searching her eyes, her face lifted trustingly to his, Dan seriously asked, "Do you?" Whispering, tracing the contours of her face with the roughened tip of his finger, he breathed, "Do you? You must forgive me, Lydia. There is nothing for me in this life if you cannot forgive me. Survival is empty, blacker than death, without you." Black lashes swept down to shield his golden eyes as he raised her face for a tender kiss on the mouth. His touch was blazing fire in a raging blizzard, lighting her path, warming her. Lifting his mouth from hers, he vowed in a rough whisper, "I love you."

Smiling expectantly, hopefully, she took his hand and kissed the palm, sealing him to her. He had told her last night that he loved her, but there was no way to measure the difference. This declaration was of giving, not taking. He spoke from the heart and sealed the vow with his very life.

God had answered her impossible prayer. Dan loved her, finally. No lies marred the beauty of it. This love would carry her into eternity with all the effortlessness of flight.

"I sailed after you," he continued, his voice raw with emotion barely contained, "as if demons drove me. To ask you to marry me. You must marry me."

Lydia smiled, the tears blurring her vision of the man God had given her. The sun, before plunging joyfully into the blackened sea, turned the sky a brilliant gold touched with rose and wine and purple. The warm wind was a gentle and constant friend pressing a comforting hand to her back. In this quiet light, Dan's golden eyes lit her world.

It was no demon that had driven him.

Leaning up to kiss him, she breathed against his mouth, "I know."

Lair of the Wolf

CHAPTER FOUR

Emily Carmichael

Lair of the Wolf also appears in these *Leisure* books:

COMPULSION by Elaine Fox
includes Chapter One by Constance O'Banyon

CINNAMON AND ROSES by Heidi Betts
includes Chapter Two by Bobbi Smith

SWEET REVENGE by Lynsay Sands
includes Chapter Three by Evelyn Rogers

On January 1, 1997, *Romance Communications,* the Romance Magazine for the 21st century made its Internet debut. One year later, it was named a Lycos Top 5% site on the Web in terms of both content and graphics!

One of *Romance Communications'* most popular features is The Romantic Relay, an original romance novel divided into twelve monthly installments, with each chapter written by a different author. Our first offering was *Lair of the Wolf,* a tale of medieval Wales, created by, in alphabetical order, celebrated authors Emily Carmichael, Debra Dier, Madeline George, Martha Hix, Deana James, Elizabeth Mayne, Constance O'Banyon, Evelyn Rogers, Sharon Schulze, June Lund Shiplett, and Bobbi Smith.

We put no restrictions on the authors, letting each pick up the tale where the previous author had left off and going forward as she wished. The authors tell us they had a lot of fun, each trying to write her successor into a corner!

Now, preserving the fun and suspense of our month-by-month installments, Leisure Books presents, in print, one chapter a month of *Lair of the Wolf*. In addition to the entire online story, the authors have added some brand-new material to their existing chapters. So if you think you've read *Lair of the Wolf* already, you may find a few surprises. Please enjoy this unique offering, watch for each new monthly installment in the back of your Leisure Books, and make sure you visit our Web site, where another romantic relay is already in progress.

Romance Communications

http://www.romcom.com

Pamela Monck, Editor-in-Chief

Mary D. Pinto, Senior Editor

S. Lee Meyer, Web Mistress

Chapter Four

by Emily Carmichael

A quarter of the way down the staircase to meet her fate, Meredyth paused. Dame Allison stopped beside her and peered anxiously at her face.

"My lady? Is aught amiss?"

"Is there aught that is not amiss this day?"

The gathering in the Great Hall had swelled from Sir Garon's immediate retainers to include what appeared to be a whole troop of yeomen and men-at-arms. The English drank and ate with a coarse disregard for manners or courtesy. Glendire's servants scurried among them with platters of tidbits—bread, cheese, and cold meat—that were precursors of the wedding feast to come. A pack of hounds, usually confined to the kennel, dodged around feet and under tables, rooting through the floor rushes and fighting among themselves for scraps. And at the head table was Sir Garon Saunders. His black tunic echoed the darkness of his hair and eyes—of his soul as well, Meredyth reflected. Indeed, he looked like Lucifer himself—God's most beautiful, most wicked creature, presiding over a rowdy celebration in hell.

"Look at them," she moaned to Dame Allison. "Glad I am that my blessed mother is not here to witness such scum making use of her hall."

The keep, with its Great Hall, had been a haven of peace and orderliness under the rule of Meredyth's mother. Beyond the keep's walls, the upper and lower baileys, with their thick fortifications and high watchtowers enclosing the top of the hill, had bustled with industrious activity under her father's wise gaze. The village of Glendire, nestled in the shadow of the castle against the lower slopes of the hill and crowding the shores of a deep blue lake, had boasted fat sheep and sturdy cattle grazing in the commons. Pigs had rooted and chickens had pecked busily around the mud-and-timber huts. Bertha, the alewife, had sung so loudly as she worked that her voice had carried over the castle walls all the way to the keep.

Now Glendire was a sad mockery of what it had once been. The meadows were weed-choked, the livestock sparse, and no one had the heart left to sing. Castle and village alike were missing too many beloved faces. And an arrogant Englishman sat in the high seat from which Meredyth's father once had reigned.

"My lady," Dame Allison said gently. The older woman reached for Meredyth's hand and squeezed.

"I know. We must go down."

Meredyth managed a smile for her attendant as she descended to meet a future she didn't want, a defeat she couldn't endure. Bitterly, she remembered her bold claim that she would never accept the Wolf as husband. How she longed to think of a way to make good that claim.

Garon was feeling well pleased with himself that afternoon. When he had first claimed Glendire in the name of King Edward, the task had seemed onerous, requiring that he, a warrior, learn the sedentary ways of a landed lord. Now, sitting in his own hall, his body warmed by a fire and good mead, he began to appreciate the benefits of the reward Longshanks had given him. Glendire was a jewel—a battered jewel, 'twas true, but beneath the damage of war still a strong, well-situated fortress surrounded by rich and fertile land. A jewel indeed. And the brightest facet of that jewel was just then descending into the hall—the Lady Meredyth.

The sight of her warmed Garon even more than the mead he drank, although *warm* would certainly not describe the expression upon the lady's face. As her eyes surveyed the noisy hall, her delicate brow puckered into a troubled frown, and her generous mouth tightened to a thin line of distaste. The scowl couldn't disguise her beauty, however. It was little wonder that she'd been unable to pass herself off as a boy, even with shorn hair. Her skin was too fine, her bones too delicate. She could dress herself in a grain sack and shave her head to the scalp, and Garon would still know she was a woman.

He rose from his chair and crossed the hall to meet her at the base of the stairs. "My lady." If there was a bit of unchivalrous mockery to the smile he gave her, Garon couldn't blame himself, considering the circumstances of their last encounter.

A flood of desire filled his loins as he remembered the softness of Lady Meredyth's lips and the lush promise of her naked body. Suddenly, he was impatient with the silly ceremonies of nuptial feast and wedding vows. He wanted to carry her to his chamber and claim her as thoroughly as he had claimed her home.

Meredyth regarded his offered arm with contempt. "I am not your lady yet, Sir Wolf," she said with a bit of mockery herself.

"Soon you will be—and I promise, you will have no doubt of it."

"Not if God is inclined to mercy."

"God seldom shows mercy, my lady. And at times, I show even less. You and your people will do well to remember that."

Behind them, Dame Allison muttered something about blasphemy. Garon gave the woman a quelling glance. "I will have silence from you, Dame Allison, unless you prefer kitchen work to serving at my lady's side."

Dame Allison gave Meredyth a despairing glance. Garon knew it was cruel of him to cow the old woman with the same tone of voice he used on recalcitrant squires and fractious knights, but he wasn't accustomed to women behaving in such an insolent manner. If this was what they had to put up with at home, no wonder Welshmen were so surly and anxious to fight.

Meredyth was stiff as a block of ice as he appropriated her arm and brought her with him to the high table, seating her in the chair to the right of his. The old woman trailed them at a safe distance.

"You are cruel as well as arrogant," Meredyth accused. "Dame Allison is not a servant. She is a beloved companion and part of my family—the only family you English barbarians have left me."

He smiled dryly. "Beloved companion, she may be, but I hope she is not accustomed to sleeping in your quarters."

"She is."

"Then you will need to find her a new place to sleep, unless you crave an audience to the activities of the marriage bed. From this night forth, you will have a new companion in your chamber."

Meredyth sliced him a glacial look at this reminder of her upcoming doom.

He smiled wickedly. "The marriage bed is not such a frightening thing, my lady. If you would cease fighting it so fiercely, you might find your new situation in life not so horrible."

She turned her face away.

Garon's patience, never vast in any situation, was nearing its limit. "Enough of this sulking. This is your wedding feast. Your people have labored all morning to prepare a celebration worthy of our marriage."

"Our marriage merits no celebration, Sir Garon," Meredyth snapped. "And Glendire can ill afford such luxury. Our livestock is depleted, and game in our woods is scarce, since every band of English marauders has seen fit to help themselves. Even the fields are barren, poisoned by the blood of the men who used to tend them, and many of our storerooms harbor only dust and mice."

A hesitant servant set a steaming bowl in front of her. After seeing the soup tasted, Garon handed Meredyth a spoon and fixed her with a stern look. "Eat, my lady. All eyes are upon you."

"Then they will see my distaste for this mockery of a marriage."

He set the spoon beside her bowl, and before she could blink, he captured her defiantly out-thrust chin, grasping it gently and forcing her to face him full on. Green eyes snapped up at him.

"Lady Meredyth, if you love this land you call yours, then you would do better to kneel at my feet, as a proper wife should, not snap at my heels like an ill-tempered bitch from the kennels. Wounds of war can be healed, but not if they are slashed open again and again. The game will return, the fields will bear crops, and the village can be rebuilt under the husbandry of a conscientious lord."

"Not an English lord," she scoffed, her eyes flashing her contempt. "Or an English husband."

"My lady," Garon growled quietly, his voice pitched for her ears alone, "I warn you now that I intend to make my mark on Glendire. I will make this place, its people, and its lady mine, in fact as well as decree. And 'twill go easier for all concerned if you are at my side willingly, not held prisoner in my chamber and my bed, where you serve only me and not your people."

Held still in his grasp, she inwardly quailed at his words but defiantly met his gaze. "Not all things can be won with brawn and sword. Think you that Wales, or a daughter of Wales, will so easily bend to your conquest? You think your battle is over, Sir Garon? I tell you it has just begun."

The sizzle of challenge in their locked gazes grew hotter than the blaze in the fireplace.

"My, my, my," came a voice like a dash of cold water. "You're supposed to save the arguments until after the wedding, my lord and lady. Your faces could sour the wine before the seal is broken."

Meredyth exhaled a shaky breath, unaware up until then that she had ceased to breathe. It was frightening how Sir Garon so easily stirred her emotions. This morning he had coaxed her to passion with a kiss, and this afternoon, one look at his arrogant face had set spark to a cold fire of anger. Passion and anger—the two sensations were frighteningly similar, and equally hard to control.

The newcomer regarded Meredyth with interest. Though he addressed Sir Garon, his eyes remained on her. "My lord, I crave your pardon for coming to the hall late, but there was a matter to be settled in the bailey."

Sir Garon raised an inquiring eyebrow.

"Nothing that need take you from your wedding feast, my lord."

"Bring Sir Olyver hot soup and bread," Garon instructed the servant who was removing empty bowls—and Meredyth's still full one—from the table. He motioned the knight to take the seat on his left. "My lady Meredyth, allow me to present Sir Olyver Martain, who will command the castle garrison. Sir Olyver's family has been fighting beside England's kings since William crossed the Channel from Normandy."

"Indeed."

Sir Olyver was a comely man of middle years, whose graying temples and weather-seamed face added to rather than detracted from his looks. A neatly trimmed beard defined the strong line of his jaw, and carefully curled hair gave him the look of a courtier, not a warrior. Meredyth took his measure and found that his polished smile did not seem to match the watchful cunning in his eyes. He reeked of subtlety and subterfuge, neither of which were to her taste.

"Sir Olyver." Meredyth inclined her head in a bland nod.

The knight ignored the coolness of her greeting. "My lady, I am honored. I thought Sir Garon a fortunate man for the rich fief our king has given him. Now that I see what treasure resides within Glendire, I know he is wealthy beyond any man's dreams."

Meredyth was tempted to laugh at such flattery, but when she saw how the extravagant compliment brought a dark furrow to Garon's brow, she smiled pleasantly instead. It was worth enduring such drivel to see Garon tipped off his arrogant high horse. Indeed, beside the smooth Sir Olyver, Garon appeared as rough as a block of granite next to polished marble. The unkind comparison inspired her smile to widen.

353

"Thank you, Sir Olyver. What a relief to know that some among the English include courtesy among their accomplishments. I was beginning to fear that all of Edward's knights were fit only for the society found in barracks and stables."

Garon's face darkened ominously, but before he could comment, a page plucked at his sleeve with the news that a messenger from the king waited without.

"Bid him come into the hall."

"Your pardon, my lord, but the messenger says his words are for your ears alone."

A muscle jumped in Garon's jaw as he excused himself from the table and, with a warning frown at Meredyth and Olyver, left them to each other's company.

As Meredyth watched Garon follow the page from the hall, Sir Olyver gave her a smile of sympathy.

"You must forgive Sir Garon, my lady. Though he has the advantage of a strong arm, he is somewhat deficient in manners."

"You do not think highly of your lord, Sir Olyver?" Meredyth surprised herself by resenting the veiled contempt she heard in the knight's voice. Garon was her enemy and therefore to be despised, but surely Sir Olyver owed more respect to the man he followed into battle.

Sir Olyver's smile was placating. "Sir Garon has few equals in battle. In times of unrest, as now, fighting skills are valued above sophistication. When the country is calmer, perhaps Garon can acquire enough finesse to remain in favor with the king. It is a shame that more knights cannot endeavor to excel at both war and peace."

"As you do?" Meredyth inquired dryly.

"I would not be so immodest as to claim such."

"Of course you wouldn't. Immodesty is so unsophisticated, is it not?"

The arrival of great platters of venison gave Olyver an excuse to ignore her sarcasm.

Conversation everywhere fell to a mere mumble while the English invaders stuffed themselves with the fruits of the morning's hunt, along with leeks and onions, potatoes that had spent too much time in the vegetable cellar, and boiled eels swimming in a rich sauce—all made from resources Meredyth had so frugally conserved during the long, hungry winter.

The English pigs seemed to have no compunction about gorging themselves in a frenzy that would leave the storerooms much the poorer. Of those at the high table, only Glendire's chaplain, who well knew what the people had suffered this past winter, did not have cheeks bulging with food and a chin running with grease. Mayhap in him lay Meredyth's last hope.

Meredyth pushed away her untouched plate and got up. "Excuse me, Sir Olyver, but I must speak with the chaplain."

"By all means, my lady. Seek your peace with God."

As she turned away, Meredyth thought she heard him mutter that she would need it. Incensed by his presumption, she turned back to give him a setdown, but before she could open her mouth, a woman's cry cut through the rumble of conversation and eating.

Meredyth whipped around in time to see a maidservant cry out again and try to dodge the blows coming at her from a man-at-arms sitting at one of the lower tables. He held her arm in his meaty grip while his fist battered her face. Blood squirted from her nose, and the spurt of crimson brought shouts of approval from others at the table who cheered the soldier on.

The maid was Alyce, who had been born at Glendire and had served the Llewellyn family from the time she could walk. She and Meredyth were of an age, and many was the time the daughter of the castle had slipped away from her nurse to play with the soot-smeared, cheerful little kitchen drudge. Now, seeing Alyce mauled for the entertainment of men who were little better than animals, Meredyth became enraged. Something inside her snapped as all the indignities and injustices visited upon Glendire by the English became embodied in one squalling maid struggling against a man twice her size.

Meredyth uttered a low growl and hurried into the fracas, grabbing a pitcher of mead from the table as she passed. Without ceremony or warning, she emptied the pitcher over the head of Alyce's attacker, and then she hit him with it.

The pitcher shattered, and for a moment the man-at-arms swayed while everyone in the hall fell silent in stunned surprise. Then the dripping soldier came to life with a roar. He grabbed Meredyth and raised one beefy fist for a blow, only to freeze in place when a sword smoothly slipped beneath his chin.

"Touch her at your peril," warned Sir Garon's calm voice. His iron-hard gaze threatened as sharply as his weapon. Meredyth found herself freed so quickly that she lost her balance and nearly fell backward.

Relief vying with chagrin, she stared at her rescuer in surprise. "You're back."

"Aye, my lady, I'm back. Can I not leave you for a moment before you manage to cause trouble?"

The soldier's mouth opened and closed several times, like that of a beached fish gasping for life. "I din't know it was the lady," he squeaked. "Really I din't!"

Slowly, Garon lowered his sword, but his eyes still pinned the man with deadly intensity. "Why were you beating the maidservant?"

"She's a slow and sloppy bitch," the man whined. "Half the time our cups're empty, and she turns up her nose when we call fer more. An' then she spills hot gravy right down me crotch. She deserved a beatin'."

Alyce had tried to flee, but one of the other men at the table held her fast. Garon shifted his punishing gaze to her, and she seemed to wilt in her captor's arms. "Go to the kitchen, woman. Your mistress will deal with you later." As the maid fled, Garon sheathed his sword and reached out to grasp Meredyth's upper arm, drawing her close to him. "I trust you will mend your servants' attitudes, my lady."

She stiffened in protest, but he ignored the gestures, looking instead at the man in front of him. "Five strokes of the whip for you, John Trainor, at dawn tomorrow. Until then, you can cool your temper in the barracks."

With hard eyes, he surveyed his restive men. "Heed my words, you men. The next one who lays a hand upon the lady of Glendire will not escape so lightly. I tell you now that every man, woman, and child of Glendire is mine, and they will be treated with consideration by those whose job it is to defend them. As for the Lady Meredyth, she is mistress here and this day will become my wife. What is mine, I guard well. Remember that."

Meredyth burned with the heat of a hundred eyes that fastened onto her with merciless intensity. The need to be free of all those eyes rose in her so strongly that it threatened to choke her. With a gasp, she pulled away from Garon and turned to flee. His heavy hand on her shoulder spun her around, and he impaled her with a look that showed no more mercy than he'd shown the offending soldier.

"I go to the chapel to pray. Surely you cannot deny me that comfort!"

His grip loosened. "You are facing your wedding this day, my lady. Not your execution."

"One has very little to recommend it over the other," she shot back.

He did not attempt to hold her as she turned to stalk out, but she felt the weight of his gaze as she pushed through the great wooden door and fled into the upper bailey.

The cold air calmed her temper as she headed for the little wooden chapel crowded up against the bailey wall between one of Glendire's several stables and the forge. Here in the bailey, her upcoming nuptials were being celebrated by those too lowly to gain entrance to the hall. Trestle tables had been set out in the open in front of the keep, and there goose girls and kennel boys, the herb wife and her seven children, woodcutters, wheelwrights, fire tenders, dairy maids, and the displaced peasants from the village ate and drank. Their eyes followed her passage with a curiosity equal to that of the soldiers and celebrants inside. Meredyth covered her shorn head with her mantle's hood and ignored them, until a deep voice reached out and snagged her.

"What's your hurry, lass?"

She looked up to find old Owain, the smith, smiling at her from the forge. Since she was a small girl he'd called her "lass," and no amount of maturity or dignity she acquired would ever change that.

Meredyth gave the smith a wry smile and a sigh.

"That bad, is it?" he asked.

"Nay, Owain. I am fine."

"Are ye now?" He frowned into the forge's fire, and the flames cast his scowl into ruddy relief. "They whipped Mott, the kennel lad, nay but an hour past. Ten strokes for giving an English pig a bit of sass."

"Oh, no," she moaned. "Is he . . ."

"He'll weather it. He's a strong lad."

Meredyth closed her eyes, a sad sickness washing over her. "Was it Sir Garon who had him whipped?"

"Nay. 'Twas a piece of pig shit with the name Sir Olyver."

"Sir Olyver," she sighed. "He is to be commander of the castle garrison, second only to Sir Garon in authority."

"Lass, what manner of man is this Sir Garon you're forced to wed?"

Meredyth did not try to keep the bitterness from her voice. "He is hard as iron, Owain. A warrior with no softness in him."

"He will learn soon enough that the Welsh can be pushed only so far."

"Do not cross Sir Garon, Owain. I fear the best we can do is pray to God for a miracle to deliver us."

"I've always thought 'twere better for a man to make his own miracles."

"Mayhap. But I am not a man, Owain. I cannot lift a sword and defend my home as my father and brothers did."

"There's many here that bless you for not running away and leaving us to face the English without our lady. Don't be forgetting you're not alone, lass."

This time Meredyth managed a real smile as she laid one hand on the smith's sooty forearm. "I won't forget, Owain. Thank you."

The smith's words brought little comfort to Meredyth some minutes later as she knelt upon the cold floor of the chapel and prayed for deliverance for both herself and her people. She needed a miracle akin to the parting of a mighty sea or a bolt of holy lightning from above, if God would only hear her plea. Her knees ached from kneeling, and her knuckles turned white from the force of her praying. She was scarcely aware of the chill of the chapel or of time marching toward the hour when Garon would lose patience with her delays and insist she take her vows—until a rumbling sound from outside erupted into a furious clamor.

The sudden outbreak of violence did not take Garon completely by surprise. He had hoped Glendire's Welsh obstinacy wouldn't lead to more bloodletting, but he hadn't survived years of warfare by simply hoping for the best. He always planned for the worst. Therefore the half of his garrison not drinking in the hall was available and eager to fight when the first sullen group of shovel-wielding and ax-bearing peasants, led by an aged blacksmith, attacked four English archers on the practice field. By the time word reached the hall, the little uprising had spread throughout the upper bailey. Garon calmly donned his chain mail—there was no time to bother with full armor—set a guard on the hall, and dampened the servants' restive speculations with a warning not to be fools—not unless they would die this day.

Outside the keep was chaos. Tables that had held the wedding feast were overturned. Some were broken, and more than one Welshman used the shattered plants as weapons. Others fought with shovels, axes, crowbars, buckets, rakes—anything they could find to break an English head or pierce an English heart.

If the insurgents had hoped Garon's men would be drunk and clumsy, however, their hopes were quickly dashed. The yeomen Garon had posted earlier in the bailey fought with long practice and calm determination, and the knights and men-at-arms who poured from the keep were not so far gone in drink nor heavy with food that they didn't relish a good fight. There was little doubt of the outcome.

"Try not to kill the Welsh fools," Garon instructed his men.

"Aye," Sir Olyver agreed, grinning ferociously. "With the peasants all dead, who will do the work?"

Garon's mail easily deflected a crude spear that flew his way. He cursed, raised his sword, and waded into the fray.

Fighting always brought an icy calm to Garon's mind. But as he knocked heads and disarmed the doltish peasants and servants who fought so hard to free their home and their lady from his clutches, a slow burn of anger began to melt the ice. He hated fighting these pitiful

fools—peasants armed with only farm tools and mis-
guided fervor. Even women and children were fighting.
One old crone shouted "For our lady! For our lady!" and
wielded an iron pot that laid out more than one
Englishman before Garon yanked the crude weapon from
her hand.

He wrapped the hag's arm in a grip capable of crushing bone. "Where is your cursed lady?"

She shrieked an oath at him, and he tightened his grip
until her shrieking diminished to a frightened squeak.
Before she could speak, however, a wide-eyed Meredyth
emerged from the chapel.

"Go you with the others." Garon pushed the old
woman toward the center of the yard, where the rebels
still on their feet were being herded into a sullen group.
His gaze fastened upon Meredyth as she quickly looked
from the tattered remnants of the uprising to Garon, the
color draining from her face and her eyes widening in
horror.

Garon's anger grew to fury as he looked about him at
the damage wreaked upon his bailey and his people, for
the peasants were now just as much his people as the
English men-at-arms. The natural target of his fury stood
frozen upon the chapel steps. If Meredyth had not incited
this foolishness herself—and he wasn't sure she hadn't—
surely her recalcitrance and determined hostility had
egged the peasants on.

He sheathed his sword and stalked slowly to the group
of rebels in the yard. As he swept them with cold eyes,
they visibly cringed, the fight drained out of them.
Abruptly, he turned toward Meredyth.

"Do you realize the consequences of rebellion?" he
asked in a voice that was quiet yet carried the heat of his
anger across the distance that separated them.

She stood in grim silence, a slender pillar of grace rising above the broken remnants of Welsh pride.

Garon was unmoved. "Do you care so little for your people that you lead them to slaughter?"

"No." Her fists were clenched at her sides, and her eyes glistened with what could only be tears. "Sir Garon, do not harm them. I beg you."

He laughed, and even to his own ears the sound rang with ominous promise. "You beg me, do you, Lady Meredyth? Tell me why I should show mercy. Why should I care if you beg? What will you yield me, my treacherous lady, for the lives of these fools? What will you yield me?"

Watch for Chapter Five, by Martha Hix, of
Lair of the Wolf, *appearing in April 2000 in*
White Nights *by Susan Edwards.*

Compulsion Elaine Fox

On the smoldering Virginia night when she first meets Ryan St. James, Catra Meredyth knows nothing can douse the fire that the infuriating Yankee has ignited within her. With one caress the handsome seducer has kindled a passion that threatens to turn the Southern belle's reputation to ashes—and with one torrid kiss she consigns herself to the flames. Ryan has supped at the table of sin, but on Catra's lips he has tasted heaven. A dedicated bachelor, Ryan finds that the feisty beauty tempts even his strongest resolve. In the heat of their love is a lesson to be learned: The needs of the flesh cannot be denied, but the call of the heart is stronger by far.

Lair of the Wolf

Also includes the first installment of *Lair of the Wolf*, a serialized romance set in medieval Wales. Be sure to look for future chapters of this exciting story featured in Leisure books and written by the industry's top authors.

___4648-2 $5.99 US/$6.99 CAN

Cinnamon and Roses
Heidi Betts

A hardworking seamstress, Rebecca has no business being attracted to a man like wealthy, arrogant Caleb Adams. Born fatherless in a brothel, Rebecca knows what males are made of. And Caleb is clearly as faithless as they come, scandalizing their Kansas cowtown with the fancy city women he casually uses and casts aside. Though he tempts innocent Rebecca beyond reason, she can't afford to love a man like Caleb, for the price might be another fatherless babe. What the devil is wrong with him, Caleb muses, that he's drawn to a calico-clad dressmaker when sirens in silk are his for the asking? Still, Rebecca unaccountably stirs him. Caleb vows no woman can be trusted with his heart. But he must sample sweet Rebecca.

Lair of the Wolf

Also includes the second installment of *Lair of the Wolf*, a serialized romance set in medieval Wales. Be sure to look for future chapters of this exciting story featured in Leisure books and written by the industry's top authors.

___4668-7 $4.99 US/$5.99 CAN

Dorchester Publishing Co., Inc.
P.O. Box 6640
Wayne, PA 19087-8640

Please add $1.75 for shipping and handling for the first book and $.50 for each book thereafter. NY, NYC, and PA residents, please add appropriate sales tax. No cash, stamps, or C.O.D.s. All orders shipped within 6 weeks via postal service book rate. Canadian orders require $2.00 extra postage and must be paid in U.S. dollars through a U.S. banking facility.

Name_____
Address_____
City_____State_____Zip_____
I have enclosed $_____ in payment for the checked book(s).
Payment <u>must</u> accompany all orders. ❑ Please send a free catalog.
     CHECK OUT OUR WEBSITE! www.dorchesterpub.com

Elaine Fox
Untamed Angel

Bestselling Author of *Hand & Heart of a Soldier*

With a name that belies his true nature, Joshua Angell was born for deception. So when sophisticated and proper Ava Moreland first sees the sexy drifter in a desolate Missouri jail, she knows he is the one to save her sister from a ruined reputation and a fatherless child. But she will need Angell to fool New York society into thinking he is the ideal husband—and only Ava can teach him how. But what start as simple lessons in etiquette and speech soon become smoldering lessons in love. And as the beautiful socialite's feelings for Angell deepen, so does her passion—and finally she knows she will never be satisfied until she, and no other, claims him as her very own...untamed angel.

___4274-6 $4.99 US/$5.99 CAN

Dorchester Publishing Co., Inc.
P.O. Box 6640
Wayne, PA 19087-8640

Please add $1.75 for shipping and handling for the first book and $.50 for each book thereafter. NY, NYC, and PA residents, please add appropriate sales tax. No cash, stamps, or C.O.D.s. All orders shipped within 6 weeks via postal service book rate. Canadian orders require $2.00 extra postage and must be paid in U.S. dollars through a U.S. banking facility.

Name_____

Address_____

City_____State_____Zip_____

I have enclosed $_____ in payment for the checked book(s).

Payment <u>must</u> accompany all orders. ❏ Please send a free catalog.

The Outlaw Hearts

Rebecca Brandewyne

Pistols at the ready and blond hair blazing, Luke Morgan gallops out of the Ozarks' deep valleys to seize golden treasure. But his plan is thwarted by a lovely, grey-eyed schoolmistress traveling to her new position. Owing to a twist of fate, only she can identify him as the feared outlaw. And to silence the beauty he has only one choice: marry her. Moving to Missouri to forget memories of a day filled with terror and tragedy, Jennifer Colter finds herself face-to-face with a frightening renegade. But the passion burning in his eyes tempts her to enter a world fraught with danger—to surrender to a lawless passion that will become the legend of the outlaw hearts.

___52360-4 $5.99 US/$6.99 CAN

Savage Grace
Cassie Edwards

From the moment he sees her, her lovely flame hair spread about her shoulders like a glowing halo, Standing Wolf thinks of no other. She is a vision—an angel with beautiful blue eyes that look deep into his and see his every emotion. She has rescued him, body and soul, and he knows that when he has finally claimed her as his one and only love, he will never leave her side. Shaylee has never dreamed that she will be given another chance at life and love. But Standing Wolf needs her as no one ever has: He is her destiny. As she nurses the handsome Cherokee warrior back to health, she longs to feel his hard muscled body beneath her fingertips and taste his sweet kisses. For only his touch can erase the pain of her past and unite them as one.

___4666-0 $5.99 US/$6.99 CAN

OFFICIAL ENTRY FORM

Win a romantic island getaway for two on Eleuthera in The Islands Of The Bahamas! Just correctly answer the following three questions based on Lydia and Dan's story from *Tell Me Lies* by Claudia Dain. Be sure to give your complete and correct address and phone number so that we may notify you if you are a winner. (Please type or legibly print.)

1. What is the name of Dan's ship?_____

2. What is the name of the plantation that Dan will inherit?_____

3. At what time of day does Dan propose marriage? _____

NAME:_____

ADDRESS:_____

_____

PHONE:_____

E-MAIL ADDRESS:

MAILING ADDRESS FOR ENTRIES:
Dorchester Publishing Co., Inc.
Department CD
276 Fifth Avenue, Suite 1008
New York, NY 10001